The Dangers
of
Doing Good

Also by
Rebecca Connolly

An Arrangement of Sorts
Married to the Marquess
Secrets of a Spinster

Coming Soon
The Burdens of a Bachelor

Also from
Phase Publishing

by
Emily Daniels
Devlin's Daughter

The Dangers
of
Doing Good

Rebecca Connolly

Phase Publishing, LLC
Seattle

Phase Publishing, LLC first paperback edition
November 2016

ISBN 978-1-943048-13-7
Library of Congress Control Number 2016957763
Cataloging-in-Publication Data on file.

Acknowledgements

To my awesome, generous, wise, and *very* patient mother who has always been a great example to me, who taught me all the good stuff that moms teach their kids, like you can have pie or cake for breakfast if you do it right, breakfast for dinner is perfectly normal, and going to the doctor means you get a treat... The greatest compliment I can ever receive is anything along the lines of remotely resembling you in any way, shape, or form, and I hope to live up to it. Thanks for being my mommy, my fan, and my friend. And, you know, for teaching me to love hot chocolate so much.

And to Diet Coke, since I couldn't have written and edited this one without significant support from it. You are a mighty miracle worker, curing everything from headaches to stress to heartache, and I love you in all your varieties.

MASSIVE shout out to my favorite team of people. Chris Bailey and Phase Publishing for sticking with me and letting me dream big dreams, and then working with me to fulfill them. Deborah Bradseth for the incomparable cover and vision that brought everything to an entirely new level. Whitney for helping me get rid of the bad and improve the good. Hannah and Alicia for beta reading and being the best fangirls ever. The A-Team for being the blossoms in my stressful life.

Thanks to my family for being the nicest weirdos I could ask for. Big fan.

Last, but not least, a baker's dozen of donuts to my Musketeers. No distance, no danger, no diet is too much to keep me from being devoted to you. Except I'm sick of the diets, so let's not do those anymore, please. Replace that with dark chocolate. Lots of it.

Chapter One
Yorkshire, 1820

Duncan Bray thought he was a content man.

Riding through the wintery chill of Yorkshire, he could easily convince himself that he was.

His life was not perfect, not by any stretch, but neither was it overly complicated or full of much to distress him. He had a younger sister who was bent on turning him into an overprotective grizzly bear of a guardian, and an aunt who frequently put him at his wit's end, but he adored both of them with such inexplicable fervor that even their best and most concentrated efforts were not enough to set his life awry.

He had also been blessed to be friends with some of the very best men England, if not the world, had to offer, all of whom would give all they had, even their very lives, for any of the others. And all of them were deliriously happy, which could only leave Duncan with equally delighted contentment.

Well, Colin was perhaps merely delirious, but he thrived in that state and thus did not require concern or additional attention from anybody, let alone Duncan.

More than that, three of his friends had married and were beginning families of their own. Marriage itself was not something so very shocking, everybody seemed to be getting married these days, and very rarely was true affection to be had. At least, not in his view. But all of his married friends had done so with the purest and deepest of loves.

He mentally winced as he remembered that Derek's marriage, now going on seven years, had not been one of love initially, and hadn't even been pleasant at all until recently. Indeed, he had never met a couple who had hated each other more, and Duncan had been privy to details of quite a few unhappy marriages. He had despised Kate himself before he had known just how delightful she was, and before he could see how perfect she was for Derek.

Now he could hardly imagine thinking anything less of her than near-complete adoration. And it was the same with Moira for Nathan and Mary for Geoff.

Duncan was not prone to overenthusiasm, but if he could be half as happy in marriage as his friends were, he would want for nothing else in his life.

Not that he was pining to be done with his woebegone state of bachelorhood. On the contrary, he quite enjoyed it. He had freedom to go wherever he wanted, whenever he wanted, and he took that opportunity as often as he could.

He absolutely abhorred London. The city life was too much for him; there was never a time or a place for peace and contentment. One always had to be about and doing something, or seeing someone, and when one had nothing to do, there was always someone else who was doing something or seeing someone in such a way that made for quite a scandal and everybody had to hear about it and make it their business.

Duncan hated knowing other people's business. What right did he have to know what other people did with their time or who they chose to spend it with or in what manner? He could not have cared less.

His sister did not feel the same way. Marianne relished the high society and fashionable airs of London. But, of course, she was a beautiful young woman who did not want for attention. He rather wished she were a bit plainer and not so infectious in her charms, as he was tired of fending off her ill-advised suitors and troublemakers who only sought her fortune or fame.

Marianne had quite the fortune and more than enough fame. She was bold, she was cold, and she was intoxicating, or so he had been informed. This made her fodder for gossip and speculation, which was something else he detested. But there was no stopping it, and Marianne thrilled with the knowledge that she was a household name.

It was why she chose not to spend Christmas with him at their cousin's castle in Scotland. Graeme had insisted they come this year, as they had not been in the Highlands for almost four years, and Duncan was pleased to accept. But Marianne had no desire to spend the holidays in "a stinking, freezing castle in the middle of a frozen wasteland surrounded by five grown men with the manners of boars." Somehow, Graeme and his brothers had not been offended by that, and each had sent presents home with Duncan for their "favorite girl" along with their love and compliments.

Duncan shook his head, bundled up with furs against the snow and the wind and the cold. He was not generally prone to such elaborate measures nor such grand taste as to be seen wearing furs, but his cousins had insisted. And as he had won the fur from his cousin's castle fair and square, he felt a little bit of pride in now using the fur for warmth.

It had been his well-deserved prize, as he had trounced all challengers in a surprise brawl the day after Christmas. In theory, it was the fur of a bear that was killed by their great-grandfather, Angus MacLaine, one of the boldest and bravest men to ever roam the Highlands. Of course, there were many rumors and legends tied to this ancestor, most of which Duncan suspected to be wildly untrue, including the bearskin. If he had it properly inspected, he was half convinced it would have been revealed to be made of an astonishing number of rabbits.

But nevertheless, he was grateful for it. And he missed his cousins fiercely. They were his brothers in blood and had shown immense support for him and Marianne when their parents had passed, remembering their aunt with grace and honor.

Duncan often thought of removing himself to Scotland entirely. The remote nature of the Highlands was far more suited to his reclusive lifestyle and contented nature.

But he could never leave Marianne. Or Tibby.

3

He scoffed as he thought of his aunt. The great Lady Raeburn would have thrown a massive fit of blazing proportions if her favorite nephew had left her side. His father's sister was truly the most eccentric woman he had ever met, but he was fond of her. Far more so than he would ever confess. She alone had been his saving grace in the darkest hour of his life.

She would find his furs delightful and no doubt try to convince him they should belong in her house rather than his. He could hear her voice now; "No, no, dear boy, far too masculine, think of what Marianne's suitors would say when they came to call! No, they shall come home with me and I shall find a place for them. Furs are so deliciously rare these days, no one will think of it. Perhaps I could present them as from India…"

He grinned and shook his head. Tibby. What a rare old bird she was.

So in truth, he was content. He was. He was just fine, nothing to complain about at all.

But…

His horse, Balthazar, snorted suddenly, ears at the alert. Duncan sighed and patted the horse's neck. The creature had been fidgety ever since they had left the Highlands and was determined to either race home as fast as possible or trudge in a funeral procession. It made for quite the exchange between the two of them.

"Steady there, laddie," he murmured, letting his well-practiced Scottish brogue roll on. "Don't you be keeping me from a good bed and a warm fire tonight. "

The horse calmed under his touch, but his ears still stood tall. Duncan frowned. Balthazar was not normally so concerned about his surroundings. He scanned the vicinity and saw a small creek and a stand of trees nearby.

"Thirsty, are you?" he asked with another pat. He nudged the horse in that direction, with no resistance in return.

He chuckled and allowed Balthazar to take the pace he chose. Fastidious animal.

The snow crunched beneath the horse's hooves, and the tips of grass blades could occasionally be seen poking through the blanket of white. Duncan loved when the world was like this. The air was brisk and made his lungs feel alive, everything was soft and still, and there was something about snow that he had loved ever since he was small. He would not be sorry to reach the warmth of an inn, however, for even bundled up as he was, the chill was growing fierce.

Again, Balthazar snorted restlessly, and this time, Duncan's senses went on the alert. He had been away from the army for almost eight years and his skills had become dormant, but, he flattered himself, they were not yet lacking. He looked around for what had disturbed his horse, what danger could await them in such a place.

The creek was sluggish, almost silent as it kept its pace, and the banks were shallow; there could be no danger from either. He turned his attention to the stand of trees, and as he did so, something within shifted.

Duncan froze, his horse stilling beneath him. He was still too far away to make out any sounds, and whatever the beast was, it hardly moved. Well, he himself had always been a creature of stealth. He pushed Balthazar gently forward, the horse seeming to sense his master's wishes and trod lightly.

The closer they drew, the more Duncan wondered what creature they were to come upon. Its movements were slow and careful, almost hesitant, and it barely made any sound. It obviously had not heard him or his horse in their approach.

Ah, he loved having the advantage.

With as much silence as he could manage, he dismounted, and rubbed Balthazar's nose when he did not so much as sniff. Then he turned and crept, with surprising stealth considering his size and stature, towards the trees. The closer he got, the slower he moved.

Still the creature did not notice him.

It shifted to one side and suddenly Duncan was brought to a complete halt.

It was a woman!

And given the slow, halting manner of her movements, he suspected she was very old. She shuffled towards the creek and he was filled with compassion. Her clothing was thin and tattered, and she looked very frail. What was this old woman doing out in the middle of nowhere in this frigid cold near a creek? He could have snapped her between two fingers, and the flimsy shawl she wore around her head and shoulders would not have been sufficient as a serviette, let alone apparel of warmth.

He did not want to startle the poor thing. That could send her into the creek and then he would be in a difficult place. He continued forward without his previous designs of a soft step, and still she did not move. Was she also hard of hearing?

He frowned as he studied her from his distance. Why was this unfortunate woman out in this bitter cold alone? Surely she should have someone helping her, a child or grandchild, or even a servant. Perhaps her state of life was more destitute and she had no one at all. But couldn't a neighbor have been assisting her? She was so small, so slight, and she shivered visibly against the winter breeze. It was then that she heard it: the soft, unmistakable sniffle that came with tears.

He could not leave her in such a state.

He cleared his throat as gently as he could. "Can I be of some assistance?"

The woman jerked and whirled around, clutching her wrap tightly.

A young face and striking green eyes stopped him in his place, and all of the air in his lungs rushed out as if he had been kicked in the stomach. She was no old woman at all. She was young. Quite young, if he was any judge. Younger than Marianne, he would guess, but only just. She was also hauntingly beautiful, though in a tragic sort of way. Her cheeks were gaunt and pale, and they held traces of tears, the faintest hint of dirt erased by their paths. Darker smudges of the same dirt and grime marked her prominent cheekbones, and underneath her eyes she bore dark circles that told of sleepless nights.

And she was utterly terrified.

"I am sorry to disturb you," Duncan said softly, recovering his surprise as best as he could. "Do you need some help?"

She said nothing as she stared at him, did not even move. Her small fingers clutched her wrap even more tightly around her head and shoulders, her knuckles white as the snow beneath their feet. Her eyes were fixed on his, and she did not shift or blink.

"Miss?" he asked, trying his best to keep his voice as gentle as he knew how. He took a step forward, and she scampered backwards, faltering slightly as she nearly went into the creek.

"Careful!" he pleaded, coming forward.

She looked back at him with those emerald eyes, and the smallest whimper escaped from her.

Duncan sighed and looked at her with concern. He knew he was intimidating in his size, and it was often very useful. Except when it was not. But a lifetime of being his size and shape had given him ample time to adjust accordingly.

"I am not going to hurt you," he told her with a smile. "I just want to help."

She looked him up and down, then looked around in panic.

"I am alone, and I will not harm you. I promise."

She considered him for a long moment, still shaking, whether from cold or from fear, he could not tell. He did not know what to do; he could hardly help her when she was so afraid of him. A great shiver racked her tiny frame, and that, he knew, was from the cold.

"You must be freezing," he commented unnecessarily. "May I offer you my coat?" He began shucking his great coat off.

"N-no."

The word was spoken so softly he nearly missed it amidst the faint sounds of the creek.

"No?" he asked, pausing with his coat half off.

She shook her head very slightly. "No, thank you."

He looked at her, concern rippling across his features. "Are you sure? You look quite chilled."

Again, she only shook her head.

He returned his coat to his shoulders and, feeling quite useless, put his hands into the pockets. "Might I help you, Miss?"

She gripped her forearm suddenly, wincing at the clench and his eyes darted there. There were distinctive signs of blood soaking through the faint grey fabric.

"Are you injured?" he asked, his voice rising just a touch as he moved towards her.

She tried to move backwards, but again found the creek there.

She faltered and was going to tumble into the creek. Duncan lunged for her and seized her arms, pulling her safely away. She released a panicked yelp at his touch, crying out louder when his grip on her wounded arm tightened. He set her a safe distance away, then released her and sat back. She scurried further away still, and her wide, terrified eyes went back to his as she clamped down on her bottom lip.

He halted at once, his breath coming out in visible clouds as he panted. "I will not hurt you, I give you my word as a gentleman. I only want to help. Will you let me see to your wound?"

She blinked her large eyes, a single tear leaking its way out and running down her frozen cheek. Then, just when he thought she would refuse, she slowly released her clenching hold on her wrap and held her injured forearm out.

The rush of elation that coursed through him was nearly embarrassing. He walked the few steps to her and went to his knees as he took her arm gently in his hand. She jerked noticeably at his touch, and he met her eyes.

"Easy," he murmured softly, as if speaking to a skittish colt. "It's all right."

Her eyes darted down to her wound, and his followed.

Her sleeve had already been rolled back to her elbow with ease, the fabric both loose and worn. Halfway down the forearm was an angry cut that was not so very deep, but was nearly a hand span in length. Her skin was cold to the touch, and bore the faintest pink color.

"Did you put snow on this?" he asked, his fingers grazing the edges.

She nodded. "Mama said cold slows bleeding and takes away pain."

His brows rose just a touch, surprised that she had spoken a complete sentence to him. Encouraged, he nodded in return. "Yes, she was quite right. She is a very intelligent woman."

"She's dead."

A boulder seemed to fall into his stomach and his breath caught rather awkwardly. "Sorry," he finally murmured, keeping his eyes focused on her wound. The margins were clean, and the blood was turning sluggish.

"Have you cleaned this yet?" he asked, keeping his voice businesslike.

"Just water."

He frowned and looked up at her. "From this creek?"

She only nodded, her eyes darting to the water.

Duncan followed her gaze, humming a noise of uncertainty. He leaned over and cupped a hand into the freezing depths, then brought the little water to his mouth. Bits of water dripped from his thickly stubbled jaw, and he winced as he remembered that he had not shaved in some time. No wonder the girl was afraid of him, he rather resembled a bear at this moment.

"Bad?" she asked in a worried voice.

He turned to look at her with a reassuring smile. "No, no, the water tastes clean. I'm sure you won't be harmed from it. I would like to wash it once more, and then see if I can help to stem the bleeding some."

"It's not that bad," she said softly as she looked at it.

"No, it's not," he agreed, smiling again. "But it does seem to have bled quite a bit. How did you injure it?"

She stiffened and looked away quickly. "I fell."

He did not believe it for a second. He tried to hide his frown, but knew he would not be entirely successful. "And did you fall on a sharp object?" he asked, regretting instantly the bite in his tone.

Her emerald eyes clashed with his and he saw the briefest glimpse of spirit, but then it was gone and the hollow gaze returned. "No."

He gave her a serious look, and she held his gaze steady. She might have been afraid of him, might have been the size of a twig, but she was no weakling. She had strength within her. However dampened and hidden away it was.

He sighed and cupped water in his hand once more, then poured what little remained onto the wound. She hissed and bit her lip, looking away.

"I'm sorry," he murmured as he scooped yet another handful. "That must sting."

9

She nodded, still clamping down on her lip.

He poured water on yet again, then reached into his coat pocket for a handkerchief. As gently as he could manage, he wiped the older blood from her arm. Some of it had been there a while, if the crusting was any indication. That worried him.

He trained his attention now to the wound, which looked better for having been rinsed, at least. He sponged it with his handkerchief, murmuring "Hold still," to her, though it was unnecessary. She hadn't moved in some time. She was as still as a statue during his ministrations, her eyes fixed back on him in apparent fascination.

He felt her gaze upon him like fire and was oddly unnerved by it. She was so steady, so calm, though her entire being was tense, as though she would flee at any minute. Who was this winter creature that struck his manner so?

"There," he said as he removed the now bloodied handkerchief. "That seems better, doesn't it?"

She did not reply, did not even look at it. Her eyes were still on him.

He swallowed nervously. "How are you going to agree with me if you don't see for yourself?"

Her eyes darted down, then looked back at him. "It does."

He tried not to smile and nodded at her. "Thank you. I think we should apply some pressure to it, as it is still bleeding and might for a bit. May I use my handkerchief?"

Her smooth white brow furrowed briefly. "You already did."

One side of his mouth quirked up in a wry grin. "Ah, but a true gentleman always carries two handkerchiefs at all times." He reached into his inner pocket and produced another with a bit of flourish.

That coaxed a small smile from her and it was as if the morning had dawned anew.

He swallowed back his surprise and folded the handkerchief crisply. "Now, we will set this over the wound, and apply pressure for a time. May I?"

She nodded immediately, that small, maddening smile still fixed upon her lips.

He laid the fabric on her skin, and gently took hold of her

forearm, which fit easily in one of his massive hands. He tightened his hold, keeping his eyes fixed on her so she would see he was not threatening. She looked right back at him, eyes still hollow and yet so impossibly alive.

"What is your name?" he asked softly, unable to help himself.

She blinked, her face tightening with discomfort.

He cleared his throat, anxious to make amends. "I apologize, I should have asked you before. In fact, I should have introduced myself. My name is Duncan Bray. I come from London."

"London?" she asked slowly, her tone confused.

Poor thing had likely never left this area. Might not have even been aware of the world outside of it. "Yes, London. Do you know it?"

"Of course," she said simply.

Oh. Well, that made him look a right idiot.

She tilted her head ever so slightly. "London is far away. Why are you here?"

He grinned up at her. "You never answered my question."

Her lips came together in a line, and her eyes narrowed just a touch. As if she were assessing him. Determining his worthiness. She had what he wanted and she knew it.

"Your name," he said with a shrug. "Then I will tell you why I am here."

The corners of her mouth quirked, tickled the edges of her cheeks. Really, she needed to stop smiling so delightfully; he was not immune.

Perhaps it was the light, perhaps he was only now paying proper attention, but the smudges on her cheeks caught his eye. They were not on the surface of the skin to be brushed off, as he had previously thought. They were beneath it. Deeper. And the coloring was wrong.

He looked a little closer, and saw her smile fade as her eyes grew worried.

"Are these... bruises?" he asked in surprise, reaching a hand out to touch her cheek.

She jerked back so quickly and with such force her arm was ripped from his hold. Her eyes were wide and terrified, as if she had

11

never seen him before, as if he had brandished a knife, as if…

As if he would hit her.

"Have you been hit?" he asked, his voice rising.

She skittered backwards, clutching her forearm tightly. Her wrap fell down around her shoulders, revealing long golden hair that was matted and tangled, yet still managed to glitter in the light of the day. Her breath escaped in foggy pants, and her entire frame shook again. She was still beautiful and it hurt him somewhere deep inside.

She should not be this frightened, she should not even know this fear. She should not fear anything.

"Are you being hit at home?" he asked in a softer tone, taking one small step towards her.

She shifted uneasily, and looked away, unconsciously displaying more of her cheek to him, where the bruises seemed to glow against her pale skin. Some of them were relatively fresh, but some were older. Much older. He sucked in a breath, wondering where else she was bruised, how many injuries her body bore. No wonder she moved with such hesitation, she was in pain!

"Let me help you," he pleaded, wishing she would let him take her hand. "I can help you. You should not have to endure this. Please. Trust me."

Her eyes widened, and in them he saw the faintest pooling of tears.

It nearly buckled him.

"Please," he said again, holding a hand out to her.

She looked at his hand for a long moment, and shifted the slightest bit towards him.

A rifle shot exploded in the silence of the morning. Duncan jumped at the sound, but the girl screamed, then clamped the injured hand over her mouth, squeezing her eyes tightly shut.

"Annie!" an angry male voice shouted. He sounded far away, far enough that he may not have heard the scream.

The girl flinched and looked up at the hill behind them with no small amount of apprehension.

"ANNIE!"

She dropped her hand, and took a slow, steadying breath. Then she looked back at Duncan, her eyes completely unreadable.

He shook his head, and held his hand out further. "Please. Please, let me help you."

Her jaw quivered.

"ANNIE! BLOODY IDIOT, WHERE ARE YOU?"

She whimpered, and then took off running towards the hill, towards the sound, towards the man yelling.

Duncan stood there for an unconscionably long time, hand still outstretched. His chest was tight and breathing was difficult. He was not even sure what had happened to him. But that shy little thing had struck him more deeply, more thoroughly, than anything else in his life. And he did not even know her name.

It could have been Annie, if the man yelling was any indication. But it might not have been. He knew nothing about her except that she was injured, and was being beaten, if her bruising and behaviors were any indication.

All he really knew was that he would have moved heaven and earth to help her.

And the thought terrified him.

He was a generous man, he knew. His friends joked with him about being hard and burly on the outside, yet soft on the inside. Perhaps he was so. He helped his fellow man as often as he could, willingly and without judgment or expectation of a return. It was simply his nature.

But this… This was different.

This was entirely different.

Heart heavy, chest aching, he turned and walked back towards Balthazar, clenching and unclenching his hand.

It was not until much later that evening he realized he was no longer in possession of his handkerchief.

Chapter Two

*A*nnie Ramsey was a thief.

Not intentionally, of course, for no girl of sense would ever intentionally steal anything unless positively desperate. Which she was not.

Not yet, at any rate.

She ran her fingers over the stitching on the handkerchief… *his* handkerchief… and released the smallest of sighs. She hadn't meant to steal it. She had never stolen anything in her life and had never had the desire to. But now she had it, she couldn't say she minded very much.

Her fingers absently traced the monogram. D.B. Duncan Bray. Even his name sent a warm tingling sensation down her back and into her toes. Which was a silly, nonsensical thing for her to be feeling. The man had been very kind, tending to her wound and wanting to help her, but he could hardly have meant to give her his handkerchief. Even if he did carry two.

She smiled to herself as she remembered his brandishing of the second. It seemed absurd that a man should ever have two handkerchiefs, let alone ones of such high quality. She might be a bit of a simpleton, but she did know quality fabric and handiwork when she saw it. And his handkerchiefs had been the very best of fabric she had ever seen.

She studied the stitched monogram for a moment. It was done with such delicacy, such intricate work. The dark green contrasted so beautifully with the crisp whiteness of the fabric. It was beautiful work.

Had it been stitched by a loving wife at his home in London? Did he have children whose tears he had wiped with this very handkerchief? Was it a treasured possession?

Or would he even miss it at all?

It made no difference, either way. She would never see him again. He could have searched high and low to get it back and he would never have found her. No one ever did.

She had been shocked at being discovered at all yesterday by the creek. Her only focus had been to hide from Frank and to clean her arm off. No one had ever come that way before. She was not even sure Frank knew that spot. It had been Annie's refuge for years, the only place she could find any kind of quiet or peace.

Until yesterday, it had been her secret place.

It would always be secret. Duncan would never come looking for her. Why should he? She was just a pale, pathetic creature with no sense and no hope of anything. He was a fine gentleman from London, a real life knight aiming to aid a poor girl in need, only to ride off into the sunset for greater adventures and fair damsels in real distress.

He would not think of her at all. Ever.

She sat back against her rough wooden chair and glanced over at the fire where her pot of soup was cooking. Frank would be home soon and he would be starving. He was always starving after hunts, and if she did not have food ready and waiting…

She jerked a small shudder of apprehension.

Her brother had a temper. And it only got worse when he drank, which he always did. She had made it her life's work to avoid angering him, but there always seemed to be something. And if it was not anger, it was boredom. He did not like boredom.

He did not like her.

Which made no difference, really, because she didn't care for him much either. But he was her brother and her mother had asked that they stay together after she died. And even if that had not been the case, where would Annie go? She had no friends, no other family, no money, and no skills.

She rolled her eyes at herself. Well, all right, she could cook a little and mend a little, and she had learned to read years and years ago, even if she was so out of practice she only remembered letters and very small words. But her very limited skills and abilities would make it impossible for her to get any sort of employment. Unless she became a laundress.

That was a possibility. She had gotten very good at getting even the most stubborn stains to fade so much they were no longer noticeable. Her brother's frequent drinking had given her ample opportunity to practice, considering his difficulty to even bring his drink to his mouth when in such a state.

She had managed to clean Duncan's handkerchief almost completely. It had taken a good deal of work, and she had been forced to do it in secret, but now it was done and she was rather pleased with it. One would never know that this fine handkerchief had once been used to stem her bleeding.

She glanced down at her forearm now, turning it over. The bleeding had stopped last night, and she had kept a rag of hers tied on it ever since. It still stung, but it was really nothing. It would heal.

They always did.

Frank had been in a foul mood yesterday, even crueler and meaner than normal. He blamed her for the dinner being burned and cold, though it had been he who had insisted she leave the food in the fire and tend to his horse. When she came back to it, it had burned. So she had taken it of off the fire and set it before him, only for him to order her to feed the horse before they ate. She generally did not mind feeding the horses, but she had not eaten all day and was starving. When she asked if she could eat first, he had taken her out by the hair and watched as she fed the horses.

When they did finally eat, his first bite of dinner sent the entire plate into the fire and he roared how she was useless and he would teach her a lesson. They had gone out into the snow and he had suddenly aimed his rifle in her general direction. He was an excellent shot and they both knew it. Something snapped inside of Annie and she took off running. He yelled after her, and fired once, the bullet hitting a tree near her. He called her again, but Annie knew better than to stop.

Then he shot again, and fire shot across her forearm. She had cried out between clenched teeth, but kept going. She did not stop until she had reached the creek, where she had collapsed in a pile of tears.

She huffed a sound of irritation now as she looked at her wound again. She had been so terrified the entire time Frank had been shooting at her, but was unable to show it or allow herself to truly feel it until she had been alone. She ought to be used to being afraid by now. She knew when she was about to be hit, and the same jolt of fear shot through her every time.

She feared everyone these days. Frank brought men to see her, to look at her, his so-called friends and associates, all talking about her like a horse or a dog, and they all laughed when he threatened her or when he hit her. The others never touched her, it was not permitted, but none of them ever stopped Frank from his actions. It was all a game to them.

It was why she didn't trust anyone. It was why she had reacted so strongly to Duncan's approach.

It was why she could not let him touch her.

She was not a brave person, she never had been, but something about the fire in his blue eyes had strengthened her, and told her to try, just this once, to not be so afraid. And so she had offered her arm to him, a small part of her mind screaming it was a horrible idea. But, she reasoned, it could not get any worse than it already was.

His touch had been so gentle, so soft, so totally different from any other she had ever known. His manner had confused her. How could one who looked so formidable behave so mildly?

Then he had smiled.

Annie was not a girl who had seen much of men, but she felt very certain that there could not be anything more perfect than that man's smile.

She knew full well that she had been an idiot before him. She had been fully incapable of saying anything of substance and had been reduced to a shivering, whimpering mess. It was not possible for her to explain why she had only stared at him, why he held her so captive. Why should he have paid any attention to her at all? Why should he care that she was injured?

It didn't make sense, even in her imagination. All she had ever known of men was that they would harm her.

Yet he had wanted to help her.

He had seen her bruises and the shame and embarrassment that had swelled within her had brought more tears. Then he had reached out to touch them and she had reacted instinctively, defensively, and he let her go without scolding or objection. She was never allowed to do so at home. She could never escape.

The horror on Duncan's face at her reaction was something she would never forget.

She expected him to leave, to turn and run, or to send her away.

But then she watched as his horror turned to compassion, almost worry, and he reached for her.

And that, too, was something she would never forget.

What would have happened if Frank had not fired his rifle and called for her? What if that moment had extended and she could have made the choice? She was a weak, fearful creature, and she had never imagined escape or help, or that she needed it.

And yet...

A loud hissing shook her from her thoughts and she shrieked as she saw the soup beginning to bubble over and spill into the fire. She grabbed a cloth and lifted the pot onto the table, then picked up the nearest spoon and gently stirred the soup, sighing when it returned to normal and did not seem to be the worse for the wear. She put the lid on the pot and moved it back near the fire, but far enough away that it was in no danger of boiling over.

She couldn't ruin dinner again. Not when he was still so upset about yesterday. He had been furious when she had finally appeared from the creek, demanding to know where she had been and why she had taken so long to come. He had accepted her answer of washing by the creek and had not even glanced at her wound. He'd merely told her he was going to the village and she needed to make sure the horses were all in before she went to bed, then he'd left, warning her not to ruin his dinner ever again.

Her mind still frazzled by the shooting and by her encounter, she had stood like a fool for a good number of minutes. Then some eager, wild part of her she did not recognize made her whirl around and run back to the creek, hoping against hope that her mysterious stranger would still be there, possibly even waiting for her.

Of course, he had gone. All was as if he had never been there.

Reality crashed down around her and she scolded herself soundly for losing her head. All girls were permitted their little whims, she supposed, but hers went above and beyond all idiocy. She, Annie Ramsey, was not the sort of girl that a gentleman from London would even look at twice, except with the utmost of pity. She could daydream and have her fanciful moments all she liked, but she knew very well how the rest of her life would play out.

She would marry a man her brother picked out for her based on the sum of money he would earn from the transaction, be forced to endure childbirth however many times her husband saw fit, and then raise the children in the best manner she could, given her poor upbringing, poor and loveless marriage, and potentially poorer future.

It was bleak and she was well aware of it. But perhaps her husband would not be as cruel as her brother. Perhaps they could have a congenial relationship.

Or perhaps things could get worse.

It hardly seemed possible, but she supposed things could always get worse.

She glanced at the soup again, trying to remember what else was required of her before Frank returned. She groaned as she realized she had not gone for bread yet. Frank would never take soup without bread, but there was hardly money for it. He had not given her wages this week, and she dared not ask for them. The little left over from last week would only buy the smallest of loaves.

But it would be better than nothing.

She shoved Duncan's handkerchief down the front of her dress, then picked up her shawl and her fingerless gloves. She donned them both as she slipped out the door, wincing at the bitter cold. A frigid storm had blown through in the night, bringing a great deal of snow as well as even colder temperatures than what they'd had before. She wished she had thought of bread earlier, before it had started to grow dark and colder, for now the snow that reached her mid-calf felt even colder than it would have before. But there was nothing for it.

She hoped Duncan had made it safely to wherever he was headed and that the snow last night had not adversely affected his journey.

She hoped he always had good things rather than poor.

Annie shook her head and exhaled sharply, sending a cloud of air into the darkening sky. She needed to stop thinking about him. He was out of her life, and pining like a silly schoolgirl for a man about whom she knew so little was foolish.

Dreaming about him had been even less sensible.

She tightened her shawl around her as she shivered with the memory. From the beginning it had been a fantasy beyond her wildest yet. She'd been soaking in a warm bath filled to the brim with bubbles. It was the grandest tub she had ever seen in her life. She'd only ever seen one, and it had only been half the size and far dirtier. The dream one she had bathed in was pristine and so large she could stretch out entirely without exposing the slightest bit of skin. She had been in heaven, and every moment she lingered, she remembered less and less of the cold of her past.

Then a maid had come in, looking far better dressed than Annie had ever been in her life, and offered her a dressing gown that looked as though it was more suited for a queen than for her. Yet she had smiled and donned it, gingerly stepping out of the mountainous tub that was still steaming.

Then, impossibly, the maid helped her dress. Undergarments, stockings, a corset... she had only ever *heard* of corsets and one of the milkmaids in the village had shown her a very old and probably outdated one, but she had never imagined she would wear one... and though Annie was a slender girl, the dream version of her was just a little fuller in places. Still small by any standard, but not so frail looking. And the corset gave her the most perfect posture and figure she had ever seen.

Her shock only increased when the dress was brought forth. It was exquisite. It was the palest of pinks, the color of a blush, and the faintest hint of a golden shimmer flickered in the delicate embroidery along the neckline and skirt. Even the dream version of herself was stunned by its beauty. The maid helped her to put it on, then buttoned up the back. But still she could not see herself, for there was no mirror in the washroom.

She walked into an elegantly furnished bedchamber, where the mirror was covered, and sat herself into a chair. The maid followed her in and began doing the most elaborate twists and turns and curls with her hair. Annie was amazed, as her hair was and always had been hopelessly straight. Yet it curled with ease under the skilled hands of the maid.

Just when she thought it was imaginative enough, she heard a deep voice that made her toes curl in heated delight.

"You are exquisite."

She turned her head to see Duncan standing in the corner next to the covered mirror, his face clean-shaven, and only halfway dressed himself. His pristine linen shirt was properly tucked into his breeches, but it lay open at the collar, exposing the very top of his blatantly well-muscled chest and his strong neck. She swallowed at the sight of him. Faintly, it had occurred to her dream self to wonder where the rest of his clothing was, but it seemed a small matter.

"Thank you," she murmured, feeling her cheeks flush.

"I think you need to see yourself," he replied, pulling the sheet from the mirror.

Annie looked back at the maid, who grinned and nodded at her in encouragement.

"Annie," Duncan said in a low voice, instantly bringing her attention back to him. He held out a hand. "Come."

Nerves tingling, she rose and took his hand. He pulled her directly in front of the mirror, and she gasped at the sight.

She looked like a completely different person. A fine lady, a woman of fashion and airs, one of importance and worth. The only thing she recognized were her eyes, which were exactly the same as they had ever been, except now they sparkled with an unfamiliar light. And her smile, which grew on her face until her cheeks began to ache.

Duncan moved to stand behind her, his large hands resting on her shoulders. "Beautiful," he whispered, moving his hands down to wrap around her waist and pull her securely against him. She covered his hands with her own and leaned back against him.

"You make me so," she said in her own soft whisper.

He pressed his lips against her hair, and then dropped his head to place a startlingly hot kiss to the nape of her neck, his breath dancing along the sensitive skin there. Her eyes fluttered shut and a breathy sigh escaped her lips.

Annie stumbled on a rock in her path and fell into the cold snow, only just catching herself with her hands before her face would have directly landed in a snow pile. She exhaled slowly, collecting her wits, and pushed herself back up. She wiped her hands off on her apron, tightened her shawl around her, and moved forward once more, the baker's shop in sight.

Even now, the dream left her wanting something. She had thought of little else all day, ridiculous and fanciful though it was. She had always considered herself a creature of sense and calm, yet here she was imagining the most scandalous things about a man she had only known a day, and for barely fifteen minutes at that. He could have been a true scoundrel, a thief, a duke, or next in line for the throne.

She doubted the last one, but then, she had never been able to keep straight the monarchy and all its dealings.

It would not do for her to dream any more. Nothing good would ever come of it.

She was nothing more than Annie Ramsey, the pretty daughter of a horse tradesman who had been killed by his partner, raised by her illiterate mother who died of a fever, and further brought up by a drunken and vicious older brother who viewed her as his personal servant and the means to an end. She was not worth the spit beneath the shoes of a man such as Duncan Bray. And she would do well to remember it.

The baker was kind enough to give her a slightly larger loaf than she could afford, but he and his wife had always been considerate where she was concerned. They could not offer her butter this time, but she did not care. So long as she had the bread, she would be safe tonight.

She hurried back to the house as fast as she could manage in all that snow, feeling her brow perspire in spite of the freezing temperatures. Her fingers still ached from the cold, even though they now held a warm loaf. She would warm them by the fire later.

She arrived at the house when there was just enough light to see without help. She rushed over to the pot of soup, and was relieved that it was still very hot. It seemed that, for once, fate would not frown on her. She set the bread on the table, removed her shawl and gloves, and began slicing the bread.

At that precise moment, her brother burst into the house, already scowling. The hunt had not gone well, then. And based upon the smell currently coming from his general direction, it was not difficult to imagine why. He glared at her, but couldn't seem to find anything to fault, so he merely grunted a greeting and set his rifle against the wall. His hat went flying into a corner and he sank into his customary chair.

Annie turned to the soup and filled a bowl for him, then handed it to him with a spoon and a large slice of bread.

He didn't look at her as he ate, nor did he take any care for table manners. This wasn't surprising, but she wished he would at least pretend to be human.

She scolded herself soundly in her mind. She ought to keep a civil tongue in her head or she would speak these things out loud someday, and that would not serve her well at all.

"This is better than normal," Frank managed around a mouthful of soup and bread, ignoring the few drops that fell onto the table.

"Thank you," Annie replied softly as she sat down with her own small bowl.

He snorted. "Don't go thinkin' it was you. Must be better spices from the shop."

She ignored that comment. "How was the hunt?"

He ignored her and continued eating.

It was destined to be a typical meal eaten in silence, until Frank pushed his now empty bowl away and cleared his throat. Annie looked up in surprise.

"I've picked a man for you," he said, looking at her at last.

The soup she had just swallowed suddenly felt like rocks in her throat. She tried several times to clear it before the sensation vanished. "Oh?" she asked finally.

"Yes. The price is good and you won't get anything better around here."

Considering the quality of people considered as "around here," that was something she could agree with him on.

"Who will I have, then?"

He barked a laugh and stood, taking his jacket off. "You will have no one. But Albert Thorpe wants you badly and is going to pay a considerable sum, considering what a disappointment you are destined to be. But he's determined and he's outbid all the rest, so there it is."

Annie's blood ran cold and she had to latch onto the table to keep from collapsing out of her chair and into the fire. "M-Mr. T-Thorpe?" she stammered, stuttering so badly she nearly bit her tongue.

Frank's brows rose in surprise, knowing she hadn't truly spoken with such difficulty since she was a child. "Yes, that's what I said."

She shook her head and released a gasping breath. That was beyond the worst she could have imagined. Thorpe was a recent addition to her brother's group of potential bidders, and the one she feared the most. He enjoyed cornering her, whispering his plans for her, his black eyes glinting with such danger she trembled.

He never touched her, he knew that was forbidden and would cost him, but she felt more filthy after his encounters than she imagined any touch feeling. His plans for her included all the same types of beatings her brother was prone to and beyond, and then he ventured into darker, more disturbing details that she had nearly vomited from hearing.

If Frank knew, would he have stopped it? Would he have chosen someone else? Anyone would have been a better choice, and anyone else at all she would gladly accept as alternative.

"I can't," she hissed, clenching her eyes shut.

"What?" Frank drawled, clearly no longer paying attention to her.

"I can't marry him," she said a touch louder.

Suddenly her head was forced back and her brother's stench threatened to choke her. "Open your eyes, and say that again," he growled.

Unable to restrain the smallest of whimpers, she opened her eyes. His face was directly before her, eyes bloodshot, chin stubbled, breath horrendous and potent. Her jaw quivered and she bit her lip hard.

"Say it. Again," he ordered.

"I can't marry Thorpe." She tensed in anticipation.

"And you think you have a say in this?" he sneered, his fingers digging into the back of her head.

"He is horrible," she tried, her chest beginning to heave in panic. "He will do things to me that you cannot even…"

"You think you have a say in this?" he bellowed, screaming into her face so fiercely she could feel the drops of his spit flying onto her face. "You will marry who I tell you to when I tell you to and you will obey me in all things!"

"Frank…"

He slapped her across the face so hard she fell from the chair and clattered onto the floor. "You obey me, Annie! You obey me!"

She crawled to the other side of the table. "I won't marry him, Frank. I won't!"

He roared and turned the table onto its side, stalking towards her. "If I say you will, you will! You have no choice! Do you understand me?"

"Frank," Annie tried, shaking as she tried to evade him, unable to stop the tears that flowed helplessly down her cheeks. "Frank, please."

"Shut up!" he yelled, still coming at her. "I've had enough of you! You will marry him and you will do everything that I say! Do you understand me?"

"Frank!" she screamed as he latched onto her and hauled her backwards.

"I'll teach you to mouth off to me."

He threw her against the nearest wall and her head crashed painfully against the stone. Her vision spotted for a few moments, then cleared as he began rolling his sleeves up, his chest heaving like an angry bull. He was a small man by height, but in this moment, he might as well have been a giant.

"All these years," he seethed as he glared at her, "and still you disrespect me. Clearly I have not done a very good job. But you'll learn. Before you marry Thorpe, I'll have you crawling on the floor if I order it."

"Frank," she whispered, feeling the faintest sense of something trickling down the back of her head. "Please."

"I said shut up, Annie," he said in a quiet, dangerous tone. "Shut up, or lose your teeth."

She clamped her lips together, shaking all over. She felt the handkerchief at her heart and her mind seized upon that faint glimmer of imaginary hope. Frank started towards her again, and she shut her eyes, waiting.

Chapter Three

"*D*oes it always snow this much at once up here?"

"Very rarely, sir. Never, in recent memory."

Duncan grunted and looked out of the window at the blowing snow and the drifts that had formed. He had been forced to remain an extra day and night due to the storm that had come in, and he was not happy about it. Not that this place or this inn had been such a terrible thing, but now he was headed home, he really would just rather get there.

Still, staring out into a winter evening when he was warm and comfortable was something he always appreciated. There was something so peaceful about a clear night sky above with a blanket of snow beneath and he was half tempted to go walk in it. He could let his thoughts wander freely and gaze at the stars in wonder and awe.

He knew very well where his thoughts would go. They had remained on the same subject the night before and throughout the day.

A pair of emerald green eyes, haunted by the cruelty of her life, filled with tears...

Annie.

If that was even her name.

He sighed as he looked out of the window. He ought to have gone after her. He should have sought her out, done more to help. What exactly he could have done for her he couldn't have said, but doing nothing made him feel lower than the dust. He was not a man accustomed to inactivity. He could not stand idly by.

Yet he had. He'd stood there like a fool and let her run back to the man who was hurting her. He hoped she was safe. He hoped she had someone to look out for her. He hoped she was not alone or afraid. He hoped she was well.

He should have gone after her.

He thumped his fist against the wall in irritation.

"Mr. Bray, are you quite all right?"

He turned to the concerned woman standing near him. Her cap was perched on her head a bit askew, and her corkscrew silver curls stuck out at odd angles beneath it. She had a voice like a warbling bird and her clothing was just a bit too snug in places, but she had a kind smile and a good heart. She really had taken quite good care of him during his visit, and though he had not wanted to stay and had made no secret of that fact, she had remained cheerful and accommodating.

"Yes, Mrs. Burton," he said with a smile. "I am well. Thank you for your concern."

She beamed and the corners of her eyes twinkled. "Can I get you anything, sir? A bit more dinner, perhaps?"

As if awaiting that exact suggestion, his stomach roared its approval. He smiled in embarrassment and Mrs. Burton chuckled.

"I take that as a compliment, Mr. Bray," she told him as she moved back towards the kitchen.

"As you should, Mrs. Burton, as you should," he replied. He turned away from the window and situated himself by the fire and looked around the room. There were only a few other patrons at this inn with him, though it was along a busy street. He suspected that the storm the night before had kept others from their journey, same as he.

The village nightlife trickled in a few at a time, all bundled up against the bitter cold and snowflakes. From what he had seen the night before, these were a higher class of people than one might expect to come to an inn at night purely for the drinking. These were hard workers and good people, and they were the sort of people he would enjoy knowing.

The sound of the room rose to a dull roar and all were pleasant and cheerful. Even the fire seemed to glow a little brighter, burn a little hotter, and his worries melted away with the cold.

Impossibly, over the tumult, he heard a faint knocking. He glanced towards the front door, but no one moved towards it. No one else seemed to hear it. He frowned and looked towards the kitchens. Mrs. Burton bustled around, fetching drinks and handing out bowls of her cook's excellent stew.

Then the knock came again, and this time, Mrs. Burton heard it as well. But she didn't look towards the front door. She glanced off to her left and a crease appeared in her high brow. She nodded towards her maid, and the young girl rushed to a side door that Duncan had not noticed before.

He quickly glanced around the room to see if anyone else was paying attention, but everyone in the now almost full room was otherwise occupied.

He looked back just in time to see the door open and felt the sudden blast of cold air. Mrs. Burton looked at the door, paled, and then pressed her lips together in a thin line. She nodded once, then tilted her head towards the kitchen door behind her.

The maid reached through the door and pulled in a small woman, wrapped in a shawl that covered her head and kept her face obscured from the view of the room. The woman moved haltingly, her movements stiff, and favoring one side. Mrs. Burton continued stirring whatever she had on the counter, her motions now agitated and brisk. The woman went to her side and said something, to which Mrs. Burton only nodded again, not even looking at her.

Then Duncan saw Mrs. Burton's jaw tighten. And he did not imagine the glisten of a tear that appeared in one of her eyes.

The woman tightened her hold on the shawl and turned slightly to glance around the room, her face still mostly hidden.

But Duncan could see enough.

Emerald eyes clashed with his and she stilled, frozen, and at the same moment all time ceased to exist.

Annie.

What he could see of her face bore fresh marks and bruises, and one of her eyes was beginning to swell.

She gasped... how could he have heard her over the entire room?... and whirled for the kitchen before he could do more than drop his foot from his knee to the floor. The kitchen door swung shut behind her, with only the faintest glimpse of swirling skirts to catch his eye.

What was she doing here? What had happened to her that rendered her so completely injured?

Why did she seem to fear him?

He stared at the closed door, feeling rather thunderstruck. He had thought of her all night and all day, worried for her and about her, and now she was here.

The world could have rolled into the sun and he would not have been more shocked.

Somehow, the rest of the room had not noticed anything out of the ordinary. Nothing to make anyone even slightly curious about the goings on in this place. All had been as it was before.

Except for him.

He saw Mrs. Burton hand the bowl to the maid, who continued to mix whatever had been so viciously stirred, and then she herself went back into the kitchen. Duncan craned his neck to see as far as he could into the room, but he could see nothing. He nearly growled in his frustration.

The maid suddenly was before him, handing him a fresh bowl of stew. He looked at her in a sort of bewildered confusion, but she had already moved on to another guest. He could not remember asking for food nor was he even remotely hungry. Still, he could not very well sit here and do nothing. So he began to take absent spoonfuls, and it really was very good, as it had been before.

He looked at his pocket watch, and watched it tick, waiting to hear something, anything.

Only after he lost count of the ticks did he realize that no one would tell him anything. And why should they? Who was he to know anything about her?

He would never know.

Just then, Mrs. Burton came back into the taproom, her expression maddeningly unreadable. She smiled for all present, but it did not reach her eyes. She moved around the patrons until she reached a middle-aged local who appeared as though he had imbibed the least out of all present. She leaned down and murmured something to the man, whose smile faded into a hard line. He nodded, then rose and followed her back to the kitchen without a word.

Duncan would go mad.

He looked around, desperate for someone to tell him something. His eyes fell on the nearest local, a rotund man with a wide smile and who was not so far gone as to be insensible. Duncan leaned over the table and tapped the man on his arm.

"D'you know what's going on?" he asked, again mimicking a Scottish accent and lifting a cup of water to his mouth. "What's that man to do with Mrs. Burton?"

The man turned his great beefy self to look where Duncan had indicated and sighed so heavily the bench beneath him creaked audibly. "Oh… Annie Ramsey must have got beaten again."

He choked on the water and sputtered. "I beg your pardon?" he finally managed.

His companion's eyes turned surprisingly soft and sad, nodding sympathetically. "Local girl. Her brother is a mean drunk with an awful temper and he takes it out on her. She comes in every now and then to get help and Mrs. Burton does what she can. But if she pulled George Lyman back there, it must be a pretty good one. He's the closest thing to a doctor we have."

"And he is?" Duncan all but growled.

"Animal doctor. Horses, mostly."

Duncan had heard quite enough. He pushed off of his table and marched in the direction of the kitchen.

"But he's really very good!" the man called after him, as if that fixed everything.

He snorted. Animal doctor. It might have been better than nothing, but it was certainly not good. And apparently everybody knew about Annie's situation, yet nobody had done anything about it. How common was this? Weekly? Monthly? Or was it random and sporadic?

He needed answers and he needed them now.

31

He shoved the kitchen door open and entered the warm room with a bit more gusto than he had intended, but nobody paid him any attention. The cook and her two helpers were busy, but looked over at the trio by the fire frequently.

Mrs. Burton and Mr. Lyman were crowded around Annie, whose shawl now lay draped around her tiny frame, and they actually appeared to be attempting to restrain her.

"No, no," Annie was saying, shaking her head. "I shouldn't have come, I need to leave."

"Annie," Mr. Lyman said, keeping a firm, but not tight, hold on her arm, "you need to let us see to your wounds. I will keep it quick, I promise you, but…"

She shook her head frantically. "I need to go. I can't…" She tried to rise, but Mrs. Burton would not let her.

"Please," Annie said, her voice turning pleading. "Please let me go."

Duncan had heard quite enough. He started towards them, and such was the force of his footfalls that all present turned to face him. Annie made a noise of distress and turned her entire frame towards the fire.

Instantly, Mrs. Burton was on her feet coming towards him. "Is there something I can do for you, Mr. Bray? What do you need? Was dinner to your liking?" Her words came fast and with a distracted, false optimism.

He found it irritating.

"What is going on?" he asked, ignoring her questions.

"Nothing, not a thing," she replied with a fluttery laugh that did not suit.

He gave her a pointed look and gestured with his head. "That does not look like nothing."

Mrs. Burton's eyes turned a shade cooler, but still her smile was bright. "It is nothing, Mr. Bray. Nothing to concern yourself with."

Ah, now that was what he had expected. He forced his ire to calm and smoothed out his features. "I merely wanted to see that the girl was all right. I saw her come in, and I was concerned. Might I be of some assistance?"

Mrs. Burton clucked with her tongue and put a hand on his arm. "Kind, my dear, but no. I am so sorry she disturbed your evening. But have no fear, she is just a poor local girl who has had an accident. She will soon be gone and then we will all return to the taproom for far more pleasant things. Forget you saw anything, Mr. Bray."

There was no staying calm after that.

"An accident," he repeated coolly.

She nodded quickly. "Yes, she's quite the clumsy little thing, and…"

"Excuse me," he interrupted firmly, pushing past her and walking towards the others. Annie had stopped trying to leave, and might as well have been frozen but for the slight tremor that ran through her. Mr. Lyman looked helpless as he crouched before her, trying to tend her wounds while she was turned away.

Annie tensed further when Duncan approached, but he turned his attention to the man before her.

"Mr. Lyman, is it?" he asked, his voice still rough.

Mr. Lyman looked up at him and nodded. "Yes, sir. George Lyman, at your service, Mr. Bray."

He nodded. "Pleasure. Would you give us a moment, please?"

"Certainly, sir." He rose and moved to go past him, but paused at his shoulder. "I think she may have a broken rib or two on her left side," he murmured very low, "but I cannot say for certain. She really must get something on those cuts and bruises. I can ride home for some salve, if you don't mind."

Duncan felt the knot in his stomach loosen slightly. Here, at least, was a creature of sense. "Thank you, Mr. Lyman. That would be much appreciated, I am sure."

Mr. Lyman nodded, then moved out of the way and exited the kitchen. Mrs. Burton still stood where Duncan had left her, her expression hooded and wary. But when Duncan looked at her and gave her a simple nod, she sighed in resignation and she, too, left.

Duncan moved in front of Annie, who still remained turned towards the fire and kept her eyes shut, her expression hidden.

"Annie," he said softly.

A sharp tremor ran through her and he heard the faintest

whimper escape.

He released a sigh and crouched down before her. "Annie," he said again, his voice gentle.

She sniffled and a short sob seemed torn from her throat. He'd never heard a sadder sound in his entire life. He reached out and took one of her small, frozen hands in his.

He swallowed an unexpected lump. "Annie, please look at me."

She shook her head, her free hand covering her mouth as more cries broke free.

"Why not?" he asked. "You remember me, don't you?"

She nodded and hiccupped.

He felt an unexpected burst of pleasure, but he quickly tamped that down. "Then we aren't strangers, and you know that I want to help. Please look at me."

She shivered and he saw her lips move, but heard no words.

"What was that, Annie?" he asked, leaning a touch closer. "I couldn't hear you."

"I can't," she gasped, her words hitching.

"Why not?"

Sobs fairly exploded out of her, each jarring her injured ribs, and she grabbed her side instinctively. He rose slightly and moved to rub her back, trying to soothe her as best as he could.

"It's all right," he murmured, feeling utterly useless. "It's all right, you're safe here." He wanted to take her into his arms, as he had so many times when Marianne had cried, but that was too forward, too much, and he couldn't.

Slowly, Annie's cries faded and her tears, though still flowing, were mostly silent. "I'm so ashamed," she whispered at last.

Duncan closed his eyes and restrained a groan of his own pain. He shook his head and moved back to crouch in front of her, still clutching her hand.

"Annie, look at me," he ordered, keeping his voice gentle, but firm.

She inhaled shakily, then turned and looked at him. Her left eye was more swollen than he'd thought previously, and there were angry scratches along her cheeks and jaw. Each had been bleeding at one point, but now all seemed dried. Fresh bruises surrounded them, and her mouth bore an angry cut that puffed her lip. She looked as though she had been through hell, and as he looked at her, he saw more blood in her hair. Still, through it all, her eyes were just as vibrant as he remembered, their color just as bold.

He smiled softly at her and squeezed her hand. "You have nothing to be ashamed of, sweetheart. Nothing. Do you understand me?"

Her swollen lip quivered and a few stray tears fell.

Without thinking, he reached up, holding her fast as she jerked in surprise and fear, and gently wiped the tears away. Her eyes widened as he touched her skin, and she winced, ever so slightly.

"Does that hurt?" he asked.

She nodded, another tear leaking free.

He quickly swiped that away, then dropped his hand back to her lap. "Annie, did your brother do this to you?"

She looked away, back to the fire, and she swallowed several times.

Duncan watched her for a long moment. So she wouldn't tell him either. It didn't matter, not really. He knew the answer. Or at the very least, he knew enough.

He released a slow breath, then squeezed her hand once more. "Annie, look at me. Please."

Almost hesitantly, she looked back at him.

He smiled and rubbed her hand between his. "You do not have to tell me what is going on in your life. You do not have to tell me what he does to you. But I have eyes, Annie. I can see what you are going through, or its effects, at any rate. And it makes me sick."

She closed her eyes and looked away.

He swallowed and shook his head. "No, look back at me. Come on, stay on me."

Those emerald eyes, filled with tears, met his once more.

"I have a sister," he began, "who is probably fairly close to your age. And she means everything to me. I practically raised her, poor thing, and I am far too overprotective for my own good or for her taste. The thought of ever raising my hand to her turns my blood to ice, and the idea that any brother would feel differently…" He shook his head again, then squeezed her hand tightly. "No one deserves this, Annie. You should not have to live like this."

In a small, very shaky voice, Annie replied, "It's all I know."

"It doesn't have to be," he said with a renewed energy. An idea struck him with such force he felt dazed, but his mouth apparently didn't notice, for it continued on. "I also have an aunt who lives near me in London, and she has no one but my sister and I. She does not say it very much, but she gets lonely. She needs a companion."

What was he doing? Was he *insane*?

Annie apparently thought so, for her expression turned bewildered.

"Annie, you could come back with me."

Saints above, he was mad.

"What?" she gasped, her eyes searching his frantically.

He was nodding before he knew what he was doing. "Come to London with me. You can stay with Tibby. That's my aunt, Lady Raeburn. She would take excellent care of you, and you would be safe and warm and comfortable, but also providing her with the company she craves."

"You're mad," she whispered sadly.

It was true, he was. And yet…

He shrugged. "Probably. But you deserve better than this, Annie. I want to help you. I need to help you. And I can, if you let me. Come with me to London. You will be safe. You will be protected. You will never have to be afraid. Leave all of this and come with me."

"Leave?" Her voice broke and her hands shook beneath his.

He tightened his hold. "I know you don't know me. But I swear to you, on my sister's life, I will never do you harm. I will protect you as fiercely as I would her. I can help you, Annie. You can have a different life."

She stilled and stared at him for what seemed like hours. He held his breath and waited.

"You don't want to get involved," she finally said, shaking her head and wincing. "I'm not worth it. It's too…"

"I already am involved," he interrupted gently, "and nothing is worth more right now than you. Than this. I hate that I could not help you yesterday. I have thought of little else. And so help me, Annie, I will help you now. I refuse to let you live like this one day more. So I am begging you, quite literally on my knees, to let me help you. Come to London with me. Start a new life. Be free."

A more impassioned speech he had never given in his entire life. He'd never had a reason to. But suddenly, everything in his world hinged on her answer.

"I... I don't know if I can," she murmured, looking at him with worry, hesitation, and sadness.

He swallowed a lump of disappointment, but that was hardly her fault. He had dropped a mountain before her and asked her to climb. She would have been just as mad as he to accept at once. "I understand," he said slowly, offering her a reassuring smile. "I truly do. But I cannot wait. Tomorrow morning I will leave here for London. If you come, I will most willingly take you with me and help you start a new life. If you do not..." He trailed off, the thought to horrible to comprehend. "Well, I don't very well know what I would do. But you would always count me as a friend. The offer will always stand. Always."

"You don't even know me," she whispered.

"I know all I need to."

They stared at each other for what seemed an age, not speaking, and not needing to. There were no more tears, and her hands beneath his were finally beginning to warm. He was still crouched before her, and his back and legs were beginning to throb.

But he couldn't even feel it.

He was, in fact, remarkably content.

The kitchen door swung open again, bringing Mrs. Burton and Mr. Lyman back into the room. Annie slid her hand out from his, and Duncan rose, stepping back to let them tend to her. He made additional suggestions as needed, but remained mostly apart. Annie did not look at him again, nor did she speak another word in his direction.

When he was assured she was in good hands, and after receiving multiple assurances from Mrs. Burton that Annie would be properly escorted home, he left the kitchen and headed for his rooms.

He could not be entirely sure what had just happened, but upon reflection, he would not have changed a single thing.

He prayed Annie would come with him in the morning.

He could never live with himself if she did not.

The morning air was frigid. Much colder than it had been in days past. But the sky was clear, and there had been no snow in the night, so it was time to continue on. Duncan waited next to Balthazar, wrapped in his warmest clothes, and the furs lay on the horse.

He had been waiting for nearly an hour already.

He ought to just go. He was freezing and Balthazar was growing restless. He had walked the horse around a bit to keep him moving as best as he could. His eyes wandered across the horizon, wondering where she would come from.

If she would come.

Mrs. Burton kept bringing him things for his journey and additional blankets to ensure he stayed warm. At this rate, he would have more blankets than he had acquaintances. He suspected the woman was trying to make up for her behavior the night before, and he forgave her. He had seen in her eyes how much she had truly cared about Annie, despite what she wished to show outwardly.

It seemed everyone cared about Annie.

Just not enough to do anything about it.

He had asked around this morning, and everyone he spoke with knew that Frank Ramsey beat his sister on a semi-regular basis, regardless of timing or reason. He had done so for years and nothing had ever been done. He was not a man of high regard in the area, nor of great importance. He did sell a number of relatively good horses to several of the townspeople, but all in all, he generally kept to himself. He was not well liked, and certainly no one approved of his behaviors, but getting involved in someone else's private affairs was not of interest to anybody.

Duncan was the same way.

Most of the time.

He shook his head in derision. He was a mad fool. Waiting in this freezing cold weather for a young woman he had encouraged to break all ties with her family, her friends, and her reputation to come away with him and start a new life, not because of some wild, frantic, passionate love affair, but simply because he couldn't mind his own business.

He did not regret it. He could not.

But still, he was a fool.

She wouldn't come.

Or would she?

She was a timid creature, terrified by the world, and rightfully so. What had the world ever given her to make her fond of it? She had spirit, but she had likely never done a brave thing in her life. Someone had tried to crush her spirit and make her smaller.

He prayed they had not succeeded entirely.

He glanced down at his pocket watch and sighed heavily.

It was time to go.

He turned to Balthazar, rubbed his nose, then moved to the side and prepared to mount.

Then he heard it. The unmistakable sound of snow crunching beneath feet, and a soft, timid call. "Wait."

He turned towards the sound and exhaled sharply, waves of relief washing over him so poignantly he could not breathe.

She had come.

Chapter Four

$\mathcal{I}$t was only three days all told to London, and Annie grew more and more anxious with every mile. After the first day, Duncan had decided it was not wise for Annie to ride all the way to London on horseback in the winter weather, so he had hired a coach for her. It was unfathomable, but he seemed to have endless amounts of money.

He paid the coachman handsomely, he paid for the meals of other people, and he paid for their nights in inns so fine Annie had been afraid to touch anything. She knew they must have seemed very ordinary to him, but to her it might as well have been a palace.

And the beds! She could have slept for three years straight in them. She had never known anything beyond her straw-filled pallet at home, and now she could quite plainly see what she had been missing.

The coach itself was rather spacious for one person, and she felt a slight twinge of disappointment when she saw that Duncan would continue riding his horse alongside. She didn't flatter herself that there was a bond between them of more than allegiance and the possibility of friendship, but that first day, when she had been so uncertain and afraid, his warmth and strength had carried her through. Now she would be alone again.

She was under absolutely no illusions. She knew she had not actually run away with Duncan nor would he ever consider her actions as such. There was nothing romantic about a man helping her to escape from her abusive brother and indifferent townspeople.

No one had ever taken such an interest in her before. Mrs. Burton and Mr. Lyman had certainly tried their utmost where she was concerned, being acquainted with her parents in the past and certainly always helping when she asked for it. She was grateful for their efforts in her behalf. But no one had done what Duncan had.

No one had stood up for her. No one had ever insisted things change.

No one had offered a way out.

The thought of escaping had never actually occurred to her, as often as she might have wished for it. It was simply not a course of action that she could rationalize. Alone it would have been impossible, foolhardy, and probably would have ended with her dead or worse.

With Duncan, not only had it seemed possible, but also remarkably clear. She'd *had* to go.

She had not missed his surprised, yet relieved expression when she had arrived, wrapped in her meager shawl and tattered dress. He had given her a very searching glance, then asked, "Are you sure about this?"

Something within her had forced her to be brutally honest with him. After all, she was trusting him with the rest of her life, in a manner of speaking.

"No," she had told him, "but I'm doing it anyway."

Now they rode on, destined for London and her unknown future.

He had been the height of consideration where she was concerned. He asked after her needs so often it was repetitious, but she never minded. He had lined the coach seats with sheep skin so she might be warm, had asked for additional blankets and pillows so she might have comfort for the journey, and he ensured that at every inn they stayed she had all the privacy she could want.

She didn't want privacy. Privacy gave her time to think on her actions, and so many doubts flooded her mind that she almost asked if they could stop several times. But some small thread of courage kept her from it. She had made her bed and she would lie in it.

Besides, going back would ensure her a beating so terrible she might never recover.

And Duncan wouldn't be at all pleased about that.

Her ribs were finally starting to cease in their constant throbbing, her bruises were fading, and the cuts had healed over well enough to only be noticeable if one truly looked. Whatever faults she had, she was a fast healer, which she was most grateful for at this time.

She couldn't face Duncan's aunt and sister looking as though she had come out the loser in a tavern brawl. They would have tossed her from the house at once and she would have had to fend for herself in London, of all places.

They might do so anyway.

London.

The very idea of such a large place was enough to make her shiver with fear. She wondered how she would manage. Would Lady Raeburn like her? Would she even want her as a companion? Would Duncan turn her over to his aunt and then wash his hands of her? Would he feel his good deed done and take no further interest?

She hoped he would take at least some interest. He looked at her with such concern, such compassion, and she didn't think she imagined the intensity in his blue eyes when he spoke with her. But perhaps that was merely his nature. She had seen him behave with kindness and charity to several along their journey, so it was likely that his nature was one of giving, of helping, and of asking nothing in return.

He was too good for her.

But of course, she knew that already.

She leaned her head against the plush sides of the coach, tucking her shawl more tightly around her, and restrained a heavy sigh. She had rested well in this coach, had certainly been taken care of, and treated far better than she ever had in her life, but she was ready to be done with travelling. She wished to begin her new life as soon as possible.

Why prolong what one feared?

The carriage slowed, then stopped.

"Annie."

42

She raised her head and looked out of the coach window. Duncan smiled down at her and gestured for her to look. "We have arrived."

She rose as best as she could manage in the coach and looked out of the window. There, ahead of them, in all its glory, was London. It was bigger than she could have imagined and far more imposing.

"Oh my," she breathed, her voice coming out more like a whimper.

Duncan's smile turned infinitely warm. "You will be fine, Annie. You're not afraid, are you?"

She could only whisper, "Terrified."

"There is no need. I will be with you every step of the way. I promise."

She looked up at him, and again felt her insides heat at the raw power and utter sincerity in his blue eyes.

She swallowed and nodded, then leaned back against the carriage as it moved once more. Her fingers began to knot themselves together, and her stomach began turning over in anticipation. There would be no turning back now.

It was not long before they stopped once more, and a brief glance out of the window told her they truly had arrived now. The buildings were so tall and so grand. And people *lived* in these? Regular people?

She almost laughed.

Regular people.

She was a regular person. These people were high society, lords and ladies, people of grace and power and influence. And untold wealth.

They would never be regular people.

And she would never fit in.

Duncan opened the door to the coach and offered her a hand. She looked at him uncertainly, knowing she should not be afraid. And she wasn't. Not of him, at any rate. But actually taking this first step into her new reality?

Of that she was more than a little afraid.

She met his eyes, knowing her fear and hesitation was clear. He smiled at her, the corners of his eyes crinkling just a touch, and he crooked his fingers at her. "Come on, Annie. Time to be brave."

"I've never been brave a day in my life," she muttered, pushing a bit of hair out of her face.

"Not true," he told her with a shake of his head. "You did the bravest thing I have ever seen only three days ago. This is nothing in comparison." He extended his hand a bit further. "Come on."

She sighed, and placed her hand in his, ignoring the way her fingers seemed to tingle in his hold. She stepped out of the coach and glanced up, craning her neck to see the top of the grand edifice. There were no words for what she felt, for the pressure that had begun to pool in her chest.

"It's a bit grand for me," Duncan said, seeing her dazed expression. "Marianne thinks it needs more, but I refused."

"I like it," Annie murmured.

He smiled at her and squeezed her hand. "Good." Then he dropped his hold and took her by the elbow.

Annie looked up at him. "So this is…?"

"My home," he finished for her. "I want to introduce you to my sister before we go to Tibby's. It is not far, three blocks perhaps."

She nodded, swallowing hard. His sister. She had imagined so much these last three days and Duncan's sister was one of them. She would be regal and elegant and refined, and just the smallest bit spoiled, by Duncan's account. But she would have his coloring, dark hair and bright blue eyes and a ready smile. Annie hoped she would not be too proud or too fine, for she wished to make a good impression, and dressed as she was, and by her nature, she wasn't going to have an easy time of that as things stood.

And then there was Lady Raeburn. She subdued a shudder and bit her lip instead. She was glad she would have some time to prepare for that introduction. It was the most important one she would have.

Duncan squeezed her elbow briefly. "I promise, you will be fine."

Annie nodded again, a bit too quickly, and swallowed once more. She wished she had the courage or the will to smile for him, but she couldn't. She was surprised her legs actually moved as they neared the door, as she could not feel her toes. As quickly as she could, she glanced down, just to be sure they were still there.

What a relief. If all else failed her, at least she was still in possession of her toes.

Duncan rang the bell and stepped back. It seemed ridiculous that a man should have to ring the bell at his own home, but perhaps that was how things were done in London.

A middle aged man with a receding hairline and an impressive frown answered, then stepped back immediately, his frown turning into a straight line. "Mr. Bray, welcome home, sir."

"Thank you, Wilson," Duncan replied in his usual low tone, which seemed to reverberate in the entrance as they stepped in.

Annie had never seen a place so grand in her life. She couldn't see enough of it as she craned her neck in every direction. The entrance was almost entirely made of marble, and the slightest sound echoed on and on.

The stairs were marble, but they held a green rug that ran along each step then seemed to spill into the same shade of rug that sat on the entrance floor. The railings were a pale stone as well, and even from her present spot, she could see their smoothness.

The walls were hung with tapestries of such exquisite details and designs that she could hardly imagine the intricate work that had been required. Sconces hung along the walls with ivory candles in each and there were halls and rooms beyond that she itched to explore.

What secrets and mysteries could such a grand place hide?

"A bit much, is it not?" Duncan said softly, leaning towards her.

"It's very grand," she answered, marveling at how even her soft tones echoed.

"As I said, too grand."

It was not too grand, in her opinion. It was perfect.

"Wilson," Duncan said in a louder voice, turning to the butler, "will you send for Marianne? I should very much…"

"Duncan?"

They all turned to the nearest doorway, where a young woman in a simple grey day dress stood.

Duncan grinned and opened his arms. "Minnow."

The woman squealed and ran into his arms, and allowed him to pick her up and swing her round, laughing and giggling all the while.

Annie hung back and watched the reunion with interest. Was this what it was supposed to be like?

Duncan set her down and kissed her cheek. "Have you missed me?"

"Dreadfully," she replied. "This place is so dull without you."

Annie was mostly correct in her imaginations, but she had fallen *far* short of the glory of Miss Marianne Bray.

No woman could have been more beautiful, or appear so unattainable.

And Annie was suddenly very aware of how very much she lacked.

Even the simple dress Marianne wore was exquisite. Silvery-grey and clinging to every curve without being the slightest bit revealing, and she bore a burgundy wrap around her arms that did not make her seem the slightest bit matronly. She looked positively regal, and the rich darkness of her hair reminded Annie of coal, which seemed a poor comparison indeed.

Suddenly, the siblings turned to her and Marianne's expression changed from delight to disbelief.

"Marianne, I would like you to meet Miss Annie Ramsey, from Yorkshire."

Was she supposed to bow or curtsey? She had no idea, so she simply stood there.

Marianne looked at her brother in confusion, then back at Annie. Her eyes were wide, confused, and a bit pitying. She turned her head towards the hallway. "Tibby!" she called, her voice musically echoing off of everything. "Come quickly! Duncan has brought home a stray!"

Duncan swatted his sister sharply, his face burning at her rudeness. Annie's cheeks flamed a brilliant pink, her eyes lowered, and her fingers clenched their hold on each other. She was positively mortified. "Marianne!" he hissed.

She looked up at him innocently. "Yes?"

He hardened his jaw and glowered at her. "Be nice."

She quirked her brows at him. "You have a better description?"

He pinched the bridge of his nose and exhaled quickly. This was not going well. "You are being intolerably rude to our guest."

Now Marianne looked thunderstruck. "Our guest? Surely you do not…"

"Marianne," he interrupted as gently as he could with his teeth grinding, "she is standing right there."

She looked over at Annie and Duncan could see her superior expression soften as she really looked. There was the sister he so adored, not the creature she had taken to being.

"My apologies, Miss Ramsey," Marianne said in a very kind voice. "Please, forgive my rudeness."

"It's fine," Annie murmured so softly Duncan could hardly hear it. Her eyes were still trained on the floor.

Marianne looked up at him. "What did she say?" she mouthed at him.

"She said it was fine," he whispered. "But obviously, it is not."

Marianne had the good sense to look ashamed. "I am sorry."

"Then act like it."

She nodded once and cleared her throat. "How long are you here for, Miss Ramsey?" she asked, keeping her voice kind and polite.

Annie looked up sharply, her eyes panicked, and she glanced at Duncan, biting her lip. "Um…"

"What is all this? Have we been invaded by gypsies?" Tibby's voice echoed in the halls before she made her presence known.

Duncan rolled his eyes heavenward. This day could not get any worse.

Annie jumped as if startled when Tibby came from the room nearest her and grandly entered the entryway. And much to Tibby's credit, it was an entrance to be proud of. The woman was dressed in a vibrant Alexandria blue silk dress and a matching turban, which made her fiery red hair seem more violently red than normal. Her eyes appeared the very color of her dress and turban, and her wrap and slippers were apparently made from pure spun gold. And for some inexplicable reason, she had colored her cheeks, making her look more like a star of the stage than a well-colored lady of fashion. It was impossible to look anywhere except at her.

But she was, after all, Tabitha, Lady Raeburn. She never did anything by half measures.

"Oh, it is just you, nephew," she crowed, smiling brightly at him. "My, my, you look quite unchanged. I expected your dear cousins to send you home in a tartan and raving on and on about the delights of haggis, but I am pleased you still seem resoundingly English."

He could not help but to grin at her. "Lovely to see you, Tibby, as always. To what do we owe the pleasure of your presence in our home?"

Tibby laughed a tinkling trill of a laugh. "Oh, darling boy, I am living here now."

Duncan could only blink his shock. "You're what now?"

"Living here, Duncan," Marianne said from his side, her voice thick with amusement. "Isn't it grand?"

"Not forever, mind you," Tibby said with a dramatic wave of her hand, her many rings glinting in the light of the day. "Just until the renovations of my own house are completed."

"Renovations," he repeated, feeling rather staggered by the news. "When did those begin?"

Tibby put a finger to her chin in thought. "Hmmmm, two weeks, was it, Marianne?"

"Nearly, yes," his sister confirmed.

"And they will be finished…?" Duncan asked, glancing over at Annie, who seemed positively transfixed by Tibby. In fact, she looked terrified.

Tibby gave him a hard look. "Why, when I approve of the work, my dear. I should not expect them to even be ready for inspection for another month, perhaps two. And then it may be some time until I approve it."

Two months. With Tibby, and Annie, under his roof.

He swallowed and tried to look complacent. "I see."

"It has been a vastly entertaining Christmas," Marianne quipped, nudging him with her elbow.

48

He could only imagine.

Tibby looked at Marianne now. "What were you saying, dear? Duncan brought home a stray?"

Marianne bit her lip hard to keep from laughing.

Tibby looked back at him with a scolding glare. "How many times have I told you to stop saving animals? I have four dogs as it is, all living here with us, and your two pointers will not appreciate any further intruders. Really, I wish you had a harder heart, my love, you are so generous and soft, despite your gigantesque stature."

Duncan had the absurd urge to laugh, but he resisted. "I did not bring home a dog, Tibby."

"I am relieved to hear it," she said with a heaving sigh. "So what did you bring, then?"

He smiled and looked at Annie. "I have brought a young lady." He gestured politely in Annie's direction, pleased that her fearful expression seemed to have faded to one of utter bewilderment that was quite charming.

"Praised be the heavenly saints! I never thought I would see the day!" Tibby crowed, raising her hands to the sky and turning on the spot to see who he had indicated. Her eyes widened, her arms slowly dropped, and she was somehow able to only look mildly surprised. "Oh my. You are a tiny wisp of a girl, are you not, my dear?"

Annie looked horrified at being addressed.

Tibby turned back to Duncan with an expression of concern. "Is she well?"

"Very," he said, still smiling. "Her name is Annie Ramsey, Tibby. Annie, this is my aunt, Lady Raeburn."

Tibby turned back and nodded regally. "Charmed, my dear, charmed. Tell me, did my nephew fish you out of a rustic and filthy wishing well and wed you on the journey home?"

Annie flushed so suddenly Duncan thought she would either swoon or burst into flames.

"She is not my wife, Tibby," Duncan said, feeling his neck heat under his collar. "I have brought her back for you."

"For me?" Tibby asked, her brow furrowing. "Whatever for?"

"She is to be a companion for you."

Tibby looked at him for a long moment, looked back to Annie and appraised her, then turned back to him and put her hands on her hips. "What in heaven's name gave you the idea that I need a companion?"

Chapter Five

$\mathcal{A}$nnie wondered if she could sink into the marble floor beneath her feet. It would probably be painful, but not nearly as agonizing as being forced to stand here and endure what had just happened.

Duncan had been mortified by his relations, but Annie had expected nothing less. She did not, however, expect Lady Raeburn to have no desire for a companion.

So even in London she was useless.

Brilliant.

Duncan had pulled both of the other women into a near room, begging Annie to excuse them for a moment, and shut the door. It took all of her strength not to go listen at the door. So instead she stood where he had left her, fingers mangling each other, clothing tattered and torn, looking like a clump of dirt on a pristine floor.

If she had anywhere to go, she would leave this instant.

But she did not.

So she stayed.

And waited.

"When have I ever needed a companion?"

Duncan paced back and forth in his study a bit frantically, running his hands through his hair. "You are always saying how lonely you are and how no one pays any attention to you."

Tibby sighed and put a hand to her brow. "Darling, I was being dramatic. I have many, many friends. Far too many, in fact," she added as an afterthought. "I am due to cut some out. I am ridiculously popular and invited everywhere. It is an exhausting way of life."

Marianne giggled from where she sat in his chair, then covered her mouth.

He threw his hands up in the air. "Then why would you say differently?"

"Because, my dear, I want *you* to pay attention to me." She looked at him as if that should have been obvious.

He gave her an exasperated look and put his hands on his hips. "I do! I always have; I am very attentive to you and your needs."

She smiled fondly. "Yes, dear, of course you are, that is why you are my favorite and will inherit my vast fortune and my massive collection of antiquities. But it is always a bit more fun when you think you are being the hero."

Duncan gaped at her for a long moment. "I never think I'm being a hero," he finally stammered.

Tibby's smile turned a bit patronizing. "Yes, you do. You always have. It's really very sweet."

"You do, Duncan. You save everyone and everything," Marianne pointed out with a smile.

"I do?" he asked, looking between the two of them.

Both women nodded.

He leaned back against the nearest wall a bit inelegantly as he took in the impact of those words. "I had no idea."

Tibby let him digest in silence for a bit, then cleared her throat. "So, to answer your query; no, I do not need a companion. Besides, I always have Marianne." She waved a hand in the direction of his sister.

He glanced over and saw Marianne meet his gaze with an expression of pure and unfettered panic. She quickly recovered and turned back to their aunt.

"But Tibby, think how fun it would be to have a companion of your very own," Marianne said in a would-be calm voice. Duncan could hear her straining for a note of excitement and he had to restrain the urge to grin.

Tibby gave her a strange look. "How do you mean?"

Marianne seemed to choose her words with great care. "Miss Ramsey would be entirely at your disposal. When Duncan is with his friends or I with mine, she could be available for you, to read or play or escort you wherever you wish to go. You could have a great influence on her. Think of that."

"I have a great influence on everyone," Tibby said with a sniff, winking at Duncan.

Marianne rolled her eyes. "I am trying to be encouraging, Tibby."

"Oh, really? After you called her a stray?"

"You asked if she was fetched from a dirty wishing well."

"Well, did you see the poor thing? She looks like a starving waif!"

Both turned their eyes to Duncan expectantly. He was unprepared for such intensity. "What?"

"Really, Duncan, what were you thinking?" Marianne asked with pity.

"Wherever did you find that girl and why in heaven's name did you bring her here?" Tibby shook her head sadly. "If I wanted a companion, there are several more suitable, not to mention better fed, candidates floating around London. Why that one?"

"Her name," he said, losing a bit of his patience, "is Annie. And you both can think whatever you like about me, but let me tell you a little bit about her."

Quietly, and trying to leave as much emotion out of it as possible, he relayed the facts of Annie's story and situation and how they had met. He didn't elaborate, nor did he speculate. He fully admitted to not knowing everything, but told what he could. He spoke of his meeting her, of her fear and her injury, of seeing her again at the inn and her fresh wounds, of the indifference of nearly everyone there. Perhaps he ought to have been more delicate, but they deserved to know the facts as they stood.

When he finished, Tibby had sunk onto the sofa nearest her, a handkerchief over her mouth, whimpering. Marianne sat still, tears streaming down her cheeks. Duncan looked at them both and relaxed a little.

"And now you know why I have brought her," he said softly. "You can only imagine what else she has endured in her life. It was not easy for her to come with me. She was probably terrified the entire time. But she did come. The strength that must have taken… It might not have been the most proper thing in the world, but I could not leave her there, not like that."

"Of course not!" Marianne sniffled and dabbed at her eyes with her own handkerchief. "I am a horrible creature," she wailed.

Duncan moved to her and pulled her into his arms. "No, sweet, you are not."

"That poor thing!" Tibby cried, her voice wavering dangerously. She blew her nose loudly into her handkerchief. "Duncan, you… you saved her!"

He pulled away from his sister, shaking his head. "I did no such thing, Tibby. She saved herself. I simply gave her a way. And I hope that I can count on the two of you to continue to help me and her in this. She is starting a new life without family or friends."

"Except for us," Marianne said fiercely with a final sniffle. "I am adopting her."

"As am I!" Tibby announced, getting to her feet. "She will be my companion and my godchild. I always thought I would make an excellent godmother, and here is my chance."

Duncan grinned and looked at the both of them. "And this is why I adore you both."

"We know," they replied as one, then burst into laughter.

Duncan shook his head. "Now, don't mention anything to Annie. She is uncomfortable as it is, I'm not sure she would enjoy being reminded of what she has left behind. So please, try to be tactful and sweet."

"When are we anything but?" Marianne asked as she pinched at her cheeks and headed for the door. "Honestly, it is like you expect us to be cruel."

He could have said so many things to that, but he chose to keep his mouth shut.

He knew when he could not win.

The two of them swung the door open and headed directly for

Annie, who instinctively backed up at their approach. Duncan followed with his own reservations, but he kept those carefully hidden. Annie would need someone who appeared calm and comfortable.

"It seems, Miss Ramsey, that I have need of you after all," Tibby said with a wave of her hand. "Truly, I have always wanted a companion, but not a loud or ostentatious one, and you shall suit perfectly."

Annie looked at Duncan in bewilderment, but he merely smiled and shrugged. What could he say? There was no explaining Tibby.

"Miss Ramsey," Marianne began, taking Annie's hand in hers, "I do hope you will forgive my abominable rudeness. I am really not that heartless. Slightly heartless, but not entirely. I should never welcome anyone into my home with such behavior. Say you will forgive me, Miss Ramsey, and allow me to make amends."

"Annie," she replied in her soft, shy tone, still looking confused.

"Pardon?" Marianne asked, rubbing her hand.

"Call me Annie," she said louder, her cheeks turning pink at her apparent daring. "Please."

Marianne smiled brightly. "Annie, then. You must call me Marianne. And am I to be forgiven?"

Annie looked surprised at the question. "Of course," she replied in her simple, soft way.

"Oh, you delightful child!" Tibby squealed, embracing her quite suddenly. Then she stepped back and wrinkled her nose in distaste. "Darling, you smell like a wet dog."

"Tibby!" Marianne and Duncan cried together.

"What?" she asked, looking around at them both. "She does."

"I'm sorry," Anne murmured, ducking her head and stepping back as far as she could.

Tibby waved her hands dismissively. "It is not your fault, dear girl. If my nephew were any sort of gentleman, he would have seen to your comfort properly. But all men are useless, and as you have, I am sure, noticed, he falls rather soundly into that category." She clucked her tongue. "But really, we must have a warm bath drawn for you and a fresh set of clothes, you must be positively perishing with dirt and fatigue from all that travelling."

"Yes, yes, where are your things?" Marianne asked, peeling Annie's shawl from her shoulders, hiding her appalled expression from her. She handed the garment off to a servant who also wrinkled her nose and carried it away with only two fingers touching it.

Annie looked down at the floor again. "This is all that I have."

The women stilled and looked at each other with wide eyes. Even Duncan had no idea what to say. He had not said anything to Annie as yet about her lack of luggage or belongings. It had occurred to him, of course, but what could he say? She could hardly have brought everything she owned with her.

Or had she done so?

The girls sprang into action.

"I will write to Mary Harris straight away," Marianne said as she recovered. "She will have several things that will suit until we can get her some proper things."

"I don't want to cause a fuss," Annie replied, her eyes startled.

"Mary Harris?" Tibby squawked. "She is far too tall. Our Annie will be walking on more of the dress than she wears."

"Mary is not so tall," Marianne countered, peeling the fingerless gloves from Annie's hands.

Tibby gave Marianne a look. "She is half a head taller than you, dear, and though her figure is as slender as a reed, everything will still be too long."

Marianne sighed in irritation. "Diana Beckham?"

"Better, but she has gotten so plump with her child bearing that she will be too large. Annie will swim in it."

"Please don't make a fuss," Annie tried again, looking between them.

"Well, I am sorry that I do not know anybody as small as Annie, Tibby, but she has to have *something* to wear," Marianne huffed, signaling for Annie to remove her shoes.

"Nobody is as small as Annie," Tibby commented as she looked her up and down. "Mary Harris might have some of her sister's things that will do. Cassandra was quite small once upon a time."

Annie looked down at herself, then looked up at Duncan, her

emerald eyes wide. "Am I really so small?" she asked.

He opened his mouth to reply, although what he was going to say he had no idea.

"Skin and bones, darling, skin and bones," Tibby sighed shaking her head. "If we wrapped you in white linen, people would think you a corpse."

"Tibby!" Marianne screeched, cheeks flaming.

Duncan put a hand over his eyes briefly, unsure whether to laugh or groan.

"What is it now?" Tibby asked with no small amount of irk. She shook her head and leaned closer to Annie. "This is why I do not like living in England. Abroad is so much lovelier. You can say the most astonishing things on the Continent and nobody thinks anything of it. But here in England, it is all prim and proper, polite behavior all the time. I have no idea how we became so high and mighty, but there it is."

Annie actually smiled at that, which sent a warm jolt into Duncan's midsection.

Tibby smiled back and patted Annie's hand. "Never fear, my dear. We shall take good care of you here. Between Marianne and myself, you shall want for no fashion or conversation, and with Duncan we are sure to be well protected and well fed."

"Excuse me?" he asked, attempting to appear affronted.

"Time for that bath, I think!" Tibby said loudly as she took Annie's arm and began leading her towards the stairs. "Marianne, which room should she take?"

"Oh, the one next to you, of course, Tibby," Marianne said, taking up position on the other side of Annie. "Agnes! Have a bath drawn up in the room next to Lady Raeburn, as quick as you can! And bring the lavender soap!"

"What am I supposed to do?" Duncan called after them, feeling slightly worried about leaving Annie alone with his overly exuberant sister and aunt. They would overwhelm her beyond anything he could have imagined.

"Something manly!" Tibby called down.

"There is a pile of correspondence in your study!" Marianne

reminded him. "We shall not be long, and then we may all have dinner together!"

Annie looked back at him before they reached the turning of the stairs. He was correct, she was overwhelmed already. He took three steps forward, then stopped. Was not this what he wanted? For his sister and his aunt to adore her and take care of her? To have her take her life by force and start living in earnest? To have someone take care and take an interest in her?

She did not need rescuing. Not now.

And he was no hero.

He smiled at her encouragingly and nodded.

She bit her lip and gave him the slightest nod in return. Then she was out of his sight, and he could only hear his aunt and sister tittering on about soaps and gowns and stockings.

All too soon, the entryway was silent. And he stood there alone.

He put his hands on his hips and hummed a brief sigh to himself.

Surely there was something he was supposed to do, but on his life, he had no idea what it was.

He barked a laugh and shrugged to himself, then strode off to his study, whistling as he went. And most determinedly *not* thinking about what was going on upstairs.

"Your hair is stunning, Annie!" Marianne gushed as she rinsed it once more. "It is as pure as gold and glitters just as bright!"

"Thank you," Annie murmured, tucking her chin into her knees.

"Such a pretty little thing." Tibby sighed and shook her head. "It is so sad you have had such an unfortunate life thus far."

"Tibby," Marianne scolded from behind Annie. "Hush."

"Do not hush me, child," Tibby barked, coming over with toweling and a simple dressing gown. "Annie is a grown woman and she has been through enough. She can certainly take a bit of sympathy."

Annie did not know what to make of Tibby at all. The woman was outrageous, audacious, and vibrant about absolutely everything.

She was quite intimidated, and yet helplessly fascinated by her. Here was a woman who did not care what anybody else had to say or think. What would it be like to live such a life?

"I don't mind," Annie said softly as Marianne rung out her hair. "Truly."

Marianne sighed. "You are kind. But really, you must tell us when we ought to stop talking or we will just keep going."

Annie smiled into her knees.

"All right, stand up now. I believe it is as clean as we will get you." Marianne stood and wiped her slightly perspiring brow, handed the soap to a servant, and dried her hands on the apron she wore. Even thus, she was beautiful. Exquisite, yet so natural and at ease. No trace of the airs from before.

What a mystery Duncan's sister was.

Annie shakily stood, her knees trembling from cold and fatigue, and yes, from her injuries. Marianne had not said much as she had washed over the bruises, but she had felt when Annie had tensed at the ribs. Yet she had been careful and kind, attentive and soft. Annie appreciated the discretion. She didn't mind sympathy, but she did not wish to discuss it.

She had rinsed her hair that first night at the inn, hoping to rid it of the blood. As no mention of it had been made, she supposed she had been successful. Her scalp still tingled from the cuts there, but not enough for her to make any sort of outward appearance of discomfort. She knew she was not so fortunate in the rest of her body. Her face was mostly healed, but the rest of her still bore ugly discolorations.

Tibby stepped forward with the gown, then she saw the bruises, and she was not as discreet as Marianne.

"Oh, my dear child," Tibby moaned as she took in the bruises on her sides, her arms, and her thighs.

Annie's face flushed and she dropped her eyes, covering herself in embarrassment.

"No, no," Tibby said, sounding serious for the first time yet. "Do not be ashamed, Annie. May I look more closely?"

Annie nodded, her eyes burning.

Tibby came closer and peer intently at the bruises Annie bore, occasionally bringing two fingers out to touch them, but never applying enough pressure to cause a reaction. She met Annie's eyes, then set her hand against her sore ribs and pressed lightly, making Annie wince a bit. Tibby nodded, then brought the dressing gown over and helped her get into it.

"I think we may want to have a doctor examine you, Annie. Just as a precaution," Tibby said softy. "The bruises are healing well, but I am concerned for your ribs."

"How can you tell?" she asked quietly, stepping out of the tub with assistance from Marianne.

"I once volunteered as a nurse with the British army," Tibby replied with a smile, her tone becoming more her usual self. "It was quite exciting. That was how I met my first husband."

"I did not know that, Tibby," Marianne said in surprise as she began drying Annie's hair with a towel.

Tibby smiled rather deviously and her eyes glinted. "Well, he did not marry me for another seven years, but I made quite the impression on him."

Marianne laughed loudly, while Annie merely smiled. "Of course, you did!" Marianne squealed. She saw Annie's uncertainty, and whispered, "You will have to get used to Tibby. She is quite eccentric. Absolutely no inhibitions whatsoever."

"I can see that," Annie murmured, still smiling.

"Come, my dear," Tibby said, taking her arm. "Sit by the fire while we wait for your dresses to arrive."

Annie let herself be led, still not sure if this was real or not. Nobody ever took care of her, let alone to such an extent. They obviously knew some of her story, perhaps all that Duncan did. But no one knew the whole story, and no one ever would.

"You don't have to fuss over me," she murmured as she sat where Tibby had indicated. "I know you have other things to do. Better things."

Tibby gave her a harsh look. "Tosh, my dear, that is quite enough of that. You are to be my companion and that is as much my responsibility as yours. Do you think I would let any companion of mine stand there any longer in such dirty things after so long a journey? Or fail to see after her welfare? How would that reflect upon me?"

Marianne snorted and sat on the ottoman near Annie's chair. "Really, Tibby, she will think you only care about your own reputation."

"Pah! She will not." Tibby winked at Annie. "I am merely pointing out that a person of my standing and reputation takes a great deal of care with the things to which she is entrusted. Or the people."

"Thank you," Annie told her, her eyes burning again as tears swirled.

"Oh, do not cry!" Tibby insisted, reaching out and taking her hand. "I cannot help but to cry when others do!"

"Since when?" Marianne laughed, stretching her toes out to the fire.

Tibby glared at her. "Mind your tongue, girl, or you will be out of my will."

Annie looked at Marianne in abject horror. Could such a thing really be done so quickly?

Marianne giggled and leaned closer. "Tibby is always threatening to cut me off. She has not followed through yet."

"Now, Annie," Tibby said with a sharp clearing of her throat. "As you are to be my companion, I feel that I must ask you a few simple questions. Nothing too pressing or personal, mind you, for personal details always complicate matters of business."

Business? Since when was their relationship going to be purely business? Still, if that was how she wanted to view it, Annie would not argue. But perhaps she ought to consider a salary or something, if that were one of the questions. How much money did one even expect with these positions? She had no head for figures, and was quite slow with these things.

She swallowed and nodded, wishing she were back in that warm bath where Marianne and Tibby had taken such care with her.

"What skills do you possess?" Tibby asked in a very formal voice.

Annie swallowed, unsure of how to answer. She didn't think that the making of edible substances out of very few ingredients would count with this particular setting, but would her mending?

Tibby tilted her head slightly. "Do you play?"

She shook her head.

"Do you sing?"

"O-only to myself, probably not well," she stammered.

Tibby hummed. "We shall see about that."

"Tibby," Marianne scolded softly, setting a hand over Annie's, "you are making her nervous."

"I make everybody nervous, darling. She will get over it." Tibby turned her fierce gaze back on Annie, but tempered it with a smile.

"Do you enjoy reading?"

"I used to," Annie replied quietly, her hands quaking beneath Marianne's hold. "When I was small, I learned to read and I think I enjoyed it. But I don't remember much." Her cheeks warmed in embarrassment, and she felt Marianne squeeze her hands.

"That can be improved upon," Tibby told her with an approving nod. "We can certainly help you with that. I do not read much myself, it makes my head ache, but I enjoy listening. Perhaps Marianne can teach you and then you can read to me."

"Or Duncan," Marianne broke in suddenly. "He enjoys reading very much, and has quite the good storytelling voice. I am a very poor reader myself. I can read, of course, but I have no patience for it." She smiled at Annie and patted her hand. "You, on the other hand, seem a very patient person."

Annie smiled back. "I try."

Tibby sniffed. "We all try, darling. Some of us succeed more than others." She cleared her throat again. "Now, what about embroidery? Have you any experience there?"

Annie bit her lip. "I can mend very well, and sew as well. I had to make my own dresses."

Tibby and Marianne reared back in shock. "Truly?" Marianne gasped, looking both impressed and horrified.

Annie nodded, unsure whether she should be ashamed or proud.

"Did you make that gown you wore earlier?" Tibby asked, peering closely at her, as if trying to determine if she were being truthful.

Again, Annie only nodded.

"My, my," Tibby said in a soft tone, sitting back. "In that case, we really can send for dresses from whomever we like, can we not? Annie can fix them herself."

"I'm not so very skilled," Annie admitted shyly. "I can do basics, and some slight detailing, but…"

"Darling, the basics are all that is required!" Tibby said with a grin. "I hate embroidery, I am terrible at it. But I do love embroidered things. I would pay you to embroider for me."

"I could do that," she said a bit more confidently than she might have otherwise, but she would do whatever Tibby wanted. The woman was taking great pains with her and she was grateful. "Would I… um… that is… will I have a… salary?" she asked, knowing she sounded rather forward.

Tibby looked thoughtful. "I do not think that is necessary."

Annie's mouth gaped in shock.

"After all, no godmother would pay her godchild," Tibby continued without noticing. "That would make me rather peculiar, employing relations and all that."

"We are not related," Annie stammered in confusion.

Tibby waved a hand. "Of course, we are, darling. I am your godmother now. I will provide everything you need."

"Lady Raeburn…"

"Call me that again and you may take a turn as a scullery maid in the kitchens," she scolded, looking quite fierce. "I am to be Tibby and nothing else, even Aunt Tibby, if you wish to be polite. Back to your situation. You shall have room and board with me, all clothing that you or I see fit, as I suspect you live quite simply, and I, most assuredly, do not, and an afternoon off whenever you like."

This was not at all what Annie had expected. How long was she to remain, then? Would she never have further opportunities in the world? Not that she could ever imagine leaving, but what if things changed? And to live so freely?

"And of course, you shall have an allowance."

"An allowance?" Annie repeated. "How would that be different from a salary?"

"Yes, Tibby, how?" Marianne asked, having watched the interchange with amusement.

"An allowance is my being charitable, a salary is something you have earned," Tibby explained patiently. "As Annie is not actually under my employ, she is to have an allowance. And now as to how much…" She put a finger to her lips and pursed them.

Annie looked over at Marianne, who was grinning and only shrugged.

"I shall set up an account for you with funds to spend as you like," Tibby said slowly. "And I shall add to it each month. How much does a companion make these days, Marianne?"

"I do not know."

"Of course not. Hmm… Fifteen pounds a month?" she asked, looking at Annie.

She gasped. "Fifteen pounds?" It was a fortune!

"Oh, very well, then. Thirty pounds?"

She could not even gasp. She mouthed the amount that was so extravagant she could not fathom it.

Tibby sighed in mock frustration. "Mercenary girl. If you keep reacting thus, I shall increase it again."

Annie clamped her mouth shut on a helpless giggle, and Tibby nodded with a smile.

"Thirty it is, then."

"But what am I to spend it on?" Annie asked, truly stunned.

"Anything you like!" Marianne told her with a nudge. "Bonnets, books, gowns, sweets…"

"Although it is wise not to spend it all on sweets," Tibby said with a finger in the air. "People will talk." She looked at Annie thoughtfully. "I suppose you could spend a few months' worth on sweets and get away with it. You could use a bit of extra weight."

"Oh, Tibby," Marianne sighed, rolling her eyes.

A knock on the door interrupted the most ridiculous conversation Annie had ever been part of. A maid entered with arms full of gowns and undergarments that were quite reserved, which suited Annie perfectly, but were of such quality she gaped. She never *seen* clothing so fine!

"Ah! The gowns!" Tibby leapt to her feet and Marianne was hard on her heels. "Excellent. And you are sure Mary will not tell Geoffrey? We must keep her presence quiet for as long as possible, and you know how those men are…"

"Positive," Marianne replied. "He is with the rest of them and not due to return until Friday."

"Excellent." Tibby said again.

Both turned to Annie with nearly identical grins. "Come along, Annie," Tibby said with a crook of her finger. "It is time to play dress up."

Chapter Six

$\mathcal{I}$t was not unusual for Duncan to eat alone when in London. It was, however, unusual for him to eat alone for two consecutive meals.

Dinner the evening before had turned out to be just him at the table. The women had been enjoying themselves too much above stairs with the borrowed dresses to be bothered to come down to eat, and had instead requested a tray be brought to them.

He couldn't say that he minded so very much. How could he resent them for taking Annie under their care so immediately and with such fervor? If she were enjoying herself, he would certainly not stand in the way of that.

But the dinner had been surprisingly lonely.

He shook his head as he pushed aside his breakfast plate and glanced around the room. Eating alone at breakfast was not nearly so uncommon. His aunt and sister were hardly to be seen before luncheon, while he could not sleep much longer than the sun had risen on any given day, no matter how exhausted he was.

He wondered if Annie rose early.

The thought had crossed his mind to invite her to dine with him, but he would not want her to feel forced or that it was expected. He was not entirely sure his aunt had been very clear on what she expected from Annie as a companion or how she could comport herself. Having never been a companion before, he doubted she had the slightest inclination of the rules and expectations of Society, least of all Tibby, who obeyed Society's boundaries only if she wished it.

Why, Annie probably didn't even know anything about the house beyond what she had seen last night. She would have no idea where anything was or where she ought to go and do and say.

Had there been a maid arranged to help her? Would she want one? What sort of freedoms did she expect? Or, far more likely, how restricted did she believe she was?

He groaned and put his head into his hands. He hadn't thought anything through and now he would look a pompous fool. He had brought a woman into his home for his aunt's express purposes without explaining anything at all to the woman about what she should do or in what capacity she would serve or where she ranked in the hierarchy of the house.

Duncan didn't believe in such standings, and would have told her such straightaway, but he knew enough of her to know that she would expect herself to be around the level of the rats that attempted to enter the kitchen. Which, of course, was the single most ridiculous notion on the planet.

He would have to correct her misguided and foolish perspective of herself.

She was... extraordinary.

Where was she at this moment? Still abed? Wandering the house? He suddenly had the strongest desire to seek her out, and though he knew it was an idiotic notion, he missed her.

How did one miss someone they had known not even a week? And yet...

He shook his head. He didn't need to go and seek her out, not this early, not for any reason. Not if he valued his sanity.

He headed directly for his study, determined to distract himself from thoughts of her. There were several letters on his desk as he entered. He would need to concern himself with matters of business, replying to letters from his friends and solicitors, and one in particular in a now familiar hand.

Duncan had grown quite used to these letters, which came from an anonymous source, in which was shared with him the latest gossip surrounding his sister. They were delivered every so often, without a pattern, always written in the same hand with the same seal on the back, and always spoke of Marianne and her dealings.

There was no elaboration or hyperbole in the details shared with him, merely a bald declaration of the facts. Duncan's own investigations into early reports had proven the source correct in every aspect, but he could not even come close to identifying the man, which drove him mad.

If the man had an interest in Marianne, Duncan wanted to know. If he was protecting her, he wanted to thank him. Most of all, he was desperate to make sure that his sister was not being put in danger by someone who was apparently following her. But he was elusive, even for Duncan's efforts, and no harm had come to Marianne. So he had reluctantly come to regard this stranger as trustworthy and reliable. He still didn't know who it was, but he was grateful that someone out there was also looking out for his sister.

She had been in rare form of late and this report claimed no different. She had been bolder in her flirtations, crueler to her suitors, and raised more comment from the women of Society than ever before. Her number of suitors had increased, even during the winter months, and those that had joined the ranks were not the sort of men he would wish for his sister to keep company with.

He would need to speak with her before the Season began. He simply could not deal with more trouble than what he already had.

He groaned and sat back, pulling at his lip in thought. How did this stranger know so much? Why did he take pains to alert Duncan about Marianne?

How long would these letters continue to come?

If this one had just arrived…

He bolted from his chair, determined to ask about it yet again, to see if anyone had seen it delivered or could give him details.

He was nearly to the door when it opened, nearly hitting him in the face. He stepped back as a slightly red-faced Wilson appeared.

"A thousand apologies, sir," Wilson said, his voice still remarkably calm.

"No trouble, Wilson," he replied with a slight wave and a sigh. "What is it?"

"You have guests, sir."

Duncan's brows shot up. "More?" His house would burst at the seams.

"Indeed, sir."

He put a hand over his eyes. Who in the world would call at this time of the morning unannounced? He slowly dropped his hand, his eyes narrowing slightly in suspicion. "Who is it, Wilson?"

Wilson's mouth twitched the barest hint of humor. "Your friends, sir. Lord Beverton, Lord Whitlock, Mr. Harris, and Mr. Gerrard."

Duncan stood before his trusted butler with his mouth gaping for an astonishingly inappropriate time.

"Sir?" Wilson finally asked, looking rather worried for a man with no expression.

"I thought they weren't in London until tomorrow," Duncan managed, his voice raspy.

"I know nothing of that, sir," Wilson replied, apparently relieved his master had not lost his ability to vocalize.

Duncan half nodded, half shook his head. Of course his butler wouldn't know that. What the devil were they doing here? Could they have already found out about Annie? No, it was not possible. They had only just arrived yesterday and they had not seen anyone.

But Marianne had requested the aid of Mary Harris…

No, Mary was a good sort who would never divulge such sensitive information so unwisely.

Then again, she was remarkably weak where Geoffrey was concerned.

He glowered. This would not be pleasant.

"Sir?" Wilson said again, his voice ringing with concern and not a little fear.

Duncan cleared his expression, having forgotten that his glower tended to make people hide. "Very good, Wilson. Where are they?"

Wilson visibly relaxed, as much as the stoic man ever did. "The drawing room, sir. Mr. Gerrard requested a tray, should I have one sent in?"

He nodded. "Yes, or he will go out in search of food and disturb the whole house. Wilson, did they say what they were here for?"

Wilson shook his head. "No, sir. They only said they understood you had returned and would wait upon you at your convenience."

"My convenience would be in another week," he muttered, rubbing the back of his neck.

"Indeed, sir."

He tried not to smile at his butler's placidity. "Thank you, Wilson. That will do."

Wilson bowed and left the room.

Perhaps they knew nothing.

Unlikely, but perhaps.

He would pretend *he* knew nothing. It wouldn't be difficult. After all, these were his friends. He had nothing to hide.

Except he had everything to hide.

He took a deep breath and released it slowly, then walked towards the drawing room.

The door was open, no doubt for Colin's sake, as he enjoyed watching people, so his presence was fairly quickly noticed.

"Duncan!" Colin crowed from his lounging position on the couch. He grinned and waved like a child.

Blast. He knew.

Duncan raised a brow in his greeting. "Good morning, Colin. Did you sleep well last night?"

The rest of the room snickered, and each man rose to shake Duncan's hand in a more typical greeting fashion.

"I did, I did," Colin cheerfully replied as he remained in place, but shook Duncan's hand all the same. "Slept like a baby, as always."

Derek laughed and shook his head. Duncan glanced at him and noticed the dark circles and tired expression. The youngest heir to the Ashcombe title was almost eight months old, but according to his parents, young Henry Thomas Charles Alexander, known as Harry to them, was no easy child and had yet to master the art of sleeping at night.

"If that were true," Derek muttered, "you would wake every few hours and cry without hope or chance of consolation."

Nathan chuckled and patted Derek on the back. "Still not

70

sleeping through the night?"

Derek groaned and put his face in his hands. "Three times last night. Three. At this rate, he will be twelve before I get a full night of sleep."

"This is why people have nursemaids for their children," Colin informed the fathers.

Both looked at him with interest. "Oh, really, Colin?" Nathan asked in amusement. "Is that what worked for your children?"

Colin didn't even blink. "You need not get so uppity, my dear earl. Your son sleeps better than I do, so even you do not fully comprehend Derek's suffering."

"You cannot compare Robbie with Harry," Derek said, shaking his head. "It won't work. Nathan has more patience than I do, and Moira…" He trailed off and looked at Nathan suddenly. "Actually, Moira and Kate are on the same level with their patience and temperament, so it must be me."

"I wasn't going to say anything, but…" Colin trailed off, shrugging.

"Probably wise," Geoffrey commented, speaking up for the first time. He had always been the quieter member of the group, which made him a favorite with Duncan, if favorites were allowed.

"Well, I am going to be losing sleep again myself in the not too distant future," Nathan sighed, leaning back against his chair.

All perked up at that announcement.

Nathan grinned and laced his fingers across his midsection. "Moira is carrying again."

They all cheered, and despite their previous tussle, Colin crowed the loudest and rose to congratulate him. Nathan beamed brightly and chuckled when Derek shook his head mournfully.

"You will be there again soon, my friend," Nathan chortled. "You'll see."

"Perhaps," Derek said with a grin. "But the next had better be an angel."

"With Kate as the mother?" Colin laughed. "Please."

A throw pillow was suddenly soaring through the air and smacked Colin's face. Another man saying as much would have been thrashed within an inch of his life, but considering every man in the room knew that they all, especially Colin, were entirely devoted to the wives of the others, it wasn't warranted.

This time.

"How was Scotland?" Geoff asked Duncan as the room quieted. Duncan shrugged and settled into a chair. "About as I expected. Good food, good company, freezing cold castle, and a few brawls to keep things interesting. I even partook in a clan skirmish, which was won in our favor. And then there was a clan challenge, in which I claimed victory, and returned with many spoils from my relations."

"I would like to meet your cousins," Nathan told him with a grin. "They sound like my kind of people."

"You would get along very well," Duncan replied with a nod. "I should like to pair you against Aiden. He is about your size, but I think you could take him." He slid his glance over to Colin. "You could fight Gwen, but she would likely tear you to shreds."

The others snickered, but Colin gave him a devious smile. "I think I would very much like to try her on for size. It would be most entertaining, and the results might be equally delightful."

Duncan glowered at him, knowing his friend would never do what he suggested, but warning him off all the same. "You would not make it five paces towards her before your carcass would be torn apart and left for crows."

Colin held up his hands in surrender. "Fair enough. Down, boy, down. I shall stick to my harmless flirtations with the London misses and leave your fair and charming Celtic cousin to her fate."

Duncan nodded and turned back to the others. "It was a good visit, though I am glad to be back." He looked around at them all with narrowed eyes. "Speaking of which, what are you all doing in London at this time? I didn't anticipate any of you returning so early."

Derek shrugged and looked at his hands. "We have been finishing the work on our town home, so Kate wanted to stay and see it through. You know how she adores ordering people around."

That was undeniably true.

"Mary's brother wanted their country home this holiday," Geoff chimed in, "and Cassandra and Simon were staying and begged for her company, so she decided to remain. I am powerless to resist when Mary commands."

The room snickered as Geoff also shrugged. Geoffrey had been in love with Mary his entire life, but hadn't realized it until last year, when he had gone completely mad for her. He still was.

Nathan grinned and said, "Moira heard Kate and Mary were staying and decided I wasn't enough company for the winter, so here we are."

Colin scoffed loudly and looked at his fingernails. "Obviously you're not enough. Hence your wife's remarkable fertility."

Only Colin could say such improper things and not shock the polite world.

Nathan returned the look with an arched brow. "You have something to say, Colin?"

He waved his hand dismissively. "No, no, not a thing… Where is the food, Duncan?"

Duncan shook his head and gave his friend a pitying look. "It's forthcoming, Colin."

"Good. I'm starving."

At that precise moment, a maid carried the heavily laden tray into the room. Colin sprang up and took the tray from her trembling hold. He offered her a bold wink, which sent her cheeks flushing. She met Duncan's eyes nervously and bobbed a quick curtsey, then scurried from the room.

"I wish you wouldn't upset the servants, Colin," Duncan sighed as he watched his friend set the tray down and begin his foraging.

Colin looked at him with wide eyes. "Did she seem upset to you? I rather thought she was happy about it."

"Colin…"

He scoffed and sat back down with a plate of the light food. "Duncan. She won't think anything of my winking at her, and she will now have something fun to report to the girls below stairs. What harm has been done?"

Duncan looked to his friends for help, but they all looked as clueless as Duncan felt. There was just no helping or excusing Colin.

"So, Duncan," Colin announced with a slight clearing of his

throat as he settled back in. "Anything else happen on your trip?"

Duncan pretended to think on it. "No, I've told you everything."

Colin's eyes narrowed, but he looked unperturbed. "Anything else you feel like telling us? Any changes in your life that your friends might deserve to know? Any… anything?" He gestured faintly with his hands, as if attempting to draw the information out of him manually.

Duncan gave him a curious look. "No, I don't think so."

Colin frowned, his high brow wrinkling. "Nothing that ought to be shared between friends of such extent and degree as we are? Nothing that has altered from your previous way of living? Nothing… new?"

Duncan cocked his head to one side, keeping his expression very carefully blank. "Colin, what are you talking about?"

Colin threw up his hands and set his plate aside. "Oh, for heaven's sake, polite behavior is highly overrated."

"This is getting us nowhere," Derek told Colin irritably. "Get on with it."

Colin nodded, folded his hands and turned back to Duncan. "We want to know about the woman."

A sharp jolt of panic hit Duncan's stomach, but he hid it as best as he could. "What woman?" he asked innocently.

Colin looked at him in disgust, then turned to Geoff. "He thinks we are imbeciles."

"That's a bit insulting," Geoff agreed with a shake of his head. "Honestly, as if we don't have connections enough to know when he brings a woman into his home."

Duncan felt beads of sweat form on the back of his neck. "I don't know what you are…"

"Lying to your friends is never a good idea, Duncan," Derek interrupted firmly.

"Particularly when they know you are lying," Colin added.

"And you, my friend, are lying," Geoff informed him.

"Badly," Nathan chimed in.

Duncan looked around at them all, then exhaled sharply. What was the point of hiding anything now? They obviously knew about

Annie, and hiding things from them would only make things worse when it eventually would come out.

He glared at Geoffrey. "Tell your wife I will kill her."

Geoff looked truly shocked and reared back a bit. "What does Mary have to do with anything?"

"She's the one who told you, right?" Duncan asked, confusion rolling over him.

"Mary knows about this?" Geoff looked around at the others. "If Mary knows…"

"Then Kate and Moira will know soon enough," Nathan finished. "Heaven help us all."

Duncan rubbed at his eyes hard. "Then how did you all know?"

Colin patted him on the arm too hard to be comfortingly. "You forget, Mr. Bray, that I am the very heart of gossip in London. Nothing happens without my finding out."

Duncan removed his hands and glared at Colin. "You have spies in my house?"

"Stop avoiding the point, Duncan," Nathan said with a grin. "Tell us about this young woman you have brought home."

"First of all," he said, holding up a finger, "I have not brought her home. I have brought her to London."

Colin snorted and took a sip of his tea. "And that is an important distinction. Your home is in London, she is in your home in London, yet she was not brought home, but to London. I see."

"Shut up, Colin," Duncan growled ruthlessly.

"I think I am agitating the bear," Colin whispered loudly to Geoff, who clamped his lips together.

Duncan felt another growl rumble in his chest and got to his feet. "Thank you all for coming, but I have other things to attend to." He started out of the room, but Nathan and Derek rose and stopped him.

"Come on, Duncan," Derek said, ushering him back. "Colin will stop being an impertinent whelp, I promise."

"Will I?" Colin asked with interest.

"Yes, you will," Nathan ordered severely.

"Fine," he grumbled moodily. "But make Duncan eat something. He is so cranky when he does not."

Duncan glanced back down at his oldest friend, and sighed. Would he never be able to remain angry at the man? He returned to his chair, took the offered plate, and put a few small things on it.

"Very well, I'll tell you what you want to know," Duncan told his friends. "But you are sworn to secrecy and to support me."

Colin looked the most surprised. "Did you think we would do anything less? I may plague you worse than a pox, but you know you have my loyalty."

"Hear, hear," Geoff murmured.

Duncan felt a surge of warmth and nodded. "Her name is Annie Ramsey," he said in a low voice, "and I found her in Yorkshire."

"Found her?" Derek asked in bewilderment. "How is that?"

"Exactly as I said. I was riding Balthazar, went to a creek to water him, and there she was." He thought back to that day, the stirring moment that he first saw her, the sudden need to right all her wrongs…

"So how did she come to be here?" Geoff inquired, breaking through his reverie. "Finding her is one thing, but bringing her back to London…" He frowned and tilted his head in concern. "Did something happen, Duncan?"

"No!" Duncan said immediately, shaking his head viciously. "No, nothing of the sort. No. She was… in need. I saw an opportunity to be of some assistance. I have brought her back to be a companion to Tibby."

The room was so silent he would have thought them all dead.

"Does your aunt need a companion?" Nathan asked carefully.

Duncan sighed and winced a bit at his lack of foresight. "No, she doesn't. But that does not mean she won't enjoy one. Annie will suit her very well, I can assure you."

"So you brought this poor girl… who was in need… to London to be an unnecessary companion for your aunt because you… saw the opportunity?" Derek said, his voice slow and confused. There was a slight twinkle in his eye that Duncan did not care for at all.

"That about sums it up, yes," Duncan said, feeling his defenses rise. Really, what was so difficult to understand about that?

"It all seems rather rash," Geoff murmured. "A bit hasty, if you

76

will. And not at all thought out. Did you even discuss with Lady Raeburn the possibility of a companion?"

"Is this girl qualified to be a companion for her?" Colin asked on top of that. "You know how unconventional your aunt can be, and if this Annie creature is not fit for her, it will…"

"Why are you all attacking my actions?" Duncan interrupted a bit loudly.

"Why are you so defensive about it?" Nathan asked, looking far more interested than he had been previously. "What does this all mean to you?"

"It was nothing!" Duncan insisted. "I saw the opportunity to help someone, to do a good deed, and I did it! Why should you…?"

A movement out in the hallway caught his eye and his agitated mind seized upon it, his attention flying to it, and his words trailing off.

Annie had come down the stairs, dressed in one of Mary's old gowns that had been lightly altered to her size, but still hung loosely on her. It didn't matter. She looked beautiful. The gown was a muted shade of green that would make her eyes stand out brilliantly against the pale porcelain of her face. He longed to see them, to be seized by their power again. Her golden hair had been simply braided and hung over one shoulder, but it glinted in the morning light.

She had not seen him, wasn't even looking for him. She moved carefully, cautiously, yet with a grace that could not be taught. She bit her lip, looked about, then walked out of his line of sight, hopefully towards breakfast.

So she was an early riser. Like him.

He would have to remember that.

And suddenly, he wished his friends far, far away.

"Yes," Colin said slowly, his voice ringing with blatant amusement. "Yes, I see the good deed you have done. Very good, indeed."

Duncan very slowly turned to glower at Colin, who was grinning like a cat who had found a bowl of cream. He then became acutely aware of the number of eyes that were upon him. He glanced around him to see his other friends watching him with eerily identical expressions of fascination.

"What?" he asked grumpily, fidgeting slightly in his seat.

"Annie?" Nathan asked with a quirk of his head.

Duncan exhaled sharply, knowing he had been painfully obvious. There would be no secrets anymore. "Yes, that was Annie. And there is something else you might as well know about her."

He confessed everything he knew about her, never once defending his actions. And much to their credit, they did not say anything. The amusement left their faces and their jaws all set. When he had finished, no one spoke for some time. It said much about each of them that their expressions were bordering between angry, disturbed, and determined.

Derek suddenly cleared his throat. "The duke has some properties in Yorkshire. Would you like me to make inquiries about her family?"

Duncan smiled faintly at his most powerful friend. "No, I think not. Annie has left that all behind, and I don't want to pry without her consent."

"Brave girl," Nathan murmured, shaking his head. "Courageous, indeed, to leave her former life behind."

"She must be terrified," Geoff said. "Leaving everything she knows and coming to Town without knowing anybody. If you don't mind, Duncan, I'll send Mary over. I won't tell her anything you don't wish her to know, but…"

"Tell her all," Duncan insisted with a swift shake of his head. "Your wives are all welcome at any time. Perhaps not today, as Annie is more than likely already overwhelmed. And remember, she is my aunt's companion. She isn't… one of them."

"Are you quite sure of that?" Colin murmured, his eyes glancing out of the door, where Annie had once again reappeared and softly walked down the hall towards the back of the house, still unaware of their presence.

Duncan swallowed the breath that had caught in his throat.

No, he was not sure.

He was no longer sure of anything at all.

Chapter Seven

The house was a maze.

Annie had never been in a maze, of course, but she couldn't imagine one more confusing than this. Everywhere she turned was another door or another hall, a part of the house she dared not venture into, and another sign that she didn't belong here.

She had nibbled very briefly on bites of the incomparable breakfast spread that had been in the dining room, but she couldn't bring herself to sit and dine. Not here. And not alone. It didn't matter that she was clean and dressed in a finer gown than she had ever seen in her entire life. She knew exactly who she was and what she was worth.

It was part of what made this morning so difficult.

Where was she to go? What was she to do with her day? Were there places she ought not to go?

And what of the servants? She would know how to converse with them, should she need to converse with anybody at all. But even they seemed to sneer at her, sniff in disapproval. She knew very well she had a thick Northern accent that many would dislike, but surely their families were of a similar descent and fortune.

Agnes had been very kind to her last night, but Agnes was a bit older and had seen her bruises. She had been sworn to secrecy by Marianne, and Annie had no reason to doubt that the good woman would break her word.

But she couldn't find Agnes.

She couldn't find anyone.

She sighed and pushed a strand of her blond hair behind her ear. She didn't know what the protocol was for the morning, but she could not remain in that luxurious bed one moment longer. It felt wrong, like such a dream she knew she would soon wake from. Someone would recognize the mistake and cast her away.

When would they remember who she was? She was no fine guest they had invited into their home. She was a poor little waif that Duncan had taken pity on and found a way to help. She worked for them. Though Tibby had said she would adopt her, Annie knew it was not so easy. She would soon prove that she had very little use at all, hardly fit for any sort of reference.

Oh, she had no doubt they would find her a fine situation once they had educated her enough to fend for herself. They were, after all, quite decent people, even if they were exorbitantly wealthy. And Duncan would… He would…

She shook her head and plucked at the fine dress. She ought to stop herself right there. She did not know Duncan Bray at all. She had no idea what he would do.

Some far-fetched corner of her mind had the errant thought that perhaps they would let her keep a few of the gowns when they came to their senses and sent her away. They were so fine, yet not half so extravagant as the gowns Marianne and Tibby wore, and those were purely for around the house. What in heaven's name did they wear when they went out in public? Or, more astonishing, to a ball?

Annie knew she would never be able to afford the quality of gowns she currently wore on her own. It did not even matter that it didn't fit. She and Agnes had spent a bit of time last night altering what they could while still keeping the integrity of the dress itself, and it was much better than it had been.

But the fit of the gown was rather like the quality of it. Too much for her.

She ought to find a servant, to ask if there were any spare bolts of their fabric she might buy with her eventual allowance. Their clothing was obviously made from a higher quality fabric than she would have worn before, and they were the servants here. She would

80

feel much better wearing their sturdy and functional attire than this costume they had forced upon her.

Forced.

She shook her head and opened the door to yet another room that didn't lead where she wished.

She hadn't been forced into anything. They were not forcing her to be here or to dress this way. She had not been forced to leave her home and her brother. They did not force her to sleep in that grand bed last night or to bathe in that enormous tub or to come to London at all. They had offered. She had accepted.

She had chosen.

What was she thinking? She was choosing a life so far above herself that it was laughable. Imagine her being a companion to a fine woman of influence and Society like Lady Raeburn! She hardly spoke at all unless directly addressed, and even then she was a soft spoken, shy girl and never said anything of consequence. She had always been this way, and years of fearing the world had not done her any favors in that category. She had grown used to not speaking, to living in silence and simplicity, and to being ignored. She was more content to sit and watch life than participate.

This was one farce she no longer wished to participate in.

And yet…

She had felt bold upon leaving Frank and leaving home. Something inside of her had been excited at the prospect of the future. Some part of her still dreamed of something greater. She might not fit in here, but that didn't mean she would not fit in anywhere. There were possibilities she had not explored yet, and perhaps through the misguided and undeserved efforts of Duncan and his relations, she would gain the experience and knowledge to entertain those possibilities and perhaps turn something into a reality.

So she was using them.

That hardly seemed right at all.

But she could hardly be anything more.

She sniffled back the slight sheen of tears that had formed and shook her head to clear it. She must remain a sensible creature amidst all this insanity. She could not lose herself and think her place higher than it was.

Another door ended up being a closet, and she groaned. She would never find the library at this rate, and it was the one place she longed to go.

"Annie?"

She winced and closed her eyes. Of course, Duncan would come across her when she was aimlessly wandering his home.

Her face flamed and she turned to face him. "Good morning."

He smiled and his eyes crinkled at the corners. "Good morning yourself. Have you eaten?"

"Yes." It was true. She had. Just not very much. But there was no need for him to know that. She knew very well he would have forced her into the room to eat some more and she was simply not willing to be made to eat like a child. And the way her stomach was clenching, it would not have gone well anyway.

He gave her a look that told her plainly that he did not believe her.

She kept her expression composed and blank, which she imagined not many people could do in his presence. But she had been partially raised by Frank Ramsey, who seized upon the first sign of weakness he could see. She had learned long ago that a lack of expression was the safest way to live.

Finally, Duncan sighed and his smile returned. "Very well. What are you doing up so early?"

"I couldn't sleep," she replied as the burning in her cheeks subsided.

He nodded thoughtfully. "It would be expected. You are in a new place, surrounded by new people, and your bed is not your own. It will take some adjustment, but I do hope you will find yourself comfortable before long."

She dared not tell him that her bed at home had been a hard pallet of straw, and she would no more be comfortable in this finery than he would have been in her home. But the earnestness of his gaze, the hopeful look in his eyes, and that charming smile took her heart and twisted it so she could only smile shyly in return.

The warmth that grew in his smile made her knees quiver and

her breath catch.

No one had ever looked at her like that.

Steady, Annie, her mind scolded. *He is not for you.*

She swallowed and barely resisted the urge to nod in agreement with herself.

"Can I help you find something?" Duncan asked, his gaze searching.

Now she was embarrassed. What if he did not want her to go into the library? What if she was expected to wait upon Tibby hand and foot? She would do it, whatever her expectations were, but she simply did not know… Perhaps she ought to return to her room and wait to be told what she needed to do.

"Annie?"

Duncan broke into her internal debate and Annie flushed again. At this rate, she would permanently stain her cheeks a bright pink before she ever said anything of value to him.

He smiled at her again, as if he could hear her thoughts. "You can go wherever you want, sweet. Anywhere at all. But you will get there much faster if I help you find your way."

Her ears tingled at his endearment and she could not help but smile a little. "I was… That is, I thought I might sit in the library for a time."

"The library?" he asked, looking surprised.

"Yes." She cleared her throat, desperate to explain without being misunderstood. "I could read as a child, and I thought I ought to see how bad I had got before… before it was expected…"

"Before Tibby asked you to read aloud," Duncan finished, his brow clearing as understanding dawned.

Her eyes suddenly felt dry. She blinked rapidly and it took more effort than it had ever taken before. Her failings were becoming more and more apparent by the moment, and she couldn't bear it.

"I would love to show the library to you," Duncan murmured softly, laying a gentle hand on her shoulder. "It's one of my favorite rooms."

She looked up at him as her heart pounded against her chest painfully. And suddenly, she lost what little pride she possessed and asked, "Will you help me, Duncan? If I… if I can't…?"

"Of course," he said immediately, the pressure of his hand increasing slightly. "I would be delighted."

"Thank you." Her breath caught and she could not tell if it was the fervency of his voice or the delight in his eyes that caused it.

Whichever it was, she was helplessly vulnerable to it.

"Well, well, what have we here?"

Annie's instincts took over at the unexpected sound of an unfamiliar male voice and she skittered backwards out of his grasp, her eyes flying open wide, a startled whimper escaping her.

"Easy," Duncan murmured softly so only she could hear. "Easy, now. They are only my friends."

"I can't, I can't, I can't," she babbled as her breath came in panicked bursts, her body quivering.

The men were drawing nearer, a tall, slender one leading the pack, but they were still far enough that she was slightly obscured and they couldn't hear her.

She shook her head frantically. "Don't make me, don't make me…"

"Annie." Duncan's voice was firm, but still so gentle she felt her breathing begin to calm. "They are my friends. They will not harm you. Do you trust me?"

Did she? Did she truly?

She met his eyes and her knees quaked. She grabbed onto his open arms for balance. "Yes," she gasped, her voice as shaky as her body.

He nodded, a spark of something flaring in his eyes. "Then trust me."

She looked behind him and saw that the men had stopped and waited just far enough off that she still had privacy. "What do I do?" she eventually whispered to Duncan.

"About?"

She bit her lip, and inhaled shakily, the last of her tremors vanishing. "Do I bow, do I curtsey, do I…?" She shook her head. "What do I do?"

He smiled and stepped back just enough that he only held her hands. "You could always just say good morning."

As if that was so easy.

She swallowed and nodded, then steeled herself as Duncan stepped to the side, releasing her hands.

She nearly swallowed her tongue. The men before her were four of the handsomest men she had ever seen. What was this, a collection of beautiful people gathering to admire each other? It was as if God had taken every possible attractive feature He could create and divided them amongst the group. It was simply unfair that so much attractiveness should be so condensed among five wealthy and powerful men. Really, they ought to do *something* to reduce their combined power. How was a single, able-minded woman to think a concise thought?

"Good morning," she managed limply.

"Good morning," the darkest one replied, smiling crookedly.

"Miss Annie Ramsey, I presume?" the tall, thin one said, his pale eyes twinkling with unspoken humor.

She only nodded, unsure what manners ought to be employed here.

The man smiled pleasantly, then turned to Duncan with a wave of his hand. "Well, Duncan, don't just stand there like an overgrown suit of armor. Introduce us!" He rolled his eyes and looked back to Annie. "I am so dreadfully sorry, Miss Ramsey, how mortifying. But Duncan needs reminding of politeness from time to time, he tends to forget such things. And really, one cannot introduce one's self if this is to be done properly. I should not even be speaking to you yet, but I have always been a bit hazy about the particular boundaries of Society."

Annie's brows shot up in surprise. Was he teasing her?

Duncan heaved an impatient sigh. "Annie Ramsey, permit me to introduce to you my friends. In the back there is Nathan, the Earl of Beverton."

The dark one who had greeted her bowed, and Annie had no idea how to respond, so she nodded her head and tried to smile.

"Next to him is Derek, the Marquess of Whitlock." The most attractive man in the group smiled and also bowed.

An earl *and* a marquess? Duncan kept high company, indeed!

"The blonde one is Geoffrey Harris, newly married and still glowing," Duncan said, bringing laughs and smiles to his friends' faces.

Geoffrey shrugged with a broad grin and gave her a jaunty, but very polite bow. "It is true, I'll not deny it."

Annie could not help but to genuinely smile in return.

"And last… and most definitely least… the scarecrow in front of you is Colin Gerrard." Duncan waved his hand dismissively.

Colin sniffed in a playful manner, then bowed deeply. "Charmed, Miss Ramsey."

"It… it is very nice to meet you all," she said, her voice more than a bit shaky.

"Our pleasure, to be sure," Derek told her, his green eyes twinkling.

She was getting more and more overwhelmed by the second. What did one even say to such men? Her palms were beginning to perspire and her stomach twisted itself into knots. But she must not embarrass Duncan, no matter what…

"A question for you, Miss Ramsey, if I may," Colin said with a slight incline of his head.

She was startled by being addressed so directly and suddenly by one of his friends. "I… I suppose you may…" Really, as if she had any reason or power to refuse him should she have wished it.

Colin nodded, putting his hands behind his back. "Thank you. When you first met our Mr. Bray here, what was your initial impression?"

Annie froze so completely winter might well have focused on her entirely. Her impression? Of Duncan? Oh, she had been part terrified, part mystified, and part helplessly devoted from the first. How did she adjust that to sound polite and proper?

"My… impression?" she stammered.

"Colin…" Nathan said in a warning tone, watching Annie. Duncan had stiffened and the other two watched with caution.

"Yes," Colin told her, ignoring the others completely. "On a scale of a tiny kitten to a ferocious bear, how intimidating was he?"

The entire room, paintings, statues, and suits of armor alike, seemed to release a breath of relief with the rest of them at those words. All of the men grinned and looked to Annie.

How was she to respond? She looked up at Duncan, biting her lip anxiously.

He shook his head, smiling. "Don't look at me. You must answer him honestly on your own."

Honestly? She would never manage that. She looked back at Colin, who waited with infinite patience, his smile warm and inviting, so much so that she simply had to trust him. And she could play along.

She forced a timid smile. "You know those little dogs carried around by fine ladies? The fluffy ones that bark incessantly and bare their teeth and jump as high as your hip?"

Snickers began tumbling from the others, but Colin kept his expression very composed. "Hmm, perhaps your hips, my dear, not mine. But yes, I do know. Go on."

She blushed a bit at her own daring. "He was a little more frightening than that."

The snickers turned to barely restrained chuckles.

Colin frowned. "Truly? Not a bear?"

She shook her head. "No, sir."

He hummed and glanced at Duncan in confusion, then back at her. "Not even a cub?"

Annie looked at Duncan herself, who was watching her with unfettered glee and a bit of pride. She would keep that image in her mind always. She somehow turned back to Colin and said, "Well, perhaps a sleeping cub."

The rest of the men, Duncan included, laughed aloud, the sound ringing from the hall.

Colin laughed, then sighed. "Well, take care not to disturb the sleeping cub. He has been known to bite, on occasion."

She smiled warmly and allowed him to take her hand when he reached for it.

He pressed a kiss to the back of her hand and bowed. "A sincere and rare privilege, Miss Ramsey." Then he turned, nodded to the others, and swept from the house.

Surprised by the shortness of the conversation and the suddenness of the departure, Annie looked around. The rest seemed as stunned as she. Then Derek whistled and looked back at them all.

"Well," he said, "now I have seen everything."

"Sorry?" Annie asked, not understanding and forgetting for a moment that she was shy and he was a handsome marquess.

"Colin did not even attempt flirtation with you," Duncan explained, leaning towards her a bit. "It is simply unheard of. He would flirt with a street light if it gave him the proper inclination."

Her cheeks flamed. "Oh."

She could not help but to look down at her toes. So the cheerful and friendly Mr. Gerrard would be the first one to realize she was not suited for this life and therefore unworthy of his usual attentions. She could not say she did not expect it, but she wished she had not been so ill a judge of character as to presume real warmth there. She must learn to be more discerning if she were to retain any sense at all.

"Miss Ramsey?"

She glanced up slightly at Nathan, who looked more gentle than she would have expected a man of his physique to appear. He smiled faintly. "Colin also never kisses hands. He is never so polite or respectful to anybody. I think you ought to consider yourself quite flattered by his manner just now."

He could not be serious.

And yet the rest were smiling at her with the same expression. Encouragement. Agreement.

Approval.

She was undoubtedly going mad.

"How are you finding London, Miss Ramsey?" Geoffrey asked, his tone and expression warm.

She swallowed her panic, her throat burning with its dryness. "I... I can't say, sir. I've not seen it yet."

He seemed entirely unperturbed by that. "Well, you must as soon as you can. If you do not mind, I could have my wife Mary come pay you a visit, and she could show you around."

He wanted his *wife* to do that? With her? It was unfathomable.

"W-wouldn't a servant be better suited, sir?" she asked, her face tingling with embarrassment. She shouldn't be so forward as to suggest he was wrong, but neither should he saddle his wife with being forced to spend time with her.

Now the men looked surprised and looked at each other. "Why would a servant be more suited?" Nathan finally asked.

She looked up at Duncan, who seemed to view her with a sense of bewilderment that didn't suit his features. Really, what could he be so confused about? She was little more than a servant, why should a fine lady like Mrs. Harris spend any time with her at all? It was one thing for Tibby and Marianne to give her attention, she worked for them and they no doubt had her best interest at heart. But they would not have her mingling with finer people of Society unless Tibby had need of her.

Why should she know London at all?

"Annie," Derek said softly, breaking through her internal reverie. "I apologize, may I call you Annie?"

She nearly laughed. He could have called her Fred and she would have answered. But she merely nodded.

He tilted his head slightly. "Why do you think a servant should show you London instead of Mary?"

Was he under the same delusions as Duncan? It had to be a contagion. "Because I am only a companion to Lady Raeburn. And not a very good one. Nothing special."

The room suddenly felt as if all of the air had been sucked out and replaced with ice. Each of the men stiffened and gave her such a look that she would have run for it had her feet any power at all.

"Let me tell you something right now, Miss Annie Ramsey," Nathan said with his impressive glower. "You know that Duncan will not tolerate your speaking that way, I presume. Especially with the thunderstorm brewing in his eyes at this moment."

She barely glanced in his direction, but she knew it was true. She nodded once.

"Well, neither will we," Nathan continued. "You are under his protection while you are here, but you will also be under ours. And furthermore, I think Mary Harris is the perfect person to show you around London and you are more than special enough for her to be seen with. And further than that, I will have my wife Moira come with her. And unless I am mistaken in his character, I believe Derek feels the same about his wife Kate."

"I do," Derek said firmly. "And they are much meaner than we are, Annie, so you had better speak highly of yourself indeed."

She swallowed hard, but nodded obediently.

"You're scaring her," Duncan murmured, his stature softening the slightest.

"You will love them within minutes," Geoff assured Annie with a smile. "We did."

They all nodded with smiles.

"Well," Annie managed, when her mind caught up with their actions, "if Lady Raeburn won't mind…"

"She won't," came a chorus from all of them at once.

She smiled softly. "Then I would be happy to meet them."

"As if you have a choice," Duncan chuckled. "They would have descended in a flock regardless."

"Prepare yourself, my dear," Nathan said with a sigh, patting Annie's shoulder softly. "You will need all your strength to endure it."

She laughed at his teasing expression. "Yes, my lord. I shall."

"No formalities, Annie," Derek said with a shake of his head. "No more 'my lord' or 'sir' or any such nonsense. You are one of us now. We take care of our own."

If she could believe him, she would have cried.

But she did not.

She could not.

So she smiled and ignored the burning in her eyes, and agreed.

But someday soon, this charade would end and she would have little to rely on. She could not presume that these men, as charming and polite as they were, would align themselves with her then. And their wives certainly would not. She knew enough of women to know they always held reputation to a high standard, and they could be brutal when theirs was in danger.

No one would solicit her society.

But for now, she would let these nice men think it possible.
They need not know how the world truly worked.
Not yet.
She needed to get out of here before the dream ended. She
cleared her throat awkwardly and looked at Duncan. "Could I go to
the library now? I would like to be available when your aunt wakes."
He seemed to sense her discomfort and his warm eyes showed
understanding. He nodded. "Would you like me to show you?"
She shook her head. She needed time away from the delusion
she lived in, not to embrace it. "You have friends here. I can find it if
you will direct me."
He did not looked pleased, but she dared not call it
disappointment. She wished she knew what he was thinking, but then,
that was none of her business. He could think whatever he liked of
her. She would never know.
The men looked at Duncan hesitantly, but said nothing.
He quietly told her where to go and she smiled to the rest in
farewell, hoping she was not expected to curtsey, and fled as calmly
as she could.
The sooner Tibby's house was finished, the better. She needed
to get out of this house.
She could not stay here for long, or she would start to believe.
She would start to hope.
And life had taught her that hope was dangerous.

Chapter Eight

The afternoon light streaming through the grand windows of the library made for a surprisingly warm patch amidst the relative frigidity of the room. Wrapped as she was in the thickest shawl that had been able to be procured for her on short notice, Annie found herself quite comfortable when that light was warming her.

Others would probably have disagreed with her, but considering she had spent a good portion of her life become accustomed to freezing, she was quite content at the moment.

Although she had to admit that she wouldn't have complained had there been a fire blazing in the large fireplace nearby. But she was not yet brave enough to inquire after one. After all, she had barely been in the house a week, and hardly been any sort of a companion at all.

One must be able to read in order to read aloud.

And she was far worse at reading than she had feared.

Not that she was giving it all of her energy at the moment. She was a bit distracted by her memories. She had spent the last few days being entertained by some of the finest women she had ever met. The very first time had been excruciatingly awkward for Annie. The maid who had brought her the news that three ladies were waiting upon her in the parlor seemed to think there had been a mistake and laughed when Annie had risen from her chair and had gone, red cheeked and embarrassed, to meet them.

They had talked for over an hour.

Annie had really said very little, answering their questions just enough that they asked more or would discuss her answers amongst themselves. It had given her ample opportunity to study these women more carefully.

Lady Beverton and Lady Whitlock were imposing, yet surprisingly warm, and had an understanding between them that Annie wondered at. They were rare beauties and the perfect matches for their husbands. Mary Harris, on the other hand, was remarkably plain. Mr. Harris had been one of the most attractive men Annie had ever seen, and yet this woman was quite simply average-looking. Kind and gracious and certainly had a portion of the majesty the other two seemed to possess, but in looks she was certainly no match for her husband.

It made her instantly like Mary and she was in no way intimidated by her. It had only taken a few minutes with the woman for her to forget all about the inequality of looks and to find her irresistibly charming.

She had expected them to depart with all politeness when their hour had been reached, but they had surprised her by insisting that she fetch her coat and some sturdier boots so they might take her about London.

They had only spent a short time out and about and she was convinced she had seen it all, until they promised to call on her in another two days to show her more of it. And they had come, with more energy and excitement, more familiarity, and more interest in her. By all accounts and appearances, it seemed they did not care one way or another that she was to be nothing more than Tibby's companion. They were as comfortable conversing with her as if she were an equal.

How was she to ever keep her head when surrounded by such women?

No one had ever wanted to spend such time with her.

A cold shiver raced up her spine.

Some had. And if she did not improve her situation quickly, that future would still be a possibility.

She returned her attention to the book before her. She was

pleased that she had discovered a collection of fairy tales upon her first visit to the library, which she could only tell by the illustrations within. She had spent every morning and as much time as she could in the afternoon or evening trying to read, but she hadn't managed to get beyond the first two pages. And none of it made any sense to her.

After struggling for what seemed an age, she closed the book and put her head into her hands, letting the frustrated tears flow. How could she hope to escape what lay before her if she were so utterly useless? She would never be able to earn a decent wage if she couldn't obtain basic skills needed to work!

Though Tibby and Marianne and Duncan were generous and kind, not all employers would be. And though they denied such a relationship, she knew the truth.

She was nothing. She would always be nothing. It didn't matter if she could read or not, if she knew how to spell her name, or if she could play a simple tune on a pianoforte. She could be as accomplished as any lady of London and she would still be nothing. It would all be lies.

She could keep company with a countess and a marchioness, with a future duke, and with the debutantes of fashion and Society, and she would still be nothing. They could change her clothing and give her an allowance and freedom, and it would not change anything. She couldn't change who she was.

She was plain, poor, pathetic Annie Ramsey from Yorkshire. Her brother had sold her to the vilest of men for the best profit he could find. Her future was destined to be as dark as her past. And she had run away from it. What horrors would wait for her when she returned?

And she would have to return. There was nothing for her here. Nothing.

The tears came faster, harder, and she couldn't stem them. What had she done?

She had to read. She *had* to. It was the key to everything. If she could not read, she could not work. She would have two choices then: to stay in London and try to survive, or to return home. She would never survive in London alone. And she could not go home. She could not marry Mr. Thorpe. She could not go back to Frank. She would die if she did. As surely as she lived and breathed at this moment, they would kill her. Her soul first, and then slowly and surely her body would follow.

She might be nothing; she undoubtedly was. But she wanted to live.

Although, for the life of her, she could not see why.

The door to the library opened and she turned her face more fully away. She wasn't hiding from sight, but it wouldn't be difficult to miss her. She had yet to be disturbed by anyone when she was in this room, so barely used was it. Duncan had said it was one of his favorite places, yet she had never seen him. She wiped at her cheeks as quickly as she could and quietly reached for the book on the floor. She prayed that whoever it was would be so surprised when they saw the room was in use that they would leave just as soon as they had come.

She opened the book to somewhere in the middle, and prayed she looked serene.

"Here you are, Annie. I've been looking for you."

Her eyes closed of their own accord and more hot tears flooded them, even as a now familiar warmth settled in her stomach.

Duncan.

"Why are you sitting on the floor?" he asked, his voice nearly a laugh. "And away from anything?"

She inhaled slowly, wishing her tears would subside so she could respond without betraying her emotions.

But Duncan did not notice.

"Have you been in here all afternoon?" he continued, his footsteps sounding closer. "You should have... Annie, why is there no fire in that grate?"

She winced at the bite in his tone. "I..."

"It is freezing outside!" he scolded, moving around her to the empty fireplace, where the last of the small flames had gone out some time ago. "Did you not notice that it has snowed again? And you are in here with only that flimsy shawl and sitting on the floor. You only need to ask, and a fire would have been built for you!" He turned away from the fire and marched towards the door, still having yet to actually look at her.

He called for someone to build up a fire, then came back towards her. "Honestly, Annie, you are going to freeze if you don't…"

Annie's breath caught as she realized he had trailed off and was standing directly in front of her. And more horrifying, a pair of tears leaked from the corners of her eyes and made their way steadily down her cheeks. They dripped from her jaw and splashed helplessly onto the pages below.

"Annie," he said softly, his voice as tender as a sigh.

More tears fell, helpless before his warmth and gentleness. She closed her eyes more firmly and tucked her chin down. Why must he always find her at her most vulnerable? Why could he never see her when she was strong?

Why was she never strong?

She heard him move, then nearly jumped at the soft pressure of his hand under her chin. He tilted her face up and against her will, her eyes fluttered open.

He gave her a small smile and his thumb stroked the side of her jaw. "What are these for, Annie? What has upset you so?"

"Nothing," she managed, though her voice and fresh tears betrayed her. "Nothing, I'm… I'm fine."

He shook his head. "No, you're not. Annie, will you never trust me?"

"I hardly know you," she whispered, another tear falling and landing on his hand.

"You know me," he insisted, his words tinged with real feeling and warmth. "Not in ways words can yet describe, but you know me." He left those words to hang in the air, their meaning as heavy as the feeling in her chest. Again, his thumb stroked her skin and she felt it like fire to her toes. "And you have trusted me thus far. Can you trust me again?"

Could she? Could she dare that far? Her heart yearned to tell him everything, to beg him to save her yet again.

But he was destined to be someone else's hero. Someone else's champion. Someone else's future.

She opened her mouth to protest, but his eyes stopped her. They glanced down at her barely parted lips, then slowly dragged back to her eyes. But they had changed in those brief moments. They were no longer the calm, clear blue from before. Now they were as stormy as the sea and twice as dangerous, yet she felt no fear. She had never felt so safe, so well-guarded, so warm…

Too warm.

Too much.

Too…

"Annie…"

Something in his voice snapped her resolve and she released the sigh she did not know she had within her. "I don't belong here."

He tilted his head and his hand dropped to where hers rested in her lap. "I don't understand. Are you unhappy?"

She instantly shook her head. "Your friends are wonderful and kind, and their wives are… They were so… I've never met women like them before."

"No, and you never again will, I daresay," he offered with a quick smile. Then he went back to being sober and attentive. "Go on."

She swallowed hard and jerked when a servant entered and began building up the fire.

"Annie." Duncan's voice was firm, commanding her to focus back on him. He squeezed her hands, and her fingers twitched in his hold.

"I don't belong here," she repeated softly. "I shouldn't be having such people call on me. Even if I were just Lady Raeburn's companion, it wouldn't be right. But I'm not."

"Not what?" he asked, his expression furrowed.

She nearly huffed a frustrated sigh. Could he really not understand?

"I'm not her companion," Annie said, her eyes dropping. "How can I be? I have no qualifications, no skills, I… I cannot be her companion."

"Of course, you can," Duncan insisted, his other hand coming to seize hers. "In case you have not noticed, Tibby is not your usual lady of Society. She does not have the same expectations that others would. I told you that you would suit her, and I stand by it. She adores you."

His faith in her only made her feel worse and she would have looked away if she had the power.

"Why did you save me?" she whispered as another tear fell. "What could you possibly gain from bringing me here? Just... why, Duncan?"

He released a soft exhale as he reached up and smoothed the tear away with his thumb. "Honestly? I couldn't help myself. I had to. Anything else was unthinkable and impossible." His thumb moved across her cheek almost absently, as if it was involuntary. "So you see, you do belong here. Because I had no choice but to bring you here. That must mean something, right?"

Annie did not think she could breathe. She had felt the same way about coming with him. There was no reason she should, and yet she had no other choice. She had to.

That *had* to have meant something.

Didn't it?

Again he stroked her cheek, and then he smiled a bit crookedly. "You belong, sweet. Trust me. And trust yourself."

There it was again. Trust. If only she knew how.

But for him, she would try.

She glanced around and noticed that the servant had left, and they were alone again. Taking a chance with the fleeting burst of faith she suddenly had in him, she squeezed his hands in return. "I can't read," she murmured.

Either he was a really magnificent actor, or he actually had no reaction. "No?" he asked innocently, as if that was a normal statement to make.

She shook her head. "I have tried and tried all week and I remember almost nothing."

"Why didn't you come to me? I already promised I would help you." His words were a scolding, but his voice was kindness itself. She was beginning to wonder if he was ever anything else.

"It's hardly an easy thing to admit," she told him. "And I didn't want Tibby to regret her acceptance of me."

"She wouldn't," he assured her with a firm shake of his head. "You should have heard her this morning, she is so delighted with you already."

"But I haven't done anything yet!" she protested, feeling sure he was lying.

He shrugged. "You have made an impression on her, it seems. You've impressed all of us." He winked at her, then finally moved enough away that she could draw in a full breath. "Now, come away from that freezing window and sit by the fire with me. I will help you read."

"Truly?"

He glanced back at her. "Yes, truly. Come here."

She gave him a curious look. "You will sit on the floor by the fire and read with me?"

He grinned broadly, and she had learned enough about him recently to know that did not happen often. "There is no better way to do it. Now, come over here."

She couldn't help it; she grinned back and scrambled like a child to his side, that tiny spark of hope bursting into a flame that burned as brightly as the fire before her.

Duncan sat alone later that night, staring blankly at the fire.

"You know me," he had said. Those words echoed through his mind again and again. He had never thought of it before, but it did feel as though Annie knew him.

Tibby would say something at breakfast and Annie would get this look on her face that was so close to a smile he could almost see it, and she would meet his eyes, almost as if she knew he had also been amused by it. And he always had been. She always seemed to look at him right when he was looking at her, which was happening with a startling frequency of late. And she would smile that small, barely-there smile just when he needed reassurance.

It had been barely a week that she had been in his house and he already dreaded the day Tibby's renovations would be complete.

He exhaled heavily as he considered the fire. He had not felt as contented in ages as he had when he and Annie had sat before the fire reading together only hours ago. She had not been so bad as she had led him to believe, and with his help and encouragement, she had improved greatly just in that one sitting.

He loved to hear her read. Her voice was filled with such wonder, so much light, that he was captivated by stories he had heard, and read, thousands of times before. It was as if he was hearing them for the first time. They had laughed over the antics of the characters, had drawn a bit closer when lovers were reunited, and he knew he could not have imagined the warmth that he felt between them as they took turns reading a page.

He could not explain it. How could he feel so much in so short a time?

But what exactly did he feel? He had a connection to Annie, that much was certain, but to what extent? She needed him, it was clear, but for how long? How much could he give her before she would find her wings and take flight?

His friends were curious about her, about him. How could they not be? He had hardly done anything this week that he was supposed to because he was too worried about how Annie would fare with the women and with her adjustment. It had taken every ounce of self-control he had possessed to remain in his study when she had returned instead of pouncing and interrogating her. He had to remember that she needed time and space to adjust, that it was not his place to become overly invested.

He was fooling himself.

He was overly invested.

Her success, her happiness, had become his primary goal. Everything was focused on that.

Why? What was it about her that drove him so?

He hardly knew how to respond when she had asked why he had saved her. He didn't think he had saved her. He rather thought she had saved him.

He had been used to helping people his entire life. His parents had instilled it into him to reach out to others, to help whenever and wherever he could regardless of the personal cost. It was how he would be able to pay back the kindness he had received from others. He knew firsthand what it felt like to want, to need, and to not have. Not many people knew about his family's true past or what they had endured before they had entered Society. Even less knew what they had endured when they had entered. It was not something to discuss openly.

But he was accustomed to service and charity. He always felt he would be less of a man if he did nothing. He was constantly trying to make up for where he had come from, to earn the position he now had.

Helping Annie was the first time he had ever felt he could be more than he already was. He had been completely truthful with her, but he could not have told her just how forceful the need to help her had been.

There had been no other choice.

He rubbed his hands over his face and groaned. Annie was partially right, though. She was to be his aunt's companion, and he was taking a shocking amount of liberty with the attention he was ensuring she received. If any knew about it, rumors would undoubtedly fly. He could only imagine what the servants were saying below stairs.

Not that he cared so very much about that, but Annie would.

Annie.

What was he supposed to do with her?

"Duncan?"

Tibby's voice broke into his reverie and he glanced towards the door. She was dressed far more simply than he had seen her recently, wearing a simple cap on her head, her gown plain and unadorned, with only a shawl wrapped around her. She looked more like the Tibby he had known in his youth, the one who had encouraged him so, nurtured him when others would not. The woman he had always thought of as his other mother. The one who had saved him first.

"Tibby," he said, his voice a bit rougher than he had intended it to be. "What are you still doing up?"

A gentle smile lit her features. "I've been talking with my

companion."

He nodded absently, then realized what she had said. "Annie?"

She nodded as she approached and took the seat near him. "I thought it was high time she and I had a private conversation. I have sensed, as I am sure you have, that she was not quite comfortable. I think she is trying to find her place, where she fits in with all of us. She doesn't, you know."

"Doesn't what?"

She gave him a look. "Fit in."

He restrained a growl. "Tibby…"

"Duncan, I adore her. You know I do, and you know how rare it is for me to feel that way about anybody." She reached out her hand and set it over his. "Annie is a special young woman. I am grateful you have brought her to me. But you must know she does not fit in. She has had such a hard life. She has suffered, Duncan. As much emotionally as physically."

He swallowed hard and nodded. He knew that. He had seen that. And he ached because of it.

"You can introduce her to your friends all you like," Tibby continued gently, rubbing his hand. "You can have Moira and Kate and Mary parade her around London if you wish it, but she will not fit."

Her words struck something in him and he looked at her, feeling very much like the child he once was. "I know. But I want her to." Then he shook his head and looked away. "But it isn't about what I want."

"No," Tibby replied quietly. "No, it isn't." She hesitated a moment, then sighed. "Tomorrow Annie and I will begin in earnest, and I will help her where I can. Even if she is not my companion for long, Duncan, I want her to fit in as well. She deserves to. And I think one day she could."

He suddenly had the urge to swallow again, but something blocked its way. His eyes burned a bit and he looked back at the fire, desperate to clear them.

"Duncan," Tibby said, her voice tinged with a bit of amusement, "what do you want me to do with her?"

"Make her feel useful," he replied. He cleared his throat. "Make her feel wanted. Give her no reason to fear the future. Let her see a brighter way to live. Make her feel..." He trailed off, unsure he could put words to what he wanted for her.

"Loved?" she prodded gently.

He nodded once, swallowing. "Make her feel loved. I don't think she has ever had that."

"And what about you?"

He glanced over at her. "What about me?"

Tibby considered him carefully. "What will you receive in return for all you have done?"

"That does not matter."

"Doesn't it?" She heaved a sigh and stood, still clutching his hand. "My darling boy, someday you will have to decide if you deserve the same happiness you insist on giving to others." She squeezed his hand tightly, then left him alone with his thoughts once more.

Chapter Nine

*F*ive days. How could it have only been five days? It might as well have been a lifetime.

Duncan was pacing in his study like a madman, knowing he deserved every jab his friends had leveled at him. They called him a loon, a mother hen, and dozens of other equally ridiculous names, and he had laughed them off. But inside each chipped away at him.

Because they were all true.

He was going crazy. How could he have seen her so little over the course of five days? What in the world were those women doing to her? Ever since Tibby said they would "begin" and Annie would start to fit in, they had all been as elusive as mist over the Thames.

It was driving him to complete and utter distraction.

What was even more maddening was the fact that he *had* seen her. Every day. Or evening, as it happened. Their reading in the library together had become ritual and he craved it. He loved being able to hear her improvements, which were significant and rapid. He cherished wandering the rows of books with her as they finished one after the other.

She was destined to be as avid a reader as he was, and he was utterly delighted by it. But their conversation did not stray far from the books. She remained aloof as to the dealings of her day and he did not pry. He wanted to, desperately. In fact he yearned to know everything. But he did, after all, possess some restraint.

He had only remained sane by forcing himself into activity with his friends. But one could only examine horses or advise on remodeling or admire infants for so long. Even Colin, his once trustworthy source of entertainment, was shockingly unhelpful. Colin had been as mulish as a bull of late and he suspected it was due to newfound rumors circulating about his brother Kit, but for one reason or another, Colin was not talking about it.

It was very unlike Colin.

But that only registered faintly in Duncan's mind right now. A far more pleasant topic was entrapping him far more completely than he would dare fathom.

Today he had thought he would be able to distract himself once again with some sort of useful employment with them, but each had his own tasks to see to this morning. So Duncan was left to his own devices, none of which would be even remotely plausible in his current state. What he needed was to see Annie.

He glowered and sank into his chair. He had learned very early in the week to stop mentioning her name. Every time he did his friends would look at each other with the same amused, knowing smiles. He found it irritating beyond reason.

They did not know anything. They knew nothing about Annie, or even himself. Granted, they knew more than most people did about Duncan's past and his family history, but he was not a man prone to sharing thoughts and emotions, even with his friends. His had always been more of a silent role, not for any particular reason, but merely because he had never felt a need to converse when conversation was not needed. Excessive vocalization irritated him.

Which did not explain why he was friends with Colin, but there it was.

A loud burst of laughter interrupted his reverie and he looked at the door of his study in confusion. He had suspected everyone to be out on such a fine day. The snow still lay crisp and white outside, but the sun was shining at last. Surely they would have gone for some fresh air.

Music filled the halls and wafted into the study. It was elaborate and intricate and beautiful, he thought with a smile. Then he frowned. It was also entirely beyond Marianne's skill.

Oh, his sister was quite accomplished, more so than a typical London girl of Society, that much he knew for certain. But while she was talented in all things, she was not especially excellent in anything, particularly with music. No one hearing her would suspect she lacked in any respect at all. But Duncan, who had endured hours upon hours of her recitals as a test of will, knew that her talent only extended as far as her patience, which was limited. And what he was hearing right now from the music room was not something she could have played without significant practice.

Which she never did.

Curious enough to investigate, he rose from his chair and snuck out of the room. The music was spritely and joyful, reminding him of a certain young girl who used to dance in flowerbeds before she was informed it was improper. Before such things became important to her. He smiled at just the sound of it. The closer he drew to the music room, the more he knew it could not be Marianne.

Or at least, not Marianne alone. Could it have been a duet?

If he suspected Kate were in the house, he would have said no, it was simply her. But Kate was madly gifted and accomplished musically. And he knew for a fact she was not in the house.

Who could duet with his sister? Tibby did not play, much to her apparent dismay, and often bemoaned her lack of musical accomplishment loudly and publicly. But she was a great appreciator of music and held musical galas annually. Had she decided to learn the basics of playing? At her age? He would not be surprised, the woman had recently vowed she would also learn Italian, and she was dreadful, but determined.

He would certainly tease her endlessly if she had taken up music as well.

Another burst of girlish giggles met his ears and he frowned briefly. Definitely not Tibby.

The music grew louder and faster and his pace matched it. He peered around the door of the music room and his breath caught in his chest.

His sister was at the pianoforte. And next to her was a small, slender wisp of a woman with golden hair that looked like the sun.

She looked at Marianne with a wild, carefree smile and her complexion was rosy and warm, the very picture of beauty and health. And they were playing with such delight and laughter, they might have been the best of friends.

Astonishingly, his eyes and his chest burned and he struggled to know which he ought to soothe. He found himself breathlessly laughing when they laughed, uncertain why or how, but he felt as light as feather and twice as flimsy. A weight he had not known he had been carrying was suddenly lifted from his shoulders, and he could breathe as freely as he had ever done.

The girls raced to the end of the song with gusto, Annie trying furiously to keep up with her far simpler part, but she matched Marianne note for note. The final chord was struck and both burst out laughing again as one of Marianne's notes was a trifle off, then they adjusted for the actual notes and raised their hands from the pianoforte, still giggling like children.

He did not want to disturb them, but he could not remain. He shifted his weight and the doorjamb creaked with its relief at his movement. The girls turned in surprise, and Annie's emerald eyes went wide with shock even as her cheeks flushed with embarrassment.

Marianne had nothing of the sort. She grinned as her eyes twinkled merrily. "Found us, have you? Took you long enough."

He regarded his sister with surprise. "I beg your pardon?"

"That is the fourth time we have played that song this morning and no one has even peeked in at us." She looked at Annie with a look of mock consternation. "Perhaps if we put words to it and sang at the same time, we might receive our due attentions."

The two of them snickered helplessly, and Annie covered her mouth with one of her delicate hands. Good heavens, had she ever laughed this much in her entire life? She was a fairy of joyful innocence when she laughed, and the sound was more musical than anything he had ever heard, including their playing just now, or even Kate's excellence.

"I did not know you played," Duncan said softly, his eyes only for Annie.

"I don't," she quipped. She smiled brightly, her expression still so full of joy and delight he was strongly tempted to kiss her.

The impulse took him by such surprise and force he felt himself falter just a bit. But given his size, it was noticeable and awkward. Annie did not react at all, but Marianne gave him a look that spelled trouble for him later.

Frantically, he swallowed and attempted to recover some semblance of control and normalcy. "Then how did you…?" he asked, gesturing to the pianoforte.

Annie's smile widened and her blush deepened. "Marianne has been good enough to teach me a little here and there this week. I am not very good, but…"

"You are doing *very* well for a beginner!" Marianne insisted with a squeeze to her arm. "Even I am impressed, and I am never impressed."

"You sounded like Tibby just then!" Annie squealed with wide eyes.

Marianne looked positively horrorstruck. "I did? Good heavens. Time to go for a walk. Come on, Annie." She jumped from the bench and took Annie by the hand, leading her from the room.

"What, you're leaving now?" he asked, knowing he sounded far too concerned.

Marianne rolled her eyes at him. "Yes, Duncan, we are. I have to change, I cannot go walking like this."

He saw no reason why that should be the case. She was looking very pretty today and it would have been entirely suitable for a walk about London.

"Do not look at me like that," his sister huffed. "You have no idea about fashion."

Duncan gave Annie a bewildered look and received only a shrug in return. She was apparently just as clueless.

"Well, I would like a word with Annie, if I may," he said suddenly, not willing to let her out of his sight just yet.

Marianne looked more put out than ever. "Well, Annie needs to change as well!"

"Do I?" Annie asked in surprise, looking down at her dress. It was a new one and Duncan had never seen it before, but it looked rather fetching on her. A simple blue day dress, hardly fine or expensive, and certainly something his sister would never have worn. But Annie needed no such finery, and it heightened the green in her eyes in such a way that they were the very first thing anyone would notice.

"No," Duncan said forcefully at the same time his sister screeched, "Yes."

Annie looked between the two in confusion, and the siblings stared at each other in a silent battle of wills.

Typically, Marianne would win these battles. She was headstrong, determined, and incredibly opinionated. She was accustomed to getting her way and thrived with that knowledge and self-proclaimed authority.

But where Annie Ramsey was concerned, Duncan would accept no defeat. And he could stare at his sister for an exceptionally long time until she, too, understood that fact.

Finally his sister threw her hands into the air with an exasperated huff. "Fine! See if I care! But she will change her boots. I have to insist upon it. I will send Agnes down with her coat and boots, you impossible louse." She whirled from the room in a flurry of skirts.

"You love me!" he called after her, sending a crooked grin at Annie, who had not handled the tension well and hesitantly gave a small smile back.

"God alone knows why!" his sister replied.

Duncan chuckled and shook his head.

Then he realized he was alone with Annie and had no idea what he wanted to talk to her about.

Blast.

She watched him expectantly, her eyes still filled with mirth, though a bit diminished. He had not failed to notice how she had nervously shifted her glances between the two of them as they had tested wills. Two weeks with his family and she still expected the worst. How long would that go on? When would she witness enough goodness to replace the underlying fear?

She tilted her head at him, no doubt curious as to why he had said he wished to speak with her. He could not have said why or on what subject he wanted to speak, could not have said he actually wanted to speak at all. Looking at her seemed to be quite enough at the moment.

But he knew she would hardly see it that way. So he would have to think of something to say.

Anything.

Anything at all.

"Good morning," he finally said softly.

That maddening hint of a smile reappeared and he would swear hours later that her eyes twinkled. "Good morning."

Excellent. Now what?

"Are you… enjoying your time here? With us?" He sounded like a frightened schoolboy stammering before a particularly fierce master.

Annie, it seemed, didn't notice. "Oh, yes. I have loved learning music and drawing from Marianne. She is sweet and kind and ever so patient to teach me. And Tibby has been helping me to improve my manners." She blushed a bit and looked down at her toes. "I'm still so rough and unrefined, but I am learning."

"And your reading is much improved."

She beamed at him. "Yes. Thank you for helping me. I have enjoyed our reading time together. You have been very kind to me, Duncan. All of you have."

His mind was swirling with the amount of speaking she was doing. He was used to the timid, shy creature from before, the one who hardly spoke at all. Not that he minded, quite the opposite. He was delighted that she was opening up in such a way.

"I am very grateful," Annie said in her soft, sweet voice.

Grateful? He did not want her gratitude. He did not care.

He wanted… He wanted…

What the devil did he want, anyway?

"Are you happy, Annie?" he asked suddenly.

Annie's pale brows rose and she bit her lip. "Yes, I think so. Why shouldn't I be?"

Why indeed?

"I have more than I ever dreamed I would," Annie continued slowly, seeming to choose her words with great care. "I still feel very out of place... I doubt that will ever change no matter where I am employed. But I am learning how to fit in. To want to fit in." She smiled up at him and again his heart stopped. "I have so much to learn, so much I still need to be, but I am happy." She shook her head faintly, and her voice took on a hint of wonder. "I don't know when I last felt that."

His chest ached at her words and he took her hand without even noticing he had. "Good," he murmured, stroking it. "I want you to be happy. Wherever you are, whatever you do, I... You should be happy, Annie."

A soft blush appeared on her cheeks and her smile turned shy. "Thank you." She shifted almost uneasily, looked out of the door, then back at him. "Do you think I need to change my dress? I don't want to distress Marianne by wearing something... inappropriate."

He sighed a small laugh and shook his head. "You don't need to worry about distressing Marianne ever, Annie. She will always get over it. And your dress is perfectly appropriate. In fact, if I might say so, you look very pretty."

Her eyes lit up and searched his eagerly. "Really?"

He swallowed and nodded. "Really." He brought her hand to his lips and pressed a warm kiss to the back of it.

He heard her breath catch and felt his match it. Her eyes turned a shade darker and a bit of anxiety entered them, the barest shadow of fear reappearing.

"What?" he asked softly.

She swallowed and stepped away. "Nothing. You're sure this dress is all right?"

He smiled again. "Do you like your dress, Annie?"

"I think so..." She said it almost as a question and looked at him as if for approval.

He shook his head at her. "I told you my thoughts, Annie. But my thoughts on the subject matter very little. All that matters is what you think of it."

She bit her lip again, chewing in indecision. Then she looked out

111

of the door again. "Marianne was so upset. I think I should go change."

Duncan felt a twinge of disappointment, but shrugged as if it made no difference. "If you like, Annie."

She nodded. "I would." She turned to go, then winced and turned back. "That is, if I may? If we are finished? I don't want to be rude."

He could not help the smile that formed on his lips. She was still as uncertain and timid as ever, checking on every little detail. Her confusion amused him, and made her even more charming. What would he do when she no longer asked for permission or his opinion? When she was no longer afraid or uncertain? When she tired of his protectiveness and his lurking? When she had grown enough to have real and gainful employment?

He forced himself to smile at her as kindly as he knew how. "You may, Annie. You don't need to ask. We are finished here."

She nodded and gave him his favorite barely-there smile. "Thank you for speaking with me, Duncan. I enjoyed it." She bobbed a hint of a curtsey and walked out, then turned suddenly. "We will still read tonight, won't we?"

Inexplicably, his chest was seized with a burst of pain. How long would that go on? When would she tire of their evenings in the library? Her uncertainty unnerved him. He would always want to read with her.

Always.

He nodded, unable to say a word.

She smiled with what he hoped was relief. "Good. I… I enjoy that, too." She averted her eyes and turned away.

Duncan exhaled sharply and ran a hand over his hair, laughing ruefully at his own distracted behavior. He used to have such composure, some might even call it poise, if he weren't so massive and oafish. Now he was a babbling mess of a man who hardly knew which way was up. The change was laughable. It was also terrifying.

"I have an idea."

He froze as he turned around. Tibby stood a little ways behind him, her arms folded over her bright green silk gown, several feathers sticking out of her elaborate hair. Her expression was superior, knowing, and altogether mischievous.

It was eerily too much like Colin Gerrard's typical expression.

"How long have you been there?" he asked, knowing a defensive tone was clear.

She smirked. "Long enough."

He frowned at her, attempting to appear menacing. "How did I neither see nor hear you?"

His aunt made a harsh sound and paired it with a matching look. "You have a second door to this room, Duncan. You should pay more attention in your own house. How can you expect to know anything if you cannot remember the basic logistics of a house that has been in your family… Well, not very long, actually, but you've certainly lived in it long enough to…"

"Tibby…"

She raised her hands and waved him off. "Never mind, never mind. As I was saying, I have an idea."

"Do I want to know?" he asked politely, knowing he probably did not, but neither would he have a choice.

The smile Tibby offered was neither comforting nor encouraging. "Yes."

He doubted that very much.

"And, I suspect, very much no."

That certainly caught him off-guard. When she did not continue, he raised a brow and gestured. "Well?"

"I want to sponsor Annie for a real London Season."

Duncan's mouth gaped open for a long moment. Then it worked noiselessly. Eventually, his voice caught up. "No," he said firmly. "No, no, absolutely not."

Tibby's eyes narrowed. "You misunderstand me, my dear. I have already decided. She *will* have a London Season and I *will* sponsor her, and if we have any luck, she *will* find herself a husband before the Season is out. I was merely informing you. Thought you ought to know." She turned on her heel and swept out of the room grandly.

He stood there for several heartbeats, then his brow snapped down and he marched after her.

"Tibby!" he barked, his voice booming throughout the house. "Tibby, wait!"

"Explain it to me again," Duncan sighed, putting his head into his hands.

"Quite simple, my dear," Tibby said from the far corner of his study. "Annie is far too good to be a companion or a governess or anything of the sort. Her station is all that limits her."

"I know that," he grumbled, grinding his eyes with the heels of his hands. "Don't you think I know that?"

"Of course," his aunt replied a bit too gleefully. "We all know it. Even Marianne."

He lifted his head and looked at her in disbelief. "Really?"

His sister was not the sort to let that detail slip by. She held firm beliefs about station and fortune and the like. It was irritating, but there it was. He could hardly believe she would ignore something so monumental, in her estimation, as a difference in situation.

Tibby smiled, no doubt understanding precisely where his thoughts were at the moment. "You saw them on the pianoforte today. She loves her, Duncan. Marianne has a sister at last, or a true friend, at the very least. When was the last time Marianne had any such young woman? Annie would be far more a companion for her than she could ever be for me, though I daresay I would take her in an instant."

"So why don't you?" he asked, his head feeling like it would split in two.

"Because I want her to have more."

It was said so simply, so honestly, and he felt the same way. But a Season in Society? With fawning cads and daring debutantes and the criticism and scrutiny of snobs and fools and good-for-nothing tiresome gossips the likes of Lady Greversham? He could not allow Annie to be subjected to that, she would not be able bear it.

Or perhaps he would not.

"So," Tibby went on when he did not reply, "obviously we shall change her name. Not that anyone here should know her, but you never know these days. Obviously, the Season is still some weeks away, so we shall test her out while London is quiet, and it will give us plenty of time to prepare her. And she shall be a long lost relative of mine. Some niece of a late husband from his previous marriage or some such nonsense, and her fortune shall be rumored at some twenty thousand pounds."

Duncan gave his aunt a look of sheer and utter bewilderment. "Twenty thousand pounds? Where in the name of Christendom is she going to obtain twenty thousand pounds, Tibby?"

"Why, from me, of course."

Now he was positively thunderstruck. His house could erupt in green flames and he would not be any wiser.

"What?" he choked out.

Tibby dropped her chin just a touch, her bright eyes leveling him to the ground. "I am giving her twenty thousand pounds. I have the fortune to do whatever I please, and it will not infringe upon Marianne's portion, nor yours. Though I daresay neither of you need anything from me, given your own living, however reluctant you are to spend it."

"That is not the point," he growled, resenting her for even bringing it up.

"I know," she replied firmly, her amusement dimming. "I know, Duncan. What I am saying is…"

"It's your money and you can do what you like with it?" he suggested with more than a hint of irony.

"Exactly so."

He did not like the smug expression on his aunt's face. He did not like this plan of hers. But he also knew his aunt well enough to know that if he got in her way, she would run him over with her coach and team of horses, then back the whole rig up and run him over again for good measure.

"I will not agree to this scheme of yours," he said slowly, keeping his voice level and his words careful, "nor support it…"

"Duncan!"

"…unless I am sure that Annie wants to participate." He gave

Tibby a hard look of his own. "She has to want it, Tibby. You cannot force her. She must understand completely what will be expected. You thought she had a hard time fitting in here with us as a companion? She will now have to blend in seamlessly into the most vicious pool of carnivorous monsters that has ever existed. She has no idea how Society is."

He saw his aunt stiffen, saw the way her expression froze, and the worried light that entered her eyes. She had not considered all of that, he could see. Why should she? She was one of the wealthiest and most influential people in Society. She could go where she liked however she liked and not care a sniff for the opinions of others.

Annie was a fresh young face with no history, no fortune, and no accomplishment to speak of.

London would eat her alive.

"And what will you do, Tibby," Duncan continued, his tone remaining even, "if she does find an eligible man who wants to marry her?" His throat dried at the thought and he had to swallow, praying his composure was still intact. "Will he find her true identity a betrayal? Will he find her past abhorrent? What will your ideal potential husband for Annie do when the truth comes out?"

"It should not matter," Tibby muttered stubbornly.

"It should not," he agreed, "but it will."

She studied him for a long moment. "Would it stop you?"

Duncan jerked where he sat, and barked, "What?"

"If you loved a young woman, and you found out a truth like Annie's, would it stop you?"

He felt as though he were walking on ice and the slightest misstep would send him flying into danger. He wet his lips and released a brief sigh. "No. But not all men have my past, nor my opinions."

"Can we not try?" Tibby asked, leaning forward eagerly. "I am not saying that we will parade the sweet girl around like a peacock, or even turn her into a debutante. We saw the trouble that created for Mary and Geoffrey last year."

Duncan sat back and raised his brows in surprise. "You knew about all of that?"

116

Tibby waved a hand at him. "Please, darling. You underestimate me."

He had to chuckle. "Apologies. Of course, you knew."

She nodded, then folded her hands and sighed herself. "No parading, Duncan. No debutantes. No snobbery, no false behaviors. Annie will be entirely herself. But in the sort of places and among the sort of people that will give her the best chance for happiness and security. Don't you want that for her?"

"I want her to be happy," he murmured. "Nothing more, nothing less."

"So… I may try?"

He smiled at her, finally, shaking his head. "I told you, only if Annie understands what this entails and she wants to. If she agrees to it willingly… not forcibly," he broke off with a final warning look that she nodded at, "then I will agree." His smile turned rueful. "And since when do you need my permission to do anything?"

She sniffed and sat back, already looking victorious. "I do not. It is merely a formality."

"Of course," he replied, nodding obediently. "Formality."

"I will take care of her, Duncan," Tibby said quietly, all pomp and airs gone. "I give you my word. I will be her dragon."

"And I her defender," he murmured. "Don't turn her into Marianne, Tibby."

"God forbid." Tibby crossed herself and rolled her eyes. "One is quite enough."

He nodded, feeling a twinge of guilt at saying such things about his sister. But at the moment he feared nothing more than seeing Annie change into something she was not. He wanted nothing to change about her. Ever.

"Annie would never be Marianne, though," Tibby said thoughtfully. "She is too sweet, too shy, and too innocent to ever be so. And I intend to keep her that way. We shan't let Society change our girl, now shall we?"

"No," he breathed, still feeling his heart wringing itself out in his chest. He was uneasy about this plan, and probably always would be.

But he could not deny that the prospect of dancing with Annie at a ball surrounded by his friends did have a certain appeal to it.

He looked back at his aunt, who watched him steadily. "A niece of your late husband's from his previous marriage? Really?"

Her eyes narrowed. "It was a thought, Duncan."

"Which late husband, I wonder?"

Tibby scoffed and rose. "Rupert, you impertinent man. His family was riddled with all sorts of random relatives, the likes of which most people had never heard of."

"I did not know that." He smirked as he leaned back and looked at the ceiling. "I always liked Rupert. How shocking is his family?"

She turned to face him with a look. "Some things, Duncan Bray, you honestly do not need to know."

He burst out laughing as she boldly left the room without glancing behind her even once.

Chapter Ten

"*I* won't do it."

"You won't? I don't understand."

"What is there to understand? I will not do it. I refuse. Absolutely and emphatically no."

Duncan pinched his nose between his thumb and forefinger and exhaled sharply. "Why not?"

"You have to ask? You do not see any potential problems here?"

He snorted. "Of course, I see potential problems, this idea has nothing but problems in it for most parties involved. But I don't see any reason why it should keep you from helping."

Marianne did not reply, which was unlike her, so Duncan raised his head to look at her. She stared at him with her mouth agape, her entire being apparently offended. "Why it should…? Duncan! She does not belong in Society! Do you even hear yourself? You and Tibby want her to raise herself so far above her station that it places her on a level with…"

He glowered at her, his ire rising within him. "What, Marianne? With you?"

She closed her mouth, but her glare remained fixed. "Yes, as a matter of fact. You said Tibby is giving her twenty thousand pounds? Preposterous. Even with extensive training and an entirely new wardrobe, she could hardly pass for five."

"Don't be mercenary," he growled, patience rapidly wearing thin.

"Nay, I *will* be mercenary!" his sister cried, rising out of her chair.

"Money is everything! Money brings position and power and influence. Without it, you cannot get anywhere. Annie has nothing to offer anyone. She has no fortune, no family, and no talents! You think she can survive for one hour in a London ballroom? She will not fool anyone. She is too poor and too plain to entertain such aspirations. You cannot raise her to this level, it throws everything Society holds important into complete degradation."

"You place entirely too much importance on the opinions and appearances of Society."

"And your complete lack of regard makes you stupid to the point of imbecility."

Duncan looked at his sister in shock. She had never spoken to him in such a way before, and he had never imagined she would have reason to. "Tread carefully," he threatened, his tone far more dangerous than he had ever allowed with her before.

But it seemed Marianne would not heed him. "You cannot hide what she really is, Duncan. She is a poor little urchin who deserves the pity of the world, but not their welcome. She is not well-bred, in fact she could hardly be more *ill*-bred. A horse tradesman is all the relation she has in the world, and from your own account, he is a woman-beating drunk. Yes, I can imagine that will go over quite well with the bachelors of London."

"Marianne, I am warning you." Any sensible being on earth would have heard his barely concealed rage and stayed far away from rising temper. His sister had no such sense, and no such cares. She did not fear him.

"You will make our family a complete laughingstock!" she cried. "When these lies, these fabrications come to light, and mark my words they will, it will be the end for us. By association with her, we will all become ridiculous and the stuff of mockery!"

His knuckles were white as they clenched the arms of his chair, though how he was still seated, he could not have said. "No more," he said, his voice low, seething, and taut, "than you have already made yourself."

Marianne looked as though he had slapped her.

Faintly it registered to him that his words were harsh, but not enough to force him to stop. "Do you think that I am so ignorant as to what people say about you, Marianne? And what they say about me because of it? Do you even know how many rumors I have had to quell, how many lives I have had to threaten to protect your reputation, or what shreds actually remain of it? I have never in my life cared about what is said about me. And neither, it seems, have you. So forgive me if I do not take your opinions into consideration with regards to Annie. You are spoiled, self-centered, and in want of discipline, which I have neglected to give you, and that is my fault. I gave you too much freedom, and now it's too late. But mark *my* words, Marianne, if you don't check yourself, you will fast find that you will turn into..." He trailed off, even as his chest heaved with his fury.

Marianne lifted her chin, daring him to finish, but having no idea what he would say.

He shook his head, unable to complete his worst fear vocally. He exhaled slowly, fighting for control. "You have your own say in this. I cannot force you. Stay out of it, if you will, but you will not make things more difficult for her. You will not insult, degrade, or deride her. You will keep your mouth shut where she is concerned if you cannot say anything good. I dare not ask you to defend her, because I know that is asking too much of your pride, but you will not injure her. Do you understand me?"

Perhaps it was the eight years between them, perhaps it was the authority in his voice, perhaps it was nothing other than a bit of sense smacking her in the face, but she only held her stubborn chin high for a fraction of a moment before she nodded. Her eyes were misty, but she shed no tears. His words had been brutal and he knew it, but they had also been truth. And it was long past time she heard them.

"Are we done here?" Marianne asked bitterly, her voice not nearly as steady as it had been.

He gave her a single nod, torn between wanting to hug her and wanting to rage at her.

She rose and turned to leave his study, then turned back to him. "I like Annie. I admire her. I daresay I even love the girl, as much as one might love someone like that. But that does not make her my equal."

"I thought you were going to adopt her."

She sniffed with far too much conceit and gave him a look of complete and utter superiority. "Rather as one might adopt a puppy, Duncan. Not a sister. She could not aspire to equal me."

He considered his sister with sad resignation. "No, Marianne. You could not aspire to equal her. But you should."

She inhaled and stiffened visibly, her eyes widening a touch. Then her jaw tightened and she whirled from the room, stomping down the marble halls, her steps echoing each angry stride.

Duncan closed his eyes and barely restrained a moan of pain. His sister had several points, all of which he had considered long into the night and continuing through the morning. But she was also quite mistaken about several things, and he was horrified at the creature she was becoming. How could she be so cruel and heartless?

His fears were coming true. She was turning into their mother.

Not that his mother had actually been heartless or cruel. In fact, she had been anything but. If, however, one had asked any member of Society who knew her, they would have disagreed. Their mother had put on the same sort of show for the world that Marianne now was, only Marianne acted the part in private as well.

She didn't know what the rumors said about her. She didn't know what they said about their mother. Oh, she had heard some things, enough to know that she didn't want to be accused of becoming her, but she had no idea. He had shielded her from that.

She also did not know the truth about their family.

Perhaps it was time she did. But it would mean admitting to the past, and Marianne would be ashamed of it. Of them.

Of him.

Did he dare risk that?

After their conversation just now, he did not know.

He was disappointed that Marianne would not help Annie, should she agree to Tibby's proposition. But thinking back on it, he couldn't say he was surprised by it. Luckily, he had other alternatives, ones who might not share his sister's opinions.

But then, he could never be sure. They had surprised him in the past.

Annie needed to agree before he proceeded any further.

And at this point, he was not sure he wanted her to.

"I'm afraid I don't understand." Annie fumbled anxiously with her hands in her lap as she considered Tibby. "You don't want me to be your companion anymore?"

Tibby reached across the small table in the morning room and took Annie's hand. "No, dear girl. I want you to be my niece."

That made no sense of any kind. "Your… niece?"

"Well, the niece of my late husband from his previous marriage." Tibby shook her head, sending her tightly curled hair dancing like flames. "It will all be such a mess to sort out that no one will ever take the time to unravel it. But I want you to join us in Society. I want you to have a debut like all the other pretty young girls in England and have a real London Season with balls and parties and suitors. I want you to be a lady."

Annie felt the breath leave her lungs in a massive exhalation. "What?"

Tibby nodded, smiling as if she had not just asked for the impossible. "You are a delightful girl. So sweet and kind and patient, and you will do anything to please anybody. You have had such a hard time of life and yet you have no bitterness or hard heartedness in you. It shows remarkable maturity for one so young. Anyone would be blessed to have you as a companion." She squeezed her hands tightly, so tightly that her large rings began cutting into Annie's skin. "But I do not want you to merely be someone's companion. I think you can be more."

"More?" Annie felt as though her brain were working through mud and mist. How could she be more than a companion when she was barely capable enough for that?

"Yes, Annie. More. I think, with enough training and adjustments to your hair and wardrobe, you can be just as graceful and elegant in public as you are in private. Enough so that you could even find a match out of the highest society of London."

Lightheadedness suddenly hit Annie and she clung to Tibby's hand as if it were a rope tossed to a victim of the sea. Waves upon waves of dizziness rolled over her and she closed her eyes tightly to get her bearings.

"Take a breath," Tibby's voice soothed, sounding very maternal indeed. "Breathe in slowly…"

Annie tried to do as she was instructed, and found very little air going in, but quite a bit coming out. Her heart began to race, pounding against her ribs brutally.

"Breathe, Annie." Her voice was now commanding and firm, and Annie was instantly obedient.

Slowly, the room stopped its spinning, though her face and brow were now covered with a sheen of anxious perspiration that mortified her.

"That is better," Tibby sighed, coming to sit by Annie and rubbing circles on her back. "I can see I shall have to be more careful with you than I thought."

"I'm sorry," Annie whispered shakily, moving to wipe her face with her sleeve.

"No, no, my dear," Tibby said, holding Annie's arm to stop her. "Handkerchief. Do you have one?"

Annie nodded and pulled the one in her pocket. Her fingers trembled as she wiped her face, her lungs still aching from her panic.

"Where did you get that?"

Annie jerked as Tibby's voice reminded her that the only handkerchief she possessed was, in fact, Duncan's. She shot a terrified look at his aunt, fearing the worst. But Tibby's eyes were soft, just as her voice at been, and she took in Annie's clutching hold on the fabric with interest.

"Is that what he used on your wound?" she pressed.

Annie nodded. Her cheeks were flaming and she could not manage to swallow. What in the world would Tibby think?

Tibby sighed and smiled at her. "Sweet girl. I am going to be remarkably impertinent at the moment and ask you something terribly personal. Do you have feelings for my nephew?"

Annie would have run for the hall if Tibby's hold on her weren't so tight. Her blood suddenly felt hot and her toes tingled with anticipation. "I... I... don't know," she admitted finally, her voice quivering unsteadily.

"Why do you not know?"

She moved a damp lock of hair from her forehead and twisted it behind her ear. "He... he saved me. He helped me to escape. He brought me here and helped me to read. I am... grateful to him for that. But..."

"But you do not know if there is more than that."

Annie nodded, swallowing hard.

"Do you find him handsome?"

Again, she nodded, her cheeks flaming again. What a thing to admit to one's employer!

"Kind?"

"Yes." He was the very description of the word.

"Why did you go with him?"

Annie glanced over at Tibby and saw genuine curiosity, but also something else. Something she could not define. But it gave her strength. "Because when I was with him I felt... safe." She suddenly had to swallow once more. "I hadn't felt safe in so long, I was afraid to go back. And also..." She blushed at her own daring, uncertain if she could complete the errant thought.

"I see," Tibby said slowly, one side of her mouth curving upwards. "Yes, I see. Well, I stand by what I said. I want you to become a lady and take London by storm."

"I'm not a lady."

"Well, not yet, but you will be when I am through with you."

"I doubt I could take anything by storm, Tibby," she laughed, her nerves fading a bit.

"Tosh," Tibby scolded, patting her hand. "It will be a very quiet storm, hardly any noise at all, just a few waves here and there. Maybe a stray bolt of lightning where it is needed. Nothing scandalous."

Annie laughed a little and sighed as she wiped a stray tear from her eye. "What will I need to do?" she asked with a sniff. Her mind reeled with the possibilities and expectations and confusion.

Tibby straightened up and gave her a very serious look. "First, I need to tell you what you can expect from this all of this. You've not experienced London at the height of Society, and thankfully, the official Season does not start for some time, so you will get a taste before the insanity commences. After I have told you all, then the rest is up to you."

Annie reared back in a bit of shock. "To me? Why me?"

"Because when it comes down to it, my dear, you must be the one to decide what to do. I shall not force you, nor try to dissuade you. If you choose to do it, I will be thrilled and help you every step of the way. If you choose not, then you will still be my companion and I will be delighted by your company."

The older woman's words were so sincere, so encouraging, that Annie almost cried again. But she was so terrified at the prospect of being on display for all of London that she could only nod jerkily and attempt to regain sensation in her fingertips. There was no way she could do anything so impossible as what Tibby had suggested. But she would hear her out.

She absently gripped at the fabric of her plain day dress while Tibby began, rather rapidly, to talk about what London was like during the Season. What the people were like. It was plain that Tibby adored being on display and that the hustle and bustle of the Season poured life into her veins. Annie listened with half of an ear, knowing that this was important for her, but also knowing there would not be any point. The dress she wore now was a borrowed and refurbished gown belonging to Mary's sister, though Mary said it suited Annie far better.

She doubted that.

It was impossible to deny that she had not thought once or twice about what it would be like to be a fine lady with the sort of gowns and manners that Moira, Kate, Mary, Tibby, and Marianne all possessed. She had even dreamed about it a few times. But she had never imagined that she would ever have the chance to actually… That anyone would *want* her to…

Could she really do something so farfetched?

"Are you even listening to me, child?"

Tibby's voice broke into her reverie and she snapped up to look at her. Clearly, Tibby did not think she had been.

But Annie had long been used to listening and thinking at the same time.

"Yes, ma'am."

Tibby raised a brow suspiciously. "What did I just say, then?"

"That I can still be as reserved as I am and will not have to speak to anybody that I don't want to so long as I speak to someone," she recited nearly word for word.

Annie felt a rush of pride at seeing Tibby's expression of surprise. At least something from her past was useful.

"Well, well," Tibby murmured softly, "you may do far better than I expected in Society if you can listen without listening."

Heat rushed into Annie's cheeks and Tibby grinned. "You will have to manage your blush better, my dear, or the men will be all over you. You look quite charming with such color."

"Tibby..."

"I never flatter, darling, not at all," Tibby continued with a wave of her hand, "and I know that I have described quite a bit just now. But think it over, won't you? I promise you, you will not regret a moment. We can stop it at any time, just say the word. I think you will enjoy it, though. And I know a certain someone would love an opportunity to see you all dressed up in fine clothes and dance with you as such."

Annie's mouth fell open and her eyes widened. "What?"

Tibby smirked. "Did I say something? No, no, I don't believe I did. Well, I shall leave you to your thoughts. Say the word and I shall wave my magic wand over you, my dear. Ta ta!" She rose and swept from the room in one fluid motion, leaving Annie alone on the sofa in the drawing room, feeling as though her stomach had dropped to the floor beneath her toes.

There couldn't be any truth to what Tibby was saying. None at all. Duncan would never want... He could never...

But what if he did?

Her breath caught in her chest and a strange sound sprang from her. Could it even be possible? She knew she was not indifferent to him, far from it, but would he ever be more than simply protective and kind where she was concerned?

A twinge of something sharp hit her stomach and she shifted uncomfortably. What would he want her to do? He had brought her here to be a companion; would he be offended if she went beyond his expectations of her? Would he think her impertinent or improper?

Or would he approve of it?

Before she could think twice about it, she was on her feet and moving quickly from the drawing room and practically running down the hall to his study. She needed to see him, to know what he thought, to watch his eyes when he answered…

The door was open and he sat at his desk, head down, writing a letter of some kind. Somehow, he had not heard her frantic approach. She swallowed thickly and knocked lightly on the door.

He looked up instantly and smiled. "Annie. Please, come in." He rose and came around the front of his desk, then leaned against it, the fawn of his trousers contrasting brilliantly with the rich mahogany wood of his desk. She ought not to look at his taut, muscular legs. It was most certainly not proper.

"What can I do for you?" Duncan asked, apparently not noticing her attention.

She lifted her eyes and bit her lip, suddenly more terrified than she had been since arriving in London. Her fingers began mangling each other and his eyes darted there. A small smile lit his features, and he looked more impossibly handsome than before. His clear blue eyes met hers and he tilted his head slightly.

"Let me guess," he murmured. "You've just spoken with Tibby about her idea."

Relieved, she nodded.

"And?"

And what? He was supposed to tell her what to do! Yet his face was remarkably devoid of emotion.

"And I'm terrified," she whispered, feeling that at the very least she ought to be honest with him. She *could* be honest with him.

"You don't have to do it, you know," he said gently, folding his arms over his chest.

His kind words weren't helping her situation. She had to know what he wanted. What he thought.

How he felt.

"Tell me what to do," she pleaded, wishing it didn't sound so desperate.

He slowly shook his head, maintaining eye contact, and smiling. "No."

She closed her eyes and clenched her hands, exhaling slowly. "Please."

"No, Annie." His voice was so soft, so tender, and she could hear his smile in it.

There was no sound then, save for the fire crackling in the hearth, and the sound of her breathing, which she struggled to maintain control of. So much weighed on this decision, and no one would help her make it. What was she to do? How was she to…?

"Annie."

She opened her eyes and met Duncan's gaze instantly.

"You don't have to do it," he repeated. "You don't have to do anything you don't want to do."

"Do you want me to do it?" she suddenly asked, a little louder than she had planned. Her cheeks heated at his arrested expression and it took all of her strength to avoid fleeing the room in the face of such impudence on her part.

He considered her carefully for a moment. "Does that really matter?"

"Yes." It mattered. It was everything.

"That is why I cannot tell you," he replied softly, still smiling. "I'm sorry, Annie, but if you are going to do this, you will need to decide all on your own. Not for me, not for Tibby, not for anyone. Just for you. Don't worry about disappointing anyone or gaining anyone's approval. We will act on your wishes. You must choose what to do, and what you want."

What she wanted? She had no idea what she wanted. She wanted to be told what to do. She was a very obedient person, she would do whatever she was told. What she wanted had very little place in her life.

What she wanted was…

She wanted…

"You can choose, Annie. Whatever you want. Whatever will make you happy. You have that freedom. I will stand by you, whatever you decide."

A spark of something hot filled her chest and spread throughout her limbs. She nearly gasped at the sensation, and suddenly, she knew what she wanted; what she would do.

"I'll do it," she whispered, unable to keep the wonder out of her voice. She cleared her throat and repeated, "I'll do it." She laughed and nodded. "I'm going to do it."

He grinned, his eyes crinkling at the corners. "All right then. Let's do it."

She returned his smile with one of her own. "Now what?" she asked breathlessly.

"Now, I think you had better go and tell Tibby before she perishes from curiosity."

She giggled and nodded, then ran from the room, feeling as light as a fairy and twice as magical.

Duncan still sat in his study when Annie returned barely a half hour later. He looked up in surprise, unable to keep the smile from his face. She had a sparkle of excitement in her eyes still, and it was enchanting. Her expression when she had made up her mind had been captivating and taken hold of him.

"Yes?" he asked teasingly as she bounced back into the room.

She bit her lip, looking uncertain again. "Did I do the right thing?"

He chuckled. "You've already told Tibby, the thing is done."

"I know," she said, wrinkling her nose a bit. "She's beside herself."

"She usually is." He tilted his head and looked at her closely. "Second thoughts?"

She nodded, then shook her head. "No, I… I want to do it. I

may never get anything like this again, and Tibby... She believes in me."

"So do I," he said before he could stop himself.

To his surprise, Annie's smile deepened and she kept his gaze. "I know."

He suddenly had to fight hard to swallow. "If this will make you happy, Annie, then you should do it. That is all I... all we want for you."

She did not miss his correction and her cheeks tinged with pink. "Thank you," she said softly.

He was quite sure he had never smiled so much in his life, but he could not help it when another touched his cheeks.

"Annie!" Tibby's screech echoed in the hall. "Annie! Come quick!"

"Oh lord," Annie muttered, drawing a laugh from him. She turned to call out to his aunt. "What is it, Tibby?"

"You have... callers!" Tibby's voice was ringing with excitement and delight.

Annie reared back in shock, then looked at Duncan. "Callers?"

He shrugged and gestured. "Ask who it is."

"Who?" she called loudly.

Duncan put his head into his hand, laughing. This was going to be entertaining.

"Moira, and Kate, and Mary! They are demanding you come and see them in the drawing room, and are quite excited, if I do say so myself!"

Duncan clamped his lips together to keep from laughing at Annie's surprise, and released a few chuckles when her smile threatened to break her cheekbones. She tossed a wild, excited look at him, and he waved her on, knowing he looked too involved, too happy, too delighted himself.

But he was.

And he would be lying if he did not admit he was a bit curious about Tibby's scheme, and what could come from it.

Chapter Eleven

"*I* think your hair is perfect just the way it is, though we may need to instruct your maid how to do it properly. It suits you now, but it should have more movement and intricacy to it for you to really shine."

Kate hummed and made yet another circle around Annie, a finger to her lips, her eyes wandering the length of her. She looked rather like a cat circling a trapped bird, a suspicious gleam in her dark eyes. But she also had a small smile on her face that was encouraging.

"I don't have a maid," Annie told her softly, feeling more self-conscious than she ever had in her entire life.

Kate looked up in surprise. "Then who does your hair?"

"I do."

Moira snickered from where she sat in the straight back chair next to the fire and put a hand over her eyes. "Now what have you to say, Kate? Would you like some help climbing out of the hole you have suddenly found yourself in?"

Annie and Mary snickered as Kate gave her friend a quelling look, then turned back to Annie.

"I am very impressed," Kate replied, giving Annie a broad smile. "You would never know."

"I cannot do that," Mary admitted, pushing off of the wall where she had been leaning. "I am absolutely hopeless when it comes to my hair." Her arms were folded over her chest and she cocked her head as she studied Annie carefully. "Still, I think a maid would be helpful.

Is there anyone who can help you?"

"There most certainly is!" Tibby's voice called from the hall, where she was eavesdropping.

The women snickered and Annie shook her head. "She said she would leave us to it," Annie murmured softly. "I am learning that means she will listen at the door and voice her opinions later."

"Or now, it seems," Moira added with another laugh, shaking her head. "I am, however, surprised that Marianne isn't here. She would be a great asset to these discussions."

Annie felt her cheeks heat and looked down at the floor. Tibby had informed her of Marianne's decision and opinions, and while Annie could understand her reservations, she could not deny that she was hurt. She had not seen Marianne since their walk yesterday and she had wondered why. Now she knew.

Marianne liked her well enough, but only with a certain understanding between them.

Annie could not fault her for that.

"Marianne doesn't approve," Annie whispered softly, not wanting to speak ill of her. She still liked Marianne a great deal, and she hoped that as long as she kept things as they had been here at the house, they might still be friends.

If that was still possible.

Again, Kate hummed, pressing her lips together, her eyes flashing dangerously. Annie faintly hoped that she never angered Kate. It was a rather intimidating look.

"Don't worry about it," Mary soothed, coming over and putting an arm around Annie's waist. "She will come around. And you've got us."

"Hear, hear!" Moira cried jubilantly from her chair with a grin. "We are your champions."

Kate gave a short laugh and shook her head. "Moira, are you going to help us or not?"

"What?" Moira asked, cocking her head. "Analyzing Annie as if she were a pig for slaughter or a horse for market? Finding her flaws and where she needs improving? No, I thank you, I shall sit right here and only voice my opinion when necessary."

"But her accent…" Kate said, biting her lip.

"Her manner of speaking…" Mary added, squeezing Annie tightly, which assured her that she was not being cruel, merely honest.

"Her vocabulary, her dress, her skills," Kate rambled off, taking Annie's hand and smiling.

Moira shook her head. "Not saying a word. I am here for moral support only."

Annie gave the woman a strange look. "Don't you think I need improving?"

Moira snorted in a rather unladylike way. "Not a bit. You are sweet and kind and far too good for any of us here; yes, including you, Mary Harris," she added as the others chuckled and Mary curtseyed in response. Moira grinned and looked back at Annie. "All I would say is find a better fitted wardrobe because, really, darling, you are a tiny thing and that must be appreciated. But I rather like your accent and I like you just as you are, so unless you are to be the next sovereign of this nation, no, I do not think you need improving."

Annie swallowed the sudden lump in her throat and raced over to Moira and kissed her cheek fondly, which Moira returned with a grin and a wink.

Kate huffed in mock exasperation and put her hands on her hips. "Really, Moira, you say the most extraordinary things when you are expecting." They all laughed and she took Annie's hand once more. "We all like Annie excessively or we would not be here. Now stop being so high minded and help us get this girl a proper debut!"

All of the women laughed and Annie felt a weight lifted off of her shoulders. She might be in for a rude awakening of just what Society expected and what she would have to endure and become, but these women seemed to like her in spite of her many flaws. They knew where she needed adjustments and were willing to help her make them.

She had never known what it was like to have friends, but she suspected this was as close as she would get.

"I don't need much by way of clothing," Annie said, trying to be helpful. "I can mend and alter myself."

All three women looked at her in surprise.

"Can you really?" Moira asked, her eyes lighting up. "Excellent. I am coming to see you to help me let out some of my gowns. As I grow larger, my dresses grow smaller, it is most inconvenient."

Kate shook her head. "Moira, you are not going to employ Annie as a seamstress. She is a lady now."

"Who said I would pay her?" Moira shot back, making Annie giggle helplessly. "I was thinking of a trade. She helps me with my gowns, I help her learn how to navigate Society."

"Yes, since you do that so well, dear."

Moira narrowed her eyes, but could not help the smirk on her face.

"Ignore them," Mary murmured into Annie's ear. "They always do this."

"I like it," Annie whispered back. "I've only ever known fighting. This is much better."

Mary squeezed her again. Then she spoke in a slightly louder voice. "First thing I think you should know, Annie, is that there is always a better dress. My sister had to teach me that unfortunate lesson myself not too long ago. You look very pretty just as you are, but for a lady, I am sorry, but you must have some new dresses."

Annie wrinkled her nose, unsure if she liked that idea. New dresses were always appealing, but she did not think she would enjoy the extravagance. Not when this would not last. Not when she already felt so in debt to them, to everyone.

"I have never met a woman who looked so uncomfortable at the prospect of new gowns," Moira announced from her chair, looking a little concerned. "And I was there for Mary's fittings. Are you quite well? Are we overwhelming you?"

"A bit," she admitted shyly, her cheeks blushing.

"Sorry," Kate told her with a sigh. "I know we are overbearing. We bombarded Mary last year. But we would not do so if we didn't love you."

"You barely know me," Annie reminded them as her cheeks warmed and her eyes burned.

Moira came out of her hair and went directly to her, wrapping her arms around her and pulling her close. "We know you well enough," she insisted fiercely. "And we adore you. So you will just have to put up with us, all right?"

Annie swallowed hard and nodded against her, blinking back the tears in her eyes.

Moira pulled back and grinned. "So. For starters…"

"I thought you did not think she needed improving," Kate said from behind her, looking a bit misty-eyed.

Moira sniffed a bit superiorly. "I still don't. But that does not mean a little refinement could not help. Even Mary could be more refined."

"Excuse me," Mary protested with a laugh. "Have you met yourself?"

Moira ignored that comment. "You ought to know that all polite members of Society address each other as Mr. or Miss or by their title, if they have one. So in public, I am Lady Beverton or my lady. Kate is Lady Whitlock or my lady. And Mary is Mrs. Harris."

Annie nodded carefully, trying to absorb it all. "And I curtsey?"

"In greeting, yes. But not deeply. In private, you must still call us by our first names. None of us permit formality out of company." Moira looked so severe that Annie had to laugh. Duncan's friends had said the same thing, and it was evident that these women were quite suited to their husbands.

Kate cleared her throat and stepped around Moira. "Now. We must figure out how to introduce you. I know Lady Raeburn had some ideas, shall I call her?"

"I think she can hear," Mary muttered as Tibby entered the room right at that moment.

"I have always loved the name Tabitha," Tibby announced grandly. "But then, I am quite biased…"

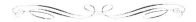

It was too quiet in the house. Far too quiet, considering he knew that at this moment, Moira, Kate, Mary, and Tibby were all in a room together plotting over how to help Annie make her debut.

Knowing that, the quiet made him uneasy.

They'd been together for nearly two hours, and he knew Annie would most likely be going mad under the scrutiny and her mind would whirl at the complexities. It was quite a lot to deal with for even those who had been used to Society, let alone one who had never even seen a dance hall. No doubt she would rethink her concession to the idea and would search for ways to escape.

He would not blame her.

His stomach growled angrily and Duncan groaned in response. He had worked through the luncheon hour and now, far too early, he was famished. He would not be able to have a true meal until later, as Tibby took control of everything no matter where she was, and she insisted on family meals at set times.

It was probably for the best. After all, Marianne had been remarkably absent since their fight and she would have to make an appearance there. Even in her foulest of moods, she did not go against Tibby.

But that did not mean he could not find something to eat to tide him over.

He set aside his diminishing pile of correspondence and pushed off of his desk. His kitchen staff was used to him wandering down there at odd times. No one so much as batted an eye at it now.

He slowly opened his door, desperate to not make any sound at all if possible. If Kate knew he was venturing down to the kitchens, she would force him to bring back pastries. More than one of their kitchens had been suspiciously depleted of pastries when Lady Whitlock was visiting.

When he was assured of his safety and secrecy, he ventured forth, feeling the slightest bit ridiculous about sneaking around in his own house.

He got halfway down the hall when he stopped.

Annie came out of the drawing room, closed the door behind her, then leaned against the wall and closed her eyes. He saw her exhale slowly, and tip her head back just a bit.

She was so beautiful it made his teeth ache.

And she looked tired.

Before he could stop himself, he changed course and headed in her direction.

"Good day," he said softly.

Her eyes snapped open and she hastily pushed off of the wall.

"No, no," he insisted, waving her back. "Please."

She gave him a careful look, then took up her position again.

"Good day," she replied, leaning her head back once more.

"Are they wearing you out?" he asked as he came and stood next to her against the wall.

Annie released a heavy sigh. "Yes. And no. There is just so much to learn and remember and understand, and I can't... I cannot," she corrected with a furrow in her brow, "keep it all together in my head."

"Yes, it can be a bit daunting," he admitted. "Would you believe that I had to learn all of this myself at one time?"

She turned her head and raised a brow. "No, I would not."

He nodded, surprised at what he was going to tell her, but not wanting to stop. "My family was not always wealthy. In fact, my parents were fairly poor. My mother was the youngest daughter of a powerful Scottish laird, and her father was desperate to marry her off. My father happened across her by accident and they fell in love, married, moved to England, and started a life together. Hardly any money at all. My father's family was a once well-respected family, but his oldest brother hated him and cut him off. He started to work in trade to make up for the lack of funds, and that is hardly something Society likes to hear."

Annie was listening with such intensity that Duncan felt the need to say everything perfectly, yet he was entirely at ease, as if talking to her was the most natural thing in the world. As if sharing his family's less-than-reputable past was perfectly normal.

"I was born during all of that," he continued, swallowing the dryness that began in his throat. "I was used to running around like a street urchin without manners or cares. I went to a local school with other boys, but it was hardly a decent education. Sheer basics were all that we received, and we were content with it." His mind was suddenly filled with memories of a long-forgotten past, and he felt himself becoming lost in it. "We were all content. We wanted for a great deal, I know that now. There was so much we didn't have, but we were happy."

"What happened?" Annie asked softly.

Duncan shook his head and looked back down at her. "When I was eleven, a man came to our home and said a distant cousin of my father's had died without children and we were the only relative eligible for inheriting his estate and fortune, which was quite extensive. We all removed to Brockleton Park in Shropshire and started a new life. A different life. And I had to learn how to be a gentleman." He shook his head, remembering the agitation of a young man trying to please his relations, live up to expectations, and yet still be himself. "Marianne was just a little girl," he said, "she doesn't remember any of this, and very few members of Society still recollect it. But my father never felt he deserved that fortune. Mother had no such reservations, she had been used to a sort of station in Scotland. But Father rarely expended any money at all. He used what he could to help others, as he remembered too clearly what it was like to suffer." He trailed off once more, remembering his parents with a deep ache in his chest.

A soft hand reached out and touched his arm. "They sound like wonderful people," came Annie's gentle voice.

Duncan covered her hand with his own. "They were." He smiled at her with too much emotion in his heart and his throat. "I am telling you this so that you can know that you can do it. You can learn and remember and become all that you need to. And I will say again, Annie, that you don't have to do this."

"I know," she replied, her emerald eyes searching his, "but I want to. Don't you think I should?"

"I already told you that I am not telling you what to do," he scolded gently. "I will never tell you what to do."

She huffed a bit, and a strand of hair danced on her breath. "That is going to be frustrating."

He chuckled and touched the underside of her chin. "You are just going to have to make up your own mind."

"That is not so easy for me," she whispered.

"I know."

She sighed softly and twisted her lips. "They want me to choose a name."

His brow furrowed in surprise. "A name? For what?"

"Well, I can hardly be Annie Ramsey in Society, can I?" She shook her head and rubbed at her face. "So now I must pick a new name, and I can't. Who am I supposed to be if not myself?"

He frowned and held her hand a bit tighter. "You can be whomever you want. Be yourself. Don't let them change you."

She smiled and it took the breath out of him. "They won't. But even you must admit that choosing a new name for yourself is not easy."

She had a point there. He exhaled and thought for a moment. "Well, are there any names you have ever wanted to be called?"

"Not really."

"Any other names you have been called before? Anne, perhaps?"

She bit her lip and chewed for a second. "My mother called me Annalise," she finally said.

Duncan felt a slow smile start on his lips and spread into his cheeks. "Annalise? That is beautiful. Why did she call you that?"

Annie looked away quickly, her cheeks becoming tinged with pink. "It's my real name."

Duncan stood stock still in shock. The very name was music to his ears, would roll off of the tongue and lips like a sonnet. "Why don't you use it?"

She shrugged. "My father didn't like it. He insisted I only be called Annie. She only called me Annalise in private. Then she died when I was thirteen and nobody has called me that since."

Duncan swallowed and tilted her face back to him. "I am going to call you Annalise from now on."

Her eyes widened and she shook her head quickly. "No, don't."

"Why not?" he asked her. "It is such a beautiful name. Why not use it?"

She lowered her eyes. "It's too beautiful for the likes of me."

He felt as if he had been kicked in the chest and anger curled in his gut like a flame. "I am going to call you Annalise," he said again, choosing to ignore her absurd statement.

Again, she shook her head, this time with more force. "No."

"It is your name, Annalise," he ground out, trying to keep his voice calm.

"It's too…"

He put a hand over her mouth and glared at her. "Don't let me hear you say that again," he warned in a low, dangerous voice. "I will not let you put yourself down like that. Your mother gave you a beautiful name, and you are more than worthy of it."

She looked up at him with wide, almost hopeful eyes. He removed his hand, trying to ignore the fire that was starting in the center of his palm.

"Do you really think so?" she asked him.

He nodded firmly. "I know so."

She licked her lips quickly. "No, I mean… Duncan, that is… Mr. Bray…"

"Duncan will suffice," he growled.

"Do you… Do you really think…?" She ducked her chin and looked away, her cheeks positively flaming.

Duncan's heart lurched and his pulse quickened. He put his hand under her chin and slowly tilted her face back up to him, almost succeeding in not looking at her lips.

"Yes, Annalise," he murmured, his voice far too rough for comfort. "I think you are beautiful. I think you are very, very beautiful. A man would be blind to think anything less."

His eyes looked down at her lips again, and heaven help him, they parted slightly under his gaze.

Annie did not breathe, and neither did he.

He felt himself leaning towards her, pulling her chin closer.

He exhaled a puff of air and fought for control. It was too soon, too much, he could not…

He lifted his chin a fraction and pressed a soft, lingering kiss to her brow, the taste of her skin like the sweetest honey.

He heard her small gasp, and he felt the faintest shudder course through him. He needed to step back, to let go…

He needed…

"Annie! Where are you?" Moira called from the room. "Tibby says you can play a little and Kate is dying to hear it!"

Duncan's hands were suddenly empty as Annie stepped away, looking at him with those wide eyes, confused, and something else. Something darker. Something his chest ached with.

He swallowed hard and nodded. "Go on, Annalise. They are waiting for you."

She bit her lip, for a moment, then nodded herself. She didn't say a word as she slowly turned and went back into the room.

Duncan turned and put both hands to the wall and exhaled forcefully as his mind and body tried to settle.

He needed to stay away. For her own sake. She was too determined to please, too unsure of her own self. He could not influence her.

He needed to let her choose.

But right now, he needed to sweat and exert himself and feel his muscles ache with too much activity. And he possibly needed to draw blood.

He turned from the hall, grabbed his long coat, and began the long walk to Colin's house, wishing his heart would resume its normal pacing.

Chapter Twelve

"Really, Duncan, if you are going to come over to fence this often, I am going to need to find you an additional partner. I cannot take anymore sessions like this."

Duncan wiped his sweat-drenched brow with a sleeve and glanced over at the also heavily perspiring Colin. "I thought you enjoyed physical activity."

Colin glared at him as his chest still heaved with his panting. "I do. I don't even mind the perspiration. I do very much mind four fencing sessions in a week when there are other things I would rather do. And when a man of my stature fences, or does anything for that matter, with a man of your stature, four times in a week is rather like twelve, and I am quite done for."

Duncan grunted as he sheathed his foil and handed it to a servant. "Fine. I will find someone else, then, and take my tiresome exertions elsewhere."

"That is not what I meant," Colin scolded as he did the same, then sat on the floor and leaned against a stone pillar. "What is going on?"

"I don't know what you…"

"I am many things, Duncan," he interrupted, "but an idiot is not one of them. What is troubling you?"

Duncan looked at his oldest friend, then sat next to him against the pillar. "My house is overrun with females."

"And the problem is…?"

He shook his head. Colin was still Colin even when he was trying to be serious. "It's Moira, Kate, Mary, and Tibby helping Annalise to become a lady."

Colin winced and shuddered. "That would get me out of the house, too." Suddenly his friend gave him a surprised look. "Wait, Annalise?"

Duncan felt his cheeks heat. "That's her real name. It suits her better, don't you think?"

"It certainly does. Very pretty."

Duncan swallowed, not feeling the need to be reminded of that.

Colin seemed to mull over the change, then asked "And where is Marianne in all this?"

Duncan shrugged his massive shoulders. "She keeps to herself and her friends these days. She doesn't want any part of it. She doesn't approve of Annalise reaching for such heights in Society. It brings her to Marianne's level."

"Spoiled brat," Colin spat, kicking his boot a bit.

Duncan raised a brow at him in surprise.

"Sorry," his friend muttered grumpily, "but you know she is."

"I know." He sighed and leaned his head back. "I told her so. I told her the rumors about her were going to ruin us faster than anything about Annie could, and with her behavior…"

"We can quell those," Colin soothed. "Between the set of us, we can stamp it all out."

"Not if your brother is around. That only makes things worse."

Now it was Colin who groaned. "Blast it, Kit…"

"Do you know anything about…?"

"No."

Duncan was not sure he believed his friend, but the finality in his voice told Duncan not to ask.

Colin cleared his throat. "So, how is Annalise?"

"She is well," Duncan sighed, "but she is so eager to please everyone she is being run ragged. I thought she was perfect as she was, but apparently the women did not agree."

"Funny how that works," Colin mused. "So Annalise enjoys all of this?"

"I think so." He twisted his lips and exhaled. "I cannot tell. She doesn't show her emotions much, but I think she might be overwhelmed. I don't know what to do or how to help, so I escape, quite honestly. Because if I see her in need or upset, I will do something. Probably something irrational."

"Get her a gift," Colin suggested with a wild grin.

Duncan snorted. "She hardly needs more things, Colin. Not when the women are continually bringing her new gowns and trinkets and such."

"You have no imagination. Women like presents. They are always well appreciated and will show you are thinking of her. I don't mean something extravagant or elaborate. Something that reminds you of her. Something not entirely obvious." Colin shrugged. "Your possibilities are limitless."

Duncan was surprised he had not thought about it. It *was* a good idea, but he would never tell Colin he thought so. He gave his friend a look. "When did you become an expert in these things?"

Colin grinned again. "I have always been an expert in women and the finer things in life. Surely you knew that by now?"

"Have you got all of that?" Tibby asked as she exhaled loudly.

Annie's head spun like a top. "Yes," she managed to say. The others had left for the moment to descend upon her wardrobe upstairs to root out what was unsuitable, though they had already been to the dressmaker's twice this week. Truly, she was exhausted by the very thought of more dresses.

"You look tired, my dear."

Annie jerked and looked at Tibby, who smiled in a very matronly way. There was such kindness in her eyes and in her person that Annie had no reservations about being honest.

"I am," she admitted softly, "but it is a good kind of tired."

Tibby nodded thoughtfully, her gold turban twinkling in the light form the fire. "You will find that sort of tired will come often once you start going out in Society."

145

Annie chewed on her lip, more than a little apprehensive about her future in those realms. She had seen the disapproval in Marianne's face when the others had brought her dresses, but she had also seen something else. Almost sadness. She wondered if she might talk with Marianne, just the two of them, to see if they might yet be friends.

"Well, Annalise, I do believe you deserve some answers."

Bewilderment surged within her, even as she jerked yet again at the use of her full given name. Duncan had told them all about his discovery, and they had agreed to side with him in their address of her. She did not necessarily mind being Annalise to them, but it took some getting used to. "About what?" she asked, still reeling.

Tibby shrugged, her vibrant copper tendrils dancing about. "Whatever you like. Whomever you like. Myself, Marianne, Lady Greversham, although I do not suggest asking after her, she is quite a harpy."

A sudden wave of need filled her and she had to bite her tongue to keep from immediately responding with Duncan's name. She practiced the composed face she had learned from the others, and carefully thought it out.

"Duncan told me a little about his past," she began slowly.

"Did he now?" Tibby mused, her eyes widening just a touch, even as she smiled.

Annie nodded, swallowing her nerves. "I wonder… could you tell me more about it?"

Tibby seemed to consider the question for an extremely long time, her clear eyes never once leaving Annie's.

Annie feared she had been too forward. She knew, of course, that she had been extremely forward, but Tibby had a skewed sense of such things and generally applauded such behaviors and thinking.

"I do not like to speak of my nephew's past without his knowledge or consent," Tibby said slowly, her voice very serious, very low, and very unlike her usual vibrancy.

Annie felt her cheeks flame and ducked her head. "I understand, of course," she murmured in a half-whisper.

There was a brief pause, and then, "But as he started it, I see no reason why I should not finish it. He never tells the whole story. Too modest by half."

It was impossible for Annie to keep from jerking to look at Tibby in surprise. The older woman's eyes were twinkling, and there was a small, barely-there smile on her face that spoke volumes about her relationship with her nephew.

"My brothers," Tibby began softly, "did not get along. Never did, and it would take years to explain why. But Duncan's father, Victor, was good-hearted and kind, for the most part. He was not perfect, but who is, besides myself?"

Annie snickered at Tibby's bold wink, but said nothing.

"When our brother inherited the title, he wished to cut us all off. But our parents had been wise and set up the fortune for their three daughters in such a way that it was out of his reach. Poor Victor, however, had no such safety. He was cut off entirely. This much, I trust you already know?"

Annie nodded and tried not to appear too eager.

Tibby sighed and her eyes took on a faraway look. "We did not see Victor for many years. He worked in trade, which is impressive, considering his lack of training. And he was madly in love with his wife, Eleanor, and she with him. She was an impressive woman, a rare Scottish beauty who commanded all attention to her. You can imagine, I suppose, who takes after her."

"Marianne," Annie breathed, feeling a bit caught up in the story.

Tibby nodded slowly. "Eleanor was more beautiful and attracted more attention than Marianne, if you can believe it. Victor, however, had grown used to his life as a hardworking tradesman and never cared much for the ways of the rich and reputable. I need not tell you how he was thought of by Society."

Annie barely restrained a shudder.

"Eleanor did her best to prove they belonged, and she had quite the throng of admirers. Rumors began to spread about why she was the way she was, and why Victor was so rarely seen. Rumors of infidelity, of towering debts, of shameless extortion... There was nothing good to be said about them but it could not keep people from wanting to surround Eleanor all the time." She snorted derisively and shook her head. "Poor Eleanor. She was determined to see to it that her children would not suffer again, and she only made it worse."

A strange sort of tension began to swirl within Annie's chest and her eyes began to water. "What kind of a mother was she?" she asked softly.

Tibby smiled at her. "As good as one might expect of her. Better, I think. She was kind and took an interest, but she was not really the mothering type. She made a far better wife than she did a mother."

The lump that had been forming in Annie's throat refused to dislodge itself. She swallowed repeatedly and blinked away tears. "What happened?"

Tibby sniffed. "Carriage accident. They were heading to the coast for a reprieve from their mess of a life."

Annie could no longer restrain her tears, and they rolled silently down her cheeks.

Tibby composed herself, though shadows still remained etched on her face. "The rumors are mostly gone now. Duncan has had to face the brunt of them, and he has done a beautiful job of restoring respectability to the name. But Marianne…"

Annie winced and glanced at the door, as if the girl would enter. "Does she know?" she asked softly.

Tibby shook her head. "Not a bit of it. How she has managed to avoid hearing things is beyond me, but she is not nearly as smart as she pretends to be. She is destined to have the same trouble as Eleanor did, if she is not careful. She is so like her. That is what has Duncan worried so. He cannot protect her forever."

No, he could not. And he could not protect Annie forever either.

"How did you manage to…? That is…" The words seemed lost somewhere between her mind and her mouth, but Tibby smiled.

"How did I become so entangled with the children?"

Annie nodded, smiling in her relief.

"My sisters are idiots."

A surprised cough escaped Annie. "I beg your pardon?"

"Were," Tibby corrected with a tilt of her head. "I should say they were idiots. Both are now dead, and good riddance. They believed my eldest brother's lies about Victor and wanted nothing to do with Duncan or Marianne." She grinned rather maliciously. "You can imagine their distress when I, the wealthiest and most popular of all, named him my heir and put him in the best universities, ensured his commission in the army, and recommended the best finishing schools for Marianne."

Annie grinned at Tibby. The woman had a flair for the dramatic, it was no secret, but she was also astonishingly brazen. It was at once a breath of fresh air and a jolt to one's senses to be around her, both refreshing and unsettling.

Annie loved it.

"You do enjoy shocking people, don't you?" She giggled softly and shook her head.

Tibby inclined her head in an acknowledging nod. "I do. But it was also the right thing to do. I never put stock into rumors. If I did, I should have to believe the most outrageous things about myself."

Annie smiled at that. "And Duncan's time in the army?"

"He was a very well respected officer," Tibby said with a warm smile. "But we all knew he would be. He was gone for a number of years, and it was astonishing he returned home unscathed. He would tell you his own service was unremarkable, but we know better. He always put his men before himself, and the way Lord Beverton tells it, the men would have done the same." She sighed a little, shaking her head. "He resigned his commission a few years ago, and made quite a fine living from it. Not that he needed to, he was well set up as it was. But Duncan is who he is, and he is his father's son above all else."

Annie sat in quiet reflection for a moment, feeling her heart warm the more she learned about the man she had come to London with. He was a far better man than she ever knew. "Thank you, Tibby," she murmured softly, leaning over to kiss the other woman's cheek. "You are the most amazing woman I have ever met."

"No doubt of it, child." Tibby patted her cheek softly and sighed. "Now. Enough seriousness. Go run and see what those girls are up to. I worry when I don't hear them anymore."

Annie obediently trotted away, then turned back. "Thank you for telling me, Tibby. I promise to keep your secrets. You can trust me."

Tibby smiled at her, and Annie could have sworn she saw a hint of tears in her eyes. "I know, dear girl. I have always known that."

Annie left quickly and had nearly made it up to her own room, where she could hear the low voices of her friends, when she passed Marianne's rooms. She had passed them several times before, but for some reason, she could not simply walk by this time. She wanted to see Marianne, to try and rekindle their once blossoming friendship. Or at least, to not have her as an enemy.

She took a brave breath and knocked on the door. Marianne was likely out anyway. It was too fine a day to be indoors.

"Come in," her clear vice rang out musically.

Annie blanched and swallowed with difficulty.

Now what?

She pushed open the door and saw Marianne sitting perfectly poised by her toilette as if she had been sitting for a painting. Every line and angle of her features was perfect and graceful, her gown so perfect for her coloring and form that it stunned her. How had someone created a shade of blue the exact color of her brilliant eyes? If Annie had needed any further reminder of how far below a person she could be, it was living and breathing here before her.

She should not have come. She should turn and run.

Marianne cleared her throat, and Annie stiffened as she realized she had been blatantly staring like a fool.

"I'm sorry," Annie mumbled, beginning to wring her hands. Then she winced and forced her hands to separate, scolding herself for her nervous habits. She swallowed and raised her chin just enough that she would not look as if she was cowering. "That is, I am sorry to disturb you, Miss Bray. But I wondered if… I might have a word?"

She dared not hope that the light she saw in Marianne's eyes was her being impressed, but she did not think it was one of cruelty. Marianne's mouth quirked ever so slightly and she indicated the chair before her. "Of course, Annie. Please, have a seat. And you need not call me Miss Bray. Not here."

Annie felt her breath rush from her and moved too quickly to the chair and sat without grace or elegance.

Marianne looked at her for quite a long while, then sighed and sat back in her own chair, all pretenses of superiority gone. "I am glad you came to see me. I have wanted to talk to you for days, but I couldn't bring myself to seek you out. I am far too proud for that."

Nothing could have shocked Annie more. "You... you did?"

Marianne nodded, and smiled almost apologetically. "It was hardly kind of me, and it is entirely unfair to you. It is not as though this whole carfuffle was of your making."

The room was suddenly a bit warm as Annie realized that Marianne was not apologizing at all for her opinions. She still felt the same way, and Annie doubted there was anything she could say or do to change that. But she could live with that, if only they could be friends again.

Marianne surprised her further by taking her hand. "I hope you know, Annie, that this is not a reflection of my opinion of you. I think you are the sweetest, dearest girl in the world, and I am grateful that you have come among us. I cannot begin to imagine what your life has been like before now, and I am pleased to be able to help you change it even a little."

Annie nodded once, ignoring the faintest wash of tears that was beginning to start.

"But," Marianne said slowly, removing her hand, "I cannot agree to Tibby's scheme. You see I have worked very hard to be the way I am. I know it is vain and silly of me, but I care very much about Society and being popular and wealthy. I am used to this life and have been brought up to desire it. And to have anyone, no matter how dear or sweet, infiltrate my world undeservingly..." She frowned and chewed on her lip for the briefest moment. "I don't like that word. I think I should have said 'without being born to it.' Do you understand what I am saying?"

Annie did understand her. Far better than she could have imagined. But she couldn't tell Marianne how false she felt in her lessons with Tibby and the other women. She couldn't tell her how her single ambition was to prove to Duncan that she could be a strong, independent woman he could admire. She could not pretend that Marianne would understand her longing to belong somewhere, anywhere, even if it was beyond her dreams.

"I understand," she said softly, forcing a small smile to her lips.

"And I respect your opinions. You're right, I would never have imagined this for myself. But the offer is so tempting, so perfectly far-fetched, that I…"

"Oh, you would be an idiot to refuse Tibby," Marianne quipped with a rare grin. "She would have found a way to convince you one way or the other."

Annie almost laughed in relief at the change in Marianne's manner. "She told me that Duncan insisted it be my choice, and that she could not browbeat me into submission."

"Did he, indeed?" Marianne looked far too thoughtful, and a brief flash of darkness entered her gaze. But then it was gone and she shrugged. "Well, good for him, I daresay. Tibby can be quite domineering. I am glad she is restricted." She paused, watching Annie carefully, and then her shoulders sagged further. "How is it going?"

Annie didn't know how to respond, as Marianne had quite plainly made it known she would not participate. What could she share?

"Well enough, I suppose," Annie said indifferently. "I have much to learn and much further to go, but Moira and Kate and Mary seem to think I have potential. Tibby is…"

"Tibby is Tibby and nothing less," Marianne commented with a dry snort.

Annie nodded. There really was no other way to say it.

"I was hoping that…" Annie began, but she trailed off uncertainly and looked at her feet.

"Yes?"

She met Marianne's eyes again, wishing she could read them more clearly. "I was hoping that, in spite of our differences in opinion on this whole affair, that we might still… be friends? Here, at least. I understand we cannot in Society, and I hardly blame you. But while at home… I could use a friend."

Marianne hesitated for so long that Annie felt her palms begin to moisten and she wondered if she had been too bold. She should leave. She should go to her friends who had undoubtedly made themselves giddy with imaginations on her wardrobe. This was a silly notion.

"I would like that very much."

A jolt of shock rippled through her visibly as she looked back at Marianne, who smiled at her.

Marianne's dark curls danced as she nodded. "I've missed you, Annie. I meant what I said before. I have the highest opinion of you. And I... I don't have many friends. With you, I need not pretend."

"Nor I," she replied quietly.

Marianne's smile was so warm and sweet that Annie was tempted to give her a hug. But they were not at that point. Not yet. Perhaps one day, but, as Marianne had pointed out before, there was her pride to consider.

"Annalise! Where in heaven's name are you? These gowns are exquisite, you *have* to try them on now!"

She groaned, which made Marianne chuckle. "Fashion waits for no one, I am afraid."

Annie gave her a helpless smile. "Apparently not."

Marianne indicated the door. "Go on, or they will come find you. I will see you at supper."

Annie nodded and rose, heading swiftly for the door.

"Annie?"

She turned to look back at Marianne.

The girl was still wearing the softest of smiles. "I think you could quite safely call yourself Anne for the public. Not too far off of your real name, yet still refined enough to be respected. Perhaps Anne Remington? It would suit you well." Her smile grew briefly. "Just a thought."

The lump that instantly formed in Annie's throat prevented her from responding more than a heartfelt croak of "Thank you" before she fled the room. But her heart felt lighter than it had in ages.

Duncan felt himself unnerved by a silent house, wondering where the ladies had gone.

Well, perhaps only one woman in particular.

He gave up all pretense and began to seek out Annalise. She

was not in the library, nor any of the drawing rooms. He frowned and asked one of his maids if they had seen her, but they had not. Where could she be?

Just as he was about to give up, she appeared from the entryway, her cheeks rosy from the cold. She rubbed her hands together and blew on them. She looked as fresh and bright as the first flowers of spring. Her wardrobe changes had only enhanced her beauty and natural grace, and whoever was now working with her hair seemed determined to torment him. Each day it was swept up differently, displaying her delicate bone structure, yet looking as though the removal of a single pin would send the whole coif tumbling around her tiny shoulders. She was, in fact, the very image of his most secret fantasies.

He swallowed hard, hoping his tongue stayed in his head, and bowed politely. "Annalise. How lovely you look today."

She stopped in surprise, her eyes widening. She considered him for a moment, then smiled. "Thank you."

"Were you out walking just now?" he asked, awkwardly descending the stairs.

She nodded, her smile growing. "Yes, Agnes and I went out for some air. I think I enjoyed it more than she did."

He grinned. "Oh? Was it too cold?"

Annie shrugged one shoulder. "Not so bad, but not as pleasant as I hoped it would be." She tilted a half smile and continued to walk.

He frowned and came beside her, matching her pace, clasping his hands behind him so he would not be more tempted to take her own and warm them in his grasp. "Oh? Why not?"

Annie laughed softly and gave him an amused look. "You were not with me."

As if she were unable to believe she had spoken the words, her eyes widened and her hands shot to her mouth. She exclaimed a stuttering "excuse me" and dashed away, her cheeks flaming.

Duncan stared after her, his mouth gaping wide, his entire being numb. She had wanted him to... He shook his head slowly, finally regaining feeling in his fingertips. His neat hair became once again disheveled as he ran his hands through it. He turned from the hall and fled to his study, heart pounding, breathing uneven. Annalise Ramsey was going to be the death of him. But oh, what a glorious death it was destined to be.

Chapter Thirteen

*S*upper was nearly silent, which never happened, and everyone knew it.

Marianne looked between Tibby and Duncan repeatedly, her clear brow furrowed in confusion. Duncan had no answers for her. The girl sitting next to him had him so distracted that it was all he could do to bring his fork to his mouth. Half of the time he wasn't even certain that there was food on it.

Tibby was giving him a hard look from across the table, but really, what did she want him to do?

And from the looks of things, Annalise was not about to strike up conversation either. Not that she ever did, but she was even more reserved than usual this evening. He knew the reason for that. She was embarrassed by her boldness.

He wished she wouldn't be. He had rather enjoyed it.

Steady on, he chided himself. It was hardly proper table manners for him to be thinking of something that embarrassed her with such pleasure, particularly when her cheeks were still flushed from it. He loved the way she looked when her cheeks were so colored. And she became quite embarrassed fairly easily. Tibby undoubtedly wanted to cure her of that before sending her out into Society, but he hoped that she wouldn't lose it entirely.

On the other hand, she was so breathtaking when flushed that her suitors would outnumber that of his sister's.

And that thought did not please him at all.

"Duncan, is the food not to your liking?" Tibby squawked suddenly.

He looked up in surprise. "I beg your pardon, Tibby?"

She gave him a hard look. "You are glowering so monstrously at your lamb that it has died again out of fright. Either you are ill or something has upset you. Which is it?"

He sensed the curious looks from the other two women at the table and felt heat on the back of his neck.

"I am perfectly well, thank you, Tibby," he muttered as politely as he could.

Her expression did not change. "Then kindly refrain from such thunderous expressions at the dinner table. It will undoubtedly give me indigestion." Her eyes flicked between him and Annalise so quickly no one would have caught it, except Duncan as he glared at her.

She returned his look with a daring one of her own.

"Chilly nights give you indigestion these days, Tibby," Marianne said with a half-smile, "so I can hardly think Duncan's expressions will affect your mutton so disastrously."

"You underestimate Duncan's power." Tibby sniffed and gracefully speared a boiled potato. "He frightens my dogs on a regular basis. Have you not seen this, Annalise?"

Annalise looked up suddenly and her charming flush vanished in favor of ghostly pale. "I... I have not..."

"Surely, you must have," Tibby pressed, her eyes twinkling in a way Duncan did not care for at all. "Tell me, do they appear frightened when you read together? His voice alone might well set them to shaking."

"Tibby!" Marianne scolded, seeing the obvious discomfort in Annalise. "Your terrified terriers are not..."

"Corgis, Marianne, corgis!" Tibby leveled a glare at her niece. "Honestly, useless alliteration is a waste of vocabulary. And it does not change the fact that Duncan really ought to make more of an effort to at least pretend he is as handsome as other gentlemen. Don't you think, Annalise?"

"I don't... That is, I don't..." Annalise flushed again and the fumble in her words betrayed her panic.

"I thought I might go for an early morning ride tomorrow," Duncan announced, desperately trying to put an end to Tibby's scheming madness.

That seemed to do the trick. Tibby only allowed one brow to rise as she asked a silent question, her lips quirking.

"You?" Marianne laughed. "You hate early mornings."

He gave his sister a glower that made her grin spread so far her eyes crinkled. "If you ever rose before luncheon, you would know that I thrive upon early mornings and am quite productive because of it."

"I have seen it myself," Annalise said in her soft, uncertain way.

Duncan allowed himself to look at her, smiling proudly.

She blushed just a bit, that maddening, barely-there smile tickling her cheeks.

"There, you see?" Duncan turned to face his sister again. "A witness."

Marianne rolled her eyes and laughed. "Very well, I stand corrected."

"Would any of you fine ladies like to accompany me for a ride?" he asked, looking at each in turn.

Marianne snorted and shook her head. "I thank you, no. I adore you, brother, but not that much."

That was not surprising. He looked to his aunt, who laughed loudly. "At my age? A horse ride in the morning? I think not, you silly boy. I would be quite bedridden for days. I only ride in carriages now."

His heart thudded and he nodded with a fond smile. He looked to Annalise, who had watched all the proceedings with only half interest. Now, however, her eyes were on her plate.

"Annalise?" he asked softly. "Would you like to go for a morning ride?"

She chewed on her lip for a moment, then caught Marianne's eye and stopped instantly. "I fear I… have not ridden in some time. It would be slow going."

"I don't mind," he replied instantly, his voice too eager. "It's

London after all, not the country. I would be happy to take whatever pace you like. If the early morning will not trouble you."

Annalise favored him with that soft smile he adored. "Oh, no, it would be no trouble at all. I… don't mind early mornings."

Marianne groaned as she swallowed her bite of food. "I do. Duncan is quite right, I dread waking up before luncheon. And it takes ages and ages to wake me."

Duncan chuckled and looked at his sister. "You sleep like the dead, Marianne."

"And gladly!" Marianne grinned cheekily.

Annalise sighed to herself. "Oh, that sounds lovely. I'm a terrible sleeper. The slightest sounds wake me."

Duncan nearly laughed at his sister's expression. She looked positively appalled.

"Truly?" Marianne wrinkled her nose and picked up her soup spoon. "That sounds dreadful."

Annalise smiled and gave a slight shrug, looking back down at her food. "I'm used to it by now. The only times I have slept through an entire night are after I've had a good beating."

The entire table froze as surely as if they had all turned to ice. Marianne had her spoon halfway to her mouth, her eyes ice cold and her mouth in a taut line. Tibby blinked repeatedly and her face tightened, her only sign of distress evident in the trembling of the fork in her hand.

Duncan stared at Annalise in horror. Not at her words, but at suddenly understanding just what horrors were in her past. She had become accustomed to those beatings. They had been a regular part of her life. He had never wanted to hold her more than he did at that moment.

Tibby slowly touched her serviette to the corner of her mouth.

Annalise looked up from her plate, realizing what she had said. Her eyes widened in dismay and her chin suddenly quivered dangerously. She put down her silverware with a loud clatter and whispered a tearful "I'm sorry" as she pushed back her chair and ran from the room.

Duncan watched her go, too stunned to do anything more than

blink.

Marianne put her spoon down in disgust. "Are we to deal with that often?"

"Be quiet, Marianne!" Tibby ordered sharply. She looked up at Duncan with pleading eyes. "Duncan?"

He nodded and excused himself from the table, not that anyone paid him heed, and went in search of Annalise.

He did not have to search long.

He found her on the stairs crying, her face in her knees.

"Here, now, what's this?" he asked gently as he came and sat next to her.

"I am so sorry I ruined supper," she said into her knees, her voice muffled and tearful.

He sighed and put a hand on her back, rubbing soothing circles on it. "You've ruined nothing, Annalise. Family supper is not a formal affair. And there was no need for such distress."

"I will be distressed!" she protested loudly, still keeping her face in her legs. She sniffled and shook her head. "I will never be a fine lady like Marianne or Tibby and pretending otherwise is ridiculous. I'm not made for it, and I am always saying the wrong things and I used the wrong fork, and I cannot make polite conversation. It's hopeless." She began to cry anew and her body shook with her tears.

"Annalise, look at me," he ordered softly.

She shook her head again.

He stopped his rubbing and set his other hand on her shoulder. "Sweetheart, I need to see your eyes. Please."

She hesitated only a moment, and then turned her head to look at him.

Those eyes. He allowed himself to look deeply into them, smiling softly. "You are a fine lady in your own right. Perhaps you don't know what to say and what not to say, perhaps you have not yet learned to control your tongue, perhaps you cannot balance four books on your head while descending three flights of stairs singing an aria."

That drew a watery chuckle from her and his smile briefly grew.

"Well, guess what, Miss Annalise Ramsey? Surprise you as this might, I cannot do those things either."

She sniffed and moved to put her head back. "Don't tease me."

"I'm not," he insisted, taking her chin and turning her face back to him. "I swear, I am not teasing you." He sighed and shrugged. "I constantly say things no one should say, speak my thoughts, blunder around like a raging bull, and make a general mess of things. I'm an oaf, Annalise. A great hulking oaf dressed in the clothing of gentlemen. Very fine clothing, I grant you; it's probably the only thing I do right. After all of these years, I'm still not a perfect gentleman. And I have not endured the horrors that you have."

"You're not an oaf," she murmured so softly he could barely hear.

"What was that, love?" he asked, leaning closer.

She cleared her throat and sat up slightly. "You are not an oaf. You are very graceful, and a perfect gentleman. And you have endured enough," she added, her eyes searching his.

He smiled and pressed his lips to her hair, inhaling her fragrance. "You sweet thing, you will make me quite arrogant."

She returned his smile, her eyes now warm, with no trace of tears left.

He stroked her cheek softly. "Don't be ashamed of who you are and what you have survived. You are brave, strong, and powerful, Annalise. I am in awe of you."

"Really?"

He nodded once. "Really." His voice suddenly sounded raw, even to him.

And she noticed. She slowly sat up all the way, turning to face him almost completely, her eyes fixed on his. They darted down to his lips, then back to his eyes, her cheeks flushing at being caught. His mouth curved into a smile as he felt her skin warm beneath his touch. The air between them suddenly seemed thin, and his chest tightened with a now familiar pain. Breathing seemed unimportant at the moment.

His thumb stroked her cheek again, and her lips parted on a breath. He leaned forward and gently pressed his lips to hers. She was so soft, so sweet, and the sigh that escaped her matched his own. It wasn't a particularly passionate kiss, but it was full of something else, a deeper emotion that began thrumming through his system. He pulled back and felt his heart skip when she innocently followed him, and he, helpless to resist, took her mouth again.

He had never felt anything like it before. The strangest, most heady of sensations swirled around him and filled his very being. It was as if his entire life had just begun, that he hadn't truly lived until his lips had touched hers.

Which was, of course, ridiculous.

He broke off again and this time, she did not follow, thankfully. He didn't think he would have been able to stop if he'd kissed her again. She opened her eyes and released a soft breath that danced across his face. In her eyes, he saw the same desire, the same emotion, the same confusion that he had felt, and it nearly undid him.

He smiled at her and dropped his hand from her cheek to take the cold hand that rested in her lap. "Are you still hungry?" he asked softly, wishing he didn't sound so winded.

"Starved." Her expression was so innocent, so lovely, so breathless…

He swallowed hastily and stood, pulling her up behind him. Then he playfully offered his arm. "Well, let's hope Marianne saved some for us. She tends to eat quite a lot when out of public sight."

Annalise giggled as she took his arm, and no sound had ever been more musical to his ears. He grinned and led her back into the dining room.

He would deal with his swirling emotions later, when he could properly decide on a sensible course of action. But one thing he knew for certain: he was in trouble.

A great deal of trouble.

The next morning was surprisingly cold, given the warm spell they had been enjoying. But London in winter was wont to be fickle. Or at least, that was what Tibby had told her.

Not that Annie minded. Being out of doors, in any weather, was refreshing, and as she was in Duncan's company, she could not have been happier.

She felt entirely overdressed in her new riding habit. It was a dark grey wool with fine gold buttons and a deep green embroidery, and it was both warm and comfortable. But she had never owned a riding habit before, and she felt like a peacock. She was a charlatan, a common woman imitating the fashion, airs, and style of fine ladies of Society. But the look in Duncan's eyes when he had seen her arrive at the stables was worth her own personal discomfort.

Riding sidesaddle was a new experience for her, and that took some adjustment. She had only ever ridden as a man does, which she knew was entirely improper. Duncan had seen her distress when she had seen the new saddle she was expected to use, and he had very patiently helped her up, then led the horse around the stable yard as she learned the motion and felt a natural rhythm begin.

Riding along now felt more comfortable than before, but only because of the comfortable pace they were keeping. She could never have galloped in such a style.

Another reason not to become a high lady of fashion.

"You ride well," Duncan commented from her side.

She glanced over at saw the warmth in his eyes and his smile. She remembered how warm and powerful his lips had been as they had touched hers. Had that really been only the night before? It felt as if it had been a lifetime. Would she ever have that opportunity again?

"Thank you," she said hastily, realizing with a flush where her thoughts had been leading her.

His smile deepened, and her knees shook, though she was quite secure upon Misty. She had learned that Duncan didn't smile often on his own, but he seemed to smile in her company often enough. She didn't dare consider the implications of that.

"You look very pretty when you blush so," he murmured softly.

Well, now *that*, of course, was destined to make her blush even more, and to her shame, she felt her cheeks flame. She dropped her eyes to the reins clenched in her gloved hands.

"Please," she whispered harshly.

He chuckled in a low, warm tone that sent shivers up her spine.

"I'm sorry, Annalise, but you really must learn to accept

compliments."

That might be true, but not from him. She would never be able to freely accept compliments from him without coloring at them.

"That's exactly what Tibby says," she finally managed to say in a somewhat calm tone.

"Tibby says a great deal too much, in my opinion," he muttered good-naturedly as he nudged his horse a bit closer. "Nothing is beyond her daring."

Annie smiled and looked over at him. "Yes, I know. I knew that from the first day I met her. She was quite outspoken then, and she didn't even know me. I daresay, it's gotten worse ever since."

Duncan groaned and set back a little more into his saddle. "What did she say to you? Tell me."

She tucked her smile back against her cheeks and shook her head. "No."

He looked at her in surprise and raised a brow in question. "No?"

More forcefully, she shook her head. "No."

"Why ever not?" he asked, one side of his mouth curving up so deliciously that her stomach growled as if she hadn't eaten in days.

She gave him an impish look. "Because I know you, Duncan. You will take what I tell you and go back to Tibby, berate her for being impetuous, no doubt making her feel guilty that she will begin treating me with more kindness and gentility, and then she won't know what she might say or do that will offend me. She will still say whatever she wants, but she will tease me about running to you whenever I am the least bit discomfited, and though it will be said with a laugh, there will be an undertone of bitter truth." She smiled at Duncan's stunned expression. "Tell me I am wrong."

Slowly, he shook his head, his smile growing. "No, you are quite right. You have got the measure of us, haven't you?"

She nodded proudly in acknowledgement. "Well, I have been making a study of you all."

"Have you now?" His eyes danced merrily, and she was astonished at how changed he became when he was happy or smiling. Duncan, as he was, could appear to some as fearsome, his features being so stark and bold, his stature so overwhelming, his persona so confident, his gaze cold and powerful. Yet when those eyes were tinged with warmth or laughter, when his mouth was graced with those rare smiles... There could not have been a man in the world more pleasant to look upon then.

She ducked her chin a touch, but did not blush, thankfully. "Yes, I have."

"And what have you discovered?"

His tone was genuinely curious and already amused. And she found herself wanting to share what her observations had been.

She straightened up and inclined her head at some passing gentlemen, whose expressions were suddenly rampant with curiosity. She paid them no mind. "Tibby sees everything, even what you think you can hide. Her loudness and impertinence serves to distract from what she thinks should remain secret and highlights what she wishes to draw out. Most of the time, she is seeking reactions. She doesn't care what others think of her, save for those closest to her. She will always do what she believes is right, whether in her best interest or not, and once she is settled on a course, there is no stopping her."

"Bravo," Duncan said softly, his eyes fixed on her with such intensity that breathing became difficult. "And Marianne?"

Annie swallowed and smiled at another gentleman on horseback, who grinned in response and touched his hat in a salute. "Marianne is surprisingly tenderhearted, but spends more time building up walls than anything else. She expects a great deal of herself, and a great deal in return for her efforts. She is easily amused, but hides it well. She is an accomplished actress, so much so that I think she deceives herself more often than not. If she felt she had truly injured someone she thought highly of, she would be mortified. She stays true to her principles and is surprisingly, and secretly, very loyal."

She saw Duncan's throat work out of the corner of her eye, and she forced herself to keep her eyes forward. She could not bear to see a loss of composure on his part. Not now.

They said nothing for a moment, and it was the most comfortable silence she had ever experienced. And she had experienced quite a few moments of silence in her life.

Duncan shifted suddenly, his soberness gone, his eyes twinkling mischievously. "And what about me, Miss Ramsey? What have you observed of me?"

She'd suspected this would come, but she would not do it. She looked away airily. "I couldn't possibly share my insights on you, Mr. Bray. Not in your presence."

"Of course you could," he assured her, laughter dancing in his voice. "I promise not to tell a soul."

She laughed and looked over at him. She suddenly saw the eager, fun-loving little boy he must have been, the one who had given Tibby a reason to act and had endured so much trouble for his family's sake. She heaved a heavy, dramatic sigh that she had learned from Tibby, which earned her a bark of a laugh from him. "Very well," she groaned, "but you must keep it a secret."

"On my honor," he said with a bow of his head and raised hand.

She gave him a look that clearly said she did not believe him. This was a bad idea. But...

She took a deep breath and looked away from him, her eyes carefully forward. "You are the protector of your friends and your family. Everything you do is for their benefit and well-being. You are determined to be a credit to the memory of your father, and to erase the horrible rumors and opinions of both your parents. You do not feel you deserve the fortune you have acquired, so you use it for others more often than not. You speak of not fitting in, but you view that as a failure, instead of your greatest strength. You may not fit in, but that is because you stand out as a gentleman of honor, respectability, and kindness. And that is something to be proud of, I think."

She had said too much. She knew it from the way his breath had audibly caught and the way her cheeks were flushing. Their pace had altered and the horses were growing restless from the tension in their riders. She swallowed several times, waiting for his response.

"Incredible," Duncan murmured from beside her.

"What is?" she breathed, not wanting to look, but feeling drawn towards him.

His eyes were dark as they met hers. Dark and inviting and powerful beyond comprehension. "You," he said simply.

She could not breathe, couldn't manage a single hint of air. She wrenched her eyes away and inhaled unsteadily. "Not at all," she managed. "You asked."

"That I did," he replied carefully. "That I did. Very astute of you."

"I see more than people think." She hadn't meant to sound so defensive, but in her distress, it couldn't be helped.

Duncan opened his mouth to reply when a shout of greeting was heard up ahead of them.

They turned to look and saw Colin and a gentleman who had to be his brother, they looked so astonishingly alike. The same chestnut-colored hair and light eyes, though his features were more angular and he seemed less prone to smile than his brother. His eyes seemed to catch every motion, though his focus remained steady and forward. She had the very strong impression that he, too, observed quite a bit more than people might have thought.

There were more people around than there had been previously, and Annie began to realize that now was the time to be the creature she had been practicing. The one who belonged. Who knew all the rules. Who was used to all of this. She ought to get into the habit of being such a woman. Otherwise the entire scheme would have to be given up, thanks to her nerves and stupidity.

She tilted her chin up and put a polite smile on her face as the brothers approached. Her heart beat anxiously in her chest. Would she ever lose the fear of meeting new people?

"Steady," Duncan murmured from beside her. "You're all right."

She spared a brief glance in his direction, hoping her eyes conveyed her gratitude.

He gave her an imperceptible nod and half a wink.

As if that would steady her nerves.

"Good morning, Mr. Bray!" Colin called out cheekily. "Fancy meeting you out and about so early."

"Indeed, Mr. Gerrard," Duncan replied smoothly. "Tell me, are you on your way to bed or were you blackmailed into such an early rising?"

Colin's brother quirked the briefest smile Annie had ever seen, while Colin grinned broadly. "Shame on you, Duncan, mentioning bed in front of a lady." His bright eyes moved to Annie and he inclined his head and touched his hat. "Good morning."

She responded with a polite nod. "Good morning, Mr. Gerrard. A pleasure to see you again." Her voice was clear and nearly free of her accent, and she was proud of the diction she had managed, exactly as her friends had taught her.

Colin looked rather impressed and winked at her. "It is always a pleasure to see me, I can assure you, Miss…?"

"Remington," she informed him, as if he really had forgotten. "Miss Anne Remington, Mr. Gerrard. Shame on your memory."

Colin clamped his lips together to avoid laughing, then he said, "I do apologize, Miss Remington. I tend to forget names of beautiful people as I spend so much time trying to remember every facet of their features."

Oh, he was good. She could well see that he would be a very popular fellow in Society.

Well, it was time to practice accepting compliments.

She thanked him with an acknowledging dip of her chin.

"Really, Colin, you grow tiresome in your flattery. I doubt Miss Remington wishes to hear your ramblings anymore," his brother said from beside him, with a smile that told Annie there was real fondness between the brothers.

Colin rolled his eyes and smiled. "I do apologize, Miss Remington. Introductions. This is my elder brother, Mr. Christopher Gerrard, and he believes that being a full forty minutes older gives him license enough to lord over me."

"Well, somebody has to," his brother muttered. "You cannot run roughhouse over everyone." He gave Annie a polite smile and bowed in his saddle. "A pleasure, Miss Remington."

"The pleasure is all mine," she murmured, returning his smile.

"You are recently come to London, are you not, Miss Remington?" Mr. Gerrard asked politely, his entire attention focused on her. The light that was so frequently dancing in Colin's eyes seemed rather absent from his brother's, but the intensity was there in more abundance. This was a man one did not trifle with.

She smiled the soft smile that felt most natural to her. "Very recently, sir. Only three weeks."

"Is that all?" he asked, looking surprised. "I daresay you've not seen much of it, the weather being so cold of late."

"Yes, it has been rather cold. But I am from the north, Mr. Gerrard, so a bit of cold air will not frighten me away."

His mouth quirked into a smile and he saluted her.

"Miss Remington is visiting my family for the Season," Duncan explained politely, his voice carrying naturally to those who were passing and no doubt wondering at the introductions. "She is a niece of my aunt's late husband from his previous marriage."

"Ah," Mr. Gerrard said as he looked back at Annie. "Most fortunate to be under Lady Raeburn's patronage."

"And I am well aware of my good fortune, sir," Annie replied. "She has been most kind."

Colin grinned and shared a look with Duncan that she could not translate. Then he inclined his head at her once more. "Well, we shall look forward to seeing you in Society soon, Miss Remington. Do save one of your first dances for me. I insist."

She blushed just a bit and smiled shyly. "I would be delighted."

"And I shall claim one as well," Mr. Gerrard said, a hint of a smile in his features. "If you shall not feel yourself overrun by Gerrards."

She giggled and nodded. "No, indeed, it would be my pleasure."

Both Gerrards touched their hats and rode off at fast clips.

"Well done," Duncan said softly as Annie released a heavy breath. "That was perfect."

She laughed again in relief. "I don't know about that. I stumbled a bit with the accent."

"It was charming," he said, reaching out to touch her, and then thinking better of it as more people began filling the park. "You should keep part of it. Besides, it was only Colin and Kit, you don't need to stand on ceremony there. And you need to stop smiling at all of the gentlemen in the park."

"Why?" she asked in surprise.

He smiled, but it didn't reach his eyes. "Because you will bewitch every one of them and we will not be able to ride without a trail of them following us home."

"Duncan…"

He shrugged. "I only speak the truth. Someday, perhaps, you will see yourself as you really are." He gave her a very serious look and then urged his horse a bit faster.

Annie caught her breath for a moment and then rode up to match him.

She had very little time until her introduction into his world.

She prayed it would be worth it.

Chapter Fourteen

"One-two-three, one-two-three, turn and curtsey, turn and curtsey... Good!"

Annie fought the urge to wipe her brow and looked at Marianne, who smiled in encouragement from the corner of the room. She hadn't expected her to attend her lessons today, but her reasoning had been that any woman could dance, not just high society ones, and she would love to have someone she could practice dancing with at home. Annie didn't mind, she was nervous enough about the ball coming in two days that would be her grand introduction. They had been dancing all morning and through luncheon, and she was exhausted. She wasn't perfect by any stretch of the imagination, but was honest enough to admit that she was getting better.

Kate clapped her hands from the pianoforte. "Excellent, Annalise!" she called. "You move with such grace, I am quite envious!"

"It's only because I am small," she replied, giving her beautiful friend a smile. "And I used to dance around as a little girl."

"Oh, I can imagine you were a precious sight!" Moira said with a hint of a tear in her voice.

Mary sighed heavily and shook her head. "Moira, you really need to retain control of your emotions." She leaned closer to Annie and whispered loudly, "Yesterday she had a potato that was boiled too soft and was so upset she burst into tears."

Annie looked at Moira in surprise, who laughed in delight.

"I did not, you lying wench. Now return to your proper position as the man. We are going to try the new one."

"Are you sure, Moira?" Kate asked from her position, eying Annie cautiously. "There are a few others…"

"No, no, I think she is ready," Moira assured her. "She's improving so fast, it will be easy for her."

Annie blanched and cast a panicked look at Marianne. She had just taught her the steps after breakfast and they were complicated. She had mastered them before, when she and Marianne could mirror each other, but when she had a partner…

"It's all right, Annie," Marianne said with another smile. "Just like we practiced."

"Her name is Annalise," Tibby muttered darkly, folding her arms over her bombazine gown.

Marianne glared at her aunt, then looked back to Annie. "You can do it. Go on."

Annie swallowed, then looked at Mary, who winked and nodded in encouragement.

Kate began to play and Annie tried as best as she could to remember the steps, but she stumbled in exactly the same spot every time. After the fourth attempt, she let out a screech of dismay and shoved her fists into her eyes.

"It's all right," Moira soothed, coming to her side. "You will get it, it just takes time."

"We don't have time!" Annie cried as she whirled around, feeling panic rise within her. "We have two days. Two days for me to be perfect in everything. Two days until everything you've taught me will be put to the test and I will have to pretend to be something I'm not. I have to do this! I have to!"

"No, you don't," came a low, rumbling voice from the doorway.

Every head turned to see Duncan standing there, his chest heaving a bit as if he had run. His coat and waistcoat were gone, and he was only in his fine linen shirt, as he had been the other day after he had returned from fencing. From the looks of things, he had been fencing again today. Faintly, the thought burst into Annie's mind to imagine what he would have looked like when he fenced. Graceful, powerful, every muscle taut and lean in his movements.

He came to her, his eyes fixed on her face earnestly. He took her arms in his strong hands and held her tightly. "You don't have to do anything, Annalise. If this is all too much, you can stop. You don't have to do this."

"Oh, but…" Tibby tried, but one look from Duncan silenced her.

"I think we need to give Annie a bit of room," Marianne murmured to the others, rising and gesturing out. "Lady Whitlock, I have a piece of music I think you would play masterfully, it is far too complicated for me. It is in my room, will you come and see?"

"Of course, Miss Bray, of course," Kate agreed, following quickly. She grabbed Moira's hand and yanked her along, and Mary followed. Tibby was the last to leave, looking at Duncan with earnest eyes.

Duncan waited until the door clicked shut, then looked back at Annie. "All right. They've gone."

"Tibby is listening at the door," she whispered, shutting her eyes and turning towards the window.

"Tibby!" Duncan called. "Away!"

They heard the unmistakable sound of stomping down the hall and then it was silent.

"Now," Duncan said, turning back to her, "tell me what this is all about."

She felt tears well up in her eyes and a tired sob escaped. "I can't do this, Duncan."

He came to her and immediately wrapped his arms around her in a warm embrace. "You don't have to, Annalise. I can put a stop to this. No one will mind, I promise. I wasn't sure I agreed at the beginning, but I thought I would stay out of it because you seemed so happy about it. But I was worried, and now I can see that…"

"No, you don't understand!" Annie cried, whirling out of the temptation of his arms. "I want to do this. I have never wanted anything more in my life than this."

He reared back in shock. "You do?"

"Does that surprise you?" she asked, looking over her shoulder at him. "That someone like me would want to aspire to such grand imaginations?"

"Annalise, that is not what I…"

Feelings that she had never imagined surged within her and her face heated without the slightest bit of embarrassment. "I have never had a choice in anything at all. I knew what my future was set to be from the moment I was old enough to understand. It wasn't happy, but nothing else was, so I accepted it. Then you came and showed me a different way to live, one where I could choose, I could have opinions, I could change things. Whatever I wanted!"

He watched her with fascination, as if he had never seen anything like her before.

She was not surprised. She hardly recognized herself. "Then Tibby offers me this chance, this once in a lifetime opportunity to go even further than the freedom I had begun to imagine. To change my station, even if only for a little while. I may become what I had never even dared to dream of. Of course, I wanted to do it. But even then I knew it was a ridiculous idea. I'm not suited for this, how could I be? I am nothing!"

His brows snapped down and he stepped towards her. "Annalise, that is not true."

"Are you blind, Duncan?" she cried, knowing she was probably going mad. "Do you really not see how foolish it was for me to think I could do this? To even want this? I couldn't even read, Duncan! What kind of young woman in society cannot read?"

"Annalise," he growled, his voice low.

She shook her head. "I am the poor, plain, obscure daughter of a horse tradesman. I have never even seen the inside of ballroom, I could not tell you the difference between a duke and an earl, I couldn't even begin to tell you what my dresses are made from or what the fashions are. I don't know if I can converse with a stranger and not make a complete mockery of everything your family stands for. Marianne seems to be the only one who sees the most likely outcome of this whole affair, and has bowed out, and who can blame her?"

He came towards her again. "Annalise!"

She moved away, the panic welling within her so strongly it did not even occur to her to be afraid of his advance. "I'm not worth this! For all your kindness and flattery and assurances, I will be a laughingstock. No one will seek me out, no one will take me seriously, and it will be a grand waste of everyone's time, not to mention money. Perhaps it would be best if I just left and..."

Suddenly Duncan was there and took her face in both of his hands, bringing his mouth crashing down on hers. Her mind went completely blank and her panic evaporated under the captivating onslaught of his mouth. She could not respond to his attack, it was too much, too sudden, too delicious to believe. And she had no idea how to respond, what to do.

Her pulse thrummed in the base of her throat, and he could feel it, as his thumbs caressed the throbbing skin there, soothing what he himself was agitating. Her head began to swim and her breathing became more erratic. Teasing and prodding and heated, his lips worked wonders and she gripped his wrists for balance.

Just as her knees began to shake, he broke off with a gasp that she faintly echoed.

"That is enough," he rasped, touching his forehead to hers. Their breath mingled, each panting desperately, the air dancing across her cheeks. He nuzzled her slightly and gave a sharp exhale. "If that does not make you feel beautiful and desirable and wanted, nothing will." He gave her another brief, but searing kiss, then strode from the room, the door thumping the wall with the force of his exit.

Annie stared at the door in bewilderment, her breath still gasping, her legs feeling exactly like jelly, and finding thought was completely impossible.

What, in the name of all that was holy, was *that*?

"All right," Moira's voice called from the hall, "we're coming back in, and the dancing *will* commence, because you really are quite good at it!"

"There is no need to shout, Moira," Kate scolded as she entered the room first. "Oh my," she murmured softly as she looked at Annie.

Annie cleared her throat and shook herself out of her rather pleasant stupor. "Yes?"

Kate's eyes were wide and she bit back a grin. "Nothing," she replied, her voice full of restrained merriment. "You are just too precious."

Annie snorted, knowing it was out of character for her, but needing something to take the focus off of her discomfort. "I am no such thing, my lady."

Kate narrowed her eyes. "Call me that again, my dear Annalise, and I will make you eat lemons. Come here."

That drew a laugh from her and she moved over to Kate's open arms and let her friend embrace her.

"Are you better now?" Kate murmured softly.

Annie nodded and stepped back. "Panicked, I'm afraid."

"Happens to the best of us," Moira said loudly as she entered, followed by the others. "But never fear, most of the men you shall be dancing with are smart enough to think they are at fault for any missteps in the dance and will blame themselves. Just let them think that and you will be fine."

"Thank you, Moira," she muttered drily, accepting her hug as well. She glanced out of the door and saw Duncan walk past, and their eyes met again.

The heat, which had simmered in her stomach, flared once more at the look in his eyes.

He moved out of sight swiftly, and she knew… or sensed… that he had felt the same thing.

"All right, enough with the niceties; you will make me cry again," Moira scolded as she stepped back. "Time for dancing. Ready?"

"Yes," Annie replied firmly, releasing a deep breath. "Yes, let's dance."

Two hours out in the cold should have been enough. He finally had lost feeling in his fingers, and his lungs were burning with the frigid air.

He was still too warm.

He shook his head and grunted as he headed back towards his

house, his greatcoat billowing out behind him like a cloak.

His feelings for Annalise were beginning to border on the obsessive. Every shift in her mood, every flash of hurt or pain in her eyes set his world adrift. After her outburst today, he was more convinced than ever that he needed to do something for her.

Besides kissing her in the middle of his music room.

Although that had been a pleasant surprise on his part as well.

He had not planned on kissing her, let alone doing it so thoroughly, but it had seemed the simplest way to shut up her ridiculous tirade about not being worth all of this and being too low for consideration. And once he had started, it had been impossible to stop.

She thought she wouldn't attract anyone? He would be beating men away with sticks and have to recruit his friends to help him. She would be irresistible to them.

She was irresistible to him.

He exhaled sharply to remove the pleasant images from his mind as he entered the relative warmth of his home. A gift. He needed to get a gift for Annalise. Something to make her smile. Something to make her laugh. Something that might take away some of his drive to protect her so desperately.

"Duncan!"

He winced at his aunt's calling him. He shucked off his greatcoat and handed it to the footman nearest him with a nod of thanks. "Yes, Tibby?"

She came out of the music room and tapped her foot impatiently. "Come here, I need you!"

He grumbled under his breath and went over to her, cursing his inability to refuse his aunt anything. "You bellowed?" he replied mulishly.

"I never bellow," she corrected with a sharp finger of reproof. "It is unrefined and far beneath my dignity."

He heard a snort of laughter from within the room that he knew belonged to his sister. He grinned at the sound and then wiped his expression clean at Tibby's glower. "Of course, Tibby. How can I help you?"

177

She took his arm and pulled him into the room.

To his horror, all of the women were still there. Kate was still at the pianoforte, Marianne sat perched on a chair in the corner, Moira and Mary stood in the middle of the floor, and Annalise was next to them, her eyes wide and uncertain as she looked between him and Tibby. What in the world?

"We," Tibby said, gesturing to the room as a whole, "have need of you."

He swallowed and said, "You all look very pretty and I wouldn't change a thing."

Moira covered her mouth as she snickered, while Mary and Annalise merely grinned in delight, and he could hear Marianne just behind him giggling. Kate had a watchful eye on Tibby, and suddenly grinned very mischievously.

Oh, that was never good.

"We need a male partner for Annalise," Tibby explained, raising her chin in that way that told him he would not get out of this one. "We females have run our course of experience and now we need two couples to get the full scale of the dance. Moira and Mary will partner, as it will not be too taxing for our sweet and expecting friend."

Moira curtseyed playfully. Mary mouthed the word "sweet" and snorted.

"But Annalise needs to practice with a man, and as you are a man…"

"Well spotted," he retorted.

"…you are the only one that can aid us," Tibby finished, completely ignoring his outburst.

"Tibby," Annalise ventured, stepping forward nervously, "I really think that…"

"So what about it, Duncan?" Tibby asked, completely turning her back on Annalise, effectively cutting off her timid suggestion.

He looked down at his aunt, then glanced at Annalise. She bit her lip and shrugged helplessly. They had no choice. He returned his attention to Tibby and nodded. "All right. But just this once. I will not be your dancing monkey."

Tibby grinned and whirled away, saying something that sounded suspiciously like "we shall see" as she approached the others.

He took his place opposite Annalise, meeting her eyes.

"I'm sorry," she mouthed, one side of her mouth quirking in an apologetic smile.

He smiled and shook his head. "I'm not," he mouthed back.

She looked surprised for a moment, then her cheeks flushed, making him grin.

She widened her eyes at him in response, and he forced his grin back.

"All right, couples set?" Tibby called.

"No, Tibby, give them another few minutes," Marianne replied in a droll tone.

"Ready!" Moira crowed in delight.

"What would Nathan say if he knew you were dancing right now?" Duncan wondered aloud as he looked over at the woman next to him.

Her bright eyes flashed in the dangerous way he knew to fear. "If you breathe a word of this to him, Duncan Bray, your aunt's plans for you will be the very least of your concerns."

He swallowed and nodded. "Understood, Lady Beverton."

Annalise covered a smile with her hand, and he winked at her.

Kate began to play and Duncan nearly groaned again. This was one of the few dances that would force him to be in close proximity with Annalise for periods of time, as it was neither light-hearted nor short. He and Moira bowed to their respective partners, who curtseyed in return. Then he took Annalise by the hand and proceeded to hold his breath.

For the first few motions, everything was fine. She did not look at him and he did not look at her... much. She was graceful and light, and there was an ease in the dance with her, as if it were the most natural thing in the world. He was not a dancer by nature, being far too taciturn and too large to be a desirable partner. But he could become quite attached to dancing if this was the result of it.

Then he spun around Moira and rejoined his hands with Annalise. She brought her eyes up to meet his and it was as if fire raced through her fingertips and coursed directly into his heart. Her eyes widened, but she continued expertly through the motions of the dance. Her hold on his hand tightened, and he felt his skin burn beneath it.

So this was why polite company wore gloves when dancing.

He swallowed hastily and forced himself to look away, to keep his gaze above the heads of the women, as polite dance partners do. He caught Tibby's eye and saw the grin on her face. Blast her, she knew there was something between him and Annalise and she was using every chance she could to exploit it. To expose him. To force him to admit something he couldn't. Not yet.

She raised a brow at him, seeing what he did not want her to see. Just as Annalise had said she did. It was Tibby's greatest skill.

He forced himself to look back at his partner, and found himself imagining how she would look in two nights at the ball. Her hair would be expertly pinned and decorated with flowers or ribbons or pearls; her gown would be fitted and flowing, her figure on display for all. Her cheeks would flush from the shower of compliments that would rain down her, and from the dance, as she would likely do so all night, and her brilliant eyes would sparkle in such an enticing way, capturing all candlelight in their beauty, that no one could help but to love her.

He nearly stumbled in his shock at the thought, but covered it so that no one was the wiser, not even Annalise, who was so focused on her own steps she could have been dancing with anyone. He did not want her dancing with just anyone. He wanted her to dance with him.

"Look at me," he murmured, his voice scratching in his throat.

She looked up at him, and he could see her nervousness swirling in them.

"You know the steps," he told her, keeping his voice low enough that no one else would hear. "Look at me. Trust me. Stay on me."

She dropped her chin once in a deliberate nod, and her eyes locked onto his.

He smiled at her, unable to help himself. Looking at her just made him smile.

Made him *want* to smile.

Made him want…

His arms and legs were suddenly alive in a way he had never known before, his entire being filled with energy. Not to dance, but to be with her. To hold her. Every motion of the dance that brought her near him was not close enough. He caught her scent as he twirled her beneath his arm. Lavender and honey and something else, something that compelled him to pull her closer than he should have, to tighten his hold on her…

Then he felt it, the throb of her pulse in her wrist, caught tightly in his hold, and it was racing.

Could she feel this too? This pull, this connection, that he was too weak to resist?

As if she heard him, she stepped closer, close enough that he could have kissed her so easily.

So close, so easily…

Without thinking he dipped his head closer to her, unable to restrain the moan of despair as the dance forced them away. But he clenched his hold on her hand all the same, and he saw the way her eyes darkened as they remained on his. He saw her breathing speed up and the heightened color in her face.

It was not all on his side.

Not at all.

"I… I don't remember any more," Annalise said suddenly, wrenching her hand away from him and stepping back, shaking her head a little. "I can't…"

"You were doing perfectly!" Marianne squealed from her chair, rising and coming over to hug her. "I couldn't believe my eyes, but you looked so accomplished! And you were nearly done, the only thing left was…"

"I thought you did not approve, Marianne," Tibby crowed with a grin, giving Duncan a bewildered look that he could only shrug at.

Perhaps Tibby did not know everything after all.

The girls began bickering, and Duncan backed away from what could have been the greatest disaster of his life.

The most enjoyable one, too, but undoubtedly a disaster.

All were fussing over Annalise except for Kate, who watched

Duncan with her steady, dark eyes. Of all the wives of his friends, she was the one he feared most. Moira was lioness, Mary the mother hen, but Kate… Kate was a mystery. Stubborn, willful, proper, loyal, fierce, and she always seemed to know something that no one else did.

She glanced over at the other women, then back to Duncan. She gave the briefest indication towards the door behind him and a bare imitation of a smile quirked at her lips. He understood her immediately. He could leave at this moment unobserved, which was exactly what he wished.

He gave her a nod of thanks and escaped without being noticed by anyone else.

There was absolutely no time to waste. He needed to find a gift for Annalise, something to ease her mind. Something to distract her from him. He would force a distance until he could control himself better. This was her greatest opportunity to find future happiness, and he would not spoil it for her by confusing her.

A gift would be just the thing to ease her away.

And he would need to get it today.

Now.

His hand clenched at his side, the only sign of protest.

He nodded to himself. This was the right course.

His only course.

Chapter Fifteen

The ball was already a triumph and they had only been here for three quarters of an hour. Of course, how could it be anything but? The girls had dressed Annalise in a gown of purest white, which served to make her appear as the goddess of the sun. Every light in the room seemed to reflect off her gown and her hair, which was twisted and curled and dotted with flowers of a similar shade as her gown. Her eyes sparkled, their emerald majesty only increased by the contrast of her gown and the rosiness of her complexion.

She was nervous, he could see it from here. Her smile was slight, timid, and very shy, which only made her more appealing. She did not hold the gaze of anybody for any period of time, making the brief moments of eye contact a rare gift for those blessed enough to receive it. She was surrounded by both men and women, all eager to make her acquaintance, but it was not so crowded as to be oppressive.

The benefit of a winter party in London was the lack of accepted invitations. There was hardly anyone in London to attend.

But he could see her fright, and he knew her discomfort.

So why did he stand here, across the room, watching the whole thing?

Duncan took a long drink of the punch he held, the taste burning in his mouth. She had only danced twice thus far, which was shockingly lax on the part of the men present, and those had been with the Gerrards. Tibby suggested that Annalise open the evening on Duncan's arm, as they were thought to be almost relations, but

Colin had insisted on the honor.

Duncan would thank him later.

He could not dance with Annalise tonight. Not if he wanted to maintain any sort of self-control or preserve his image.

He was halfway to shredding it as it was.

At long last, one of the men surrounding Annalise asked for a dance. She flushed slightly, but smiled that soft, secret smile he so adored, the one that meant she was more pleased than she would dare say. A nasty thrill of jealousy twisted his gut and he shifted uncomfortably against his pillar.

At least she danced with Thomas Granger, and not one of the more senseless creatures. Granger he could tolerate well enough, though at the moment he wished the man thousands of miles away. The man was neither fop nor fool, both wealthy and respectable, and had far more intellect than one would expect from a gentleman. He was, in every respect, the sort of gentleman that a young woman of Society should wish herself to marry, if they could be so fortunate.

Granger would never be invited to his home again.

"If you are so in love with her, Duncan," murmured a distinctly feminine voice from behind him, "why not dance with her yourself?"

He turned halfway to see Kate standing there, looking regal and exquisite as always, her gown a rich burgundy that only served to accentuate her dark, fine coloring. She always looked so composed and refined. He was one of few people, he suspected, who knew what sharp wit and good humor lay within her. She kept her attention on the ballroom floor, apparently only paying attention to the dance. He looked beyond her to see that Derek was still conversing with Sir Charles Baldwin, their host. So they had just arrived, then. Excellent. He needed a distraction.

"I can assure you, my lady," he replied, returning his attention to the dancing, "that my current observations are purely cursory. I have no personal interest whatsoever." His heart thudded wildly in his chest, still stunned by her sudden proclamation.

"Liar," she replied with a slight laugh. "You are about to make a meal of that girl and turn one of my favorite bachelors into chicken feed."

He grunted and took another drink of his punch as his glower deepened.

"I appreciate your reticence, Mr. Bray," Kate said softly as she moved to stand beside him. "You do not speak unnecessarily, which makes you both intelligent and wise. But, as your friend, and as *her* friend, I must insist that you answer as to your intentions."

"I have no intentions." He kept his eyes trained on Annalise as if she were the only woman in the room, and he the only man.

Kate sighed and leaned closer. "She isn't indifferent to you, you know. Far from it."

"I know," he whispered, his heart feeling ripped from his chest. "Then what keeps you here?"

He swallowed hard as Annalise smiled broadly up at Mr. Granger. "I merely found her. I cannot claim her as well. She deserves to choose for herself, without any notion of gratitude or debt. She deserves… the best."

"And who is to say she shall not have it?"

Duncan shifted and looked at her with warning. "Kate…"

She gave him a pitying smile. "I will not make mischief for you, my friend, nor do I wish you discomfort. But what Annalise desires is someone who loves her. And you cannot deny that you fulfill that requirement quite soundly."

His frame was suddenly wracked with a jolt of shock as he looked from Kate to Annalise and back again. "I… I don't…"

Kate hummed a quiet laugh and her dark ringlets bounced slightly. "I see. Think about what I said, Duncan. You deserve the best, too."

She put a warm hand on his arm and walked away as if they had only conversed on the weather or the state of the roads, her elegant gown swishing gracefully in her wake. Could she really have that much insight into him? He looked back at Annalise with more confusion and unease than he ever had.

Love? Could it really be that simple? Were his feelings really so easy to define as that?

It was too soon, too early to say for certain. The past two days had been anguish for him, forcing himself away from her, not even appearing in the library for their readings. He had paced anxiously in his study or his bedroom instead, praying he had not hurt her. But until he found control, he could not be near her.

Not that it had mattered. She had been in his thoughts constantly since then. Even when he wasn't with her, his mind chose to be with her.

Could it be love?

"Well, this seems to be going well," Colin announced as he came to stand by him.

"What does?" he asked innocently as Thomas Granger returned Annalise to her previous position, bowed to her, and then excused himself to attend to Lily Arden. Now *that* was a match Duncan could approve of.

Colin snorted, bringing him back to their conversation, and swiped a glass of punch from a passing footman. "Your little project."

"Cousin," Duncan corrected with a harsh look.

"Nothing of the sort," Colin said with a shake of his head as he sipped his drink. "She is a niece of your aunt's late husband from his previous marriage. As your relation is Tibby, not her late husband, and it is a niece of his from his previous marriage, and not to Tibby, the girl is no relation of yours at all."

"Why is that distinction important?" Duncan growled with a glare back at the group of people surrounding Annalise.

Colin shrugged as he, too, took in the spectacle. "Because it means you can join the throng of admirers without shocking anybody."

"Who says I want to join?" he nearly barked, only keeping his voice down for the benefit of other patrons beginning to swirl about them.

His friend looked surprised. "I thought you wished to play protector, Duncan. Wouldn't the most effective way to do that be to act a part of the collection?"

Duncan turned back to his observations with a grunt. His friend had a point, and it did not seem to him that Colin had any of the same suspicions that Kate did. That was not surprising, as Kate was a great deal more intelligent than Colin and had infinitely better sense.

"She certainly looks well, doesn't she?" Colin sighed proudly, seeing where Duncan's gaze lay. "Not quite at ease, but altogether very charming."

"Yes." He could not elaborate, not without sounding like a fool.

"It seems that our friends have done quite well with her."

"Yes."

"Any residual worries on your part? Or hers?"

Duncan heaved a sigh and leaned more heavily against the pillar. "Many, for my part. But I'm not certain about her worries. I am ready to stop this whole thing the moment it gets out of hand, assuming it does, but she wants to do this. She actually wants to. So what am I to do? I cannot force her to stop, and yet…" He trailed off, knowing it would do no good to continue the thought.

Colin made a faint noise of assent, then turned to him. "Did you get her a gift, as I suggested?"

He nodded, pleased to have a topic he could properly converse upon. "I did."

"And what did you decide?"

He smiled as he recalled the day before, when his gift had arrived. "I bought her a puppy."

Colin was utterly silent and Duncan looked over to find his friend staring at him in horror.

"What?" he asked in surprise, wondering what in the world was wrong with that. Annalise had been so pleased by the dog and he would have done it again just to see the smile that she had given him.

"Good heavens, Duncan," Colin scoffed, not bothering to hide his disgust. "When I suggested a gift for the girl I was talking of ribbons or flowers or a particularly lovely poem. Not a puppy."

Duncan frowned. "What is wrong with a puppy?"

His friend shook his head sadly. "Duncan, Duncan, Duncan. No woman is going to pay any attention to any man when there is a puppy present."

"This is not about her paying attention to me," he retorted, shifting his weight uncomfortably. Wasn't it? Wasn't that what he was craving and fearing at the same time?

That drew a snort from his friend. "Oh, very well then, give her more puppies, by all means. Then perhaps you'll go back to normal."

"She was happy with it, Colin. She was delighted." He could not help smiling at the recollection. He had settled on a pug, as it was the most popular breed among ladies in London, and it had been just as enamored with Annalise as she had been of it. She instantly named him Lancelot, which seemed far too grand a name for such a small creature, but he would never deny her anything.

And it had worked like a charm. She was so fond of the dog that Duncan had stopped worrying about her state of mind and being. There was no need to protect her now.

"Be still my ever-bleeding heart," Colin muttered sarcastically. "She would also have loved a hair comb, Duncan. Far more sensible and less troublesome. But you go ahead and be happy she has that puppy now. Let me know when your birthday is and I'll be sure to send you a cat. You'll need the attention."

He gave his friend a wry look. "Don't cats normally ignore people?"

"Do they? Much better. You will be able to relate to each other." Colin shook his head and left, muttering under his breath.

Duncan sighed irritably and looked back at Annalise, now preparing to dance with young Christian Harris. He had done the right thing. He was doing right by her.

He was.

The dark feeling in his chest would abate soon enough. And then he would be well again.

Annie smiled at the group surrounding her, feeling as though her cheeks would break under the strain she had put on them this evening alone. So many people had been introduced and conversed with her, she would never be able to remember them all. She didn't know the names of any standing around her, but as they were not addressing her at the moment, she was safe.

And she had danced. Several times now, and each had been a pleasant experience. All of the people she had met had been so kind and complimentary, it was quite an exercise in restraint as she forced herself to react modestly and without embarrassment. And as yet, she hadn't trod upon any toes, which she considered to be a triumphant achievement.

She glanced over against the far wall, where Duncan stood, where he had been standing all night. He had not come over to her at all, the whole course of the night. He had watched her, as intently as a hawk, his eyes just as steady. She could not read the meaning in them, nor his carefully vacant expression. Was he displeased? Or was he simply being watchful?

He had not spoken to her in two days, saving for his presenting her with her new puppy, Lancelot. She adored the dog, and her heart had fairly burst at such a kind and thoughtful gift from him. Lancelot brought her joy and delight, and she wished she could have expressed her gratitude more effectively. She had never been given anything of value by anyone, and the puppy was already like a friend, one who would always make her smile and soothe away fears.

In spite of that, she missed Duncan. More fiercely than she could have imagined. He seemed to be avoiding her altogether now, even during meals. And she yearned for the briefest touch of his hand. For a smile. To hear his voice. He had not come into the library since they had danced, and oh, how she missed hearing him read to her.

Her face flamed as she recalled the heat of that dance in the music room, in front of all of her friends, none of whom seemed even remotely aware of the turmoil she had endured. And she had not forgotten the steps to the dance, not at all. She simply could not continue in such a state without doing something both pathetic and shocking.

Why would he not come over to her? Couldn't he see her nervousness, which he had easily soothed before? Couldn't he see that all of this was for him?

She scolded herself and looked away as he noticed her gaze upon him. She could not pretend this was entirely for him. She wanted to live in this imaginary world he inhabited, even if for only a little while. To dream while she could, for none of this would last.

Not for her.

A lone figure entered the room then and her attention was drawn to him briefly.

Her heart lurched so suddenly in her chest that she lost her balance for a moment. Thankfully, no one noticed, but she could feel slight tremors starting in her fingers.

She glanced back up as she pretended to scan the room, and her stomach clenched again.

There was no mistaking the leanness of his body, the coldness of his eyes, the permanent sneer etched into his features.

Albert Thorpe was here.

But how? He could not have known she was here, there was no possible way for anyone to trace her. Yet here he was, in the same room as her, in London, of all places.

Was he considered a man of high Society? She couldn't imagine so, not after what he had put her through and his usual manner of dress and speech. But how else could he have obtained an invitation to the ball this evening? She knew he had money, but she had not thought it equal to those she now associated with.

He saw her group and tilted his head for a moment, no doubt wondering at the fuss, and then his eyes found her. Locked on her. And the surprised registered in his pale face so plainly she knew she had been right. He had not known she would be here.

Which meant he had no plans for her.

Yet.

His thick brows snapped together and she quickly shifted her attention to the people nearest her, engaging them in conversation on whatever she could think of first. Thankfully, they were both exceptional conversationalists and did not need much input from her. Perhaps she could convince Mr. Thorpe that he was mistaken. Perhaps he would think the idea of her being here as so far-fetched that it would be impossible.

Then again, perhaps he would merely bide his time.

Feeling panic rising, she looked over to Duncan, only to discover with a sickening jolt that he had disappeared.

She forced herself to keep breathing, and looked around for a familiar face, anyone that could help at all.

Mary and Moira were close at hand, but engaged in conversation with a few other ladies. She had seen Kate and Derek dancing moments ago, and would not have interrupted them for a fortune, not with the way they stared at each other. Nathan and Colin she had not seen, but Geoffrey and his brother were nearby. She could rush to them if need be.

Feeling slightly mollified, she looked around again. Thorpe was not looking her direction anymore, and she allowed herself to breathe a bit easier.

Marianne sat at the opposite end of the room from her, surrounded by her own collection of admirers, which far outstripped her own. That was as it should have been. She glanced over at Annie, and she saw a flicker of concern cross her features, but then it was gone and her cool, complacent demeanor was back in place. She turned away from Annalise, and back to her own group.

She didn't mind. She had expected worse.

The room was full of people now, and so it would take some time for Thorpe to get near her, if he wished, though a public scene was not his way. Flashes of memory infiltrated her mind and she forced herself not to whimper in remembered pain.

Her hands shook and she had to fight the urge to wipe at her brow, which felt warm and damp.

"Look at her, the vain ridiculous creature," a woman near her sneered.

Shocked, Annie looked at her, only to find that she was not the one being spoken of. The woman was looking directly at Marianne.

"Have you ever seen such a woman?" the lady continued, scoffing and fanning herself importantly. "Who does she think she is, to find herself so far above her company?"

Annie was shocked at the number of heads nodding near her. She glanced back where Mr. Thorpe had been, but he seemed to have vanished, thankfully. Perhaps he did not recognize her after all.

"Miss Bray has always been a cold, calculating creature," a young man muttered, shaking his head. "As impenetrable as a fortress, and just as deadly."

Annie knew her mouth was agape, but she could not muster the strength to close it. Were they really speaking so boldly of Marianne in company?

The first woman tossed her copious hair and adjusted her bodice. "She has no accomplishment, you know. Barely passable in anything at all."

"I heard she lures her suitors in with hopes and then laughs as she dashes them all to pieces." Annie did not know who spoke this, nor could she contain the fury surging through her veins. Her fears of Mr. Thorpe were now gone, banished by her indignation for her friend. She could not bear this. Was she meant to?

"Oh, I know she does," another man said in an urgent tone. "I have heard it from no less than three unfortunate men who attempted for her favors."

"Favors," a woman scoffed. "Poisonous darts, more like."

"Well, you do know who she learned it all from," an older woman... what was her name?... spoke up, looking at the rest. She had hardly spoken and had not been with this group for long. She wore far too many ruffles and beads, and the sheer volume of fabric surrounding her would have served to make three full dresses for the woman.

Every head shook in confusion, every eye fixed on her, waiting for the answer.

Annie could not allow this. She *would* not.

"That is enough," she said loudly, in a voice she did not recognize at all. It was strong and powerful and full of authority.

All eyes were now on her, but she could not look at anyone for long. She was not that brave.

"How dare any of you speak of Miss Bray in such a way! What do any of you know about her? What gives you the right to say such horrible things about her? Or to spread malicious rumors? What can any of you say about her at all that is of any worth?"

"Now see here, Miss Remington," a man began, his voice kind.

She shook her head fiercely, that warm flush now spreading to her limbs. "No, I will not see here. This is not some game you play in corners of ballrooms and parties. Marianne Bray is not an object to be mocked or slandered just because none of you have the brain capacity to focus on anything else."

Gasps of shock echoed around the group, but she was in too much of a state to consider it.

"That young woman over there has a heart of gold and her only misfortune is being so beautiful and refined that it is impossible to not be filled with jealousy and envy at the sight of her." She glared around at them all, her breath coming faster. "She is accomplished in far more areas than I could ever hope to be, let alone the rest of Society, and anyone worth any good opinion would never think of abusing her character in such a way. Shame on you all."

She turned from the group, only to have Mr. Gerrard standing before her. He looked positively murderous, and it terrified her. But his eyes were not on her. Instead, they seared the rest of the group, and she wondered if any person could stand such power. He looked down at her and bowed deeply. "Come, Miss Remington. I'm afraid I must claim the rare privilege of a second dance with you." He held out a hand forcefully and by pure instinct she recoiled.

But she would not fear him. She tilted her chin up a notch and placed her hand in his. "It would be an honor, Mr. Gerrard."

Something almost akin to a faint wink lit one of his eyes and he squeezed her hand, his touch surprisingly gentle.

"Thank you for the rescue," she whispered as he led her away. "I fear I was getting carried away. That has never happened to me before. I am generally not inclined to speak at all."

"Miss Remington, I was not saving you, I was saving them," he responded, his voice clipped.

She looked up at him in shock. "I beg your pardon?"

He glanced down, his eyes blazing. "I saved the rest of them from you. Any longer and you might have done away with them all."

Annie flushed and she dropped her chin.

"It was the most amazing sight I have ever seen."

Surprised, she looked up at him. One side of his mouth lifted at her as he took his place in the dance.

"You... you approve?" she squeaked, remembering to curtsey as the music struck up.

He nodded once. "I absolutely do. If I were less enraged, I would have applauded. I, too, am disinclined to conversation, but it is because I have no talent for it. I cannot speak or think clearly when so upset, yet you dismantled Lady Greversham in a few succinct sentences, and in obvious distress." He shook his head.

She faltered in the dance. "That was… Lady Greversham?"

He caught her and held her steady. "It was. And I feel very sure you will have a long line of admirers after that. She is nobody's favorite person."

Annie's head began to swim and thought she would faint.

"Come," he urged softly, "let me get you some air."

"I didn't know," she whispered as he escorted her off. "I didn't know it was her."

"Did it matter?" he asked, leading her to more open area.

She considered that for a moment as her head began to clear. "No, I suppose not. I would have said the same to anyone."

Mr. Gerrard was silent for a long moment, then he said, "You defended Marianne." He sounded almost surprised by it.

"Yes," she replied.

"Even though she has refused to help you."

Her mouth dropped open in surprise. "How did you know?"

He waved a dismissive hand. "I know more than anyone ever expects me to. Tell me why."

She still did not understand. "Why?" she asked, looking up at him again.

"Why, Miss Ramsey," he murmured softly, drawing a shocked gasp from her, "are you defending someone who will not defend you?"

She swallowed hard, knowing he was right. In this company, Marianne would not defend her. Not truly. She looked over at her and sighed. "Because I love Marianne."

"How?" he asked, the word seeming ripped from him.

She smiled faintly, still watching Marianne laugh in delight at one of her suitors. "Because she sees me. She knows this isn't who I am. She is the only one not pretending."

"I don't think you are pretending, Miss Remington," he told her, using her public name once more, and sounding almost proud. "I think you are quite in your element up here with the rest of us."

She laughed a sad little laugh. "Then I have become quite the actress. But away from here, away from these fanciful imaginations, Marianne is still the same sweet, kind, generous girl I knew weeks ago. And I will always love her for loving me. Even if it is different now."

"Exactly so," he murmured, his eyes now on Marianne as well.

Annie looked up at him. "You understand?"

He swallowed and nodded once. "More than you can possibly imagine." He cleared his throat and straightened. "And now I think I must return you to Mr. Bray, as he is on his way over. I think he is quite proud of you."

Annie sighed as she saw Duncan approaching, his face full of concern. "I dare say I embarrassed him."

Mr. Gerrard took her hand once more and held it tightly. "You embarrassed no one, except perhaps Mrs. Coulter and Lady Greversham, for which I applaud you most heartily." He kissed her hand and led her over to Duncan.

"Thank you, Kit," Duncan murmured softly as he took her hand from him.

Mr. Gerrard bowed. "Mr. Bray. Miss Remington. Good night." He turned from them and left the room out the nearest door, never once looking back.

"I am sorry if I embarrassed you," Annie murmured softly as Duncan led her away.

He shook his head once. "Nothing to apologize for, sweet. I don't think I have ever been prouder of anyone in my life."

She smiled up at him. "Really?"

He chuckled and squeezed her hand. "Really. You should have seen Tibby, she was in tears with pride."

"Does... does Marianne know?" she asked timidly, looking over at her friend, who still had not seen her.

He exhaled sharply. "No, I am afraid not. As you said, she doesn't notice her surroundings. I have a mind to tell her, but..."

"Don't," she insisted. "I don't want her to know what they are saying."

"You want to protect her." It was not a question, but she

answered all the same.

"Yes."

Again, he squeezed her hand. "You are a wonder, Anne Remington."

She looked up at him and her breath caught at the warmth in his gaze.

He cleared his throat suddenly and looked away. "There are quite a few people who are waiting to dance with you. Admirers of yours, if you will."

She felt a stab of disappointment. "Oh, but I…"

"Just look."

She looked where he indicated and saw each of his friends standing and grinning, their wives nearby. In almost perfect unison, the four men bowed.

"I claim the next dance, Miss Remington," Derek said, stepping forward. "And the one after that, too, if it is not too bold."

She returned his smile and looked at Duncan, who was now walking away. Her chest ached, but she forced her attention back to Derek. "Of course, my lord. It would be an honor."

Chapter Sixteen

$\mathcal{A}$nnie rubbed her tired eyes and set aside her book. Lancelot lay curled next to her, sound asleep, as he usually was these days. She smiled and stroked his soft fur, thinking yet again what a thoughtful gift it had been. Duncan had known she was anxious and overwhelmed by preparing for her introduction, and this sweet puppy had been just the thing to take her mind off of things. He walked at her heels, followed her every move, and crawled up into her lap every chance he got. And he was so adorable she would never forbid him anything.

She sighed and allowed herself to smile. For the first time in five days, she was not expected anywhere or to see anyone, and she was thankful for it. She had spent the whole morning in the library getting caught up on her reading. Her evenings had been so occupied and her energy so deprived that it had been some time since she had been able to sit in the quiet and enjoy a book. Not since before the ball.

She sighed and wrapped herself more comfortably in the blanket around her shoulders. She was exhausted. For it being winter, there were certainly a lot of events to be attended. Tibby assured her that it was her novelty that rendered so many invitations, and Annie certainly hoped so. She did not enjoy popularity.

Not that she ought to be considered popular, for compared to Marianne, she was a wallflower. But she did have some admirers. And callers.

Thankfully she had none today.

It was far easier to deal with a larger group of people than smaller numbers. There was surprisingly less attention that way. She was still rather shy when meeting one on one with people, but she was getting better. Slowly but surely, her fears were vanishing.

She discovered that most people were kind and considerate, and didn't mind her being reserved. The men she had begun to meet seemed to find it amusing, but did not tease her about it. She couldn't have said that any one particular man stood out to her at this point, no matter how Tibby interrogated her after each event, but she enjoyed meeting and associating with men that didn't have nefarious intentions for her.

A cold shiver ran up her spine as she recollected seeing Mr. Thorpe twice more since the ball. Once on her way to a card party at Lady Beckham's he had been passing on the street just as she disembarked from her carriage. His eyes had met hers and she knew instantly that he recognized her. But other than his blatant leer, nothing had occurred.

The second time he had actually spoken to her. She had been shopping with Tibby the other day and he had approached them suddenly.

"I don't believe we have been introduced," he had begun, his voice sounding slick and oozing with supposed gentility.

Thankfully, Tibby was an excellent judge of character. She had sniffed and looked him over distastefully before saying, "No. We have not," with a toss of her head and taking Annie's arm, briskly setting off towards their carriage. Annie had not looked back, but she could imagine how his expression would have looked.

"Not all men are worth knowing," Tibby had confided to Annie with a pat on her hand.

She quite agreed.

But even the sight of Mr. Thorpe could not detract from her true enjoyment. She was seeing a world she would never have been able to before, meeting people who would have passed her on the streets without a look before, and wearing clothes that she would have spent a lifetime trying to afford. She had nearly accustomed herself to her new wardrobe, much to her friends' delight. There was something to

be said about wearing fine apparel. One could not help but to love it.
In fact, in this whole affair, she only had one regret.

Duncan.

He was more reclusive than usual, keeping to his rooms or his
study, or spending time away from the house with his friends. He no
longer dined with them and never sought her out. Marianne and
Tibby claimed this was his usual way, and they had been surprised by
the amount of time he had been spending at home of late. She could
not ask more without appearing overanxious, and so her mind had
set about to wondering.

Her imagination had grown quite rampant.

Perhaps he had felt his duty to her fulfilled. This was a logical
conclusion, as he had done so much for her already, and he should
not do more. She did not expect more. She would not be surprised if
he cast her off, but it did not seem his way or his nature. He was too
kind, too giving, too generous for anything of the sort.

Perhaps he disapproved of her. He had said during her outburst
that he had his reservations about this endeavor, so perhaps his true
feelings were revealed. But why wouldn't he wish this for her? Unless
he didn't think she was worthy of such aspirations…

No, he told her time and again not to think that way.

Even if it was true.

She huffed and rose from the chair, blinking away tears. She
knew very well she didn't fit, but it wouldn't stop her from dreaming.
And if she truly wanted to do this right, she had to stop thinking this
way. Duncan and Tibby did not see her as a lower creature. Even
Marianne saw her as an equal when they were together, away from
the world. Publicly, Marianne would always reign supreme, and Annie
was content to let her.

She needed to let Annie Ramsey go. She wanted to be Annalise
now. The young woman who had no tragic past, but was strong and
vibrant. The one who had made friends with a countess and a
marchioness and was acquainted with all sorts of influential people.
The one who would take London by storm, even if it was a very small,
very brief storm.

Could she be Annalise?

Could Duncan love Annalise?

It was too preposterous a notion, more far-fetched than Tibby's scheme.

She was becoming ridiculous, being cooped up here all by herself. She needed some fresh air to clear her thoughts. The day was warmer than it had been in some time, so she could walk, which she enjoyed very much. London was such an exciting place and held so many experiences for someone who only knew a simple life. The sheer number of shops and vendors was enough make her dizzy, and the people who swirled about them were so varied and vast in their differences she could hardly countenance it.

She could see why Marianne loved it so.

And she understood Duncan's distaste for it. It was always busy and bustling, hardly the peaceful setting he would enjoy. She would no doubt feel the same way once she had grown accustomed to it.

But for now, she enjoyed it.

She inched Lancelot away, and left the library for her room. As she expected, the dog followed her, bounding excitedly as if they were headed for some great adventure. Once upstairs, she fetched her pelisse and warmest wool coat, bonnet, and gloves, taking a vain moment to admire herself. Truly, one would never know her past from her present. Her coat was a rich navy blue and fit her form so well, she ought to have blushed, but instead she felt a thrill of pride. Her friends had insisted on a matching bonnet, but thankfully one that was not so very extravagant. She was not so far gone as to forget what simple elegance was. She much preferred that to elaborate and overdone.

Apologizing to her poor Lancelot, she stepped out of the house alone. The air was fresh and clean and she allowed herself to inhale deeply. She truly loved being out of doors, and she wondered faintly what it was like at Duncan's country home. Not that she would ever see it, but she might enjoy life in the country. Long trails for walking, hills and pastures for riding, fresh air and space for picnics… Yes, while city life was grand, the country would be her true love.

She did not see many people out and about as usual, but she couldn't say that she minded. She smiled and politely acknowledged those she did see, and found herself feeling more natural than she ever had. She could not have walked down the streets of her small village and been so comfortable. Perhaps she was not so ill-suited to this life after all.

She had made her circle of her usual shops and even given a few coins to some hungry looking children, when she felt someone come up behind her.

"What a generous soul you are, Annie."

Her spine tingled and she fought a gasp.

Thorpe.

"Don't make a sound," he murmured. "Look natural."

She hastily swallowed, wishing she had thought to bring someone with her, as Duncan always insisted.

"You have been avoiding me."

"I did not know you were here."

He laughed quietly, sending shivers through her as if by an icy blast of wind. "You even talk like one of them. But you can't fool me. I know the real you. And you belong to me."

She tilted her chin up a notch. "I belong to no one."

He grabbed her wrist tightly. "Watch your mouth. We need to talk, Annie. Now."

"I have nothing to say to you."

His grip tightened and she bit her lip in pain. "You will talk to me."

She shook her head, her mouth remaining firmly closed.

She was suddenly hauled to the side as he forced her into a dark alley. He shoved her against a cold, filthy brick wall, and her head slammed back against it, knocking her bonnet off. "Who the hell do you think you are, Annie Ramsey?" he hissed, his foul breath wafting across her face as he leaned close. "You think you belong here?" He shook her roughly, his hands now at her elbows. "You are nothing, you understand that? You are *mine*. You are promised to me. I have bought you. You belong to me!"

Fear began to eat away at her stomach, but something else swirled in her, too. Something dark and powerful.

Hate.

She looked up at him with a glare, though her knees trembled. "I belong to no one."

He slapped her across the face, drawing a scream from her. "Shut up, Annie!" he hissed, hitting her once more, harder. "You know better than to scream." Again he hit her.

Dots began to appear before her eyes and she struggled to remain upright.

"You will not talk to me that way," Thorpe panted, his eyes glinting. "Your brother isn't here now, Annie. I can touch you all I want. And I will teach you to respect me."

She whimpered as fear won out and she grabbed at the wall behind her. "My name," she managed as tears began to fall, "is Annalise."

Thorpe snarled and raised his hand again.

She braced herself for another hit.

But it never came.

"Do not touch her again."

Annie's eyes popped open to find a man holding Thorpe's wrist in his hand, still raised as it was to strike her.

"Mind your own business, mangy cur," Thorpe spat at him.

The man's dark eyes narrowed, a muscle in his jaw ticked, and he suddenly twisted Thorpe's arm behind his back so violently it drew a sharp cry from him. "At this moment, she is my business," he growled. "Do not touch her again."

His voice was so venomous Annie trembled at the sound. No person she had ever met had ever sounded so deadly, not even Thorpe or her brother. This man was clearly no gentleman, as he wore the clothes of a commoner and had the fit build of a tradesman or dockworker. His face was darkened with stubble, but his features were chiseled as starkly as that of a statue.

He pulled on Thorpe's arm harder and Thorpe strained up, his breath hissing though clenched teeth painfully. "I haven't had to kill anyone in some time, but I am more than willing to start again with you."

He turned and threw Thorpe against the wall opposite. Thorpe cried out as his face slammed against the brick, and turned back, his nose already bleeding. He wiped at it and glared at the man.

"Go now," the man said in a restrained voice as he stood between Thorpe and Annie. "Before I change my mind."

Thorpe hissed and made a move towards Annie, which sent her scrambling backwards, but the man was there, and shook his head as he used his arms to shield her.

"Don't do something that will make me have to hurt you."

Thorpe glared at Annie, wiped his bleeding nose once more, and then disappeared from the alley.

Annie shuddered when he was out of sight and collapsed to the ground, her knees no longer able to hold her. She buried her face in her hands as the tears flowed in panicked sobs, shivers wracking her entire frame.

"It's all right, he's gone now," the man said, his voice far more gentle.

A hand settled on her shoulder and she jerked away with a frightened gasp, looking up at him.

He held up his hands and crouched to her level. "You don't need to fear me, Miss. Are you hurt?"

She searched his eyes for a moment, and exhaled when she saw no danger. "No," she murmured.

He reached out a hand again and helped her to her feet. He looked at her face intently for a moment, then shook his head. "Yes, you are." He touched her cheek with a gentle finger, but she winced at the pressure. "That will bruise."

She sighed and pushed back a lock of hair behind her ear with a sniff. "They always do," she murmured bitterly.

He said nothing for a moment, but she caught a flash of sadness and pity. He brushed dirt off of her shoulders as she brushed at her skirt. "Why did you meet with a man alone in an alley?" he finally asked, his tone slightly accusatory.

She glanced up at him in defense, then realized how it must have appeared. She unbuttoned her glove and rolled back her sleeve to expose her wrist, where her fair skin was already turning purple and black. "It was not by choice, I can assure you."

He hissed and brushed two fingers across it, shaking his head again. He took her hand gently in his much larger one. "You should not walk alone in London, Miss. Not with the likes of him running around. Do you need anything?"

She shook her head with a sniffle. "I just want to go home."

He wiped a tear from her unbruised cheek. "Of course, you do, pet. Do you have an escort?"

Again she shook her head, pushing her sleeve back down. "No."

He grunted and released her hand. "I will send someone back with you." He whistled down the dark alley, then put a hand on her shoulder and turned her back towards the street. "You'll be all right now, Miss. Safe as can be, I promise."

"How can I ever thank you?" she murmured, wiping at her cheeks.

She could hear him smile. "Avoid dark alleys and dangerous men, Miss. That will save me a lot of trouble."

"Who are you?"

He hesitated, then patted her shoulder. "They call me 'the Gent.' And I am someone you can trust, Miss. That is all you need to know."

She looked back at him. "Trust is not an easy thing, sir."

He grinned, displaying gleaming white teeth. "No, Miss. You'll just have to trust me on that, won't you?"

Annie found a way to smile. "I suppose I must."

He bowed to her, then gestured towards the street. "Go on, Miss. You'll be all right getting home."

She nodded again. "Thank you," she said, her voice catching.

He touched his cap and turned down the alley, disappearing into the darkness.

She looked around for whoever was supposed to follow her, but saw no one. Still, he said she would be safe. With a shiver of apprehension, she went out into the light street, now busier than before, and headed straight for Duncan's house, praying he was not at home.

He could not see her like this.

Duncan was beside himself.

A note had just been delivered to him in his study, in the same hand as his usual informant, describing an incident involving Miss Ramsey... not Remington, but Ramsey... and a man in an alley that he had intercepted, and assured Duncan that Miss Ramsey was well and whole and on her way back home, and he would keep an eye on her in the future. The note was signed only "The Gent," which was more than Duncan had known previously, but it did not account for his knowing Annalise's true identity.

Or for what had really happened.

He paced his study again, ramming his hands into his hair. His heart was racing and he could barely breathe but for fear. She had been accosted in an alley? Or had she met someone intentionally? The note had not been descriptive, but he knew better than to question it. The man's identity wasn't important now, not when Annalise had not yet arrived.

Who was the man in the alley? Why had she met with him?

Where was she?

He heard the sounds of the front door open and he burst from the room.

Annalise was hurrying towards the stairs, her eyes cast down.

"Annalise," he barked, not caring how he sounded.

She jerked and looked at him, then turned her face away. "Duncan."

"Where have you been?" he asked as he neared her.

She hesitated on the stair and he saw her hand tremble as she removed her glove. "I must... go to my room, Duncan. I am tired."

He exhaled sharply and turns towards the stairs. "I have just received this, Annalise." He thrust the note out at her. "Would you care to explain it?"

Her trembling hand took it from him, and she turned more fully away.

He waited impatiently, wanting to force her to face him, wanting to crush her to him, wanting...

She moaned and faltered to one side.

He was to her in an instant, steadying her. "What is it?" he rasped, unaware until that moment just how much he had missed her. The last week had been torture, being away from her. Forcing himself to pretend he did not care.

He did care.

Too much.

She exhaled and handed him back the note, then untied her bonnet, stiffened, and turned to face him.

He reared back at the bruising that had begun to form on her left cheek and jaw. He could not restrain the anguished growl that escaped him as he gripped her chin in his hand and turned her face to see it better.

Now her hands were not the only ones shaking.

"What happened?"

Annalise winced at his tone and a tear leaked from one of her gorgeous eyes.

He was going to go mad. He swiped the tear away roughly with his thumb. "What happened, Annalise?" he asked again, too tormented to lower his voice.

She wrenched her jaw out of his hold and seized his hand, pulling him into the nearest room. Once inside, she shut the door, still clinging to his hand, and then sat on the sofa. "Please don't shout," she whispered.

Only then did it occur to him that her hands were not shaking, but her entire frame.

He sank onto the sofa beside her and covered her hand with both of his. "I'm sorry, forgive me. I have been beside myself with worry. What happened?"

She took a deep, shaky breath, and released it slowly. "I went for a walk today. Alone."

He felt a growl start in his throat, but she cut him off with a look.

"On my way back, a man came up behind me," she continued, swallowing. "He… forced me into the alley, and he struck me repeatedly. This man… The Gent… stopped him from hurting me any further, and sent him away."

"He should have killed him!" Duncan raged, shooting to his feet and pacing frantically. "I would have strangled the man with my bare hands! I would have beaten him to a pulp! I…" He gripped the back of his neck and seethed. "Why didn't you scream, why didn't you run?"

Annalise rolled her sleeve and shoved her forearm out. "I tried!" she protested, her voice thick with tears. "I tried, Duncan."

He nearly buckled at the angry bruises that disfigured her pure white skin. "Who was he?" he begged, his voice near to cracking. "Did you know him?"

Annalise hesitated, her throat working. Then, at last, she nodded. "His name is… Albert Thorpe."

Duncan had never heard of him. "And he is…?"

She bit her now trembling lip. "I'm… supposed to marry him."

Duncan stared at her in horror. "What?" he mouthed more than asked, all of the air in his lungs suddenly gone. She was… engaged?

"My brother used to… bring men to the house," she managed, her composure breaking. "They never touched me, but they… looked. They watched while I would be forced to do chores, the most menial and dirty chores he could think of. Shoveling stables, scrubbing the fireplace, whatever would get my clothes the dirtiest and embarrass me most. Then he'd hit me. And they laughed when he hit me. And he would… take bids from them. For me."

Duncan was going to be sick. He couldn't move, couldn't feel anything. He couldn't hear anymore, he couldn't bear to…

"Albert Thorpe was the worst of them," she continued, squeaking as a few more tears fell unnoticed from her cheeks. "He would trap me into corners, never touching, but he would say the most… awful things. Ugly things. He liked it when I was being hit. He laughed the most. And he told me exactly what he would do to me when I was his. Then Frank… told me he had sold me to him. For the highest price. And then I… I saw him here in London. He knew me, but I never thought… I never…"

Her voice finally broke and she sobbed, covering her face in shame.

Duncan stumbled towards her, inarticulate sounds escaping him. He gathered her into his arms as he knelt before her. "Oh, my sweet Annalise," he breathed, fighting for control himself, stroking her hair.

"My sweet, brave girl." He kissed her hair and rested his mouth there, inhaling her scent.

She wrapped her arms around him and buried her face into his shoulder.

"Don't cry, Annalise," he murmured, tightening his hold. "Don't cry, sweet. I can't bear it. It's all right, you're safe now. I've got you."

"I've never been more terrified in my life," she sobbed, hiccupping as she clutched his shirt. "I thought he would kill me. I thought..."

"Shh, shh," he soothed, kissing her hair again. "That's enough, you're all right. It's all right now."

She released a shuddering sigh, and he felt her nod against him.

He closed his eyes tightly and swallowed the lump that had formed in his throat. "Can you tell me what he said to you today? Everything that happened?"

Her clenching hold tightened. "Don't let me go," she whispered, sounding very much like scared little girl.

He shook his head. "Not for a moment. I've got you."

She waited a long moment, then softly told him of the entire exchange.

Duncan was suddenly torn between holding Annalise close and leaving to find Thorpe and rip his heart out. He could hardly see straight for the fury that boiled within him. How dare that man torment Annalise. How *dare* he accost her in the street like some common trollop. How *dare* he lay a single finger on her head.

He released an unsteady breath and inhaled her calming fragrance. She was incredible. Extraordinary. He replayed the exchange over and over, and found himself able to give a hollow laugh. "You told him to call you Annalise?"

She released a watery chuckle and shrugged. "It is my name, after all."

He closed his eyes and took her head in his hands, pushing her back slightly. "Yes, it is, sweetheart. Yes, it is."

Her eyes glinted with unshed tears, but she smiled at him. It made his heart ache that this sweet, beautiful creature had endured so much by those who should have loved her. That she should know such pain and anguish. That he could not protect her from everything.

"I was so scared," she whispered, another tear making its way down delicate curve of her cheek.

He smoothed it away. "I know. But you will never have to be so again. He will never touch you again, I promise you that."

She shook her head and looked down, swallowing hard. "I don't want you to put yourself out for him. Don't do something that could get you into trouble, Duncan. I couldn't bear that."

He put a hand under her chin and gently forced her to look at him. "Annalise, I will do whatever it takes to ensure your protection, your safety, security, and peace of mind," he vowed. "I don't care what it takes or what it causes or what it may do to me. I will do anything. I have to. I want to. And I will."

Slowly, barely breathing, she nodded.

As softly as he could, he stroked the sensitive skin where she was struck. "He touched you," he breathed in agony. "He touched you and he hurt you. No one will ever do that again. Ever." He stroked it again and then pressed his lips to it, his mouth tracing the angry marks as if they could heal it. As if his will alone could mend her.

"I promise," he whispered against her skin. He sighed and tucked her head beneath his chin, enveloping his arms around her.

He might not be able to protect her from everything.

But he would damn well do his best.

Chapter Seventeen

$\mathcal{D}$uncan sat alone in his study, hardly any light in the room, staring off at nothing. His hand absently moved along his jaw in thought. He had finally gotten Annalise calm enough to be able to sleep, though his ears were straining to hear the faintest sounds of distress from her room. He had counted the paces from this room to hers. Fifty-three. He could cover that distance very quickly, and all the forces of heaven and earth combined could not stop him from rushing to her side if she was frightened.

The clock on mantle struck two o'clock, and he was surprised it was not later. This day felt as long as a lifetime.

Tibby and Marianne had been informed of the situation after supper, as Annalise had declined dining with the family. Duncan had made her excuses, then shared the truth after they had dined, mostly because he had been interrogated. Marianne had excused herself from the room and gone directly to Annalise's, and he had not seen her since. Tibby had sat with him quietly, occasionally asking questions of him, but most of the time she had simply looked older than he had ever seen her. He had asked if she was well, but she had barked that she was not the one they needed to worry about at this time.

Only then did it occur to him just how much Annalise meant to Tibby. She was not just an amusing project for her entertainment, Tibby truly had adopted her as her own.

She had left for her room sometime after that, saying fewer than five words to him.

He had attempted to prepare for bed hours ago, but his mind and his heart were so torn and tangled that he was beyond restless. He had to do something to protect Annalise, but beyond only letting her out of the house under armed guard, he could not think how. There was no proof that the man who attacked Annalise was Thorpe beyond her word. Even the Gent had not known his identity at the time, and he had no way of contacting him for a witness, so there could be no action against Thorpe.

He would not want to drag Annalise through that.

Much as he would like to, he could not attack the man or have others do so. Not without just cause. Not without causing more rumors and problems for Annalise. If they had been anywhere else, perhaps that would have been possible, but London was London, and it was one of the reasons he hated it so.

He had no way to avenge the woman he loved.

For he did love her.

He was an idiot to think it could be anything else. He had loved her from the moment he had laid eyes on her. It didn't matter that he was the protective sort or the kind to do a good deed. Love explained everything. Why he couldn't breathe when she was away, why he couldn't breathe when she was near, why he would go to such lengths for her, why his every thought was about her and for her, and why he hated seeing any other man in her presence.

She was his and his alone.

He winced as he recalled those had been Thorpe's words, almost exactly. Annalise did not belong to anyone. She was no man's property, and no man could claim her. He wanted her for himself, but he could never call her his. There was no possession involved.

No matter how strongly he felt it.

Because he was hers. Hers to command, to destroy, to push away.

He was not going anywhere.

And he refused to sit by and do nothing.

So he had done the only thing he could think of. He had written to his friends.

He didn't like to trouble them, particularly with something so personal, but among them were the best and most able minds in England, in his opinion. Not to mention wealth, power, and prestige. He had asked them to come in the morning to discuss an urgent matter, and had left it at that. It was best not to reveal anything until they were here in person.

He wouldn't sleep tonight. How could he, with so much at stake and so much unknown? He would sit in this room until he knew what to do. Or until his friends did. But they would not come until the morning, and by then he should have…

"Duncan?"

Blearily his raised his eyes to the open door, and his eyes surely deceived him.

Standing there in his home were Nathan, Derek, Geoffrey, and Colin, all looking as if they had been preparing for bed, with no waistcoats or cravats, yet awake and alert.

"What are you doing here?" he asked, dropping his hand to his desk.

Derek raised a brow and a half smile. "After the cryptic nature of your note? Kate practically shoved me out the door."

The rest nodded, save for Colin, who grinned raffishly. "I was just getting in myself, so I thought, why not?" Then he sobered and tilted his head a touch. "Did you really think we would wait until morning when you said it was urgent?"

He swallowed a surprising amount of emotion. "You didn't have to come."

Nathan snorted and entered the study, taking a seat. "Of course, we did. You would do the same for us."

It was true, he would. But he would never expect his friends to. Not for him.

But for Annalise…

He gestured to them to sit, and pinched the bridge of his nose. There was so much to say. So much to do. So much…

"Duncan."

He looked up at Geoffrey, who nodded in encouragement. "Start from the beginning. What happened?"

He released a slow breath, and told them of the goings on of the day. He left out the note from the Gent, feeling it was irrelevant to the matter at hand, but he shared with them the history between Annie and Albert Thorpe. As he had expected, his friends were nearly as livid as he had been. Some asked questions, but for the most part they sat brewing in fury.

"I wish the man had killed him," Geoff said in a voice Duncan had never heard from his calm and most gentlemanlike friend. "That would have solved all the problems."

The others nodded, though each seemed surprised the words had come from Geoff.

"I've thought about it over and over again," Duncan told them, "and killing him, though desirable, would not have been wise. We don't know anything about Thorpe or what his connections are. His mysterious death might have caused more problems for Annalise, not to mention the man who stopped him."

"True, I suppose," Nathan grumbled, leaning back in his chair. "So our first act should be to find out everything we can about Thorpe."

Derek leaned forward, rubbing his hands together slowly. "Do we know where he is from?"

Duncan shook his head. "Annalise didn't know. Her brother kept most things regarding the men he brought in silent. But we could start with connections in Yorkshire."

Derek nodded, his jaw firm. "I can take care of that."

"And I will see what is known of him in London," Colin volunteered with a hand raise. "I've lived here fourteen, nearly fifteen years, and my connections here are better than most people can boast."

Geoff gave him a look. "Do we want to know what they are?"

Colin offered a cheeky grin. "Probably not, you might become scandalized and never recover."

Duncan smiled and shook his head.

"What about the man in the alley?" Nathan asked, looking at Duncan. "Do we know anything about him?"

Fleetingly, Duncan considered telling him what he knew, but something held him back. He had never mentioned the notes regarding Marianne before, and how could he reveal what he knew about a man he didn't know very much about? This man was useful to him, how would he feel about a betrayal of this kind?

"He didn't give Annalise any information," he said carefully, "only that she could trust him."

"Well, thank God for that," Nathan replied, sitting back and rubbing his eyes. "All right, what can I do? I have very few connections in London, but I would be happy to put forth money or my name if it helps."

"And I," Geoff agreed.

Duncan chewed his lip for a moment. "I would not put it past Thorpe to hold a very strong vendetta against Annalise for this. He may try to discredit her, if not harm her again."

Geoff shook his head. "If he cannot have her, no one can."

Duncan laughed without humor. "Something like that, yes."

"Well, what can we do?"

"Proof," Colin said, growing somber. "We need proof that she is who we claim she is."

"I was afraid of that," Duncan murmured, putting his head into his hands on the desk before him.

Derek folded his arms and leaned back against the wall behind him. "Remind me what Tibby claimed about her."

"She is a niece of her late husband from his previous marriage," Duncan recited, his words muffled by his hands.

"Ah ha," Colin said with a nod and a straight face. "Now I remember. And which husband?"

Duncan dropped his hands and glared at Colin. "Rupert. The late Lord Moulton."

"Moulton…" Nathan mused thoughtfully. "And the current Lord Moulton is…?"

"A cousin, I think." Duncan frowned as he thought about it. Rupert had been dead for ten years, and had been quite reclusive, so there was no way to tell for certain. "I believe the family was from Kent. Tibby says they have all sorts of strange relations."

Nathan nodded. "That sounds correct, if my memory serves. I'll look into it. Perhaps the current lord might help us out."

Duncan waved his hand dismissively. "It doesn't matter. If we can find any sort of relation with mystery, we can claim her. If the family was as reclusive as Rupert, no one will know."

"But what do we do about Thorpe?" Geoff asked looking around.

Duncan glowered and wished he were not so much a gentleman. "We watch. And we wait. He does not breathe without us knowing,"

"One thing must be stated, I think," Derek said slowly, looking thoughtful.

Whether out of respect or habit, all of them looked at the young marquess instantly.

His green eyes flashed. "Annalise does not go anywhere alone. Ever."

Duncan swallowed and nodded. He had vowed that silently himself hours ago, but had doubts that he was being too protective. It was comforting to hear someone else say it. And it kept his secret for a while longer.

He was not ready to let them know.

Then again, as he looked around at them all, perhaps they already knew.

They didn't leave until the sun had risen, as they had discussed how they would go about their respective tasks, how they could assist each other, how much they should tell their wives, and ultimately, how they could help Annalise. Each man had taken responsibility for some part, and they would report back as soon as they had information that could help the group.

Duncan could not have expressed to his friends what their immediate action and attention had meant to him. He literally couldn't find the words to do so, and it wasn't in his nature to speak of such things.

Colin was the last to leave, hanging back and letting the others have their say and farewells. He waited until the door had closed behind Geoff completely before turning to Duncan with a rare look of serious appraisal.

"What?" Duncan asked after the moment had become too uncomfortable.

"Some three years ago," he said in a low voice, his eyes flicking to the closed door, "I began receiving letters from a source regarding my brother. Initially, they were not signed. They arrived without warning or cause, and did so irregularly at best."

Duncan fought the urge to stiffen as he heard the all-too-familiar tale. How was it possible that their siblings, however inextricably tied to each other in rumor, also had the same informant?

Colin continued to watch him carefully. "I didn't investigate at first. I was content to know what was being said about my brother, and if the context was of legitimate concern. And although I never knew the reasoning behind these letters, they were always respectful and considerate. Then I became curious, and, by my nature, I don't let anything go easily."

That, at least, was true. Duncan was not a curious individual and was content to let things progress on their own. But Colin, for all his lightness, had a will and drive that could not have been broken by any earthly means. When he wanted something, he made it his.

"The informant caught on to my own investigation," he continued, one side of his mouth quirking in a hint of a smile. "He had been impressed by my efforts and my own collection of informants, but he encouraged me... insisted, really... that I desist investigating him. Something about safety and security of others being at risk. All I would have would be a manner to reach him and his code name. I believe you are also acquainted with this man."

Colin smirked as he held out a sliver of paper with two words written on it. The Gent.

Duncan nodded, knowing his expression showed his shock.

Colin turned and burned the slip of paper on a nearby candle. "It seems, then, that I may be able to offer a bit of additional help in our investigation."

"So it appears," Duncan said, attempting the same calm tone, but having to cough in his surprise.

His friend winked at him. "Trust me, Duncan. Our friend is

already on it. If I know him, and I feel I do by now, he doesn't let things go either." Colin clapped him on the back and showed himself out, leaving Duncan to stare after him in stunned bewilderment.

All this time the Gent had been communicating with Colin as well? What investment did he have in their siblings? In their lives?

What madness brought him across Annalise's path just in time?

He sank back into his chair, rubbing his face. There was too much to do, too much to consider. His mind didn't have the capacity to fully comprehend all of this.

"What was Colin doing here?"

The soft, sweet voice broke into the murkiness of his thoughts and he looked up to see Annalise in the doorway. Apparently, Colin was incapable of shutting doors. Not that Duncan minded, for Annalise was a vision this morning.

Her hair was loosely braided, long strands hanging free, and she was still in her night gown, her wrap cinched tightly around her tiny waist. She had dark circles under her eyes, which meant her rest had been fitful at best. But he would have guessed that without seeing her, for it was too early for waking, even for her.

He smiled and rose from his chair, coming around the desk. "Colin is helping me with something."

Annalise might have been quiet and shy, but she was no fool. She gave him a look. "About me?" she asked, though he could see there was no question.

He would not lie to her.

"Yes," he replied, taking her hand in his and looking at the bruises on her wrist.

Her eyes remained on him. "Were all of your friends here?"

He nodded, tracing the discolorations with a finger.

"Duncan, I don't want anyone to go to any trouble for me."

He raised his eyes to hers and hoped she could see the intensity that burned within him. "I understand that," he explained softly, holding her gaze steady. "But what you have to understand, Annalise, is that there are people who care about you and we are not going to let this stand. We will go to great lengths for you, regardless of whether you want it or not."

"But…"

"I didn't ask them to come in the middle of the night," he gently overrode, increasing his hold on her just slightly. "I had asked for them to come to me today so we might discuss what we could do to help you, what needed to be done to protect you. Do you know what happened?"

She shook her head slowly, swallowing.

He smiled. "They came immediately, the moment they received my note."

Her lips parted in shock.

He gave her a slow nod. "They are my friends, Annalise. My best friends. But they did not come for me. Do you really think they would let this go? That they would let you be treated this way and not act?"

She shook her head quickly, a few tears trickling down her cheeks. "I don't deserve it."

He touched a finger to her lips, his eyes warning her. "That's enough," he murmured.

She nodded, closing her eyes for a long moment. When her eyes opened once more, he smiled and cupped her cheek.

"I've told them they can share with their wives what they see fit. I hope that is all right with you."

"Of course," she said, a faint smile. "I think they would receive mortal injuries if they didn't."

He chuckled and stroked her bruised cheek. It looked so much worse today, yet she barely winced. "I don't want you to worry anymore, Annalise," he told her. "We will handle this. I will handle this."

"I know," she whispered, gently gripping his wrist. "I trust you."

Duncan felt as though his heart had burst inside his chest and everything had now caught fire. He gently brought her to him, put his arms around her, and pressed his lips to her forehead, his mouth dancing across her hairline. "Thank you," he breathed against her skin.

She wrapped her arms about his waist and leaned into him, releasing a small sigh.

How long they stood there as such, he didn't know, nor did he care.

He had never been more content.

Only when she stirred did he release her. She appeared flustered, though no blush appeared on her cheeks. He smiled at her shyness.

"Aren't you tired?" he asked softly.

She nodded, tucking a loose strand behind her ear. "I didn't sleep well."

"Go back to bed, Annalise," he murmured, his eyes warm. "No more worries."

She returned his smile, and nodded jerkily as she turned from his study, glancing back at him as she did so.

When she had gone, he released a heavy breath and returned to his desk. There was much to do, and not much time to do it in.

It was not long after that a soft knock came at his open door. The surprises of the morning were not over, for there stood Tibby, in nightgown and wrap, her hair plaited carefully, eyes bright.

"Tibby?" There was no hiding his surprise, and he waved her in.

She did not smile, but came in and shut the door behind her. "Duncan, I need to speak to you."

He set down his pen and sat back. "Go ahead."

She nodded, but did not speak for a long moment. Then she released a quick breath and met his eyes. "Duncan, I think you have feelings for Annalise."

He prided himself on not reacting. He knew his aunt well, she had known for some time there was something there. For whatever reason, she had chosen to keep that to herself. Until now. "Do I?" he asked simply.

"I have been up half of the night thinking about Annalise, about what happened, about you... I suspected some attachment, but I know you have feelings for her. And I think you know it as well."

He looked at her steadily for a moment. "I think you are right, Tibby," he replied, keeping his voice low.

She raised a brow. "Am I?"

"Yes," he answered with a nod. "But you are mistaken as well. I don't just have feelings for Annalise." He broke off for a soft laugh. "That would put a paltry name to it."

"Tell me," she pleaded, sitting in the chair next to him.

He released a sigh and looked up at the ceiling, as if it could help him describe it. "She is the sun," he finally said. "She is the first fresh air in spring. She makes the morning begin anew and tosses the stars into the sky at night with her bare hands. Nothing beautiful was ever created without her in mind."

"Duncan?" Her voice was tinged with wonder and emotion.

He looked at his beloved aunt and smiled. "I love her, Tibby."

For the first time he could recall, he saw her eyes glimmer with tears. She smiled again and pressed a kiss to his hand. She did not speak, but she rose and left the room, quietly shutting the door behind her, winking at him as she did.

He could not help but smile. As bad as things were at the moment, as complicated as they would undoubtedly get, in this moment, he could not help but to smile.

He was a man in love.

And that was something to smile about indeed.

Scant days later, he was far from smiling once more.

"So I really think it would be in our best interest to keep an eye on Thorpe," Derek said as he gripped the back of his neck. "He is dangerous and, while I don't know his connections in London, I do not doubt they are less than savory, regardless of their standing."

Duncan nodded slowly, not saying a word. So far the reports from his friends were not good. The information obtained from Derek's connections painted Thorpe as a hard, cruel man with moderate fortune, means, and a dark history that he shuddered to remember. There was no way Annalise could be with him, willingly or otherwise. She would never last. Thorpe's associations were mostly mercenary, hardly reputable, and it seemed he enjoyed being the most powerful man in any given society.

Which did not explain why he was in London, as he was a bottom dweller there.

Why on earth would Annalise's brother condone such a

marriage? The only connection between the two men that Derek had been able to dig up had been the purchase of a horse from Frank Ramsey. That hardly seemed the sort of relationship that would lead to auctioning off his sister. But Duncan had given up trying to understand either of these men. If one could dare call them such.

They had not been successful with Lord Moulton or finding a familial connection to tie Annalise to. The family had enough trouble with their legitimate offspring, they could not afford to adopt anyone else, no matter how influential their friends were. And no other sentient relatives could be found. The rest had fled to the continent.

Duncan rubbed at his eyes and sighed heavily. They were running out of options.

"His London connections are much worse," Colin spoke up with what sounded like a wince in his voice.

"How much worse can it get?" Duncan asked, shifting to dig the heels of his hands into his eyes. Sleep had not been his ally since the attack. He was surprised to still be sitting upright.

Colin sighed and avoided Duncan's eyes. "My sources tell me that Thorpe is a notorious and ruthless gambler, and ruthless when he does so. There are rumors of his being a cheat, but no one has been able to prove it. He has allies throughout the city, in all areas both high and low. And the low can get very low. The high… well, they're not the sort of persons we would deem worthy of their station. There have been ties to financial ruin, moral ruin, even death. His depravity knows no end." Colin shook his head and rubbed at his own eyes. "I would not be surprised if he shared with the world what he knows about Annalise and her true background, to shame her out of Society and then to claim her for his own."

"That's not going to happen," Duncan growled, his fists clenching at his side.

"I also," Colin continued quietly, still not looking at him, "would not put it past him to have her abducted. What he wants, he gets. Whatever it takes."

"Not this time," Nathan muttered as he folded his arms over his chest. "Not even if we have to take shifts sleeping outside of her room and at her window."

They all nodded in near unison.

"So what do we do?" Duncan asked his friends as he looked around the room.

None of them had any answers for him. Truly, what was there to do? He ought to have wished she had never come across his path, that he had never known her.

But he couldn't.

His life would have been a bleak and boring stretch of monotony without her light in it.

Then Geoffrey shifted uncomfortably in his seat and Duncan shifted his gaze to him. Geoff wetted his lips, swallowed harshly, and looked at the floor, his hands almost imperceptibly gripping at his trousers.

"Geoff?" Duncan murmured softly.

Geoff seemed to twitch and continued to look at a floor. "I think," he began very slowly, very uncertainly, "that there is a solution we have not addressed as yet."

"Go on," Nathan urged, when Geoff did not continue.

"I think it would protect Annalise," he said in the same careful tone, "and would give us some extra time."

"So what is it?" Derek asked, looking confused by Geoff's behavior.

Geoffrey took a deep breath, then seemed to brace himself. "I think an engagement would solve it. It forces an alliance and an attachment that wards people off and ensures protection."

"An engagement?" Colin asked in surprise, looking around the room. "To whom?"

Geoff's eyes went to the wall beside him. "To Duncan."

Duncan closed his eyes as the room erupted with the protests of his friends. He had known that was the only solution, he had reached that conclusion hours ago. But he could not have suggested it, he was desperate that it should be avoided at all costs. It would take away Annalise's newfound freedom, it would force her to claim an attachment that didn't exist, and it was an action that would ensure that she would never actually fall in love with him. It would be a connection for her safety, security, and convenience. It was not for love.

It was the best and surest form of his heart's destruction.

"How can you even suggest such a thing?" Nathan roared, probably on his feet and pacing, as he was wont to do. "Duncan is already her sworn protector and everybody knows it. Why put them both through a false engagement? And it would be false in every sense, there would be no marriage, I would refuse to force that upon either of them."

"And what about Annalise?" Derek cried, no doubt shoving his hands into his hair and disheveling it, as was his way. "She deserves a man who chooses her of his own will and heart, not by force of situation! We protect her by taking away her freedom to choose? Are you mad?"

"Worst idea ever," Colin managed, his voice half gone. He, at least, seemed in control of himself. Duncan cracked open his eyes to see him sitting where he had been, looking at Geoffrey with disgust and horror. That was, in point of fact, purely Colin too.

Geoff took his friends' reactions calmly and held up a hand. "Don't you think I've thought of all of that? Do you really think I would suggest such a drastic thing if it were not necessary? Nathan, you just suggested we take turns sleeping outside of her bedroom and at her window. We are desperate."

"Not that desperate!" Nathan muttered.

"Yes," Geoff replied seriously, "we are."

"No," Colin said emphatically, shaking his head. "No, no, no. You are not allowed to suggest any further ideas, Geoffrey. From here on out, you are purely decorative."

Geoff huffed in disgust. "Well, I don't see you suggesting anything, Colin. If you have a solution that does not involve somebody dying or being abducted or being forced into a false engagement, I will gladly hear it."

"Give me some time, and I will create something," Colin assured him with a hint of a snarl. "And something far better than that."

"Time is something we do not have," Derek said quietly, releasing a heavy sigh.

It was time for him to say something. And it was something he knew he would regret for the rest of his life. He opened his eyes slowly and looked directly at Geoff.

"I'll do it."

It seemed the entire room stilled and nobody breathed. And then everything exploded. Distinguishing who was crying out what protest was impossible, it was just a cacophony of sounds bombarding his ears. He held up a hand and they all settled down. Only Geoff looked contented.

"I will do it," he said slowly. "Once I explain things to Annalise, I am sure she will consent as well."

"Duncan, no," Nathan said firmly, shaking his head.

Duncan felt a growl of his own protest rising in his chest. "I don't see you coming up with any feasible ideas, as much as we've tried and as much as we know. And this way we can surely protect her. If she agrees, then we will do it. And we'll do the whole thing. The ring, the ball, the dress fittings... No one must suspect it isn't real..." He trailed off, his heart thudding against his chest faintly at the imitation of what he really wanted.

Nathan slowly shook his head again. "This might break her."

Duncan swallowed hard. He knew that. He knew it all too well.

He also knew she would not be the only broken one.

He sighed and looked around at his friends. "Pray with all your might that it saves her instead."

Chapter Eighteen

Annalise sat at her toilette, her hands shaking and folded tightly in her lap. Downstairs in the ballroom, dozens, maybe even hundreds of people were gathering to celebrate her engagement.

She snorted and clutched her fingers more tightly. Engagement. She was no more engaged than she was a wealthy heiress. She was a fraud, an imposter, a prisoner of her wildest hopes and dreams, doomed to never see them fulfilled.

It was becoming the most painful sort of nightmare.

Duncan had explained everything to her four days ago, and she thought she recalled him asking if she agreed with the plan, which she supposed was the only proposal she would ever get. But there had been no question. They were determined to help her, to save her, in their estimation, and this was the only way they could do it. And she was determined to have Duncan in whatever way she could, and this cheap imitation of an attachment would be as close as she would ever come. So she said yes, and they were off making plans and spreading the word. Occasionally she was consulted, but for the most part, all things were now out of her hands.

Tibby had been appointed host of their engagement ball, though her home was not appropriately furnished yet. Therefore, they were using the new ballroom at the home of the Marquess of Whitlock, and Derek and Kate were sure to throw quite the soirée for them.

Faintly, it had occurred to Annalise to wonder why.

Oh, she knew very well that Duncan insisted everything appear real and sincere, so that Thorpe could never disprove it. There had been no legal documents declaring his claim on her, so there was no way to prove his tale should he have made it public. But he had not.

Yet.

He had attempted to communicate with her further, but she was always accompanied by one of the men when she was out, if not more than one. Notes had been delivered to her in his fidgety scrawl, and she had gone to Duncan with his threats. But he had merely laughed them off and assured her that they were not legitimate, that he could not get to them, nor did he have any power.

She wished he would not be so confident. He didn't know Thorpe as she did.

But she couldn't get a moment alone with him.

When they were on display as the newly engaged couple, he was charming and complimentary, adoring and admiring, and the perfect fiancé. But when out of view, he would remove himself and become reclusive, leaving her alone with Marianne or Tibby for entertainment, though neither seemed particularly inclined. They were so busy with "wedding preparations" that she, the supposed bride, would be in their way.

Marianne's inhibitions about Annalise being in Society had apparently vanished in the face of her imminent danger and protective false engagement to her brother, at which she had not even batted one of her long eyelashes. She suspected there would have been quite the protest had the attachment been legitimate, but as there had been repeated assurances that it would come to no fruition, no complaints had been put forth.

They were so eager to assure her that no one would go through with the engagement and marriage that no one ever asked her what she wanted. It never even occurred to anyone that she might want just what they were suggesting.

But then, regardless of what they all pretended, she was not one of them.

She never would be.

She glanced down at the delicate ring on her finger that served as her engagement ring. It was simple, but elegant, and it was exactly what she would have wanted for herself. An aged golden color with an emerald gem at its center and scattered imitation diamonds encircling it. It caught the light in a beautiful way and was not so elaborate that it would draw attention unless one looked for it.

It had been given to her by Duncan without ceremony before their first venture out as engaged, and for a brief moment her breath had caught, but then he had instructed her to smile and put his arm tightly around her as people began to approach.

She had cried for hours that night in the silence of her room.

And she had cried many tears since.

But tonight she was expected to glow for all to see, apparently so in love that she would cut her first and only Season short to marry the man of her dreams.

No one must see her pain.

Especially not Duncan.

She heard the soft knock at her door and shook herself from her reverie. "Come in," she called softly, heart pounding.

Mary entered with a smile, looking radiant. "Annalise, dear."

Annalise managed a smile that ought to have appeared carefree. "You look lovely!"

Mary smiled and gave a playful curtsey. "So my husband informed me, but the man has a very skewed perception."

"Not at all," Annalise corrected, shaking her head and feeling the way her hair bounced as she did so. Her maid had spent ages on it and she was very much afraid the whole thing would tumble down if even one pin was removed.

"I think you should look at yourself," Mary said as she came closer. "You are a vision."

Annalise glanced at the long mirror in the corner, eerily identical to the mirror in her dream from so long ago. And it so happened the dress was the very same shade it had been there, the color of a pleasant blush on palest cheeks, with the faintest golden shimmer. Her hair, as far as she could tell, was also nearly the same, elegantly curled and elaborately coifed. But her feelings were so different that she couldn't bear to see it. It would forever haunt her.

"I think not," she murmured, her voice shaking a touch. "It will only make me more nervous if I know what I look like. Only tell me, is it enough?"

"Enough for what?" Mary asked in a soft tone, taking her hand.

Annalise swallowed and forced herself to smile as if all was right. "Enough to convince them that I am a woman truly engaged?"

Mary's eyes told her she was not convinced, but her smile stayed fixed. "More than that, Annalise. You will convince the world that you are a woman in love."

Tears burned her eyes almost violently, but she forced them back and nodded. "Good. Then I am ready to go down."

Mary helped her stand and took her down the hall and to the stairs. "Duncan is waiting for you," she whispered. "I must go in and wait for your grand entrance. Come find me if you need anything. I know all of the secret ways out."

"Thank you," she murmured, squeezing her hand.

Mary winked and gracefully descended the stairs, her elegant, silver silk grazing the steps in soft whispers of sound.

Annalise swallowed hard and rested her shaking hand on the railing. She had never thought herself much of an actress, but tonight she must be a consummate professional one. No one must know.

Slowly, as carefully as she could manage, she made her way down, catching sight of Duncan waiting by the ballroom doors. For all his boasting of being an oaf, he truly was a glorious sight when dressed so fine. His secret love of finery delighted her, though she knew the underlying intent was to prove to the world that he belonged. Here they were, the two of them, so desperate to fit in when they felt they could not.

Except he truly did.

She did not.

But she would remember this moment, and how handsome he looked, the very image of a gentleman personified. What any sensible woman would give to be attached to such a man, if only for a short time.

If only for a night.

He turned when the sound of her shoes reached him and the look on his face caused her heart to pummel her ribs so strongly she couldn't breathe.

She wished he wouldn't look at her that way.

It would give her reason to hope.

She saw him swallow and then he came to her side quickly, shaking his head as if to clear it. "There you are," he murmured, taking her hand and kissing it.

Through the fabric of the glove she felt the heat and she shivered.

He noticed, too. His eyes met hers and turned a shade darker. "Are you ready?" he asked, his voice lower still.

She released a sigh. "As ready as I'll ever be, I suppose."

One side of his mouth curved upwards and he winked. "You will be perfect. No more worry."

She nodded, a lump rising in her throat. If only his words were true.

He turned to the doors, still holding her hand tightly. He gave a nod to the footmen, who grandly opened the doors and all within the ballroom turned and gasped with pleasure and awe, applauding as they entered. Annalise smiled as if this were all real, as if she really were the woman they thought, truly engaged to the man beside her, and fully intending to marry him. Duncan squeezed her hand and led her into the center of the ballroom.

She had forgotten they were to open the dancing and her heart sped up frantically.

Duncan must have felt the pulse in her wrist, for his thumb stroked it softly and she met his eyes. "Trust me," he whispered, his eyes warm and his smile kind.

She offered him that soft smile he seemed to enjoy, and sure enough, he inhaled sharply, his smile turning into something else.

The music struck up and he swept her through the motions of the dance perfectly. They kept their eyes on each other the entire time, and it was only his steadiness that kept her feet moving through the steps. There were no mistakes, not from either of them. The room disappeared and they might as well have been back in his drawing room practicing, only there were no nerves now. This was easy, this was natural, this was perfect.

All too soon, it was over and they were back to being applauded and congratulated. She expected Duncan to let her go and ignore her for the remainder of the evening, as had been his pattern, but he didn't release her hand. When the musicians began again he shockingly led her back into the form, taking place with the other couples.

"Again?" she asked in surprise.

He shrugged. "Why not?"

"It's not fashionable or proper," she hissed, looking around at the stunned faces.

"Says who?" he asked, giving her a grin. "I am only dancing with my new betrothed, what could be more fashionable or proper than that?" He winked boldly and her knees turned to porridge, but somehow she managed to smile.

Her heart had never felt lighter and she laughed as they danced together, in perfect harmony with the other couples, who were also delighted by the dance. It was lively and energetic, and though she was not as comfortable with the steps, she found she didn't care. She caught sight of Marianne on one side, and was relieved to see her smiling in her direction. Then she became surrounded with admirers, and Annalise could not see her.

But she had seen the smile.

Perhaps all would be well after all.

When this dance finished, Duncan led her away towards the refreshments. "Would you like a drink?" he offered.

"Please," she replied, her face still flushed from the dance. "I could die of thirst."

He chuckled and handed her a glass. "Well, drink up, then. I think you shall be dancing much of the night, and you will need your strength."

"I have never been a dancer," she said on a sigh, turning to face the room and smiling absently. "But I do enjoy it."

"I am pleased to hear it," he said softly, taking her hand. "So. Who will you dance with next?"

She snorted and shook her head. "You think I am in a position to be selective? I am perfectly agreeable to everyone tonight."

"Not everyone, surely," he laughed, setting his drink aside.

She considered his words and looked up at him mischievously. "Very well, you're right. I shall do my utmost to avoid dancing with Mr. Harrison Tarlingen."

"Shall you?" Duncan asked, sounding rather amused and quirking a brow. "And why is that?"

"Because his ability to entertain is outstripped by the trouble of concocting intelligent thought."

Duncan coughed a surprised laugh into his fist and took several moments to regain composure. "Oh my," he finally coughed, still smiling. "A little bit of bite to go with that bark, eh?"

"I never bark," she informed him in her best Tibby impression. She waited a beat, and then continued, "Snarl, perhaps, but never bark."

He grinned at her and looked so pleased that she could not even manage to find the apology she had begun to formulate. For Mr. Tarlingen was a kind man, even if he was abysmally tiresome.

"That was rather harsh," she giggled, looking at the man in question as he attempted dancing with poor Gemma Templeton.

Duncan hummed a delighted sound. "I thought it was rather accurate, actually. And far kinder than I could have said. Perhaps I should save Gemma."

"Perhaps you should."

It proved unnecessary, as Colin was suddenly there and saving her himself.

Both of them burst into laughter and did their best to hide it from the rest of the room, but Annalise turned and used Duncan's size to hide herself.

"Oh, I cannot breathe for laughing," she gasped, clutching at her chest.

"I wonder if you have any idea how adorable you are."

Her laughter died at the low, heated words rumbling in the chest of the man beside her. She glanced up at him to find his eyes fixed intensely on her, raking across her features, never missing a single pore of her skin. She blushed and looked away, tucking her chin down.

"No, no, look at me," he whispered, touching her chin. "Don't hide."

She forced herself to look up at him, cheeks pink.

His smile was soft and tender. "I know you're embarrassed, Annalise, but you shouldn't be. And you should never hide your eyes. I will always want to see them when I say something that pleases you or when you are amused. If only you could see how they dance."

She smiled, still embarrassed. "You are kind."

Duncan laughed softly. "I am rarely kind, but I am always truthful."

"Always?" she asked suspiciously, hoping to tease him out of his serious tone.

His head gave the briefest, slowest nod. "Always. And now I will truthfully say that you are beautiful."

Her cheeks flamed once more. "You're biased," she protested.

"But I am not blind." He took her hand and raised it to his lips. But instead of kissing the back, he pressed a hot kiss into her gloved palm, sending shivers of heat through her frame.

Her breath vanished and her knees shook beneath her skirts.

His eyes were like flames of cobalt blue, scorching every inch of her, though they had not moved from her face. He didn't seem steady either, his chest beginning to heave. "Annalise," he rasped, her hand still so close to his mouth she could feel his breath.

"Begging your pardon, Miss Remington, but might I trouble you for this dance?"

Annalise dazedly looked over at Lord... What was his name? ... He was married to Derek's sister, she knew that, but at the moment she barely knew her own name, let alone his. Duncan stepped back and released her hand, apparently as cool as cucumber.

"Of course," she managed, smiling for whoever it was. "It will be my pleasure."

He held out his hand and she set hers in it, allowing herself to be led. She wanted desperately to look back at Duncan, but knew she would have no composure left if she did.

So she would dance with this gentleman, and the next, and the next, until her heart and her mind could agree once more.

Duncan moved for the terrace as fast as his feet could while not actually running in a crowded ballroom. He watched Annalise dance her dance with Lord Beckham, knowing she was safe with him, but still feeling his pains of jealousy. He had barely managed to avoid actually declaring himself to her in the middle of their engagement ball.

False engagement, he reminded himself. He was not actually engaged to her.

Now she was dancing with someone else, and he could not bear it. She was too beautiful, too lovely, too sweet. He felt too much, burned too much, wanted too much. He was becoming an animal, incapable of concise thought or concrete feeling. He was simply a burning mass of sinew and limb, impersonating a controlled man.

And the vaunted control was fast unraveling before him.

"Where are you headed so fast?" Colin asked as he caught up to him.

"Air," he panted, his mind and body whirling independent of each other, senses all on alert.

"Oh dear. Are you going to be ill?"

"Too warm."

"You are? Is the room too warm?" His friend actually gasped. "Good heavens, are you going to faint?"

"Need... air..."

He burst outside and moved to the very edge of the terrace, gripping the railing tightly, his breathing rapid and heavy.

Colin came to stand beside him. "I say, are you quite well?"

He shook his head. "No. And yes."

Colin snorted. "Thank you so much for clearing that up."

Duncan swallowed, clenching his eyes shut. "I've never felt worse. But I've never felt so alive."

"Oh, well, that is much better."

A growl and a sigh combined in his chest. "You don't understand what this feels like."

"Apparently, neither do you."

He lashed out and gripped Colin's shirt tightly. "Go away."

"Excuse me?"

He pried his eyes open and looked at his friend, unmoving in his hold. "I am fraying at the edges. Either distract me or go away."

Colin glanced back into the ballroom, then back at him. "Annalise is dancing with Lord Oliver."

He tossed his friend aside, not caring if he stumbled or not. "AWAY, Colin!"

He heard no response for a moment, which was always suspicious where Colin was concerned. And then, "Saints above... You're in love with her."

He laughed without humor. "Caught on, have you?"

"I... I..." Colin stammered, which was shocking in and of itself. Colin never stammered.

"You what?" Duncan asked slowly, still gripping the railing.

"I have no words."

He did not expect that reply. He turned to look at Colin in surprise.

Colin looked rather bewildered himself.

"No words?" Duncan repeated. "You?"

"I know." Colin shook his head in astonishment. "But for the first time since any of you have fallen or thought yourself fallen, I have nothing flippant to say."

Duncan barked a laugh. "I appreciate that."

"You should," his friend said, sounding more serious than Duncan had ever heard. Colin briefly glanced into the ballroom where Annalise could be seen dancing, then looked back at his friend, his eyes somber. "And for pity's sake, man, make her yours as soon as you can manage. Bad things happen when men in love wait."

Duncan slowly raised a brow at him. "You speak from experience?"

Colin's expression changed back to his typical carefree one. "Of course. Three of my best friends have been turned into complete imbeciles over love. I have seen quite enough."

But there was something in Colin's eyes that showed a surprising darkness, a haunting, hollow look that was ill-suited to all Colin had ever been.

He wanted to ask on it, but Duncan had never been a man who interfered in another's business without cause. Curiosity was not good enough. And Colin was obviously loathe to discuss whatever it was.

Duncan pushed off of the railing and looked back into the ballroom with a sigh. Then he grinned and started forward, adjusting his cravat more perfectly.

"What are you doing?" Colin asked, sounded as worried as he was curious.

"I am going to dance with my betrothed," he informed him, as if that was obvious. Really, it should have been. Who would not want to dance with her when she was clearly the most beautiful creature in existence, let alone in that ballroom?

And he loved her.

More than anything he ever felt in his life, he knew he loved her.

And suddenly, nothing else mattered.

"You cannot possibly do that!" Colin gasped, hurrying behind him.

"Why not?" he laughed as he neared the doors.

Colin put a hand on the handles to keep him from entering. "You have already danced with her twice and we have not been here above an hour. A third time would be cause for comment. I am telling you, Duncan, you cannot dance with her again."

Duncan leveled a mischievous grin at his friend and felt the animal within him sneer. "Watch me," he growled, shoving his hand aside and re-entering the crowded room, his gaze and his intent both evident for all to see.

Chapter Nineteen

*T*hree days later, Annalise was miserably plunking out notes on the pianoforte, reveling in being alone with her distress. The ball had been the most exciting thing that had ever happened to her, and Duncan had been wonderful. For a few hours, at least, she found herself wondering if he might actually care for her as more than a friend and protector. He had been ardent in his attention, both in view of the public and outside of it. He had surely convinced the world that they were well and truly engaged.

He had nearly convinced her.

But something must have happened towards the end of the evening, for he and all the other men had vanished and none of the women knew why. They had appeared not too long after it had been noticed, and all appeared distracted by something, but there was no explanation. Duncan was back to being the aloof version of himself that she had come to despise, and she had no more hint of that man from the ball.

She had gone shopping for a trousseau with Tibby and the girls, including Marianne, but she found no pleasure in it. The gowns were to be delivered in a week, all prepared for the nuptials that had no date.

She had heard that their explanation for not having set a date was waiting for word from her family on the continent, and everybody knew that could be a laborious enterprise. Especially given that her "family" were touring the whole of the area, so no one could be quite certain where exactly they were. Duncan assured everyone he would set a date the moment he had their approval.

He would never have her family's approval.

She shivered as she recalled the end of the ball. She thought she had seen Thorpe there, but Kate had assured her that the man had been barred from the event and would not be allowed in. Everyone seemed so sure they had prevented everything bad from happening.

It did absolutely nothing to keep the feeling of dread from invading her heart.

Albert Thorpe was far more dangerous and conniving than any of them thought.

And he would not be stopped.

She had received another letter from him this morning, but it had been more of a missive. Three words only on the scrap of paper: *I'm warning you.*

She had not shown this to Duncan, nor the four others she had received since the ball. She knew he would not take them seriously. How could he? He knew nothing about this man but what others had informed him. He did not know Thorpe like she did.

He feared nothing and no one.

He did not even know fear.

Her fingers were moving of their own accord now and she played a slower, more melancholy version of the song Marianne had taught her. It was odd how perfectly suited it was when played in such a way. It was as if her heart were playing its lonely, broken song through her fingertips.

She was not a skilled player, but the song was simple enough that it didn't matter. She was not playing for an audience, no one would hear but her, so it made no difference anyway.

When the song finished, she let her hands rest in her lap and released a heavy sigh.

"What's wrong?"

She closed her eyes in agony.

Duncan.

She swallowed hard and forced herself to keep her chin up. But she did not turn to see him. She couldn't, not when her emotions were so close to the surface.

"You've never played it like that before," he murmured, and she could hear him moving closer. "It was beautiful, but also the saddest thing I have ever heard. What can I do? How can I help?"

She would have laughed had the pain in his voice not broken her heart. "You've done everything, Duncan," she whispered, willing the quiver out of her voice. "I will be well enough."

"I don't want you do be 'well enough,'" he said, his voice directly behind her. "That's not acceptable."

She sniffed and looked down at her hands. "Well, it's the best I can do at the moment."

She heard him sigh. "Will you look at me? Please?"

Unable to deny him anything, she turned on the bench and faced him. The agony in his expression sent a wash of tears into her eyes, which only made things worse.

"What is it?" he pleaded, his voice low, as he brushed a leaked tear away.

"I'm afraid," she whispered as another tear fell.

He sunk to his haunches before her and took her hands. "Of what?"

She gave him a look. "Of what? Of... him! I can't... I cannot even say his name without trembling. I worry every day that I will see him and feel that fear. That he will hurt one of our friends or Tibby or you, and I can't bear to think..."

"Shh, no, no, no," he hushed, gently overriding, and squeezing her hands more tightly. "You don't have to fear anything, sweet. We have things well in hand, I promise you."

"He was at the ball, wasn't he?" she demanded on a hard swallow.

He released an irritated breath. "Somehow he made it through our security measures, but he was quickly removed. No harm done."

She laughed bitterly. "No harm done? Duncan, he is an evil man! And he is not as easily stopped as you all seem to think! Why won't you take this seriously?"

He looked surprised by her outburst. "We are."

She shook her head hastily. "No, you don't understand. None of you understand. He is the reason why I ran away from home. I could endure Frank and his beatings if I had to, I could live my miserable normality for as long as God wanted, content to ignore and be ignored by the rest of the world. But when he told me that I would basically be sold to that man, to have to legally endure whatever he saw fit to inflict upon me... I have never wanted to die more in my entire life."

"Annalise..."

She felt her chin quivering. "It couldn't be worse than what I was living. I didn't want to live like that, always fearing, always cowering..."

"What happened?"

She raised her eyes to meet his. "I met someone who changed my mind. Someone who made the idea of living not only a pleasant one, but a necessary one." Using every bit of bravery she had ever imagined herself to have, she pulled one of her hands from his hold to reach out and gently touch his barely stubbled cheek. "And I haven't looked back since."

His breath caught and his eyes widened at her touch. She saw his throat work at a swallow as she absently stroked his cheek again.

Then suddenly he surged forward, his now free hand diving into her hair and cupping the back of her head, dragging her mouth to his. His lips were hungry, nearly crazed in their energy, and her heart hummed with delight. Her hand moved of its own accord, grasping his face near his ear, her fingertips barely toying with his hair. She sighed against him, felt herself molding more perfectly against him, and whimpered when he broke off with a violent gasp. He quickly soothed her with the gentlest, softest of encores, then wrapped his arms around her and held her to him as both of their hearts tried to resume a more normal pattern.

"Have mercy," he whispered into her hair as he stroked her back. "I have almost no control with you."

She breathlessly laughed into his shoulder. He had no control? She was ready to come apart at the seams! "Am I supposed to apologize for that?" she asked, her voice muffled.

"Heavens, no," he chuckled, kissing her head. He swallowed and held her more tightly for a second, then released her and sat back on his haunches, eying her carefully, slight color in his cheeks. "You've not been as happy lately, have you?"

She knew she looked as surprised as she felt. "I have been very happy."

He raised a disbelieving brow. "Not as happy as before. This engagement is not very fun for you, is it?"

She bit her lip and shrugged one shoulder. "Has it been fun for you?"

He twisted his mouth to one side and hummed. "That is the problem then, isn't it? We need some fun." He stood and held out a hand to her.

She hesitated for a moment as she gave him a look. "What are we doing?" she asked as she trustingly put her hand in his.

He grinned and looked rather like a schoolboy. "It snowed last night. I think the back garden is still untouched. It seems a shame to not play in it."

"Play?" she asked slowly as he pulled her to her feet.

He gaped at her. "Have you never played in the snow?"

She shook her head, wondering how one even did such a thing.

He looked sad for a moment and stroked her cheek. "Then today will be long overdue, indeed. Go change into a warmer dress and your warmest coat and things. I will meet you at the kitchen door in fifteen minutes."

"All right," she said slowly, smiling at him curiously.

He winked, then bowed over her hand and kissed it politely, though the stroke of his thumb was not so polite. "You won't regret it, I promise."

He quirked his brow and strode away for the stairs.

Regret it? How could she ever regret a single moment she had spent with him? Her lips suddenly burned in memory, and she touched them with trembling fingers. Was this all really happening? To her?

She would not doubt it long enough to question, not when there were more moments to be had. She giggled and raced up the stairs to her bedchamber, excitement rising within her.

Minutes later, she was at the kitchen door, tamping down the urge to shift her weight like an excitable child. Duncan appeared in a coat and scarf, no hat on his head, but he held one in his hand, as well as another scarf.

She took it and looped it around her neck, then took his hand and let him lead her outside.

They walked and talked for what seemed ages, all lightheartedness and fun. He showed her how to build a man of snow, and took a great deal of care to educate her on the proper foundations and methods of the thing.

Annalise spent more time watching Duncan than anything else. Even when building a snowman, he was entirely focused and meticulous. Everything he did was with a purpose in mind, intent and alert, no hint of distraction. His brow would pucker ever so slightly when he was concentrating, and it was the most adorable sight in the world, and she felt her love for him grow yet again.

Suddenly, she needed to see him smile. She chewed her lip momentarily, pretending to consider her side of the snowman. Then she bent and scooped more snow, as if to add it to the snowman, and when he was not looking, she tossed it at Duncan. It rained down upon him as if from the sky and he looked at her in surprise.

His eyes narrowed. "Was that on purpose?"

She forced herself to look entirely innocent. "Was what on purpose?"

He hummed and gave her a serious look, then returned to his work.

Fighting back laughter, she scooped up more, only to feel a bit of snow hit her in the back. She reared up and gaped in shock, but Duncan only grinned.

Suddenly they were diving for snow, balling it up, and tossing it at each other. Duncan had some particularly excellent shots, but he was putting very little force behind them. Annalise was not as effective, but the ones she did land on him were fairly sharp. He began to run after her, pelting her with small snowballs, and she ran, lobbing some behind her as best as she could. She was far too busy laughing and running to aim carefully, and she heard his panting laughter from behind, so he was not accurate either.

She found herself quite unexpectedly grabbed from behind and tackled into a small snow bank, her laughter knocked out of her only momentarily. She struggled and rolled, taking him with her and they rolled for some time, snow scattering and finding all the crevices in her exposed skin. Eventually the rolling ceased and all that was left was the two of them side by side, laughing breathlessly. She turned her head and looked at him, only to find him smiling at her, his laughter fading.

Her breath caught at his expression. It was warm and open, joyful and admiring, and entirely captivating. She could have stared at him for years and never missed anything else. His eyes scanned her face, and he was no longer laughing, though his chest was still moving with far too much force.

She felt it, too, and knew she looked much the same. There was suddenly no air for either of them. She felt dizzy, warm, cold, numb, invigorated… So many emotions and sensations all at once that she could not tell where any started and ended.

Duncan reached out a hand and cupped her cheek, stroking it softly. He shook his head as if he couldn't believe what he was seeing. Which was a ridiculous notion, he was only staring at her.

But his look said as much as his kisses ever had.

Perhaps even more…

"Duncan! Whatever are you two doing? What are you thinking, taking Anne out of doors in this cold?"

Tibby's voice was both shrill and scolding, and broke the moment so perfectly that Annalise burst into helpless giggles.

Duncan grinned and tucked her into his chest, effectively stifling it against him. "Nothing, Tibby. Just having some fun in the snow," he called back, somehow managing to sound innocent and amused.

His aunt's huff could be heard from there. "Well, stop it and come inside at once! We have several engagements this evening that require you both to be properly thawed out!"

Annalise felt his hold on her tighten briefly and his chest seemed to buzz with restrained laughter. "Of course, Tibby. We shall be in momentarily!"

242

"I am having them build up the fire in the library and fetching some blankets!" she called, walking back to the house. "Honestly, the idiocy of men, what he was thinking…"

Once clear of her, they released their laughter fully. Duncan rose and helped her up, brushing snow off of her coat and dress, and she did the same with him. They avoided looking into each other's eyes, and for Annalise's part, she could not bear to think on what had just passed, and what might have been.

She suspected Duncan felt the same.

She shivered and felt pressure at her elbow. She looked up into Duncan's warm smile.

"Come on," he said, escorting her towards the house. "Tibby waits for no one. You'll be warm again soon."

"I hadn't even noticed," she murmured, blushing furiously.

Duncan cleared his throat, and the pressure at her elbow increased.

Duncan could not stop watching her. They were wrapped tightly in blankets and sitting before the fire in the library, and her gaze was intent upon the flames, but he could not look anywhere else. She was so breathtakingly beautiful it made his chest ache in a deep and profound way. Her hair was a bit mussed, her cheeks still rosy from being outside, and she was shivering so violently he could see it from where he sat.

He had never seen anything so lovely in his life.

He was beginning to feel warmer, but she had been shaking for several minutes now, and given her slight frame, he doubted that would change any time soon.

She had to know how he felt. She had to see it in his eyes, how he couldn't breathe, couldn't think, how his control was in shambles, and he was finding moments to be near her for no other reason than because it made him come to life to be close to her. He was so in love with her that his lips burned with the desire to tell her.

He had never in his life felt more empty than he had when she had spoken of Thorpe and her fears. He was overcome with relief that she was here with him, that he could protect her, that she had come into his life at all. All he wanted was her happiness, her safety, her well-being.

All he wanted was her.

He wished he knew how to tell her just what she meant to him. He wished he knew how to calm her fears. He wished...

"Come here," he said softly.

She glanced over at him, her teeth chattering. "W-what?"

He smiled and opened his blanket. "You are freezing, and it makes me cold to watch you shiver. Come over here and let me help you warm up."

"That sounds dangerous."

She had no idea.

His smile broadened. "Well, how brave are you?"

He'd meant to say, "how *cold* are you," but he chose not to correct himself. After all, he desperately wanted to know the answer to the question he had asked, not the one he meant to.

His favorite small smile appeared and suddenly she was hurrying over to him, her blanket wrapped tightly about her. She settled into his side and he instinctively wrapped his blanket around them both, fighting the gasp at how chilled she really was. She laid her cheek against his chest, directly over his pounding heart, and released the smallest of sighs.

He'd have been quite pleased to die at this moment, had he not thought the future before him could have given him more moments like this one, and perhaps even better.

If he were so fortunate.

"I am so tired," she whispered sleepily.

He pressed his lips against her chilled skin. "Go to sleep, love. I'll keep you safe and warm."

"I know," she replied faintly, her breathing deepening.

Duncan slowly rubbed circles on her back, staring absently into the fire before them. He settled himself more fully back against the sofa, careful not to disturb the precious cargo in his hold, and allowed himself to release a sigh of contentment.

He had been considering it for some time, but holding her in his arms in this moment, playing with her in the snow before, and hearing her deepest fears earlier, combined with everything he had been feeling and had kept pent up inside, proved to him just one thing: he had to have her. This false engagement of theirs had to become a real one.

What had begun as an enterprise to save her just might, in fact, have been the thing that saved him. What he thought would break him had instead inspired him. He could never have imagined what an engagement to Annalise would have felt like, and though theirs was false and all for show, his emotions were everything but.

Somehow, he would have to convince her to take a chance on him, to accept his hand in truth, not just for the public.

This was real for him. This was all there would be for him.

It would be her or no one.

Nothing.

He had to have her.

He pressed his lips to her hair, inhaled her sweet scent, and desperately wished for his heart's desire to be fulfilled.

Chapter Twenty

Annalise had never been so happy in her entire life. Dozing against Duncan, she was not only warm, but secure and content, two feelings she had hardly ever known. If she could have anything in her life, it would be to never leave this moment.

Pity they were disturbed.

"Pardon me, sir," an embarrassed maid murmured with a curtsey. "But Lady Raeburn bid me come and see if you were ready to change for dinner."

Duncan sighed and dropped his arms from around her. She fought the whimper of protest that rose, but somehow he heard it in spite of herself and his eyes were suddenly fierce and intense, and he lightly touched a finger to her lips. She shied away, suddenly too shy to even look at him, and wrapped her blanket tightly around her, though she had not been cold for a long while.

"Yes, we are ready," Duncan answered the maid, keeping his tone polite. "I'll just be escorting Miss Ramsey to her room and then we shall both be ready soon. You may inform Lady Raeburn of that."

She bobbed a curtsey and shuffled out of the room, leaving the door pointedly open.

Annalise hid a smile at that. Even still, the servants disapproved of her. It was refreshing to know that not everything had changed.

"What is that smile for?" Duncan asked softly, reaching out to touch the corner of her mouth.

She shook her head, tucking the smile away and giving him a bit of an impish look. "Nothing at all. What am I supposed to wear today?"

He shrugged and shook his head. "I never know anymore. Something fine and flattering, I suppose, which means you could pick just about any gown in your arsenal and exceed expectations."

She giggled and blushed, rapping his chest sharply and moving away to a safer distance. "Stop."

His slow grin curved and he followed, holding out his arm properly to escort her. "I told you, I only tell the truth."

"Well, stop saying it out loud," she laughed as she looped her hand through his and let him lead her on. "It makes me blush something frightful."

"I've already told you," he murmured softly so others would not hear, "I love to see you blush. And it won't stop me from praising you just because you are uncomfortable with it."

She rolled her eyes, even as her heart skittered. They were treading on some very serious ground here, and she was not sure she could bear it. Not if she were to be disappointed in the end. Was it better to have loved and lost than to never have loved at all?

She supposed she would be one of few people who would know the difference.

Love was infinitely better.

But losing it once you had had it…

Would that pain be worse than what she had endured before?

She stole a glance at Duncan and felt her heart plummet to her toes at the thought of losing him.

Yes, her mind cried out in agony. *Yes, it would be worse.*

Duncan's gaze was intense on the steps before him, his hand now warmly covering hers, and he was suddenly gnawing on his lip. His brow was puckered, but his motions fluid. He was deep in thought, oblivious to the world around him.

His thumb brushed her hand absently, over and over, and as it had happened in the library, her skin tingled with the sensation. He had thought himself relaxing her, but she had been near ready to come out of her skin. Not that it was not a pleasant sensation, but the touch of his hand would never fail to stir her in the most shocking of ways.

Ah, so he was not quite oblivious then.

He may have been lost in thought, but she was there with him.

An intense feeling of pride, joy, and love swelled within her and she found herself leaning into him a little more than before. She couldn't help it; he drew her to him. Just as he had that first day they had met. She could not resist him then; and now? Now she knew him and loved him, and resistance was impossible, and unthinkable.

All too soon, they were to her rooms and he hesitated outside of them. He looked at her for a long moment, then reached for her other hand and held both in his.

"Annalise..." he said quietly, looking down at their hands. Hers were so small compared to his, but there was an odd sort of artistic air about the way they looked when joined.

"Yes?"

He raised his eyes to hers, then brought their joined hands up and stroked her cheek with the back of one of his hands. He shook his head and leaned forward, pressing his lips softly to hers. Feather-light, warm, grazing, his lips were a wonder yet again as the feelings said more than they could have ever expressed. Neither of them had talent for speaking.

But when he kissed her...

"Annalise," he whispered against her skin, the heat in her name sending shivers skittering across her skin. "I..."

"Fire!"

Where the cry had come from, they could not tell, but several other voices took it up, and Duncan snapped back, away from her, and the moment was broken.

"What?" he yelled to whoever it had been.

"Fire! Fire!" other voices called. "In the stables!"

They ran to the window of her bedroom and saw the stables, down a bit from her rooms, but still rather close to the house. The roof of the stables was now blazing and they could hear the horses screeching in terror.

Duncan swore under his breath and ran from the room. "Stay here," he ordered behind him. "It will be too dangerous."

Annalise covered her mouth with her hands and turned back to the window. The stables were fairly vast, considering the smaller size of the house, but Duncan loved riding so much it was a worthy investment. If there were any losses there, she prayed they would be purely structural.

The proximity to the house was a concern, what if the fire spread?

She turned to go warn Marianne and Tibby, if they were not already aware, when a footman appeared at the door, in full and perfect livery, a silver platter before him. "Letter for you, Miss Ramsey," he intoned, bowing slightly. It only took one glance at the handwriting to know who it was from.

Hands shaking, she reached out to take it. Her heart might well have left her chest and she swallowed hard. "Th-thank you, Thomas."

He bowed once more and left, apparently unconcerned about her state or the fire just outside.

She moved to the window, where she could now see Duncan fighting the fire with the stable hands. She touched the glass lightly, as if she could have touched him from here. She dreaded what this letter would say, but she had little doubt of it as well.

She broke the seal and read the lines:

I warned you that terrible things would happen if you did not agree to my demands. I will destroy the lives of those you hold dear if you should continue to deny my requests. This is simply a taste of what I am willing and able to bring about. If you value the lives of Lady Raeburn and your precious Mr. Bray, you will meet me outside of the inn at Trafalgar, unaccompanied, and without warning a single creature. Do not test me again, Annie. Lives are in your hands.

She released a pained sob that she quickly stifled, tears raining down from her eyes and onto the paper. She tore it in pieces and flung it across the room, then buried her face into the curtains that hung by her window. She knew he had been watching, had been waiting, would not rest. But even she had not thought he would resort to this.

She heard yelling and glanced out of the window again. The fire was not under control yet, and more men were coming to help fight the flames. Duncan was in the thick of the melee, bellowing orders like the army man he was, but not too proud or proper to shoulder the brunt of the work himself.

How she loved him! How precious he was to her!

She had to save him. It was her turn to do the protecting.

Sobs overtook her as she quickly went to her closet and stripped her gown off, reaching for the plainest, dullest hand-me-down from Mary's sister. The dress she had arrived in had been ceremoniously burned by Tibby, or she would have worn that one. She still had her old shawl and boots, and she pulled them out to numbly put those on as well. She removed her earrings and pins, plaiting her hair simply, her fingers aching with every twist of her hair.

She quickly picked up the pieces of Thorpe's scattered note and moved to throw them into the fire. Then she caught sight of the ring on her finger. She felt a combination of moan and whimper rise within her and she pried it off, kissed it, then set it on the table nearest her, along with the crumpled bits of letter. She pulled a few sheets of paper from the neat stack in the corner and tried to think of what she could say to Duncan and the rest that would make amends for the betrayal she was about to commit.

How could she apologize enough? How could she thank them enough? How could she ever say what she truly felt?

She tried several times, crumpling up the tear stained pages and tossing them towards the fire. Finally, she had said what she felt in the simplest of terms, set her ring atop the page, and whirled from the room, her tears blinding her way.

The fire had the entire house so distracted that no one noticed her leave. No one marked her at all.

That was as it should be.

She ran down the street, never once looking back. She could not bear to look upon her shattered hopes and dreams. They were not to be, after all. Her future was before her, bleak and terrifying and horrible as it was.

But, at long last, she was the one being brave and noble.

And that was all she could cling to now.

Annalise was gone.

Even now, hours after it had been discovered that she was missing, the words were incomprehensible. How could she be gone? She was the most vibrant part of his life, the only thing in his life that made sense.

But she was gone.

It had taken much of the afternoon and into the evening to get the stable fires under control. They had not lost a single animal, but the damage had been extensive. He would need to rebuild everything, but at least the house had not been even remotely harmed, and animals and staff were all accounted for. He had gone up before even cleaning up to assure Annalise that it was all well and to see that she had not worried too much only to discover her room empty.

He had checked every other room in the house, literally, and found her nowhere.

A search had commenced, and not a single soul had seen her leave, no one had been admitted to the house, and none of her things had been taken or were missing. On the contrary, everything was where it should be.

Except for her.

All he had found was a note, tear stained and barely legible, but there. Two words were all it said.

Forgive me.

Those words told him nothing, gave him no comfort. On the contrary, his heart felt frozen in his chest. Her ring, the one he had spent ages agonizing over for their false engagement, lay next to the note.

There could be no further proof of her absence than that.

Forgive her?

It was already done.

Whatever it was, wherever she had gone, no matter the severity or depravity, she was forgiven.

She would always be forgiven.

But even that did nothing to help him.

Tibby and Marianne had bombarded him with questions, Marianne had even gone so far as to screech that this was what ought to be expected if they were to bring someone from such a low station to such heights, saying ridiculous things such as how ungrateful Annie was, how undeserving this proved Annie to be, how deceived they all had been by Annie. Always calling her Annie.

She was not Annie. She was Annalise.

His Annalise.

He had never wanted to throttle his sister before, but her words gave him opportunity to explore the idea.

Thankfully, Tibby had whirled and bellowed, "Shut up and go away, Marianne, if all you intend is to spread poison. If you say one more word about her, I shall remove you from my will and you will be cut off without a penny to your ridiculous name!"

Marianne had burst into tears, and Duncan had been in too ill a temper to soothe her. He had turned from them both and shut himself up in his study, where he had remained the rest of the night. He sat there now, staring at nothing, no idea what to do, or how to proceed from here.

The clock on a shelf chimed four o'clock in the morning. Was that all? He would have thought it closer to dawn.

He pushed himself out of his chair and opened the door to the study, only to find Lancelot there. The pug rarely left Annalise's side, and never gave Duncan the time of day. But now he jumped up and looked up at Duncan eagerly, curled tail wagging.

He grunted and moved past the dog down the hall. He didn't know where he was going until he reached his destination. The library. It held most of his favorite memories with Annalise. The fire was only embers now, and he suddenly needed the room blazing with light and warmth. He went over and began using the tools to prod it, to brighten it. He added another two logs, and soon the grand fireplace was alight with all its intended glory.

The room was not any less dreary to him.

There, on that rug, is where he had given his first reading lesson to her. Her voice had been so hesitant, so uncertain and weak. But as time went on, she grew in both ability and confidence, until they were no longer reading aloud, but sitting in contented silence in chairs, each with their own books. The silence had been filled with contentment and peace, never once awkward.

He had imagined her sitting across his lap in one of those chairs, imagined her content to just be with him, playing absently with her hair as he read, her nuzzling against him happily.

Here he had fallen in love with her.

Oh, there were several other times and places where he had found himself in love, where he had been stunned by her, amused by her, thrilled by her, but here in this room is where he really came to see what a magnificent creature she was. Here is where he had come to know her as he had never known another human being. Here he had found what he had not known he wanted.

Lancelot whined next to him, and Duncan glared down at the animal. "She's not here," he growled, shooing the animal with his boot. "Go hang about someone else."

He went to the hearth and leaned against it, staring into the fire.

Why would she have left him? What had he said, what had he done? Had it been too much attention on his part? Had he offered too much without actually offering anything at all? Should he have said more, done more, been more?

Or had she never wanted it at all?

She had never told him what she really wanted. He had forced all this upon her. He had given her choices, yes, but never really a voice. What had she wanted? Any number of men could have given her a better life than her old one. What could he possibly offer her that no one else could?

His love, perhaps, but what was his love worth? He would give her everything he owned if she asked it, would give her himself without explanation or question. But what would be gained by it?

She would never ask for anything.

She was just proud enough for that.

If she had known how he felt, what he felt, what she meant to him, would she still have left? Or would that have been enough?

Why was he not enough?

Why had she left?

So many questions swirled about, and there were no answers to be found.

The clacking of paws met his ears and he glanced down to find the pug licking at his boot, then looking up at him with sad eyes.

"You miss her, too, don't you?" he murmured.

The dog whined as if in response.

Duncan sank down and scratched the dog behind his ears, allowing himself a brief smile when he received a nuzzle and a lick in return. "I don't know where she went," he told Lancelot, "and I don't know why. I thought she was happy. I thought... Well, I thought a lot of things. Didn't say any of them. I should have said them."

"Duncan?"

He rose to his feet to find Marianne at the door to the library, her hair rumpled and down, nightgown and wrap tightly cinched, and a shawl about her shoulders.

"Minnow, what are you doing awake?" he asked softly gesturing for her to come to him.

She sniffled and came to take his hand. "I haven't been asleep," she whispered, her voice filled with tears. "I'm a horrible creature, and I think I am the reason... That she..."

"You think you are the reason Annalise left?"

She nodded and a few tears fell from her eyes.

He lifted her chin to look at him. "You aren't. I'm the one to blame here. You've done nothing."

"Yes, I have," she insisted. "I was horrible. I wouldn't help her in Society, I stuck to my own crowd and airs and let her know I didn't approve. What sort of a creature am I?"

He sighed and pulled his sister against him. "Marianne, she forgave you for that. She knew you as I do, that you have a sweet heart and generous spirit. You are not to blame."

"Neither are you." She pulled back and looked up at him. "I have been thinking it over all night, and I cannot sleep because of it."

"Over what?"

Marianne took his hand and squeezed it hard. "She wouldn't just leave, Duncan. Not Annalise. Something is very wrong."

He didn't miss that she called her Annalise, not Annie. He knew his sister loved her, had known it all along. She merely had a different way of showing it. He wished he could give her some comfort, but he had none.

He shook his head slowly. "Nobody came into the house, Marianne. They didn't take her."

"But that doesn't mean she wasn't forced. Just... look deeper? Please?"

He looked at his sister for a long moment, wondering that her thoughts had been so close to his own. He found himself nodding. "All right. If you think so."

"I do," she said firmly, her tears gone. "And if you will get out of your own way, you will think so too."

She went up on tiptoe and kissed his cheek, then left the room.

Duncan heaved a heavy sigh and tried to force his emotions back. Logic must take precedence here, not his heart. His heart was broken and breaking, in no condition to help him. He needed to consider the facts, what he knew of Annalise, of the situation, and of her sudden flight.

He had not even informed his friends yet.

Perhaps that was a mistake, but there was nothing for it now.

He looked at Lancelot, who seemed to sense a change in him. "Come on," he said softly. "Let's go see what we can find."

And he went to the one place he swore to never enter again.

Her room.

The closet was open still, all her dresses hanging neatly in a coordinated row. Her bed sat perfect and pristine, covers not the slightest bit wrinkled. The dress she had worn earlier still lay on the floor. He bent to pick it up, and found several pieces of paper underneath. He frowned and laid them out on the table nearest him.

A soft growl met his ears and he turned to find Lancelot sniffing at one of the pelisses. He moved to it, instinctively searching the pockets. He found four letters, all very short and unsigned, in the same scrawling handwriting that the letter had been. The messages upon them were not pleasant.

You can't fool me.

Lies will be brought to light.
Come to me or suffer the consequences.
I'm warning you.

A cold shiver ran up his spine and he turned to the letter on the table, suddenly feeling as though he had been kicked in the chest.

He noticed three crumpled up pages beneath the table. He grabbed for them and smoothed them out. Each had been blurred by tears, and each was addressed to him. Not even a single sentence had been completed, but each begged for forgiveness and understanding.

He swallowed hard and moved to the pieces of letter on the table, assembling them quickly. His brows snapped firmly together and a thundercloud grew within him. He knew whose mischief this was, whose fault this really was.

Thorpe.

The threat in the letter was enough to make him seethe.

He pulled the last remaining letter from his waist coat pocket, the one he had read hundreds of times in the last several hour, the short two words written in the hand he loved so well.

Forgive me.

He shut his eyes and groaned, clutching the paper in his fist. He was the greatest fool that had ever lived.

He tore from the room and ran to his study. Taking four sheets of paper, he wrote exactly the same message on each, and after rousing four of his servants and paying them more than he ought, they rode off to each of his friends.

Duncan paced anxiously in his study while the minutes ticked by. He could not ride off on his own, not when such men had such power over the woman he loved. He would need reinforcements, and ones he could trust.

Colin arrived first, hardly decent, but determined. Duncan showed him the notes from Thorpe, and he gaped.

"The inn at Trafalgar?" Colin repeated, looking up at him. "There *is* no inn at Trafalgar!"

"I know."

Colin's mouth thinned to a compressed line. "On it." He spun from the room at a faster pace than he had arrived.

Each of the others came and scattered on various errands, asking no questions, just offering everything they had.

He would owe more debt than he could ever repay when this was all done.

As the dawn began to rise, they each returned, and the news was not good.

"Thorpe has checked out of his lodgings," Geoff reported upon his entrance.

"And a coach was rented from the station to take him and his companions to some northern destination, exact location undisclosed," Nathan added.

Derek rubbed at his hair and winced. "No news has been reported to or by the gossips regarding Miss Anne Remington or yourself, they know nothing. The fire brigade agrees with your suspicions that the fire was intentional, and you already interviewed your staff; they saw nothing and no one."

Duncan nodded, and waited for Colin, who was as breathless as if he had run all the streets of London on foot.

"A young woman matching Annalise's description was seen being forced into a carriage in Trafalgar Square," he panted, hands on his knees. "No one could positively identify her, but they said she was screaming."

Duncan moaned and rubbed his hands into his eyes.

"Also…"

He looked up at Colin, who suddenly had fire blazing in his eyes. "Our mutual friend said he could not stop the escape, much as he tried." He spat the words and wiped a hand across his lips. "Our friend also says he overheard Thorpe threatening to lash her within an inch of her life before he could claim what belonged to him. He thought you might want to know that and offers you a significant amount of power from the very highest of sources should you choose to act upon his information."

A barbaric roar was ripped from Duncan's chest and he barreled from the room and made for the stables, his friends hard on his heels.

He did not care about power or prestige, his life or his wealth, or anything in this world but getting to Annalise.

He had no doubt where she was or with whom, or what she would endure if he did not get there fast. There were also no limits as to what he would endure to get her back. He had only just realized how much he needed her, he was not willing to give her up. Especially to a man who did not appreciate, nor deserve her.

And no one took what was his.

No one.

"What if we're too late?" Colin asked, for once being the voice of reason.

"I don't care," he snarled, taking the reins from his servant. "I'll take her to the continent and live in hiding for the rest of my life if I have to. But she is not staying with them. I don't care."

"Neither do we, Duncan," Nathan said, already atop his horse.

The rest nodded firmly, eyes serious and determined.

"Whatever happens," he said, looking at them all, "know that I will never be able to thank you enough for your friendship and loyalty."

Colin snorted and tossed his head. "Enough with the emotional nonsense. We have a long ride and no time. In your lady's honor, Duncan, I insist on the pleasure of thrashing someone."

"Get in line," the rest chorused in unison.

Duncan laughed without mirth.

"Come on, Duncan," Derek said with a nudge of his head. "Your woman, you lead the charge."

He turned his horse about and faced the dawn. With a harsh bellow, he kicked his heels into Balthazar, and all the horses whinnied at once as they took off for the most important ride of his entire life.

Chapter Twenty One

$\mathscr{I}$t was the longest day and a half of his life.

It would have been much worse, had he come alone. But his friends were just as determined, and they encouraged him when his doubts and fears took control. They had stopped twice to briefly rest and take nourishment, but they were not long at all. Their strength and energy was starting to fade, and he was beginning to feel it.

His mind was not as clear, his instincts not as sharp. Thinking was more difficult than it ought to be, and his eyelids heavy. But he had enough willpower and drive within him to fight on. He would not stop until he had Annalise in his arms again, safe and sound and knowing she was loved.

There was not a word of complaint from any of the group. In fact, other than necessity dictated, they did not speak at all. He was grateful for that. His thoughts were too complex and muddled for comprehension, attempting words or conversation would have put him to the end of his wits. He knew they were all exhausted, all had doubts, and were all primed for the very worst.

The carriage would make good time, but they would also have to stop and change horses, at the very least. Colin had figured the very soonest they could have arrived would have been two days after their departure, which would put them at last night, if not early this morning. If that were the case, then all was not lost. They had not come across any hint of them yet, so they could only assume their drive to reach the end was as urgent as theirs.

Would his intentions be righteous enough to ensure success? At this moment, he would not have blinked if marrying her had been impossible, or if he had to never see her again. If he could only save her, this last time, from ever being hurt or threatened again, that would be enough. If she could be ensured of a good life, safe and warm and well, he would be content.

Miserable forever, it was true, but he would accept that.

In all the good deeds he had ever done, never had he wished for payment in kind.

He would take all of the positive debt accrued at this moment, just for her.

Hold on, my love, he thought frantically as he urged Balthazar on. *Hold on.*

They began to come across sights more familiar to him, things that were both encouraging and discouraging. The roads he had travelled with her, taking her away from her past and into the future, not knowing what would follow, only that he had to do something. Memories from the days when she had only been a beautiful stranger he simply had to help, who had captivated his thoughts and made him act irrationally.

Had he loved her from the start?

Nathan and Derek had taken up the responsibility to pick up information as best as they could along the way, and he heard their reports, but rarely responded. He knew they were on the right path. He knew they were close.

He knew she was in danger.

All too soon, her village was upon them, and for the first time in the last thirty-six to forty-eight hours, he realized that he did not know where to go once he was here. He looked at his friends in abject horror and confusion.

"What?" Derek asked, looking worried.

Duncan shook his head. "I don't know where to go. I found her in a random spot of country, I couldn't find it again without help. I…" Panic began to rise within him and he looked around frantically, but there was no one about in the small, snow covered village.

Colin dismounted and shrugged. "So we start banging on doors."

The others looked bewildered as Colin strode to the first abysmal looking home and pounded on the door. Duncan looked at his friends and swallowed the lump in his throat. Colin was right. This was no time for pride, or hysterics.

He dismounted and followed Colin's example, moving to the shops and vendor stands just beyond.

Soon all five of them were knocking at houses and begging for help, but no one seemed to know anything at all about where the Ramseys actually lived. Frank had always brought his horses to the stockyard, never showing anybody where he kept the animals in the meantime. And nobody knew much about Annie, save that she was shy, small, and usually beat up.

Duncan would have liked to burn the entire place to the ground for their incompetence, but he knew many other villages would have been exactly the same.

As the sun rose higher into the sky, Duncan became more and more distracted, his mind growing frazzled and frantic. What was he supposed to do if he could not find her? Break down every door in this godforsaken place until he had answers? He was willing to do so, but it wouldn't help.

There was no answer at the inn, so he could not even have Mrs. Burton's aid. No one paid any attention to Frank or Annie Ramsey, and no one seemed to give any heed to the fact that he was a man in distress.

He ran his hands over his stubbled face and fought the urge to groan aloud.

"Mr. Bray, isn't it?"

Duncan's head shot up and he looked around at whoever had spoken. His eyes caught sight of a familiar face, but it took him a moment to place it. "Mr. Lyman," he finally said, his voice catching with relief.

Lyman nodded in greeting. "You look like a man in need. What can I do?"

Duncan gripped the man's shoulder. "I need to know where the Ramseys live."

"Why?" Lyman asked with some concern. "What happened?"

Duncan quickly related the briefest version he could, and he could tell from the firm set of his jaw that Lyman knew exactly what all of this could entail.

Lyman sighed and squeezed the bridge of his nose. "I can take you there," he said slowly, "but I can promise you that nothing can be done without the magistrate, and he is less than inclined to help when it's against his interest."

Duncan groaned and looked at his friends, who were standing around him. "He's in Ramsey and Thorpe's pockets?"

"He is," Lyman admitted, looking up at him again. "Most of this place is. It's why no one will help you."

"Except you."

Lyman smiled briefly. "Except me. I'm new here and have yet to fall into corruption."

"Thank God for that," Geoff muttered, rubbing the back of his neck.

Lyman nodded once, then looked back at Duncan. "The magistrate here is Mr. Bridgewell. Rarely sober and even more rarely accommodating. So unless any of you are willing to actually commit a crime punishable by imprisonment or deportation..."

"I wouldn't put it past us," Derek said, seeming to consider the idea.

Mr. Lyman smiled thinly. "He does owe me for treating his horse, so if you will give me a few minutes, I'll convince him it's only a formality and some men of high standing will be most appreciative."

Derek sighed and nodded. "I'll pay him for his troubles."

"*I* will pay him," Duncan corrected.

Derek snorted. "You will beat him to a pulp. Let me do this, Duncan."

Sensing this was not a battle worth fighting, Duncan nodded his assent, and they waited none-too-patiently for Mr. Lyman to reappear with the incompetent magistrate.

Soon enough, they were back and Derek gave Duncan a grim nod. "It is done. No matter what we find, they will never be troubling Annalise again. They won't be troubling anyone."

Only slightly mollified, Duncan returned the nod. He didn't need to know what Derek had threatened, or what influence he had pulled, and he didn't care. So long as Annalise would be safe, it was enough.

The group made their way back through the village, and then turned up a country road that Duncan suddenly recollected. It was clear now, but when it was covered with snow, it had looked quite different. Which meant that patch of trees over there…

His breath caught and he urged his horse harder for the first place he had come across her. Pale and shaking and injured as she had been, she had been equally beautiful. Tragic, certainly, but beautiful nonetheless.

"What is it?" Colin asked softly as he approached him.

Duncan had not been aware that he had stopped. He swallowed and looked at the small trickle of a creek that had once seemed so vast and dangerous. "This is where I first saw her," he rasped.

They were all silent for a moment.

"Come on," Geoff urged in his quiet, calm manner. "Lyman says we're nearly there."

With no less speed, but infinitely more caution, they rode up the hill. And presumably, towards the house. He held his breath as he crested the hill, not entirely sure he wanted to see the sight of all the misery and pain Annalise had endured.

The house was still a good distance from them, but it was visible. It was hardly fit for pigs, let alone a young woman. The walls were filthy and damaged, and from his distance he could see cracks and holes that meant winter would have been torment. Smoke rose from a crooked chimney, and a well-constructed and clean barn with stables was nearby. Funny that a man should put so much care and concern into his livestock and not into his flesh and blood.

Rage swelled within his gut and he felt himself growl.

"Steady," Nathan urged him, riding alongside. "Save it."

He nodded, unable to vocalize his distress.

What state would Annalise be in? Would they have ruined her beyond what his love could heal? Would she have been beaten again? Would she be worse?

Was she even alive?

She had to be, he reasoned within himself. She was no good to either of them dead.

He would be no good to anyone if she were dead.

"RAMSEY!" he bellowed as they approached, feeling more animal than man at this moment, and not caring.

"THORPE!" Nathan roared, widening out to prevent any escape.

Two men exited the house, casually dressed, and obviously drunk, but Duncan did not miss the recognition in Thorpe's face when he saw them. The man bolted, but Derek chased after him and corralled him back towards the house. His friends all dismounted, Derek and Nathan pulling out guns that were unnervingly steady.

Duncan let his gaze rove over Frank Ramsey, the man who should have loved and cared for Annalise, who should have fought for every right and privilege for her, who should have been her prime example of love and family. The man who betrayed her beyond any hope of reckoning.

He spared no thought or look for Thorpe. Not yet.

"Who are you?" Ramsey asked, spitting on the ground.

Duncan snarled and vaulted from his horse. He marched up to the weasel and took fistfuls of his shirt, shoving him against the shabby walls of the house.

He leaned in as close as he dared, and through clenched teeth asked, "Where is she?"

It seemed Frank Ramsey had some intelligence after all. He didn't ask whom he meant, and his eyes flicked to the barn as he swallowed frantically, hands feebly trying to loosen Duncan's grasp.

Duncan flung him away and ran, full tilt, for the barn. His heart felt as if it were beating in his throat, he could not breathe, could barely see, yet his legs continued to move beneath him. He wrenched the double doors open with an agitated grunt, and stumbled in, waiting for his eyes to adjust to the sudden darkness.

When they did, he wished for darkness again.

In the dirtiest corner of the barn, just opposite the last stall, hands tied to a hook on the wall was Annalise. Her clothing was ripped, and angry, bloody cuts lay beneath the tears. Her skin was pale and discolored, her hair matted, and she hung limply from her hands as if she were made of rags. Her head was down, and she hardly moved. He had never seen anything look more lifeless.

A rough, strangled cry was ripped from his throat as he found himself hurtling towards her. He took her face in his hands, pushing the hair back from her face. A rag had been fastened around her mouth tightly, and frantically his fingers worked to loosen it.

She jerked suddenly in his hold, her eyes flying open. One eye was swollen nearly shut for the bruising around it, and a cut lashed out from the corner of her lip, though the blood was dry. A startled whimper escaped her and her breathing quickened in panic.

"Shh, shh," he soothed, his voice choked with tears. "Annalise, it's me. It's all right, it's me, shh."

At long last her unfocused eyes found him. She stared in confusion, then moistened her cracked lips. "Duncan?" she wheezed. "Duncan, is it really you?"

He laughed breathlessly once and rubbed a hand over her hair. "Yes, sweetheart, it's me." He shielded her head as he pulled hard at the ropes keeping her hands suspended, and sawdust, hay, and shards of wood rained down on them briefly. He was quick to free her hands entirely, his eyes burning as he focused on the task.

"You came...?" she asked him, as if she didn't understand. A stray tear leaked out of her eye as her now freed hands reached for his jaw. "I dreamed of you, I called out for you over and over... You really came?"

"Of course, I came," he said hoarsely, no longer in control of his emotions. He captured her wrists in his hands and stroked her abraded skin softly. "It's not that easy to walk out of my life, Annalise Ramsey, and if you ever do anything so foolish again..." He could not finish the sentence and hauled her against his chest, burying his face in her hair. "Don't ever leave me again. Ever. Do you hear me? I've never been more frightened in all my life."

"I'm sorry," she whimpered, crying in earnest now as she clung to him.

"I don't want you to be sorry. I want..." He shook his head and gripped her as tightly as he could without causing her pain. "Oh, Annalise. What were you thinking? Why did you leave?"

"They were going to hurt you and Tibby."

"You could have come to me! I would have taken care of everything!"

"I couldn't risk you getting hurt or worse." She shook her head against him. "I wouldn't risk you."

He pushed her back just enough to caress her lips gently with his own, not caring that she would taste the saltiness of his tears, or feel the yearning in his heart. She was here, she was alive, and he would be damned if he would ever let her go again. Her response was innocently eager, and not nearly so careful as his, a tender passion ringing through them both. There was no beginning and no end, just one unending series of delicate, delicious kisses that spoke volumes, yet were not enough.

He broke off and tucked her under his chin, ending the kiss before he would have liked, but there would be time for that later. There would be time for everything. All he needed now was to hold her, to remind himself that she was really here…

Her arms reached around his neck as she began to shudder with sobs. Duncan groaned and held her close, his own tears coming in earnest. He tried to soothe her as best as he could, but he was so overcome himself that all could do was cling to her and let her cry, let them both cry, until his heart was no longer racing. And he did not care how long that took.

He scattered grazing kisses along her face, her hair, her wounds, any place he could get to, and then finally, rested his face in her hair as his shudders began to subside.

When Annalise was once again quiet and still, Duncan took a clean blanket from the stall, wrapped her in it, then gathered her up and stood, murmuring soothing words into her ear as he carried her out of the barn. She shivered against the cold and he feathered his lips along her brow. They approached the others, and Nathan was instantly to him.

"Take her," Duncan ordered softly, stroking Annalise's cheek. "And send Lyman for a coach."

Nathan nodded and took Annalise from him, holding her gently. He turned her face into his chest, shielding her from her brother and tormentor as he pulled his coat around her.

Duncan stepped away from his friend as he did as he bid, inhaled slowly, and exhaled for a long moment. Then he turned and faced Ramsey and Thorpe.

Both cowered under his gaze.

Geoff and Colin stepped back a bit and let him get as close as he dared.

He looked between the two of them, feeling the seething wrath burn in him like flames. "I should do to you exactly what you have done to her," he said, his voice menacing and dangerous. "You deserve to have the same beating and thrashing and worse, and Lord knows, I want to beat you until your blood pools on the ground at my feet. But that would make me no better than you. And I am better than you."

"Amen," Geoff murmured behind him.

Colin cleared his throat. "Lucky for us, I'm more than willing to sink to your level. So once Duncan gets one good swing on each of you and turns his back, I'm taking over."

Duncan mentally applauded his friend's earnestness, but he would not dwell on it. He looked between the two men again, then swung at the brother and sent him flying across the yard. He turned to Thorpe, who looked more like a cowed chicken than a man. He thought of all this man had threatened, all the fear he had caused Annalise, and suddenly, it was easy. He grinned and forced all of his might behind his fist as it connected with Thorpe's chin.

The man lay in the dirt moaning, but Duncan no longer cared about him. About either of them. He looked up at the sound of wheels. Lyman rode up with a coach and driver, then came over to him, nodding in acknowledgement.

Duncan sighed and walked back towards his friends. "Take care of this," he hissed to no one in particular.

"With pleasure," Geoff growled, surprising him. But the others looked just as determined. Even Derek, usually disinclined to violence, was now rolling up his sleeves.

Duncan took Annalise from Nathan's hold, nodded his thanks, and turned away from them all, heading directly for the carriage.

He didn't say another word until they were sitting in the coach and heading back for London. He wouldn't have said anything at all, but Annalise stirred and slid from his lap to sit next to him.

She took one of his hands in hers. "I am so sorry," she whispered.

"No," he insisted, taking her chin in hand and lifting her eyes to his. "No. You have nothing to be sorry for. You thought you needed to sacrifice yourself to protect me. That is my fault. I should have listened to you, really listened to your fears. And I should have told you... how I felt, what I had planned. If I had, this would never have happened. This is my fault."

She hastily shook her head. "No, Duncan, no."

"Yes, Annalise." He sighed and took her hands, squeezing tightly. "If you knew... if you believed... you would never have gone away with him. You would have stayed. With me."

"W-what are you saying?" she whispered.

He looked at her with so much emotion he ached with it. "Do you really not know?" he murmured, stroking one of her soft, pale cheeks. "After all we have been through, after all we have shared..." He ran one finger down her cheek and across her chin. "Annalise..."

"Don't say it..." she whispered, her green eyes searching his. "Don't say it unless you mean it, Duncan, I can't..."

He surged forward and captured her lips with his own, swallowing her words and her soft moan of release with a satisfied growl that he felt to his toes.

"I love you," he said fiercely as he touched his brow to hers. "I have loved you every day from the moment I saw you. I wanted to give you a chance to choose, to find someone that would suit you better, someone who would be more worthy of you, but..."

Annalise brought her hand to his cheek with a sigh. "I want you, Duncan. I always wanted you."

He pulled back and looked at her in awe. "What?"

"I love you, too," she whispered as she stroked his cheek and jaw, smiling at him. "I love you so much."

He smiled and pressed his lips to her once, twice, three times, and just when she leaned in for another, he grinned and rapped on the ceiling of the coach, then moved to the door and dropped the window. He stuck his head out and yelled something to the coach driver, then sat back down and pulled Annalise into his lap.

Suddenly, the coach slowed, and the unmistakable sensation of turning around commenced. The coach lurched forward and started heading in the opposite direction.

Annalise pushed some hair behind her ear and looked up at him with a smile. "Where are we going?"

"Gretna."

She reared back. "Gretna?"

He gave her a very serious look. "I'm marrying you. As soon as possible. That is what happens there."

She shoved at his chest impatiently. "Yes, I know what happens in Gretna, but…"

He once again took her face in his hands. She had to understand. "I love you more than I have words to say," he said in a low, fierce voice, finally succeeding in silencing her protests. He reached into his pocket and pulled out her ring, making her gasp. "I love you, Annalise. We are already engaged, we had the ball to prove it, and I am holding the ring I chose specifically for you."

"Duncan…" she whispered, letting him slide the ring back onto her finger.

The hand still on her face stroked her skin softly. "I almost lost you forever, and I'm never letting you go again. Ever," he added with the briefest shake. "And I am certainly not waiting any longer to claim you once and for all as mine and mine alone."

He saw her throat work in a hasty swallow. "Oh…"

"Is that all right?" he asked, suddenly uncertain. Then, thinking he knew just how to convince her, he quirked his mouth in half of a grin. "Or would you prefer Tibby's version of a wedding?"

Annalise gave him a look that spoke volumes, grabbed his face, and kissed him hard. "Tell the driver to go faster," she rasped against his lips, sending his heart racing at a breathtaking pace.

He chuckled, returned her kiss, and obeyed, delighting in the sudden heady sensation that being merely content would never be enough again.

*E*pilogue

*A*nnalise woke far later than she usually did, she could tell from the light in the room, the sunlight scattering beams across her pillow. She stretched lazily, her body stiff and aching, but remarkably well rested. The air was cold outside of her bed, so she burrowed more deeply into the comfort and warmth of the blankets.

She smiled to herself as she recalled the events of the day before, hardly able to believe they were real and not her fanciful imaginations.

Duncan had them racing for Gretna and married by a charming old man who wouldn't budge in providing the ceremony until Duncan had assured him that her injuries were not sustained by his hand, but were what he was saving her from. He had taken Annalise aside and given her an interview of sorts, and only after he was assured of their mutual love, affection, and safety, would he proceed. She didn't think that the usual "anvil marriages" were so conducted, but she was pleased to have been slightly unconventional.

It had faintly occurred to her to wonder if Tibby might have been offended by their actions, more so by her lack of invitation, but then, Tibby always approved of independent thought and action, so long as the results were beneficial to all.

Surely there was no greater benefit or reward than a happy marriage between two people so in love.

Though they had scarcely been married twelve hours, Duncan had already outdone himself by way of husbandly duties. He had secured them the finest room in Gretna's most established inn, which was just fashionable enough for his tastes, and not extravagant enough to offend hers. His first course was to insist upon her being tended to by a physician, given her condition and injuries, and when all came back positively, he ordered a hot bath for her.

She wished she could say it had been embarrassing for her, as he had tended to her himself, sending away the maids. But on the contrary, it had been the most intimate and liberating of experiences. She had never been so vulnerable, so aware of herself and the damage that had been done. He had been so gentle and comforting, never once grimacing or looking the least bit unsettled. He had only expressed his love and admiration, showering her lips and her skin with soft kisses and caresses, washing the blood and dirt away. He had praised her so sweetly her skin had tingled with it, and his gentle reminders of her blushes only made her more self-conscious.

She would never forget the sensations of his fingers in her hair, gently massaging her scalp with the soap and water, then softly stroking it as he rinsed. His low, soothing voice gently ordering her about, always with a sweet word of praise or love. She didn't know what he had planned, only that he wanted to proudly show off his wife to the good patrons of their Gretna inn, and enjoy a quiet evening meal with his bride.

Annalise had no such desires, much preferring the simple solitude of their bedchamber and the night ahead of them to anything involving the public, but the promise in his eyes told her it would be worth it.

He unknowingly recreated everything about the dream she'd once had of him, save but one part. In her reality, he was there for the lot of it. Though her dress and her hair were far simpler, the feelings were the same. She had been scrubbed from head to toe, and her body felt alive, as if no injury had ever been placed upon it.

He had dressed her carefully, and led her to the mirror so she could see herself, just as in the dream. Again, he had wrapped his arms around her, pulling her against him as he murmured loving words. Then he had exhaled, dipped his head against the back of hers, and pressed a soft, but searing kiss to the nape of her neck.

Gasping at the sensation, Annalise had reached a hand up to his hair, tangling her fingers in his dark tresses, and pulled his mouth towards her hungry lips.

Suffice it to say, they made no public appearance last evening.

She rolled over to snuggle against her husband, only to find the space empty and cold. She raised her head and blinked her sleep-worn eyes. The space beside her was rumpled, but empty.

She turned back over and looked around the bedchamber. "Duncan?" she called softly.

There was no response.

She frowned slightly and sat up, rubbing her eyes. She looked around the room in confusion, but it was well and truly empty. She frowned and pushed herself out of bed, reaching for a morning dress borrowed from the innkeeper's daughters. She shivered in the morning air and put the wrap on as well, leaving the ties loose.

Barefoot, she padded to the door that led to the sitting room, hoping she would not have to venture out further into the general public in search of her new husband.

She opened it, only to find him opening the door beyond that led to the rest of the inn.

He stopped in surprise, gave her a quite thorough look of appraisal, and smiled at her in a way that made her cheeks flame in response.

"One would think that would get old," he murmured, closing the door. "And yet…" He set down a tray of food, shaking his head. He went to her, slid his hands around her waist, and leaned down to kiss her lips lightly, yet with so much heat she shivered in delight. "Good morning," he murmured, giving each reddened cheek a soft kiss.

"Good morning," she replied, still shy, but cupping his chin and pressing a firm kiss to his smiling mouth.

He sighed and touched his forehead to hers. "I had hoped to bring you breakfast in bed, but they were a bit long about it."

She shrugged and smiled as her stomach growled in response to the aroma. "I don't mind," she told him.

He chuckled and gave her a quick peck. "Yes, so I hear. But I would much rather you hadn't woken up alone."

She pulled back with a grin. "Then you'll just have to be more expeditious tomorrow."

He laughed and tugged her towards the table. "And the day after that. And the day after that. And…"

She covered his mouth, laughing. "Enough!"

He pulled out a chair for her and then sat beside her, smiling as they each filled their plates. He sobered just a bit. "I don't ever want you to feel alone again, Annalise."

"I won't," she assured him, covering his hand with hers. "And you can call me Annie."

He looked surprised. "But they called you Annie. I don't want you to be reminded. I don't want you to think of them ever again."

She gave him the small smile she knew he loved. "I'm not. And I won't be. Not when you're the one saying it."

His breath caught and he smiled, squeezing her hand. "You don't like being Annalise?"

She returned the smile and kissed his hand. "I love it. You've changed me, Duncan, and not just because of my name. I never minded being Annie. I will be Annalise for everyone else, and you may call me that whenever you like, it doesn't matter. But between us, because you love me and I love you, I can be Annie again."

He leaned forward and kissed her lips softly. "All right, Annie," he murmured with a wink. "It will be our secret."

She rolled her eyes and pushed him away. "Eat something, you're getting ridiculous."

They ate a bit here, a bit there, talking lightly about nothing, stealing looks and smiles meant only for the other. She told him how she loved falling asleep in his arms, how happy she was, how she felt like this was all a dream. He promised this was their reality, and it would always be this way. He asked if she wanted to live in London or the country, she did not care either way. She became quite embarrassed when Duncan mentioned how adorable her little snore was while she slept, but he repeatedly assured her that it was charming and it made him love her more. She highly doubted that, but he would not be swayed.

She loved hearing him say he loved her. She would never tire of hearing it.

"What?" he asked softly, touching her smile.

Annalise looked up at him, unaware she had done anything. "What?"

"You were thinking something, and you smiled. I want to know."

She shook her head slowly back and forth, still smiling. "No."

"No?" he asked in surprise, a strange twinkle in his eyes. "But I am your husband, you have to tell me."

"I do not. That was not in the vows."

He snorted. "I married you via blacksmith in Gretna. The vows are what we make them."

She held up a finger in warning. "You, sir, are never allowed to criticize my wedding simply because it was not in a church. The vows are binding and unbreakable, made before God, and I never vowed to not have secrets."

Duncan tilted his head and his smile became soft, warm, and melted her sternness and her bones in one breath.

"What?" she breathed when he shook his head.

"Nothing," he murmured, taking her hand and kissing the palm. "I simply have a new favorite memory of you."

She opened her mouth in confusion and his thumb reached out to stroke her now parted lips.

"I've been collecting several over the past few weeks," he continued, turning her into a soft, melted puddle. "And just when I think I cannot have more, you do something, say something, look a certain way… And my heart feels like it's going to burst. Every time. I think you are going to be the death of me, Annalise Bray. And I could not be more pleased about it."

"I love you," she whispered, unable to help herself. She wanted to cry, but was feeling so joyful she couldn't manage it.

"I love you." He stroked her cheek again, and then his smile turned mischievous. "But I will make you tell me your secret."

"You will not," she said, pulling out of his tantalizing touch.

"Oh, you doubt me?" He attempted to look fearsome. "I have ways, you know. To make you talk."

She gave him a look that she had seen Moira give many times over. "I'm not afraid of you."

One brow slowly rose. "Oh, no? Am I not a strong and fearsome creature?"

She considered it, then nodded. "Strong, yes, most certainly. But fearsome? Not in the slightest."

"Shouldn't a wife fear her husband?" he asked, his eyes dancing merrily.

"I rather think she should love him." It was true, in her estimation. She had known a lifetime of fear. She much preferred this feeling of love, and a lifetime of it.

"I see," he murmured slowly. "And do you? Love your husband?"

Again, she pretended to consider it carefully, chewing her lip a little. "Do you know, I think I do."

"More than yesterday?"

"Oh, yes," she breathed, smiling brilliantly. "Much more."

He looked the slightest bit unsettled, cleared his throat, and adopted a serious expression. "But you do not fear him?"

She shook her head, still smiling. "Not a bit."

He held her gaze steady. "I see." He sighed and shrugged. "Well, I suppose I shall have to live with that in all areas save one."

Suspicious, she raised her chin a touch. "And that is?"

He rose from his chair, then suddenly swooped down and scooped her into his arms, tossing her over his shoulder.

"Duncan!" she shrieked, laughing in surprise. "What are you doing?"

"I'm off to show my wife just how fun fearing me can be." He headed directly for the bedchamber, his strides full of purpose.

"And shouldn't you fear me in return?" she asked as they entered the room and he kicked the door shut behind them.

"Oh, I can assure you, my love, I am quite terrified of you." He swung her down again into his arms, and the heat in his eyes and his smile caused her heart to immediately race in delight. "And it is the best feeling in the world. Now, be quiet and fear me."

"Yes, my love," she murmured, sliding her hands into his hair and pulling his mouth to hers.

But she wouldn't tell him her secret. Not yet. She could hold out, endure whatever sweet torments he could give and never reveal a thing.

Because she was strong now and she knew it.

He had shown her that. He had given her everything she had dreamed, and everything she never dared to.

And forever would not be time enough to love him adequately for that.

But she could try.

Coming Soon

The Burdens
of a
Bachelor

"A fair façade hides many scars."

by

Rebecca Connolly

CPSIA information can be obtained
at www.ICGtesting.com
Printed in the USA
FSOW02n0759271116
27861FS